CHAOS

FOUR HORSEMEN
BOOK TWO

SARAH BAILEY

Chaos Copyright © 2021 by Sarah Bailey

This book is a work of fiction. Names, characters, places, and incidents either are products of the author's imagination or are used fictitiously. Any resemblance to actual persons, living or dead, events, or locales is entirely coincidental.

Please note the spelling throughout is British English.

Cover Art by Sarah Bailey

Published by Twisted Tree Publications
www.twistedtreepublications.com
info@twistedtreepublications.com

Paperback ISBN: 978-1-913217-24-2

To all my queens who dance in the darkness,
This one's for you!

ONE

SCARLETT

TEN YEARS AGO

I t felt like I'd been drowning forever. My mind was a swamp filled with vegetation and things tangling around my legs, preventing me from surfacing. All I wanted was to come up for air. To find my way back to whatever I'd left behind. Only… I had no clue what it was I was fighting for. Everything was jumbled up. Nothing made sense. It was all a blur, a haze of images I didn't recognise.

There was a beeping sound next to me. It was incessant. I tried to focus on it. On the pattern of it. The way it drummed in my ears, echoing the beat in my chest.

My heart. My heart was beating. And the noise was connected to it.

Awareness of my surroundings bled back into my consciousness. I wanted to move. I wanted to open my eyes, but my lids were heavy and uncooperative. A whooshing sound joined the beeping. It took me a long minute to realise I wasn't breathing on my own. The rise and fall of my chest was too clinical, too perfectly paced.

I wanted to wake up. Wanted to come back to the world even though I couldn't remember why or what it held for me. The only thing I knew was that I needed it. My eyes needed to open. My fingers needed to move. My lips needed to make sounds. Whoever was out there needed to know I was awake but trapped in my own body.

However long it took, I didn't know, but my fingers twitched. They moved a fraction, stroking across the soft material below me. A sound carried towards my ears. It was alien to me in so many ways, but somehow, I recognised it as words... a voice.

"She's moving."

I hung onto those two words. They propelled me forward. Someone else was here. Another person. My eyes flew open and remained unblinking for a long moment, staring up at the white ceiling. A face appeared above me. It wasn't one I recognised. Soft brown eyes stared into my own ones. He had a heart-shaped face and a lopsided smile along with a head of light brown hair.

"Scarlett, can you hear me?"

I blinked. It was the only movement I could make. There was something in my mouth preventing me from talking. A tube helping me breathe. My lungs didn't like that any longer. I choked, trying to breathe on my own. I couldn't. This thing needed to come out. It needed to disappear. The beeping sound increased with my heart rate spiking as panic constricted my chest.

2

CHAOS

"Shit."

The face disappeared. My hand twitched again. I needed to breathe. Desperately needed to breathe.

Let me out. Someone let me out, please. Help me. Let me breathe.

A hand landed on my head, stroking my hair back.

"It's okay, Scarlett. Everything is going to be okay. Just go back to sleep now," a different voice told me, soothing me from the inside out.

There was a minute more where I wanted to talk, wanted to tell them to let me out, but then I drifted off again into oblivion. Only there was nothing for me there but the swamp and vines holding me down in the water. I hated it. Every moment of it. I wanted to come back to the surface. There were people there. People who could tell me what was going on and why I was stuck in my body, unable to get out.

How long I drifted, I had no clue. The sudden rush to an alert state had my eyes flicking open. This time, there was no whooshing sound. And nothing was holding my mouth open. My chest rose and fell at a steady, more natural pace. I was breathing on my own. The beeping remained, reminding me my heart was beating. I was alive and awake.

Turning my head, I could see I was in a room surrounded by machines, but it wasn't a hospital. It was a regular bedroom. Looking down, I found myself practically immobilised in the bed. One of my arms was encased in a plaster cast and I couldn't see under the covers placed over me, hiding my legs from view. I tried to move them and found it hurt too much. At that point, I didn't think it would be the best idea to attempt to get out of bed.

"Whash hapshen?"

I had meant to say *what happened,* but my speech came out slurred and stilted.

Why couldn't I talk properly?

Why couldn't I remember what happened to me?

I had too many questions and there was no one there to answer them for me.

I lay there, trying to keep my breathing steady and even while inside, I was panicking. When I tried to focus on the hazy images in my head, I couldn't remember anything.

What was my name?

I didn't know my own name.

A tear fell down my cheek. This was too much for me to handle. My mind was a riot of images I couldn't place or see clearly. And I didn't even know who I was.

A door opened to my right. I turned my head and found the man with the soft brown eyes and light brown hair walking towards me. When he saw I was awake, he smiled at me.

"Hello, Scarlett, welcome back to the land of the living."

He took a seat in the chair next to me.

"Haaa."

I was trying to say hello, but I couldn't form words properly. Why wasn't my mouth working? I had no idea why I could understand him or words when I couldn't remember anything.

He reached out and took my hand, stroking a thumb down the back of it.

"Shh, it's okay. They said you may have trouble speaking."

I wanted to burst into tears. How could I explain to this person that I didn't recognise him? I didn't know who he was.

"I should get the nurse for you, she'll be able to explain what happened."

I shook my head and gripped onto his fingers the best I could. I didn't want him to leave now he was here.

"Paaapaaa."

If I couldn't talk, then I could attempt to communicate in another way. The man seemed to understand what I was asking for.

"You want something to write on?"

I nodded. He let go of my hand and pulled out his phone from his pocket. Fiddling with it for a moment, he then set it near my hand.

"You can write with your finger, okay?"

Using one finger, I wrote down what I could manage.

Who are you?

He frowned.

"I'm Mason."

I don't know who I am.

His eyes turned sad.

"You're Scarlett."

Scarlett. He'd called me that. And whoever had been here before had called me Scarlett as well. I sounded out the name in my head. I didn't recognise it, but if it's what this Mason was telling me, then maybe it was my name.

Where am I?

"At home."

What happened?

He shook his head.

"I think it's better if I get the nurse for you. She can answer your questions."

5

Please tell me.

He paused and then sighed as he looked over at the door.

"You were in an accident and you've been in a coma for four weeks."

I swallowed and tears spilt down my cheeks. An accident? Four weeks in a coma? Was that why my arm was in a cast and why my legs hurt when I moved them?

An accident?

"Yes. Look, let me get the nurse, okay? I promise I won't be gone for long."

I nodded at him. If this nurse was going to tell me what happened, then I might as well let him get the person. Mason didn't immediately leave. He stared down at me with sad eyes before he reached over and wiped away my tears with his fingers.

"I'm sorry, Scarlett, I really am. This must be confusing for you, but just know I'm here for you, okay? We'll get through this together. I'll keep you safe."

He dropped his hand back to mine again and gave it a squeeze. I smiled at him. If he was telling the truth, then perhaps I could trust this man, even though I had no memory of him. I had no memories at all. And it was the very worst part about waking up after four weeks of drowning in the murky waters of my mind.

TWO

SCARLETT

T he knife pierced through flesh, sinking deep into Mason's chest. I let out a wail of pain as his body jolted. It decimated me, seeing it sticking out of him with my hand and West's wrapped around the handle. West had done nothing other than hold on to me. He hadn't pushed me to stab the knife into the man's chest with his hand, only with his words. Only the command to kill the man in the chair. To kill Mason.

When I pulled out the knife, I would spill his blood. The idea of it made me sick, but I had to do this. It was the only way to make it quick and painless like West had told me to.

I jerked the knife out of Mason's chest, watching the blood pool on the white t-shirt he was wearing. Something about it shattered a piece of my sanity. This man hadn't protected me from my parents. No matter how much Mason had done for me, he'd failed to keep me safe. He'd fucking well failed.

I let out a scream, and then the knife was sailing through the air again. It landed in a different spot this time, but I was already ripping it out of Mason's chest. West let go of my hand when he realised I wasn't stopping, but he didn't move away from me. He stayed at my back, watching me as my hand came down repeatedly, stabbing over and over again. There was blood everywhere, but I couldn't stop. I couldn't fucking well stop.

"Fuck you," I screamed. "You didn't fucking keep me safe. You're a liar!"

It was as if I'd lost my mind. All I could do was keep stabbing him. Taking out all of my anger and frustration at the past ten years of my life. At the abuse I'd suffered. The heartache over not knowing who the hell I was before my accident. Being trapped in a prison and never allowed my freedom. All of it came pouring out of me until I was sobbing and my movements slowed. Then my arm hung limply at my side.

I panted, tears still flowing and mixing with the blood splattered all over my face and arms. I was pretty sure it had got on my clothes too. The thought of it made my knees give out.

West wrapped his arms around my waist, holding me so I wouldn't collapse in a heap on the floor.

"That's a good girl," he whispered. "You did so good."

I stared down at the man in the chair. Who knew how many times I'd stabbed him. His t-shirt was an absolute mess of slashes and cuts. There was blood everywhere. It looked like a damn massacre had occurred.

I'd killed my only friend. My only fucking friend. He was a bloody mess in front of me. A torn, bloody mess.

"What did I do?" I cried out. "Oh my god, what did I do?"

"You did what we asked you to."

I rested my head against West's shoulder, feeling my energy leave me in a rush. The man behind me had forced me to kill my friend, but I didn't have the strength to give him shit for it.

"I killed him."

"Yeah, you really fucking did, Scar. Just like I knew you could."

I wanted to laugh, but none of this was funny. My mind was broken. I was a murderer. I'd fucking murdered someone. And for what reason? To make them trust me and to get an in with these men who were actual psychopaths or, at the very least, sociopaths. There was nothing normal about Prescott, West, Francis, and Drake. They stood there and watched me kill someone.

I looked down at myself. My arms were blood-spattered, as were my clothes. The knife was still in my hand. I stared at it. The implement I'd used to massacre Mason's chest. This was too fucked up, all of it horrifying, and yet I'd done it. I'd fucking well done it. More tears fell down my cheeks. I thought I was done crying, but clearly not.

"Is this enough?" I whispered. "Have I paid your price?"

"Mmm, yes and then some."

West nuzzled my neck again. I shivered, the coldness of the warehouse hitting me after my stabbing frenzy. West was warm, but shock and horror were rushing through me too.

"I won't lie, Scar, watching you stab a guy to death is hot."

SARAH BAILEY

It confirmed for me how psychopathic West was, if that kind of thing turned him on. I could feel him hard against my back. Even though his body heat was preventing me from shivering to death, I no longer wanted him near me. This man had encouraged me to kill someone for him.

I shoved him off me. West let go, but not before he plucked his knife from my fingers, as if he was concerned about me turning it on him. No matter how much I hated him, I didn't think I had the energy to stab him as well.

A loud sound reverberated through the room. It took a second for me to recognise it for what it was. A slow clapping noise. I stared as the source of it appeared in front of us, walking into the light of the single bulb illuminating the room. I took him in, wondering who the hell this was. And fearing the fact he knew I'd killed someone too.

The newcomer had a black shirt on with the sleeves rolled up to his elbows and red braces attached to his dark trousers. The first few buttons of his shirt were undone, exposing his chest. He had light brown hair, grey eyes and his nails were painted black, but the thing that struck me the most about him was his tattoos. They were everywhere. All over his hands. Up his forearms. Across his chest and his neck. They even went up into his hairline. He was relatively slim, but it didn't make him any less imposing.

"That was quite something," he said with a smirk as he approached the man in the chair. "I wasn't expecting your little waif of a woman to have such a temper on her. Guess looks can be very deceiving."

He gave me a wink. Then he reached out and tugged at the hood on the man's head. I was about to tell him to stop, as I didn't want to see Mason's face, when he pulled it off completely. My mouth dropped open. And my entire world came crashing down around me.

The man in the chair wasn't Mason. I didn't even recognise him.

I backed away, my bloody hand going to my mouth.

What the fuck?

"That's... that's not..."

"Don't worry, he got what was coming to him," said the newcomer, staring down at the man in the chair with disdain.

"Who are you? Who... who is he?"

I waved at the dead man. The one I'd killed. The one who wasn't Mason.

"My apologies. I'm Penn Harlow. I... fix things." He winked at me again. "And this guy? Well, let's just say he liked young girls a little too much if you catch my drift."

I wanted to be sick. Turning away, I found the Horsemen standing together watching me and this Penn without any concern in their features.

"What the hell is this?" I waved my arms around. "What the fuck did you make me do?"

"I told you, Scar, a price had to be paid for our protection."

I stabbed a finger at West, who'd answered me.

"Why the fuck would you tell me it was Mason?"

He grinned. It made me want to slap it off his face.

"To see if you would go through with it."

"What the fuck is that supposed to mean?"

West stepped towards me.

11

"Loyalty is very important to us, Scar. We wanted to see how far you would go, whether you'd kill the person who hurt you. The one you think is your only friend."

He spat the last part as if the thought of Mason being my friend disgusted him. Right now, all four of them disgusted me. How could they do this to me? How could they make me think it was Mason I'd killed? They were insane. All of them.

"So what, you found some random guy for me to kill to prove a fucking point? You're sick. All of you are sick in the fucking head."

"He wasn't a random guy, Scar. He was a kiddy-fiddler. You did the world a favour by getting rid of scum like him."

I couldn't believe him. Any of them.

"If this is the kind of shit you get off on, then count me out. I'm done."

West tutted.

"Now, now, do you think we're going to let you leave after this?"

I stared at him. He had to be kidding. There was no way I wanted to be anywhere near them. Not after the shit they'd pulled. Not after I'd lost my mind and killed a man they'd told me was Mason, but it turned out he was some random sicko who liked kids.

"Fuck you. If you think I want to go anywhere with you lot, you're delusional."

I knew what I'd done was fucked up and wrong, but I couldn't cope with thinking about it. My mind was shattered. They'd fucking ruined me.

"You're coming home with us, little lamb," Prescott said, taking a step towards me.

CHAOS

I couldn't stand looking at him. While I was pissed off at West, I was enraged when it came to Prescott. He didn't stop this from happening. He'd made me feel like I had no choice but to kill my friend for his protection. To prove to him I was trustworthy. And yet… I had a feeling Prescott still didn't trust me, even after this. It was the way he stared at me. He shouldn't trust me, but it didn't stop it from hurting.

"How could you do this to me?" I pointed at West. "Him I can understand, but you… you… I thought…"

I didn't know what I thought. That he cared? Had he ever cared about me? Or I was another fucking pawn in their games.

"I meant what I said," I ground out. "I fucking meant it. I hate you."

Prescott flinched, a wounded look flashing across his face. He took a step towards me, reaching out his hand, but it dropped when I stepped back. There was no way in hell I was allowing him to touch me. He could burn in fucking hell for all I cared.

Are you sure? Are you sure you're not just saying that because he hurt you and you're mad at him?

My brain could do one.

"Be that as it may," Drake said. "It doesn't change the fact you are coming with us."

My eyes flicked up to his. He and Francis had remained silent this entire time.

"No, no I'm not. There is no way in hell I am going with you."

Drake stared at me with those terrifyingly calm indigo eyes of his.

"Yes, Scarlett, you are."

13

"You can go to hell along with these two." I waved at Prescott and West. "And him too." I waved at Francis. "All of you. Go to hell."

He stepped towards me.

"Where do you think you're going to go, hmm? You just killed someone."

Drake's words slapped me right in the damn face. Where *did* I think I was going to go? It's not like I could run to Mason and tell him I'd killed a man who I thought was him. Then he really would send me back to my parents. I had no one else but the men in front of me. No one.

"Him... I'll go with him."

I turned and looked at Penn, who raised his eyebrow.

"No offence, but I don't let waifs and strays tag along with me," he said with a wink.

He'd been busy untying the man from the chair and placing him down on a plastic sheet, which I hadn't noticed before. It had been under the chair the whole time. The man's blood was all over it and not the floor.

"What are you doing with him?"

"Getting rid of him. After all, someone paid me handsomely to dispose of this fucker. Your friends over there asked if I could provide them with someone to kill. Lucky for them, I had just the man."

Penn straightened. I noticed he'd put leather gloves on.

"Normally I'd send this one away to my friend who likes to rid the world of cunts, but Drake made me an offer I couldn't refuse."

I stared at him.

"What exactly do you do?"

14

CHAOS

Why I was even asking questions of this guy, I had no idea, but my mind was all over the place.

"I'm a Fixer."

I'd clearly made a face because he continued.

"I fix problems like this guy amongst... other things."

I didn't know if I wanted to know what other things this guy 'fixed'. In fact, I didn't want to know anything any longer because everything right now was fucked. And yet my mouth asked another question anyway.

"What the hell did they offer you?"

Penn smirked. My eyes were drawn to the scar on the right side of his face that ran from his ear to his jaw. It only gave him a further air of danger.

"Why, what any man in my position requires, money and a favour to be collected at my convenience."

He shrugged and went back to dealing with the dead guy. The guy I'd killed.

Stop thinking about it.

I turned back to the Horsemen.

"If you're thinking about running, I suggest you don't, Scarlett," Drake said. "You have five witnesses, not to mention the fact we have what you did on camera. We could quite easily turn you in."

I stiffened. While running hadn't crossed my mind, it could have. And after what Drake said, I had absolutely no choice but to go with them. I crossed my arms over my chest and glared at them. It drew my attention to the blood all over me again.

"You filmed it?"

15

"Yes. We need some collateral in case you decide to run from us at any point."

I had to hand it to them, they'd thought this through, even though it was messed up. Even though it meant I was trapped. My breath whooshed out of me as defeat sunk in.

"Fine, guess I have no other choice."

Drake gave me a sharp nod and stepped closer.

"First, we need to get you cleaned up. Come with me."

I didn't want to go anywhere with him, but what other choice did I have? Francis handed him a bag, and Drake strode off deeper into the warehouse. I hurried after him, not wanting to get stuck with the rest of them. He stopped outside a door and shoved it open. He waited while I walked in before following me, shutting the door behind us. The room was only illuminated by the light coming through from a window. There was a sink and a toilet, but not much else.

Drake kicked the lid closed and placed the bag on top of it. He looked at me.

"Take your clothes off."

I stepped back, banging my back against the sink counter.

"What?"

"They're covered in blood and we need to dispose of them, unless you want to leave evidence of what you did hanging around."

I gave him a look.

"Fine, I'll take them off and wash myself but you don't need to be here."

He stalked towards me. I had nowhere else to go when he placed his hands down on either side of the sink from me.

"I think you'll find I do."

CHAOS

His eyes darkened. It was the first time I'd ever seen his mask drop. There was a deadly glint to his expression. And I knew I wasn't going to like what he said next.

"You're covered in blood, Scarlett." He inhaled, making me shiver. "I like blood."

THREE

DRAKE

I'd always known Scarlett was a magnificent being, but today only proved it once and for all. The fury consuming her as she'd lost herself in killing the man Penn had provided for us was like watching a regal queen claiming her crown.

Here she was in front of me, her face splattered with blood, and fuck if the sight of it didn't make me lose my damn mind. She was stunning in her stained clothes and her skin marred by red liquid.

My little wisp. You're everything I'd hoped you'd be and more.

My hand left the sink and traced a line through the blood on her face. She stared at me as if she wasn't sure whether she should be afraid of me or not.

"Drake, what are you doing?"

"You know that's not what you say when we're alone."

"If you think I'm calling you sir after what you lot made me

I used my finger to smear blood over her bottom lip, silencing her. As much as I'd love to suck it off her, I wasn't in the habit of licking blood from a source I didn't know was safe.

"I think you're going to close this bratty little mouth of yours and let me clean you up."

Her eyes widened, but she didn't open her mouth again. Probably too scared she'd get blood in it. Leaving her by the sink, I moved back over to the bag I'd placed on the toilet seat and extracted a cloth. We had planned for all eventualities this evening, hence why we had supplies to clean our girl up.

Scarlett didn't move from her spot, and when I approached her again, she stared at me with no small amount of defiance in her expression. If she tried anything, I would have no qualms about punishing her for it.

Reaching behind her, I ran the tap and soaked the washcloth with it. Then I brought it up to her face and wiped the blood from it, taking my time as the water ran in bloody rivulets down her cheeks and chin. Placing the washcloth in the sink, I set my hands at the bottom of her bloody t-shirt and tugged it up off her head. Her skin rose in goosebumps with the cool air. She didn't stop me from removing her bra. I threw the garments on the floor before popping the button on her jeans and unzipping them.

Scarlett's bare chest rose and fell with increasing heaviness. She gripped the sink counter behind her with both hands, watching me pull her jeans from her body. She kicked off her flip-flops and stood there, waiting for me to make my next move.

CHAOS

My fingers traced a line along the top of her underwear. I didn't strictly need to take these off, but I didn't give a shit. I wanted her bare for me.

"You're such a defiant little brat, aren't you?" I murmured as I snapped the waistband of her knickers. "You should know better than to try that with me."

I tore her underwear down her legs and set her on the counter. Scarlett's eyes were wide as I lowered myself to my knees. Her gasp echoed around the room when my mouth met her inner thigh. I held her legs open so she couldn't stop me from kissing my way up towards her pussy. The moment my tongue met the softness of her lips, she squeaked. I looked up at her. If I couldn't fucking well taste the blood from her body, this was the next best thing.

I spread her lips with my fingers and found my way to her clit, flicking my tongue over it and eliciting more gasps from her lips. Dipping lower, I tasted her essence. Fuck, my woman was so wet. Moving back to her clit, I slid two fingers inside her dripping heat.

"Drake," she whined, her fingers going to my head. The ones stained with the blood of the man she'd killed. My dick throbbed in response. The idea of my woman stabbing a man to death, and being covered in his blood, appealed to me on some primal level. I wanted to fuck her while she was bathed in blood, but right now, her being splattered with it was a fucking high in and of itself.

Scarlett might not be particularly happy with me. She wasn't happy with any of us, but I didn't care. She was *mine*. And I wanted her body close. I wanted to feel her clench and strain around me.

My fingers thrust inside her, making her buck and her fingers tighten in my hair. She let out another whine and I was done. I tore her hand from me and stood. My fingers went to my trousers, tugging them open as I held her hand down on the counter with my other one. She panted, her pupils dilated and her body trembling. The moment I got my dick free, I stepped up between her legs and rubbed the tip over her wet little pussy.

Letting go of her hand, I gripped her chin, forcing her to look at me.

"Defiance won't be tolerated going forward, Scarlett. If you talk back to me, I won't hesitate to show you exactly why you need to keep your smart mouth shut."

And with that, I thrust inside her. Her lips parted in a silent gasp. I didn't give her a chance to adjust, pulling back and slamming inside her again. My hand wrapped around her hip, dragging her closer to the edge so I could have full access to her deliciously hot and wet pussy.

She gripped my wrist with her blood-stained hand, but she didn't pull it away. She held it there as if she was taunting me. The redness of the life-sustaining liquid against her skin almost fucking mesmerised me.

It spoke of violence.

It spoke of passion.

It spoke of death.

"Did you like it? Huh? Did it give you a fucking high?"

She whimpered but didn't reply.

"I think you did." I punctuated my words with my hips thrusting into her. "The first time is always the worst, but it gets easier. It becomes beautiful... watching their life fade away."

The way her eyes fixed on mine and her expression told me how conflicted she felt about the fact I was fucking her right now. How I'd told her I liked blood and death. The way I was taunting her.

"I require an answer, Scarlett. Did. You. Like. It?"

Her teeth dug into her lip. My hand around her chin tightened. The violence of my thrusts increased, punishing her for her unwillingness to give me what I wanted. This woman was sent to drive me to distraction. She was testing my patience and damn self-control. Every time she was near me, I wanted to do things to her little body. Paint her skin red. Bleed her. Make her cry.

Leaning down, I sucked her bottom lip in my mouth, pulling it from her teeth. And I replaced them with my own, biting down almost hard enough to break the skin. Her high-pitched moan only made it worse. She was in need of a serious fucking lesson.

I let go of her lip but kept my face close to hers.

"Do you like to defy me, hmm? Are you trying to test how far you can push the limits of my patience?"

"No," she whispered.

"Answer the question."

"I didn't like it."

I smiled.

"Liar."

Her nails dug into my wrist as if she hated the fact I could see right through her.

"No, I didn't want to kill him. I didn't like it. I had no other fucking choice but to do it. You didn't give me one."

We hadn't, but it was hardly the point. She could have told us all to go fuck ourselves and left. She hadn't. It meant she was more terrified of something other than getting stuck with us. And I intended to find out exactly what it was my woman was so damn afraid of. Not now, but soon.

I shouldn't have stripped her off and sunk my dick in her, but fuck if I could control myself after witnessing her rage-filled stabbing fest. All that blood called to me. Her passion lit a fire under my skin. It burnt way too hot.

I let go of her chin, pulling her grasp from mine and dropped my hand into her lap. It landed on her thigh and my thumb found her clit, stroking her while I continued to pound into her pussy like I could never get enough. And I couldn't. Just because I hadn't taken her since the night we'd drugged our woman, didn't mean I hadn't thought about it.

Her hips bucked into me and her hands gripped the counter. She moaned and made it very clear she wanted me to drive her higher no matter how she felt about this situation.

"You want to come, hmm?" I whispered, my lips dragging across hers.

"Please."

I chuckled.

"Please, what?"

Her eyes flashed with irritation. If she wasn't going to obey, she wouldn't get her pleasure.

"Please, sir."

My thumb worked harder on her clit and I kissed her, pressing her mouth hard against mine. Scarlett didn't hesitate in kissing me back even though her hands remained on the counter. Trying to convince herself she didn't really want what I was giving her, no doubt. But fuck, her mouth was sweet and the way she kissed me… so fucking raw. It's like she wanted to cry in my mouth over what she'd done, but she held her tears back.

When she came, it was violent and unforgiving. Her teeth latched onto my lip and her muffled cry echoed around the room. Her hands stayed on the counter, holding onto it while her body shook and trembled. I let her do what she wished. If she needed to hurt me with her teeth, then so be it. Seeing her overcome with pleasure was my only focus.

Releasing my lip, she slumped back against the wall, closing her eyes as her fists unclenched from the counter. I held her hips and continued to take her. Seeing the blood on her arms made my balls tighten. It was a one-way train and I couldn't get off. Grunting, I emptied myself inside her spent body, wanting nothing more than to stay locked together in ecstasy forever.

Her eyes snapped open when I slowed. She didn't look happy, but she didn't look unhappy either. More like resigned to her fate. Reaching behind her, I wet the cloth again and took her arms, wiping away the blood from them and her hands. She didn't stop me from cleaning her up the best I could. There was still blood in her hair, but there wasn't much I could do about it.

Pulling out of her, I zipped myself up and grabbed the bag, fishing out a towel to rub her down with. Scarlett didn't say a word while I helped her dress in a t-shirt, a warm jumper and jogging bottoms we'd bought for her. She slid her feet into her flip-flops after we'd rinsed them off. I stuffed the bloodied clothes in the bag along with everything else. We'd get rid of the evidence before returning home to Fortuity.

I opened the door, allowing Scarlett to stalk from the room, her flip-flops slapping along the concrete floor. I followed her, knowing she was about to unleash hell after what I'd done. It hadn't been my smartest idea to fuck her, but the sight of her overcame my common sense.

"Well, you took your time," West said as she neared them.

Penn had already disappeared with the dead guy. Probably a good thing, given Scarlett's current state of mind.

"Do you ever just shut the fuck up?" Scarlett spat at him, coming to a standstill on the fringes of the lit area.

West's eyes narrowed, but he didn't make a move towards her. He looked at me when I entered the fray.

"What did you do to her?"

"Nothing," I replied. "It's time to leave."

Scarlett's eyes blazed.

"I don't recall shoving me up against the sink and fucking me as being nothing."

I gave her a look. Clearly, someone had decided she wasn't in the mood to be a good girl any longer.

"And if you think I'm going to get into a car with you after that, you're fucking insane." She stabbed a finger in West's direction. "I'm not going with him either." Then she turned her gaze on Prescott. The venom in her eyes made him flinch. "And I would rather jump off a fucking cliff than be near him."

With that, she stalked over to Francis, who looked like a deer caught in headlights.

"You can take me back on the condition you do not fucking talk to me or touch me." She turned her head, looking at all of us. "None of you are going to touch me, you hear me? I will fucking hurt you if you come near me."

Francis gave me a helpless look, but I shrugged. I didn't think anything the rest of us said or did would calm her temper right now.

"Just take her, we'll deal with the rest of this."

We had two cars, so it wasn't an issue.

Francis let out a sigh and looked at Prescott, who dug the keys out of his pocket and tossed them. Francis caught them and put out a hand to Scarlett. She stalked away towards the door. He trudged after her.

When they left by the door, Prescott turned to me, his eyes full of conflict.

"Do you think she'll forgive me?"

West scoffed. I gave him a dark look.

"With the mood she's in right now, who knows."

Prescott looked at his feet. Clearly, he wasn't happy with all this shit, but he had to deal. His crap with Scarlett was his own problem to work out. I didn't have time to pander to his feelings.

"Anyway, let's finish this and get out of here. Be thankful you're not Francis right now. I have a feeling he'll be getting an earful from her."

"Too fucking right," West agreed.

Prescott didn't acknowledge us, merely moved away towards the door.

"You think he'll be okay?" I asked West.

"Why the fuck do you care?"

"I'd rather not have him moping around the damn place like a lovesick puppy."

"He'll work it out. Just needs to fuck her stupid after grovelling at her feet for a bit."

If only it was the solution to Prescott's problems with Scarlett. Something about the way they were together told me both of them had feelings that ran deeper than either of them was willing to admit. And I hoped he did work it out. If he didn't, having her living with us might utterly derail all of our plans.

FOUR

FRANCIS

I moved Scarlett's bag into the back of the car, allowing her to sit in the passenger seat. She crossed her arms over her chest and stared out of the window. I stifled a sigh and set off, reversing out of the side road leading to the warehouse and turning around. When we got onto the main road, Scarlett let out a breath. I didn't want to make things worse for her, so I was going to keep my mouth shut and take her back to Fortuity. Back to our home. She'd have to remain with us for the foreseeable future.

Perhaps I shouldn't feel like shit for what we'd made her do, but I did. When West suggested it, I hadn't objected. To be honest, I couldn't. He wanted to punish her, sure, but it also gave us something to hold over her head. To keep her in line. It proved a fucking point too. The power we had over the girl we'd grown up with.

However, no matter our reasons, it didn't make me feel good about it. Not after the way she'd lost it. Seeing her attack the guy in such a violent manner was like watching West butcher someone. It reminded me of why Scarlett had always been one of us. Inside her soul, there was a darkness lurking. An ugliness we all shared. One we'd revelled in as kids. She might have been our guiding light, keeping us from descending into madness, but she'd always been borderline on the crazy scale. It didn't take much to tip her over the edge.

"Whose idea was it?"

I glanced at her but she wasn't looking at me. She had told me not to talk but asking me a direct question meant she wanted an answer.

"To get you to kill someone?"

"Yes."

"I think you already know."

She traced her finger along the window.

"West. He wanted to hurt me."

It had more to do with the fact he couldn't hurt Mason than Scarlett being in the wrong. He had an extremely fucked up sense of justice, but West knew what he was doing. He knew hurting Scarlett would hurt Mason too.

"Sort of."

"What's that supposed to mean?"

I gripped the steering wheel tighter.

"West is complicated, Scarlett. You shouldn't try to rationalise his actions. It won't get you very far."

She snorted.

"He's a psycho. An actual full-blown psychopath."

I would have disputed her statement, but there would be no point. Psychopaths lack empathy. West might not show it, but he had a shred of it somewhere inside him. I'd seen it with my own fucking eyes. It had been reserved for the woman beside me. Only she couldn't remember the boy West had been. She only knew the man who could flip at the drop of a hat. If she regained those memories, she would see him differently. She'd see him like we did.

Yes, I'd come to blows with West many times, but it wasn't because I hated the guy. We were best friends. All four of us were. There just happened to be a very good reason for his animosity towards me. One I didn't want to think about.

"He's too fucked in the head to know how wrong this all is."

I didn't try to refute it. She wouldn't listen. He knew all right, he just didn't care. Or maybe he did. West was a law unto himself.

"I hate him and I hate Drake and I fucking hate Prescott."

It didn't escape my notice that she hadn't mentioned me. Perhaps I was the lesser of all the evils in her mind. At least, this evening. In mine, I wasn't any better, what with using her in the car on the way over here. It had been so fucking sweet to have her mouth wrapped around my dick, but now wasn't the time to be thinking of her in that way.

"I thought he actually gave a shit. He made me think he did. The way he looks at me like I'm precious to him, but then he goes and does this. Goes along with all this shit you lot concocted up to test me… well, fuck him. If he thinks he can worm his way back into my fucking knickers after this, he's thoroughly mistaken. No way I'm letting him anywhere near me. He can get his kicks elsewhere."

Her diatribe against Prescott didn't exactly surprise me. However, I very much doubted Scarlett meant the last part. It was clear as day to me she had developed feelings. And I'm not sure she'd be very impressed if Prescott did indeed 'get his kicks elsewhere'. He wouldn't. He was too enamoured with her to contemplate seeing anyone else. None of us would stray from Scarlett now we had her back in our lives.

"And don't even get me started on Drake. What the fuck is wrong with him? He's got serious issues."

I had some idea of what she might be referring to. I'd seen the glint in his eyes. It was obvious Scarlett being covered in blood had him all hard and shit for her.

"Do you know what he said to me? He fucking told me he liked blood. Who says that? Like what the fuck? And he asked me if I liked what I'd done. I didn't think normal people actually enjoyed stabbing a man to death, but hey, apparently, I'm living in some alternate universe where this type of shit is perfectly okay."

I held back a snort. Those were things I could well imagine Drake saying to her. He had a thing about blood and death. None of us judged him for it, considering what we were into, but we did like to rib him on occasion. He was always the last one of us to lose his temper. In fact, I'd only seen it a handful of times. None of them had been pretty. Drake could be as vicious as West when it came to people who pushed him too hard.

"Also where the fuck does he get off calling me a brat?"

I raised an eyebrow.

"If he wanted an obedient woman who doesn't speak her own mind, then he should've picked another girl because that isn't me. I'll kick his stupid arse if he tries that shit with me again. Brat indeed."

I couldn't hold back my laughter this time. Scarlett glared at me.

"What's so funny?"

I rubbed my chin before placing my hand back on the steering wheel.

"The idea of Drake wanting you to be completely obedient."

"What do you mean? You're the one who told me to be careful around him."

I shook my head and smiled at her.

"Yeah, when I thought you might not be able to handle his... quirks. But I can assure you, he likes the fact you're feisty."

She was quiet for a moment, her fingers still tracing lines across the glass window next to her.

"You think I'm feisty?"

"You're certainly not shy and retiring."

"Do you like that about me?"

I nibbled my lip, wondering if I should admit anything to her or not. This was not how I envisioned this car journey going, but if she was in a mind to talk, then I wouldn't stifle her. Perhaps she needed normalcy after what happened.

"I do."

"You barely know me though."

I wish I could tell you how well we all used to know each other. How you were our rock... our anchor. The one thing holding us together.

"I've seen enough."

"Hmm."

My eyes drifted to her for a moment. She was looking out the front window now. There was an air of melancholy surrounding her. I wanted to reach out and touch her, to soothe her somehow, but I refrained. She'd made it very clear she didn't want to be touched. And I wanted to respect her boundaries.

Turning my attention back to the road, I hoped the others weren't too far behind us. Even if Scarlett didn't want to see them, we all needed to talk about her. About what happened this evening.

A few minutes later, I pulled into the underground car park beneath our building and stopped in one of our reserved spaces right by the lift. Scarlett sat there, staring at the concrete wall in front of us. I left her to it, getting out of the car and going over to the lift to press the button. Then I collected all her bags from the car, placing them inside the lift when it arrived.

"Scarlett, you can't stay in the car all night," I called to her from the doors.

She got out and gave me a dark look. I locked the car as she trudged over to me and walked into the lift. Stepping in, I entered the code for the penthouse and leant back against the mirrors. Scarlett didn't say a word the whole way up. When the doors opened, she strode out and looked around the place. I took her bags out one by one and left them near the lift door.

"I want a shower," she said when the doors closed behind me. "And where am I staying?"

I wished I didn't have to be the one to tell her.

"With one of us."

We didn't have a spare room and we certainly weren't going to put her in our play space. It wasn't exactly sleep-friendly.

Besides, she needed to be kept an eye on. We weren't going to let her wander around our penthouse unsupervised.

"You cannot be serious!"

"Afraid so."

She threw her hands up and gave me a dirty look.

"Well, that's just fucking great."

I picked up her nearest bag and pointed towards the stairs. She let out a huff but walked up them with me following behind. I assumed, given our conversation in the car, I would be her choice this evening.

When we got to my bedroom, I opened the door and flipped the light switch. Scarlett looked around, all traces of annoyance fading when she took in her surroundings. I set her bag down by the door and watched her walk around my personal space, her eyes darting this way and that.

I had a rather rustic style with my huge wooden four-poster bed sitting against a faux wooden wall. It had large brass rings sitting above the headboard, screwed into the wall. There was a stone electric fireplace on the opposite side with a TV above it. My wardrobe doors were the same wood as the accent wall, and beside it lay the door to my bathroom. By the window, I had a large, soft cream sofa. My bedroom was pretty neutral colour wise.

"This isn't what I expected," she said, coming to a standstill by the window looking out across the city. "I like it." She turned back to me. "But I am not sleeping with you."

I gave her a nod.

"Take the bed. I can sleep there." I waved at the sofa. "It's not a problem."

It was comfortable enough to sleep on. It was also the least I could do after what she'd been through this evening.

I walked over to the bathroom door and opened it.

"Take a shower, Scarlett. I'll get the rest of your stuff. We can organise it tomorrow, okay?"

She gave me a slight smile to acknowledge what I'd said before she turned back to the window. I made my way over to the door. There wasn't anything in here she could mess around with. I kept that stuff locked up.

One last glance at her before I left the room told me she was finally coming down from the adrenaline rush of murder and sex. And I was pretty sure she would crash sooner rather than later.

FIVE

SCARLETT

W hen Francis left the room, I walked over to the bathroom door and stepped in. My fingers found the light switch. The room was fully tiled in the same neutral colours as his bedroom. He had a separate bath from his shower. There were no windows, but it was bright enough.

I walked over behind the glass wall leading to the shower and flipped it on. I didn't care about having my own products. All I wanted was to get clean. Even though Drake had washed away most of the blood from my body, spots remained. And I felt dirty… marred by what I'd done.

Tearing the clothes they'd bought me off my body, I got under the hot stream of water. It soothed me, washing away all of the horrors of this evening.

I couldn't believe I had to sleep in one of their rooms. Despite having proven to them I would kill a man on their behalf, they didn't trust me to be alone in their penthouse. It had to be the reason. That, or they didn't have anywhere else to put me. Either way, it sucked. I wanted to be alone to process everything. Yet how could I even begin to process what I'd done?

Opening my eyes, I watched the water, slightly stained red running into the shower drain. The sight of it made my stomach roil. I put my hand to my mouth, trying to push down the sickening feeling encompassing me.

I'd killed someone. I'd stabbed a man to death in the most violent manner I could think of. My mind had gone to another place and my body had taken over. My instincts. My rage. They'd sent me over the edge. Now I had to deal with the consequences of my actions. And the guilt. The fucking guilt eating me alive.

A sob erupted from my lips, my other hand reaching out to slam against the tiled wall in front of me. The floodgates opened. My knees buckled. I lowered myself to the floor, both my hands pressing to the large slab of slate covering the shower floor. Tears streamed down my face, mixing with the water from the shower. All I could hear was my horrific wails of agony and pain. I couldn't stop them. It was all too much. All of it.

They'd asked me to kill someone and told me it was Mason. All of my anger towards him had poured out of me as I stabbed him repeatedly. I thought I'd killed my only friend. And finding out it wasn't him was worse.

The Horsemen were fucked.

I was fucked.

The whole thing was fucked.

A solid body curled around mine and held me, strong arms caging me in as my hands slipped on the slate.

"It's okay, Scarlett," he murmured. "It's okay. Let it out. Just let it out."

My body shook with my sobs. My hands fell to his thighs, gripping the wet fabric below me as he sat back against the shower wall with me between his legs. Francis had got in the shower with me fully clothed. I knew it was him because I could smell cinnamon and apples on his skin. The scent reminded me of home and it made me cry harder.

"I killed him!" I wailed.

Francis held me tighter against his chest.

"I'm a killer. I… I can't believe I killed someone."

It decimated me… murdering a man I didn't know, even though they'd told me the guy had been scum. A child molester. I didn't believe in an eye for an eye or revenge. The only reason I'd even gone along with my parents and their stupid need for it was to gain my freedom. To get away from them and their abuse. I'd been trapped on their estate for so long, I thought I'd never get away. I'd never be free. And now I had a small sliver of it, I never wanted to let it go. I didn't want to go back.

It's why I'd killed a man for the Horsemen. It's why I'd paid their price. Being here with them was infinitely preferable to being at home with my parents, as fucked up as it sounded. These four men had taught me a lot about myself in the past month. Even though I couldn't remember solid details about the past before my accident, I was beginning to feel like the missing pieces of my personality were slotting into place. The real Scarlett was there, buried under concrete, but I'd dig her out. I'd fight to find her. I had to. There was no other choice.

I didn't care I was naked, crying in the shower with one of the men who'd demanded I kill for them. All I could feel was Francis' warmth. The comfort of having someone hold me while I cried and purged my emotions was everything. He had no idea how much this meant to me. How much I needed him to be here for me.

"Why does it hurt so much?" I choked out, my sobbing abating. "I didn't even know him and it hurts."

"Killing isn't supposed to be easy," he murmured in my ear over the noise of the shower. "It's supposed to hurt and bruise your soul."

"Did… did it hurt you?"

His chest deflated against my back. It was obvious to me they were killers themselves. I wasn't sure anyone who hadn't could stand to watch what I did without it affecting them. It was almost as if it was commonplace to the four of them.

"You're asking the wrong person that question."

"Why?" I sniffled, hiccupping on the word.

"You won't like the answer."

I shifted, wanting to look at him. Wanting to see his face. Francis released me enough to allow me to turn around. I knelt there in the shower between his legs, staring at him. His hands closed around my biceps, rubbing up and down my wet skin.

"Tell me."

His grey eyes were cautious and his dark brown hair plastered to his head.

I had a flash of an image in my mind. A much younger and more boyish version of Francis in the rain, staring up at the sky as it beat down on his face. I don't know why it was so vivid like it was actually real, but it couldn't possibly be. I'd never met Francis before I'd come to work at Fortuity... or had I? My past was so jumbled up in my head, I couldn't distinguish between true memories and the ones I merely wanted to be real.

"I don't have any remorse for the lives I've taken, Scarlett. I dare say I like it... the thrill of it. If you asked the others, they would tell you the exact same thing. We don't share the same morals society deems acceptable. We walk outside the lines of right and wrong. It's who we are. It's who we've always been."

Something about the brutal honesty of Francis' words had me swallowing. Coupled with the image of him as a teenager in my mind, I couldn't help but understand what he'd said, even if it was messed up. Morality was subjective. Everything in life was, on some level. And I couldn't honestly say his point of view surprised me given what I'd come to know about these four men.

"Does it scare you?" he asked when I didn't immediately respond.

"It should."

"That's not what I asked."

I leant closer to him, tugged by an invisible cord.

"No."

He cocked his head to the side and reached up, swiping his thumb under my eye. Our faces weren't under the stream of water, but we were both utterly soaked.

"The world isn't black and white," I continued. "I've always known that. If it was, then I'd know who I am inside." I pressed my hand to my chest. "I'd know the girl locked behind the wall in my mind."

"That's how you see it? Your amnesia?"

I nodded. For some reason, I felt safe to tell him these things. Safe to ask him the questions I had. There was no judgement here between us.

"Do you have any memories of the past at all?"

"I get these glimpses, snippets of old conversations, but like I told Prescott, I don't know if they're real or not."

Bringing up his name made my heart ache. I'd told Francis I hated Prescott, but I didn't. I was hurting because of him. Asking him to protect me hadn't been my smartest idea, but I never expected things would go this far. I never expected to have... feelings for him. It's as if my heart knew him inside out, but my mind struggled to keep up. My broken mind. It was split in two. The two halves needed reuniting.

His hand tangled in my wet hair and dragged me even closer until we were breathing the same air.

"You don't trust yourself."

"No."

"What did they tell you, the doctors, about your condition?"

I shifted, wanting to press myself against him. He said nothing when I straddled his lap, forcing his legs closer together. He didn't stop me when my fingers went to the bottom of his t-shirt. Tugging it over his head, it dropped on the shower floor with a splat.

I stared at his muscular body. He was beautiful to look at. A fallen god. They all were in my eyes, but not in the sense they were all-powerful. It was the way they held themselves like they knew their own worth. But they were dark and deadly too. They'd cut you down if you got in their way. And it made me wonder why they'd kept me if I was an inconvenience to them. Was I? Or did they want to fuck me that much, they didn't care I was a problem?

"My memories may never return, but it's not all doom and gloom. They simply don't know. Maybe the trauma of the accident stops me from seeing them, or I need to jog my memory somehow. They told me people and things from my childhood might help, but I have neither."

Francis' expression turned haunted for the briefest of moments.

"It's been ten years, so all I can do is hope."

He stroked my arm.

"Hope is a dangerous thing."

I smiled and shook my head.

"Guess it is."

Having purged my emotions and feelings, I felt steadier. What I'd done still hurt, but the pain had lessened a fraction. Enough for me to push myself up off Francis and stand. I put my hand out to him. He let me pull him up to his feet. Then I noticed he'd set my products down by the edge of the shower next to the glass. He'd gone out of his way to get my toiletries and bring them to me. Something about it made my heart crack.

Before Francis could do a thing, I'd pulled him under the stream of the shower and curled my body around his, pressing my face into his bare chest.

"Thank you," I whispered into his skin, unsure if he could hear me over the hammering of the water.

When I released him, he didn't leave me there alone. No, Francis picked up my shampoo and turned me around to face the wall. He lathered it up in my hair, his fingers soothing across my scalp as he washed the strands. He repeated the steps for my conditioner then washed my entire body, his soft hands entirely gentle. The man rinsed away my guilt, my shame and my pain. Tonight, I'd been the wielding force of the executioner. And somehow, Francis made it better for me. Made it bearable.

When he was done, he turned the shower off and gave me a smile. My fingers went to his jeans, tugging open the button and pulling down the zip. His eyebrow shot up and he put his hands on mine when I tried to take them off him.

"Scarlett, I'm not looking for—"

"I just want to help you. Wet jeans are a pain to get off."

It was the honest truth. I wasn't trying to get Francis as naked as me. He'd been kind to me and it was the least I could do for him.

He didn't stop me this time when I tugged the jeans from his hips, in fact, he helped. After we'd got them off him, he grabbed me a towel and wrapped me up in it, getting one of his own, which he slung around his hips before tugging his boxers off.

When I padded back out into his bedroom, I found he'd unpacked a pair of my pyjamas, hairbrush and hairdryer, leaving them on the bed for me. I hadn't realised Francis could be so considerate, but maybe I'd misjudged all of these men. Well, I hadn't misjudged West, he was crazy, plain and simple. But the others? Perhaps.

CHAOS

After I'd dried my hair and dressed, I curled up in Francis' bed. His covers were warm and soft. As I buried myself in them, my energy left me. All I wanted to do was fall into a deep sleep and never resurface.

Francis walked around the bedroom, but I barely heard him. The lights went out and I could have sworn he walked over to me, leant down and pressed a kiss to my temple, but I was drawn into the dream world before it had a chance to fully register with my brain.

SIX

SCARLETT

S omeone was screaming. The noise rang in my ears, making me wonder who on earth was that terrified. And it took me several minutes to come to the realisation the sound was emitting from my mouth.

"Scarlett!"

I shot up in bed, my body trembling all over and snapped my mouth shut. Staring down at my shaky fingers, I tried not to whimper. Why had I been screaming? I'd taught myself not to alert other people when I was having a nightmare. It had only led to pain. To beatings if I woke up my parents in the middle of the night. I wasn't at home though. Not any longer.

"Scarlett, are you okay?"

Turning my head, I found Francis sat on the bed next to me, his grey eyes full of concern. It was still dark outside. The light of the city and the moon streamed in illuminated him. He was only wearing a pair of shorts, his bare chest on display

Every part of me wanted to press myself against him all over again like I had done in the shower.

"No."

He hesitated before reaching out and taking one of my trembling hands. It wasn't enough. I needed more contact. More of him. I wanted the false pretence of safety he provided.

Although I didn't have full control over my panicked body, I tugged my fingers from his and pulled back the covers, a blatant invitation to join me. When he didn't immediately move, I got desperate. Why was he so reluctant this time? He hadn't been in the shower. He'd held me and comforted me.

"Please… I need you to hold me."

I almost let out a sob of relief when he climbed into the bed next to me, pulling the covers over himself and tugging me against his warm body. My fingers clutched him, sliding down his back and keeping him pinned to my shaky body. He stroked my hair and put his chin to the top of my head.

"What's wrong?" he whispered, as if talking any louder would break the cocoon we'd found ourselves in.

I breathed him in. The scent of cinnamon and apples filled my senses. Why did he always smell so damn good? It made him feel like home. Like a part of me belonged with Francis. Only it was crazy to think that. Crazy to feel it when I barely knew him. Why did he feel so real and familiar? I wanted to ask him, but something kept me from doing so. Self-preservation. If I asked, it could trigger a catalyst of bad events for me. After tonight, and the boys forcing me to kill for them, I didn't think rocking the boat any further would be a good idea.

"I have nightmares almost every night. Like my memories are trying to bleed back into my consciousness, but they're all jumbled up. I can't remember them clearly when I wake up either."

The only night I hadn't dreamt was when I slept in Prescott's arms. My heart burnt, feeling lost without the man who'd shown his true colours to me. Why the fuck did I care so much? I wanted to go give him a piece of my mind, but it would be pointless. He wasn't going to change his stance on what he'd done. And at this point, I had no idea if he really gave a shit about me or not. Was I only sex to him? Was I a warm body for all of them?

If that was true, then why would Francis have comforted me? He had no reason to hold me in the shower. And he had absolutely no reason to be doing so now other than I'd asked him to.

Even though he had me clutched tight to his chest, my body wouldn't stop trembling. My rioting mind was too full. I couldn't stop thinking and processing, going over in my head all of these questions I had. I couldn't ask any of them. The answers were ones I feared, as were the repercussions of probing too much.

This wasn't normal. After a nightmare, I'd calm down within minutes. Not this time. Not even with him keeping me safe. My body felt under threat. The shock of the evening and the nightmare had set off a chain reaction inside me.

"I can't... I can't stop shaking," I whispered, my fingers digging into his back.

He rubbed my back but even that didn't help. I didn't know what to do.

"Has this happened before?" he asked, his voice full of concern.

"Not… not like this."

He was silent for a beat, then he pulled back and took my chin between his fingers.

"Will you let me try something?"

I nodded. I was willing to do anything to calm my warring thoughts. To stop my senses from overloading. When his fingers went to the bottom of my t-shirt, I didn't question it. Nor when he pulled it off me. He leant over to his bedside table, tugged open the bottom drawer and took something out. Francis made me sit up, and he situated himself behind me, pulling my back to his chest.

"I've been told this can bring a person comfort, like being wrapped up helps them, contains the panic they're feeling," he told me as he took my wrists, pushed them together and knotted a length of soft rope up my arms, binding them together. He slid the rope behind my back, binding my arms to my chest. "I know it sounds rather counterproductive, but you wanted me to hold you. It wasn't working so maybe you need something tighter."

"What is this?"

"Japanese bondage," he murmured. "Shibari, also known as Kinbaku."

I stared down at his hands working their intricate knots with the rope. He watched his hands over my shoulder, making sure he tied everything just right. When he was done, he let me rest against his chest, his hands laying on his thighs on either side of me.

The sensation of being tied up was odd, to say the least. My body had begun to settle down as he tied the knots, as if having something to concentrate on focused my mind. I let out a breath. My chest was constricted by the knots and my arms against it, but in a lot of ways, Francis was right. It comforted me. Made me feel safer than ever.

"Is it okay?" he asked. "I didn't want to make them too tight as it's your first time."

I nodded, relaxing into him.

"Is this what you like?" I asked after a long minute.

"What?"

"Tying people up."

He chuckled and stroked his fingers along my hip.

"Yes, but what I've done to you now is nothing like what I would do if it was a sexual situation."

I looked at him over my shoulder. He had a smirk on his face like he was imagining it. Imagining doing it to me, whatever *it* was. I sure as shit didn't know exactly what he'd do if he was tying me up during sex.

"Are you going to do it to me?"

The way his silvery-grey eyes darkened at my words made me think asking him wasn't such a good idea.

"Eventually."

"Is that why you held me down in the car?"

His fingers moved from my hip, stroking along the rope on my wrist.

"I want to restrain you, Scarlett, either with my hands or bindings." He curled a hand around my bare thigh, resting right where my shorts ended. "You can struggle and strain against them, but I won't let you out."

I let out a breath, shivering as his fingers stroked my inner thigh. His face dropped to my neck.

"But right now, I'm going to sit here with you until you feel better, then I'll untie you and you can go back to sleep."

"Will you stay with me whilst I sleep?"

He didn't answer me straight away, merely continued to drive my nerve-endings crazy with his stroking fingers.

"If it's what you want."

"The only night I haven't had a nightmare recently is the one I spent with…"

I didn't want to say his name. To even think it. I'd already done that and it made my heart ache. It ached now, burning in my chest with the force of a thousand suns. A tear leaked from my eye. Why did it hurt so much? Why did I yearn for him even after he'd made me feel like he didn't care about my feelings? Like he didn't care how his actions hurt me. Why did I miss the way his blue eyes darkened and how he called me his little lamb?

I had to stop dwelling on it, but by fuck did I want to hurt him for the way he'd hurt me. To cut his damn black heart out of his chest and squeeze it tight in my fist. To show him he wasn't fucking well immune to me. And to prove I had as much power over him as he did me.

"Do you want to talk about him more?"

"No!"

"Scarlett—"

"Stop calling me that, Frankie. I'm Scar to you, remember?"

His stroking faltered for the merest of seconds. I don't know why. It's not like I'd said anything odd, had I?

52

"It's okay to admit you have feelings for him, Scar."

I swallowed, shifting in my bindings.

"I don't want to have them. I don't want to feel anything for any of you."

He kissed the side of my neck, giving his answer without words. Telling me he understood and wasn't going to press the issue further.

"Are you feeling better?" he whispered, his tongue tracing a line across my skin. "Seeing you like this is giving me ideas. Dirty ideas about all the ways I want to wring pleasure from your body."

My breath caught in my throat. A throbbing started below at the thought of him doing things to me while I was bound and unable to escape. I'd given up working out why I was so attracted to their darker sides. To the kinkier side of sex. Perhaps their natures called to mine.

"You can untie me."

Francis hesitated, his fingers still stroking. Then he shifted, making me sit up so he could loosen all the knots. He was so methodical about it, making sure he undid them in the order he'd knotted them.

"How did you learn to do this?"

"I had classes. It interested me and I wanted to do it safely... so I could break the rules later on."

I didn't comment on it. They all were the type to break rules and do whatever the hell they wanted.

When he was done, he carefully folded up the rope and tucked it back away in his bedside drawer. He pulled my t-shirt back over my head and encouraged me to curl up next to him. Francis pressed a kiss to my temple, stroking a hand down my arm before he lay back. It didn't take me long to fall asleep again, listening to the sound of his breathing lull me back into the void.

SEVEN

PRESCOTT

Misery. Abject fucking misery. It's all this damn shit had brought me. West's ideas had only ever led to trouble. And now I'd lost the most precious thing I'd ever had.

Her.

Not that Scarlett was a thing, but she'd been mine. She still was on some level, just not the one I wanted. No, I got stuck with her saying she hated me. I didn't believe her, but it still cut me hearing those words out of her mouth not once but twice.

I spent the entire night tossing and turning, trying to understand how one woman had me so tangled up inside. How did my little lamb make me feel so fucking much? I'd always cared for Scarlett, but seeing her again after all these years, the strong but fractured woman she'd grown into, was something else. She made me vulnerable. And I hated it. Hated how I felt so weakened by her. Like I couldn't do what I had to because she wouldn't like it. Because it would hurt her. That's all my actions had done. Caused her pain.

Remorse was an alien feeling to me. I didn't regret what we'd done, but I felt the guilt of hurting her wash over me in waves of excruciating agony. For putting her in that situation. The thing Scarlett didn't know was how fucking strong she was. How powerful she'd been last night. She hadn't been afraid to tell us all to go fuck ourselves after it happened. Maybe she didn't fear the repercussions. After all, what was worse than being forced to kill a man?

Well, in my mind, a lot of things, but I enjoyed killing. We all did. Scarlett didn't think like us, but maybe she would... in time.

"Would you stop brooding? I can hear you thinking from over here."

I looked up from where I was staring out the window of our living space. West stood in the kitchen scowling at me.

"Fuck off," I muttered.

"She's not going to stay mad at you forever."

I glared at him.

"She should be mad at you."

He scoffed.

"She knows what she's getting when it comes to me." He pointed at his chest. "Violence is in my fucking nature, I showed her from the start... but you... well, she saw something else and she hates you for destroying the illusion."

Fuck did I want to throw something at his head. Why did he have to start on me? It was too fucking early for his shit, especially after the night we'd all had.

"What illusion?"

"I saw the way she looked at you, Pres, like you're her fucking saviour. Too bad she didn't see beneath the damn mask and find the self-involved narcissist living inside that well-turned-out exterior of yours."

"I'm not a fucking narcissist."

I was sick to death of the three of them accusing me of it.

"No? Don't you love it when people worship you? When they appeal to your fucking ego, huh? You play up to it. The world revolves around Prescott Ellis, his wants and needs."

My fists clenched at my sides, but I didn't rise to his bait. I could feel Drake's eyes boring holes into the back of my head. He was sitting having coffee at the table. If I went after West, Drake would only tell me to calm the fuck down.

"Whatever, West, at least I'm not a psychopath."

Drake snorted.

"What did you just say to me?"

"You heard me."

West took a step towards me.

"West. Enough," came Drake's voice.

"He called me a psychopath."

"Well, he's not exactly wrong."

"Fuck you."

I turned and glanced at Drake who was giving West one of his 'quit being a cunt' looks. If he was going to give me shit, I'd give it right back. It's how we did things around here.

"Why am I not surprised you're already at each other's throats and it's barely nine in the morning."

All of us looked at the stairs finding Francis strolling down them with his hands in his pockets.

"Why do you look so fucking cheerful, Frankie?" West said, giving him daggers.

"For the last fucking time, it's Francis."

"And there he is, I knew it wouldn't last long."

Francis flipped him the finger before he walked over to Drake. He sipped his coffee as he levelled his gaze on our friend.

"How is she?"

"Okay, I think. Still asleep, but given she woke me up in the middle of the night screaming, hardly surprising."

Drake's jaw ticked.

"Did you do something to her?"

Francis ran his fingers across the table.

"No, she has nightmares. I think when she feels safe, they don't disturb her. At least, her sleep wasn't further disturbed when I was next to her."

My heart cracked. The night she'd spent with me she'd not woken up once. Had she felt safe with me? I'd gone and fucked it all up.

What a fucking idiot.

"You made her feel safe?"

Francis raised an eyebrow.

"It's not hard to hold a girl and let her cry. She didn't need me being a dick to her after last night."

"She cried?"

"What the fuck, Drake? Of course she fucking cried. She killed someone. Just because it's easy for you and me, doesn't mean she isn't affected. I swear it's like you lot forget we aren't the norm, and most human beings would be wracked with guilt over taking another's life."

For once in his life, Drake looked contrite, but it didn't take long for his expression to clear.

"Are you sure leaving her alone in your room is a good idea?"

Francis rolled his eyes as he strolled away to the kitchen.

"Quit worrying, she's sleeping. Even if she snoops, she won't find anything other than my ropes, which she already knows about."

"Do I even want to know how?"

Francis gave him a wink.

"Probably not."

Our intercom by the lift started buzzing. Drake hauled himself up from his chair and went over to it, pressing down on the button.

"Yes?"

"Good morning, Mr Ackley, there's someone who wants to see you at reception," came the voice of Anton, the security guy who usually worked weekends.

We had twenty-four-seven security for our building. It was needed when we lived here. We didn't get visitors on Sundays, so this was rather unusual.

"Who is it?"

"He says his name is Mason Jones."

All of us froze. What the fuck was he doing here? Had he already worked out we'd taken Scarlett? Highly likely, since we'd come and taken her without a fucking by-your-leave while he wasn't there.

"Send him up to our offices, I'll meet him there."

"Yes, Mr Ackley."

Drake moved away from the intercom, rubbing his chin.

"Well, guess we have to deal with him sooner than expected."

"If you'd let me kill the prick, we wouldn't have to deal with him ever again," West said.

"Wouldn't you rather torture the poor fucker until he cries like a baby?" Francis asked, opening the fridge.

"I suppose breaking him would be sweeter."

"No one is killing Mason," Drake interjected. "Pres, you're coming with me."

I glared at Drake.

"Fuck off, I don't want to see that cunt."

Drake pressed the button for the lift.

"Considering Scarlett hates your guts right now, you can't stay to keep an eye on her. And you know what will happen if I take West. Francis is the only one she's talking to, so deal with it."

He didn't want to go alone. A wise move. Mason wouldn't do anything to him, but you could never be too careful.

"Fine," I grumbled, walking over to the lift and crossing my arms over my chest. "But I'm not talking to him.

"You don't have to. Keep your mouth shut and watch my back."

I wanted to stay and talk to Scarlett, even if she was pissed off at me. Perhaps I could later, if West didn't wind her up first. Scratch that, he was bound to. The fucker was like a dog with a bone. He enjoyed toying with her. I didn't trust Francis to keep West off her case. And Drake wouldn't be there to keep him in line either.

I hope you're still angry enough not to take his shit, sweetness.

Our girl was so brave and strong. She could take on the world if she wanted.

The lift arrived. Drake and I walked in, me still scowling and wanting to be anywhere else. As it descended, he turned to me.

"You need to pull your shit together, Pres. We all agreed to what happened last night."

It didn't matter if I agreed to it. It hurt Scarlett and we were all fucking well responsible for it.

"When are we going to talk to her about the past?"

"She needs to remember it on her own."

I threw my arms up.

"How is she going to remember if we don't help her, huh? We are the only connection she has to it left. Us. We are her family. Everything else has been destroyed, ruined by them."

Drake's expression fell.

"Don't you think I know that? Quit acting like this isn't difficult for me."

"You sure about that? From where I'm standing, you act like you don't give a shit when it comes to her."

The lift doors slid open.

"We don't have time for this right now," he hissed, giving me a dark look before striding out.

I wanted to pull him back in here and give him a piece of my mind, but even I knew we couldn't afford to be divided in the face of Mason. Drake's apparent disregard for Scarlett's feelings had begun to grate on me. Crazy to think I'd been on board with everything… until she came back. Until she showed me glimpses of the girl I'd known before. Until she showed me her heart. And now I was fucking lost. All I wanted was her. To breathe her in. To feel her against me. To hear her laugh. To hear her moan and cry out my name.

You're falling for her, you know that, right? You're falling in love.

I told my brain to get fucked as I walked out of the lift. Drake was leaning against Tonya's empty desk, waiting for the other lift to arrive. The one containing a man we all hated with a passion. We had a very good reason for it. Hell, we had good reasons for everything we'd done. The world might not consider them right, just or moral, but we weren't mindless beasts who killed for sport. Not even West, though he acted like it sometimes.

I leant up against the window, staring down at the city below. The view always soothed me. Reminded me of how we ruled over it from high above. I'd never stopped viewing humanity as ants toiling day in, day out, for their scraps. Controlled by the rich who liked to keep them under their feet. Subservient. Capitalism was a cruel, unforgiving ruler. One that benefited the few and kept the masses from rising up. It gave us a landing pad upon which we formed our company. We rose because we knew the system. We played it to our advantage. We fucking cheated it. Now we could sit back and watch it all burn.

The second lift's doors opened. I turned in time to see Mason walking out, his face like thunder.

"Where the fuck is she?" he ground out, his fists clenching at his sides as he came to a standstill in the middle of the lobby.

Drake merely regarded him with a neutral expression.

"Where is who?"

"Don't fuck with me, Drake, where is Scarlett!"

Drake gave a semi-nonchalant shrug.

CHAOS

"Where do you think she is, Mason?"

Little did Scarlett know, but we had already encountered her friend many times over the years. It was simple. He hated us. We hated him. And the fact we all knew he clearly had feelings for Scarlett made it worse. She was ours first. She would always be ours. No matter what he did, he couldn't compete with the four of us. Scarlett would never see him the way she did us. Never. And he was fucking sour about it no doubt. Likely why he taunted all of us at the awards event when he'd danced with her. He wanted us to think he had a fucking chance with our girl. He had none. Zero.

One day, she'd find out the truth of what he'd done to her. What he'd done to all of us. Then she'd hate him. She'd really want him dead. Our woman would have no qualms about digging the knife into his chest like she did last night when she thought it was Mason. No, Scarlett would wield the fucking axe to cut him down. And we'd all watch him burn with no remorse or guilt for tearing the cunt down.

EIGHT

DRAKE

I stared Mason Jones down because I sure as shit wasn't going to let the guy intimidate me. He didn't deserve our time nor attention, but he'd left us with little choice. I didn't want him making a scene in our building. It was better to deal with him here on our turf.

"She's here. You took her."

I shoved off Tonya's desk, digging my hands in my pockets to prevent him from seeing my clenched fists. Prescott had accused me of not caring about Scarlett's feelings. I cared. The fact this cunt had physically hurt her pissed me off, but I didn't show it. I couldn't afford to allow those feelings of rage and resentment out. People often thought West had one hell of a temper on him. They hadn't seen me lose it. I could be calm and controlled, but push me too hard and you would live to regret it.

"Did you expect anything less? She's ours."

He took a step towards me, the anger in his brown eyes trying to burn a hole in me, but I remained unaffected. He could glare at me all he wanted, it wouldn't change facts. We had taken back what belonged to us. It might not have been our plan, but circumstances had changed. And now we had something to hold over her, we could keep our woman in line. We could keep her here with us where she should be.

"She's not a piece of property."

"Oh really now? Funny you say that when your employers have spent the past ten years brainwashing her into thinking we're monsters and using her for their petty and pointless revenge. Tell me how she's not a piece of property to them, because I'd love to know."

Mason let out a stuttered fake laugh.

"You are monsters."

I smiled very, very slowly, taking my hands from my pockets and spreading them.

"Are we? Pray tell me what makes us so."

He stabbed a finger in my direction.

"You fucking know why."

I tutted and rubbed my chin. If he wanted to throw around accusations, he could. Didn't mean we had to listen to them.

"Theories and conspiracies don't make up hard facts, Mason. If you're going to accuse us of something, you better have proof."

The fire in his eyes would have made a lesser man flinch but Mason didn't intimidate me. If anything, I saw him as a fuckwit who hid behind lies and deceit. I might be a master manipulator, and I was fucking proud of it, but this guy, he pretended to be nice. That's where I drew the line. Being nice was a fucking act. And one I despised.

"You know what you did. You can stand there and act like you're innocent, but I know. We know."

I wanted to laugh. Yeah, I knew what he was talking about, but I wouldn't let him know. Had too much self-preservation to ever reveal those secrets. The last thing I'd ever describe myself as was innocent, so he was barking up the wrong tree with that statement.

"You make *such* a compelling case for your suspicions. How could anyone *not* believe you."

Prescott snorted. Mason glared at him as if he'd only just noticed Prescott standing by the window.

"Fuck you. Tell me where she is."

Prescott stepped towards him, his blue eyes turning dark.

"As if you really give two shits about where she is. You're just trying to save your precious hide."

"I care about Scarlett far more than you lot ever did."

Prescott had been slightly hunched, but he straightened to his full height. He towered over Mason like he did most people.

"You care about her, do you? Is that why you hurt her, huh? I saw the bruises and I wasn't fucking impressed."

Mason took a step back, his brow furrowing.

"What bruises?"

Prescott scoffed.

"As if you don't know."

The confusion on Mason's face was evident. Did Scarlett not show him what he'd done to her on Friday morning? We'd seen them last night at the warehouse when West had held up

67

her arm. Seen the evidence with our own damn eyes. Prescott wouldn't lie about it, but the image was branded in my retinas. Mason had inflicted those bruises in anger. And I wasn't inclined to give the fucker the benefit of the doubt.

"I don't know what the fuck you're talking about."

"The bruises on her arm," I said. "You call us monsters, but we're not the ones abusing her. She wanted to get away from you."

Mason took another step back. Pain flashed in his eyes. Good, he should feel fucking pain for what he'd done. I wished I could gut the man where he stood. I'd take full pleasure in destroying him. Ripping the man apart piece by piece. I'd take his damn life, because we were fucking owed it for all the shit he'd caused.

"That's what she told you?"

"She doesn't need you," Prescott spat at him. "Stay away from her."

"As if I'm going to believe anything coming out of your mouths. You lot are a bunch of lying, cheating, murderous scum. You belong in the gutter you grew up in."

Prescott ground his teeth. Mason was getting to him. I gave him a look and he backed off towards the window again. My gaze turned back to Mason. We might have been born in the damn gutter to working-class families, but we were wealthy now. Worked our way up from nothing. And we did it to get our girl back.

"You can think whatever you want, Mason," I told him, my voice low. "Doesn't change the facts. You stole her from us. And when she finds out, she will never forgive you."

Mason looked between the two of us as if contemplating my words.

"Why haven't you told her who you are?"

"What does it matter to you, huh?"

He didn't deserve to know anything about us. He would only report back to the fucking Carvers. We weren't stupid enough to reveal anything to him, nor Scarlett for that matter.

"If you want her back so badly, why not tell her the truth? Why play all these games and toy with her?"

I almost laughed. She was an agent of his employers. Until she remembered on her own, we wouldn't interfere. There would be no point. Scarlett wouldn't believe us. She had no reason to. Not when those fuckers had taught her we were her enemies. The people she needed to take down. And if he couldn't see it, then he was an idiot.

"We don't answer to you. Our reasons are our own."

"So that's it? You're just keeping her?"

"Unless you want us to destroy her image of you completely, then I suggest you turn around and walk away."

He was right up against the lift doors, having backed off from both of us completely.

"Don't tell her."

I smiled at him.

"Stay the fuck away from her and we'll keep your sordid little secret."

Mason pressed the button to call the lift. The doors opened straight away as it hadn't gone anywhere. He stepped in, watching me with hatred in his eyes. He could hate me all he wanted. What he'd done to Scarlett was far worse than anything me or the others could ever do.

"This isn't over, Drake."

Those were his last words as the doors shut. I rolled my eyes and glanced at Prescott.

"He's going to be a problem."

Prescott gave me a scathing look.

"And? He and the whole fucking world could be a problem right now. I care more about her than that prick."

No fucking surprises there. He hadn't calmed down. Mason's words had probably made everything worse.

"We're going to do this now?"

"We sure as fuck are."

I sighed and looked away.

"How can we help her remember, Pres? If she didn't recognise us back when she first walked in here, then how is anything we do now going to change matters?"

We weren't medical professionals. Reminding Scarlett of who she was wouldn't be an easy or simple task. And it could backfire. Prescott was the one who liked to take risks. I needed to know all the possible outcomes, and work out how to mitigate them if things went sour. In a lot of ways, I admired Prescott for his ability to throw caution to the wind. He was a big part of our success. But Scarlett wasn't Fortuity. She was human. We were complicated beings. I was more cautious when it came to dealing with her.

"It's already started, Drake. She needs to be pushed in the right direction. To trust the things she's seeing. Right now, she can't tell if they're real."

My eyes flicked back to him.

"Has she told you exactly what she's remembered?"

"Well, no and now I've fucked it all up, she won't trust me with it. We're better off getting Francis to try."

He said the last part with no small amount of resentment bleeding through his words. He was clearly sore over the fact Scarlett had chosen Francis to spend the night with. Wasn't exactly Francis' fault. He was the lesser of all evils in her eyes. West had forced her to kill, I'd pissed her off by fucking her afterwards and Prescott had betrayed her trust in him. Francis was a fucking saint compared to us.

"I'll talk to him."

"You need to start acting like you give a shit about her too. I'm beginning to wonder if you even want her back."

I didn't answer to him or have to prove a single damn thing.

"If you choose to think I don't care, it's on you."

He scoffed.

"Francis makes it clear, so do I. Hell, even West in his own fucked up way shows the entire world how in love with her he is, but you... you sit there and do nothing. Own your fucking emotions for once in your life, Drake, because fuck knows bottling all that shit up has only ever brought you pain. You think we don't know how little you sleep at night, huh? We all know."

And with that, he walked over to the lift and slammed his hand down on the button. He might have said them in anger, but those words hit the nail on the head. I did bottle shit up. It plagued me at night, keeping me awake with what-ifs and what could have beens. Talking about my feelings wasn't something I did. Not since... her. And right now, I didn't trust Scarlett. Not when she couldn't remember me.

Perhaps Prescott was right. Maybe we needed to push harder. Help her recall the memories she'd lost. But if we did, would she hate the four of us for what happened that night? Would she blame us for setting off a chain of horrific events and ruining her life?

I guess the real question I had to answer was... *am I willing to risk everything to return Scarlett to the person she was before?*

NINE

West

Francis had set about making breakfast while I lounged against the counter in the kitchen with a cup of coffee. I hadn't spiked it but judging by the way he kept looking at me, he suspected I was drinking. Wouldn't be the first time I'd started on the whisky well before ten, but I didn't need to bury my feelings in booze or drugs right now. Not after last night. Not when I'd smelt blood and fear. And watched the woman I wanted for life stab a man to death with reckless fury and rage.

Scarlett had been a queen. A ruler in her own right. There was nothing sweeter than watching her give into her baser nature. To destroy a man she thought had wronged her. The rest of them might not have realised what she'd screamed at the guy, but I did. She'd called Mason a liar and told him he hadn't saved her. It made me suspicious of what had gone on in the Carver household for the past ten years. I wasn't going to ask her outright. She wouldn't be inclined to reveal her secrets to me, but it didn't make me any less curious. Somehow, I'd get to the bottom of it… eventually.

"Are you planning on pissing Scarlett off when she comes down?"

I angled my head towards Francis, giving him a grin.

"I hadn't thought about it."

He rolled his eyes, flipping the kettle on and moving back over to the stove.

"Well, I would prefer it if you cut her some slack given what we did to her last night."

"You'd prefer it, would you? Now, now, Frankie, that just makes me want to do quite the opposite."

That earned me a scowl.

"Why do you always have to be so fucking combative? Not everything needs to result in violence."

I shrugged. It was my default. And he was wrong. Violence was the best damn part of my day. It fed my warring soul and made me whole.

"Also, quit calling me that."

"What crawled up your arse?"

He turned on me, a haunted look crossing his face.

"She said it last night."

"Said what?"

He looked down at his hands and his voice turned soft.

"She called me Frankie and she didn't even realise it. She snapped at me just like she used to. For a few seconds, I saw the real Scarlett. It was amazing and soul-destroying at the same time."

Francis didn't usually have any sort of heart-to-heart shit with me, but I understood what he was talking about. The fact she'd called him Frankie was significant to him. Scarlett was the only one he'd ever allowed it from. And perhaps she was beginning to remember us.

"Did you say anything to her about it?"

"No. She was already freaked out over her nightmare, didn't want to make it worse."

Wouldn't have been the way I'd have handled it, but maybe it was for the best he didn't comment on it. I tended to take a sledgehammer to shit, but Francis had always been more subtle in his approach to anything in life. He was unassuming and it made him dangerous as fuck. Even I could admit that.

From across the room, I spied her walking down the stairs. She had a t-shirt and shorts on. Her long, wavy hair flowed down her back and her eyes fixed themselves on me. Her expression turned sour, her mouth thinning. I grinned. She'd already baited me and she hadn't said a damn word.

Scarlett walked across the room, her eyes darting away from me and going to Francis instead. He turned his head at her footsteps and gave her a smile. I clenched my fist when she went straight up to him and tucked herself under his arm, wrapping her arm around his waist.

"Morning," she murmured.

"Morning, you okay?"

She nodded and pressed her face into his chest while eyeing me. It almost felt like a fucking taunt. Her way of showing me I wasn't going to get her attention. I nearly shook my head. If Scarlett wanted to play that game, so be it. She would soon regret it.

"Hungry?"

"Mmm." She nuzzled his chest. "Yes."

Francis looked at her with a raised eyebrow but didn't ask her why she was being overly affectionate towards him.

"I'll make you something."

He carefully extracted himself from her grasp to walk over to the fridge. She leant against the counter and stared at her feet.

"Are you trying to make me jealous?" I asked.

Her head whipped up and she narrowed her eyes.

"No. I don't give a shit about your feelings."

"Mmm, I don't believe you."

And there she was, my feisty woman who wasn't going to take my shit. The way she scowled and stepped towards me had me licking my bottom lip.

"What is your problem with me?"

"You're the one out here getting all overly friendly with Frankie, whilst staring at me as if I'm going to do something about it. I merely stated the obvious."

She spluttered, clearly unprepared for my bluntness. Scarlett should know by now I wasn't one for beating around the bush.

I caught Francis giving me a look. As if I was ever not going to wind Scarlett up. It was too much fun to watch her explode.

"If I wanted to make you jealous, I'd go drape myself over some random guy who isn't on your list of approved males who can touch me."

"Is that so?"

"Yeah, it fucking is."

I shrugged.

"Go ahead... I guarantee you wouldn't like the consequences, but whatever, it's your choice."

CHAOS

I almost reached out and touched her when she closed the distance between us and stared up at me, the fire in those hazel-green eyes burning a hole in my head.

"You're acting like you don't give a shit, but I know you do."

"You've already had a warning, Scar, or did you forget how I made you come in front of all those people, hmm?"

The way her cheeks went red had me running my finger down her arm. Such a soft, little delicate thing she was. Inside lay my warrior. The woman who would go to war with me. Who'd come at me with everything she had.

"Shut. Up."

"You liked it and here you are angling for more of my magic fingers. All you have to do is ask... unless you want something else, hmm? Perhaps your pussy is craving cock, is that it?"

"I'd rather walk over broken glass than ask you for anything."

I shook my head, dropping my hand back down to my side.

"Liar."

She took another step towards me, her body almost pressing against mine.

"I just think you're fucking sour because I told you not to touch me last night and you wanted me."

I looked her over.

"If I wanted you, I could have you, Scar. You're mine."

There was a second's pause before her hand whipped up and wrapped around my neck. Her tiny fingers squeezed and the glare on her face had me wondering what the hell she thought she was doing.

"You want to own me, huh? You want me to be yours?" she ground out. "Well, how about I fucking well own you too? This right here, it's mine."

Dear fuck, what have I created? A fucking monster… and I love it.

I wasn't going to tell her I was proud of her for standing up to me. Nor how I liked this aggressive and territorial Scarlett. Her assertiveness turned me on. Made me want to pin her down on the kitchen island and fuck her senseless. But I wasn't going to reward her for any of this shit.

It started slowly, bubbling up inside me, until my laughter echoed through the room. She only glared at me harder while I stood there amused as fuck by her little display, not even trying to bat her hand away.

"It's not funny! This is the exact shit you pulled on me."

I set my hands on the counter behind me and continued chuckling.

"I beg to differ."

The lift doors opened revealing Drake and Prescott who walked out and faltered when they came across the scene in front of them.

"Do I want to know what's happening here?" Drake asked, sticking his hands in his pockets as he wandered over to the sofa.

"Scar's getting a little… possessive, aren't you?"

The only response from her I got was another glare and a squeak of frustration. Reaching up, I stroked my fingers down her neck, making her let out a breath.

"It's okay, Scar, I won't punish you for your little outburst," I murmured. "It's cute really, you worrying I might stray."

Her mouth dropped open.

"Excuse me?" she hissed a moment later.

My hand went to her cheek, brushing her jaw with gentle care I never usually used.

"My interests are with you and you alone, so you don't need to be afraid."

"If you think I care—"

I pressed my thumb over her mouth, stopping her words.

"I know you care." I leant closer. "None of us are going anywhere, Scar. We don't want anyone else."

She blinked. Then she pulled herself out of my grasp and cradled her hand to her chest, staring up at me with confusion.

"Why… why are you being nice?" she whispered.

I didn't answer her, merely winked. I don't think she knew what to do. Probably expected me to fly off the handle and threaten her, but this was far more fun, watching her attempt to work out what the hell my game was and failing.

Scarlett backed away from me and went over to Francis instead. He rolled his eyes at me while taking her over to the dining table, sitting her down at it and placing a plate in front of her. Scarlett dug into her food, but she continued to watch me, her brow furrowed as if everything I'd done had thrown her for a loop.

It wasn't until she'd finished eating when she looked up and found Prescott staring at her. He'd remained by the lift, watching her with this sad puppy dog expression on his face. Hurt flashed in her eyes. The two of them kept staring at each other as Francis took her plate away and brought it over to the kitchen, placing it in the dishwasher. When he went back over to her, she turned to him with a determined look on her face.

"You know what we were talking about last night?"

Francis frowned.

"We talked about a lot of things."

She reached out and put a hand on his arm.

"The tying up thing."

He rubbed the back of his neck as if it was the last thing he thought she'd bring up in front of the rest of us.

"What about it?"

She stood up and placed her hand on his chest, smiling at him with a wicked look in her eyes.

"Do you want to show me more… like right now?"

"Are you asking what I think you are?"

Scarlett leant into him.

"I want you to tie me up and do everything you were imagining last night."

Somehow I didn't think Francis had ever had a girl act so brazen towards him as he shifted on his feet and looked around the room. Scarlett was still staring up at him when he levelled his gaze back on her.

"I can do that."

"Good."

Then she took his hand and tugged him towards the stairs, not even throwing a look anyone else's way. She'd made her statement. It was a big fuck you to me, Drake and Prescott. I couldn't exactly fault her for it either.

It wasn't until they'd disappeared when Prescott moved away from the lift and walked over to Drake, taking a seat next to him. He crossed his arms over his chest and scowled.

"Jealous much?" I asked.

"Fuck off, West. She can do what she wants with him."

"I think she did that on purpose," Drake said.

Prescott gave him daggers, leading me to believe the two of them had exchanged words beyond speaking to Mason.

"Oh yeah?" I waved a hand at Drake. "You going to tell us why?"

I already knew but wanted to know if he'd noticed too.

"Well, she's pissed at you two…"

Prescott raised his eyebrow.

"And me. She wants us to see what we're missing out on."

"I already know what I'm missing," Prescott muttered.

Having already pressed his buttons earlier, I decided to leave him be. Prescott clearly wasn't in the mood to deal with any of us.

"I say let Frankie enjoy himself whilst he can, fuck knows he needs it after all the shit with Chelsea."

Drake turned to Prescott, ignoring me entirely.

"I'll think about what you said, okay?"

Prescott didn't respond, which made Drake sigh and rub his face. I had no idea what those two had argued about, but I could guess. And it was the woman we'd sacrificed everything for.

I wondered how long it would take before our household got completely turned upside down now Scarlett had become a permanent member of it. No matter what she and the others thought, I wasn't about to let her leave again. She belonged here with us no matter if she couldn't remember who we were. And I would damn well make her remember if I had to.

A life without Scarlett was no life worth living at all.

I should know.

TEN

FRANCIS

As Scarlett dragged me upstairs, I was sceptical about what she actually wanted. I'd seen the look passing between her and Prescott. The hurt in their expressions. While I thought they should have it out, it hadn't even been a day yet. She needed time. I was pretty sure Prescott would do anything to fix things between them. He'd changed since she came back into our lives. Not towards other people, but with her, he was softer. The last thing I'd have ever described Prescott as is soft, more like self-involved. Regardless, I couldn't help feeling as though she wanted to get back at him.

"Scar."

She paused halfway down the hall on the way to my room, looking back at me with curiosity. She'd told me to call her Scar. Maybe if I did, she might call me Frankie again. My heart

"Is this what you want? You didn't just say that to piss them off?"

Why I was asking was a mystery to me, but a huge part of me actually gave a shit about her true feelings. Knowing what I now did about her. What she'd revealed to me last night. Scarlett clearly hadn't had much agency in her life in the past ten years. We'd taken even more away from her. Guess I also didn't want her to sleep with me out of spite. Was it fucking crazy I wanted her to want me for me?

She turned around, gripping my hand tighter and pulled me closer.

"Would you be asking if we'd been alone?"

"No."

Scarlett cocked her head to the side.

"You know what I thought the first time I saw you?"

I shook my head.

"I felt a weird sense of familiarity, like I knew you somehow, which is stupid… then I thought you were hot and wondered what it would be like to kiss you. And you reminded me of home because you smell like apples and cinnamon." She got a faraway look in her eyes for a long moment. "So, the answer is yes, I do want this, but I also asked in front of them to piss them off. It doesn't change how I feel about you… especially after last night when you took care of me even though you didn't have to. You could have left me to cry in the shower and you didn't. You made me feel safe, Francis. I didn't feel stupid about being upset over what I did. I know you were complicit in it, but the fact you didn't let me drown in my own misery made me feel… closer to you."

I stepped towards her, my body brushing against hers. While I might not fully trust her, I didn't detect a trace of dishonesty in her voice or expression. And I couldn't help feeling pleased that something inside her had recognised me immediately.

"Did kissing me live up to your fantasy?"

"More than I could have ever imagined."

Reaching up with my free hand, I curled a lock of her wavy hair around my finger.

"Do you want me to kiss you again?"

She nodded, those beautiful eyes of hers darkening. My eyes went to her mouth.

"What if these weren't the only lips I kissed?"

She shuddered, clearly on board with the idea. Many times I'd envisioned having her bound so I could feast on her until she was crying and begging for the pleasure to end. Now I could make it a reality. I wouldn't use chains. After everything with Chelsea, I didn't exactly trust myself. But there were other methods to put a strain on her body. Other ways I could tie her up. The thought of it almost made me groan.

"Come then."

Scarlett allowed me to pull her further down the hall and into my bedroom. I shut the door and turned to her.

"Strip. I need you naked."

She swallowed but started to obey, pulling her t-shirt off. I walked over to my wardrobe and opened one of the doors. A whole section of it was devoted to my ropes and chains. I pulled out several sets of rope I'd need to play with, and took them over to the bed, laying them out on the covers.

Scarlett moved over to the bed having taken off her clothes and placed them on a set of drawers I had where I was intending to put some of her things. I made her kneel on the bed with her back to me.

"Do you have a hair tie?" I asked, stroking my fingers down her arms.

"Um, yeah, there's one in my purse."

She'd left it on my bedside table, so I went and rooted around for it. Coming back over, I put her hair up in a messy bun. It would make my work easier if it wasn't in the way.

"If at any point it's too tight or you want me to stop, you need to tell me, okay?"

She turned to look at me.

"What if I tell you to stop but I don't really want you to?"

I swallowed back my pooling saliva at the thought of her begging me for it to end.

"A safe word then. Say 'red' and I'll stop. Also, move towards the centre of the bed."

She gave me a nod before she shifted into the middle of the bed. I picked up one of the ropes and got up on the bed. There was a long metal bar I had bolted to the ceiling. Over that, I looped the rope, creating a series of knots to secure it. The rope hung down on two ends.

I knelt behind Scarlett and picked up the next length of rope. I wrapped it around her several times both above and below her breasts, while securing it to the rope hanging down from the pole. Then I crossed her arms behind her back and secured those to the rope like a harness. The knots were intricate and in an orderly fashion, not only because it was pleasing to the eye, but to make sure she was secure. I leant over her shoulder to check the ropes were in place around her breasts. I tried not to think too hard about how perfectly they were on show. And especially not the way her nipples had pebbled.

Even seeing her like this without having finished had me gritting my teeth. The ropes dug into her skin to create indents and it was fucking beautiful. I had to adjust myself as my cock dug into my zipper.

"You have no idea how much I want to fuck you," I murmured in her ear. "But I'm not finished yet."

I gripped her chin and turned her face towards me. Her eyes were wide as I kissed her, pressing myself into her back. She moaned when she felt me. If I wasn't so fucking patient, I'd bend her over right now and slam inside her. Pulling back, I smiled.

"I need you to stand up, okay?"

I got to my feet and helped her up to hers, then I properly tightened up the rope connecting her to the bar. Now came the difficult part, hoisting her up and securing her legs. Kneeling down, I wrapped a length of rope around each of her thighs so I could secure them to the rope around the bar.

"I'm going to need you to bend your legs for me, okay. The rope will take your weight so don't worry about that."

She did as I asked, while I pulled her up by the ropes until she was horizontal with the floor. Then I fastened her in place with her legs bent and raised above her back. Her pussy was perfectly on display for me. I wanted to devour her whole.

"Is this okay?" I asked, taking a step back and admiring my handiwork.

She turned her head to look at me.

"Yes, the rope is digging into my skin, but it doesn't really hurt."

"You look perfect."

And she did. I couldn't have asked for more. It'd taken a lot of practice for me to be able to tie the knots this well and to make sure the woman I played with was safe. Chains were different and it was why shit with Chelsea had gone so wrong. Now wasn't the time to be thinking about her. Not when I had my Scarlett bound in front of me.

Dropping to my knees, I smiled. I'd set her at the perfect height. My fingers ran along her inner thighs, making her tremble. I replaced my fingers with my lips, pressing kisses to her delicate skin. My tongue came next, eliciting a gasp from her pretty little mouth. I couldn't wait any longer. I wanted to taste her so fucking badly.

Scarlett whimpered when my tongue delved between her lips. I groaned, holding her thighs as I dipped my tongue inside her pussy, wanting her essence all over it. All I could think about was how delicious she was and how I wanted her to scream my name when she came. This was the moment I wanted to hold onto forever because I didn't know how long this peace between me and her would last. Not when I could see her past was unlocking slowly, but surely. She'd remember that night eventually. Remember us. And it might turn into a fucking disaster, but we owed the truth to her. She didn't deserve to be kept in the dark forever.

My tongue sought out her clit while my fingers plunged inside her. Scarlett shifted and moaned, but I kept her steady with one hand while the other thrust in and out of her sweet little pussy which was growing wetter by the second.

"Oh fuck," she whimpered. "Don't stop."

I focused on what she liked, judging it from the way she moaned louder when my tongue moved in a certain way. Her shifting became more frantic as if she was close to the edge. That's when I backed off slightly, not wanting her to come yet. She let out a cry of frustration.

Soon, Scar, I'll let you come soon and you'll be happy I made you wait.

I kept teasing her closer to the edge before pulling away until she was rocking in the ropes and outright begging. It was exactly the way I wanted her. All needy and unable to control herself.

"Francis, please," she whined. "Please, I can't take it, please. Let me come. I need it."

"Do you?" I murmured before burying my face back in her pussy.

"Yes! Fuck, it's too much, please let me come."

The abject misery in her voice made me chuckle. Delayed gratification was my thing, but she'd not had to experience it before. I wanted her starving and desperate for a release.

"I'm not sure you deserve it," I told her, thrusting my fingers deeper inside her. "You don't sound needy enough for me."

The low whine emitting from her lips fed me.

"Please."

My tongue moved faster on her clit, forcing her closer to the edge, but this time I didn't take it away. No, I allowed it to build inside her but kept her from falling. Her pants and cries echoed around the room like she couldn't talk any longer and had descended into an animalistic state of needing to get off.

And I let her. Watching her come apart and fall under my fucking touch was magic.

The way her body shifted and trembled in the ropes. Her moans. The way she said my name in the throes of her passion. All of it was beautiful. And it didn't stop at one. No, I made her come over and over in quick succession until she was a mess. Tears ran down her cheeks and the ropes had made marks all over her skin. I let her go then, watching her hang there in her bindings as she panted and her chest heaved.

"Francis," she choked out a few minutes later. "Please let me down."

I hadn't planned on fucking her while she was hanging in the ropes, so I allowed her request. Carefully, I let her legs down first before lowering her body down on the bed. She lay there, her arms still bound behind her back for a long minute before she stared up at me. I reached out and ran my finger along one of her tear tracks. Then I leant closer and pressed my lips to her cheek.

"I'm going to fuck you now, Scar," I whispered. "And I won't stop until you come all over me again."

ELEVEN

FRANCIS

S carlett didn't say a word as I moved off the bed and stripped out of my clothes. If anything, her eyes darkened as she watched me, leading me to assume she liked what she saw. When I got back on the bed, I gripped the rope at her back and pulled her up onto her knees before encouraging her closer to the headboard.

There was nothing like seeing a woman bound and unable to do anything. Something about her helplessness got me going. I would be the only hand who fed her. Who gave her sexual gratification and pleasure. The only thing she could do was beg me for mercy, to give her what she wanted because she couldn't do it herself.

I sat up against the headboard and pulled her over onto my lap to straddle me. Scarlett was unsteady and off-balance without the use of her arms, but I gripped the rope to keep her upright. My other hand went to my cock so I could position myself.

"Sit."

Scarlett lowered herself on my cock with my help. I wouldn't let her fall. Her pussy was soaking after I'd made her come over and over, allowing me to slide inside with ease. Using the rope as an anchor, I let go of my cock, only to wrap my hand around her throat. She swallowed against my palm, making me smile.

"You like this too?" she whispered, indicating my hand.

It took a second for me to realise she meant the throat grabbing and how West was obsessed with necks. I stroked my thumb down her pulse point. It was a power thing, not to mention it helped me with leverage. She gasped when I held onto her tighter and thrust upwards, using the grip on her rope to put some weight behind it.

"I like having you at my mercy," I told her, thrusting into her small body again and feeling so fucking high off the thrill of the experience. "You can't stop me from using you... from making you mine."

"I want you to use me."

Her eyes were on mine, the wildness in them making me give it to her harder. Her inner strength shone out of her. This woman had let me tie her up. She'd submitted. And it was a damn honour to know she'd given up a part of herself to me in the process.

"Do you want to be mine, Scar?"

She bit her lip and didn't answer. I squeezed her throat, showing her who was in control, even though we both knew if she said the safe word, I'd stop. I cared about her enjoyment. I fucking cared about her wanting this with me.

"No? Is it because you want to be my whore instead?"

CHAOS

The way she shuddered at my harsh words had me gripping the rope tighter as I pulled her closer, our bodies brushing together. My mouth drifted over hers, not quite touching her lips.

"I think that's it. You want me to treat you like you're nothing but my little plaything. My *whore*."

Her lips parted on mine, but no sound came out. The hazel-green of her eyes was barely visible with her dilated pupils. I rocked her hips on my cock, using the rope to move her body with mine.

"Say it, Scar, tell me what you are."

"A... a whore," she whispered, her lip trembling with her words.

"Whose whore?"

"Yours. Your whore."

"That's right. In this room, that's what you are. Mine."

I kissed her then, maintaining a tight grip on the rope and her throat to keep her pressed to me. There was no hesitation on her part to kiss me back and allow me access to her sweet mouth. She could probably taste herself on me. It made me throb inside her. I'd never wanted a woman more than Scarlett. Never desired to have anyone as much as I did her. She was my connection to the past and the person I wanted the future with. Nothing else mattered to me right then as we rocked against each other, devouring one another like we never wanted it to end. She was the only thought I had.

I sucked her tongue into my mouth, making her eyes fly open. My teeth gripped it and scraped along the length of her tongue. She moaned, shifting in her bindings. When I released her tongue, her head fell back, but my firm grip on her kept her from slipping further.

"Please," she whimpered. "Please put me on my knees and fuck me. Please make me your whore."

"Do you want me to press you down in the covers and fuck you until you're crying? Is that it? Fuck your pussy so hard it hurts?" My hand squeezed around her throat again. "You going to scream for me, Scar? Scream and show them what they're missing?"

"Please."

How could I deny her when she asked so nicely?

Letting go of her throat, I hoisted her off of me and set her down. No way in hell I was untying her. She could stay like this until I was done. There were rope indents on her thighs. Fuck, the beauty of them made me pause. I couldn't help wanting to stare. Scarlett was stunning. The scars on her body were too. They showed she'd survived through hell and came back from it. She'd fought. I was proud of her for it, even though I hadn't been there to see it.

Grabbing her ropes again, I shoved her face down, pressing it into the covers while pulling her up by her hips. She bent her knees and held herself there for me, offering her pussy up like she wanted me to ruin it. To ruin her.

"Please," she whimpered, her voice muffled by the covers. "Fuck me, Francis."

I leant over her, my fingers spearing into her messy bun and gripping it in my fist.

"What's that, whore? You want me to give you my cock?"

"Yes, give it to me, please. Give me your cock."

It was right then I knew she wasn't playing a game. She didn't care how wanton she sounded. No, Scarlett wanted me. She couldn't fake it. Her body trembled with the force of her need, her pussy dripping and clenching around nothing.

Deciding to tease her, I rubbed my cock along her lips before dipping the tip inside her. She shivered and whined but didn't move to try to hurry me along. Slowly, I impaled her on it, inch by fucking inch, disappearing inside her. I watched her take it, her pussy stretching around my girth and taking me so damn well.

"Such a needy whore."

When I shifted back and plunged inside her again, all my gentleness was gone. I fucked Scarlett with punishing strokes, listening to the harsh sound of our skin slapping together and her cries of pleasure.

"So fucking desperate for dick, aren't you?"

"Harder, Francis, please."

While I was slightly frustrated by the fact she hadn't called me Frankie again, I didn't say a word about it. Maybe if I made her lose herself, she would. I needed to make Scarlett forget who she was. My fingers tightened in her hair, tugging at it. I gripped her hip and gave it to her harder, making her whimper from the sheer force of my thrusts.

"Does it hurt yet, Scar? Are you going to cry?"

Her strangled moan was all I needed to hear. She couldn't escape me. All she could do was let me fuck her, punishing her pussy because it was mine.

"Please."

Nothing could prepare me for having Scarlett like this. It'd been so long, I'd built up this image of who she'd become in my mind, but the woman in front of me was nothing like the way I'd expected. She was so much more. So strong. So fierce. She'd dealt with so much from the four of us so far and, to be quite honest, it would only get worse when she remembered the past. When she remembered who we were. There was no doubt in my mind she would. She'd told me I'd felt familiar to her the moment she saw me. It was only a matter of time until her past bled into her present. We would either be the ones to catch her when she fell, or she'd want nothing to do with us. I had no idea which way it would go.

"You going to come for me, whore?"

My hand left her hip, snaking underneath her to stroke her clit. She bucked, pressing herself back against me the best she could. With how sensitive she was from my edging, it didn't take long until she screamed with her climax. I released her hair, gripping the rope to give me more leverage, fucking her ruthlessly through it while she clenched around me. Her screams turned to hoarse cries, and those cries turned to whimpers.

When her body sagged, I put both my hands on the ropes and gave it to her even harder. Her body was so wrung out, she didn't protest my brutality. It didn't take much to have me grunting and spurting inside her, the wildness and pleasure of it skating up my spine. It was a moment of complete ecstasy. The culmination of an experience I wasn't sure I'd have with this woman who'd completely stolen every part of me and the others when we'd been kids.

It took several minutes for me to catch my breath before I pulled out of her and gently lowered her down on the bed. She let out a soft sigh when I unbound her. I laid the ropes next to her and stared down at the indents all over her skin. Then I stroked them with my fingers, tracing the lines of rope.

"I'm going to run you a bath, Scar," I told her. "It'll help your muscles."

She nodded and stretched her arms before resting them at her sides.

I got off the bed and went into the bathroom, turning on the taps for the bath. When it was full, I picked Scarlett up off the bed and carried her in. I got in the bath and set her down in the water with me. She curled up on my chest, pressing her face into my neck.

"That was intense," she whispered.

"In a good way?"

"In the best way."

I smiled and stroked my fingers along her shoulder.

"Is it okay if I fall asleep?" she asked a moment later. "You won't let me drown in the water or anything?"

I laughed.

"No, Scar, I won't let you drown."

She wrapped her hand around my neck, holding me to her like she didn't want me to go anywhere. As it was Sunday, I had nothing pressing. I'd stay here with her until the water got cold if she wanted.

"Thank you for keeping me safe, Frankie."

My heart squeezed. I pressed a kiss to her hair, trying not to react to her words outwardly. My patience had paid off. Hearing her say it again was everything to me, especially after the sex we'd shared. I'd shown Scarlett a side of me few got to see, and she hadn't run. She'd embraced it.

Even as I inwardly celebrated this little win, I had a feeling it would only last a short while. If I knew anything about the others, peacefulness in our household wasn't the norm. Having Scarlett here with us was asking for trouble. And trouble had a way of finding us no matter what we did.

TWELVE

SCARLETT

I successfully avoided the others by staying in Francis'
room all day and refusing to go downstairs. After I'd
fallen asleep on him in the bath, he'd dried and dressed
me. Then he'd given me space to put my things away. Not all
of them, but at least my dresses and blouses for work were
hung up.

I sighed as I carried a mug from the kitchen down the
hallway towards Drake's office. Monday had rolled around far
too quickly. By the time I'd got up, the only person left in the
penthouse was Francis, who showed me where everything was
in the kitchen. He'd left me alone with a warning not to go
snooping. I'd listened to his words. The idea of getting caught
somewhere I shouldn't, knowing who I was dealing with, left
me with a sour taste in my mouth. I was here to get
information, but at this point, I questioned if it was even worth
it any longer.

I'd come here intending to bring them down. Things hadn't turned out that way. They had their own plan and agenda when it came to me. And my feelings only grew ever more conflicted by the day. They'd only been made worse by the intimacy I'd shared with these men, particularly yesterday with Francis. I had no idea he was hiding such a dirty mouth under that rather well-turned-out exterior of his. He appeared to be the most civil out of the four of them, but fuck had I been so very wrong. It had taken hours for the indents from the ropes to fade from my skin. And the way his eyes burnt with a possessive heat whenever he looked at them had me trembling at the memory of what he'd done. How hard he'd made me come. The things he'd said to me. The way he'd cared for me afterwards.

My cheeks heated at the thought as I continued down the hall. I'd almost reached Drake's office when I heard my name. My body tensed, but I didn't stop.

"Scarlett, please."

I had zero intention of talking to, let alone acknowledging Prescott. He didn't deserve my time or attention. The man had tricked me into believing he gave a shit about me. How could he when he'd forced me to kill? He hadn't stopped it when I'd begged him to.

"I just want to talk to you."

My traitorous heart yearned to hear his terms of endearment from his lips. My head told my heart to stop being stupid, but it didn't want to listen. It merely pounded against my ribcage in protest at my refusal to stop and look at him. To hear him out. Fuck did it long for him in ways I wasn't ready to admit.

CHAOS

Why do I feel this way about you, Pres? Is that why it hurts so much? Are you hurting as much as me? Do you feel the same way?

I reached Drake's door, rushed in and shut it behind me, hating myself and Prescott for this fucked up situation. My head rested itself on the frame. I wanted to knock some sense into myself but realised I couldn't, as I had an audience. The way his gaze burnt a hole in my back had me straightening and taking a breath.

I'd decided when I came down to the office earlier I was going to behave like a professional. It meant doing my job regardless of my feelings towards my boss. Regardless of what was going on between me and the boys. Regardless of everything. I wouldn't let them get to me.

Turning around, I strode right over to Drake's desk, avoiding his eyes entirely, and set the mug on his coaster. Then I spun around, intending to leave but remembering I'd probably get ambushed by Prescott again.

Well, fuck.

"Scarlett."

My back stiffened and my hands curled into fists.

"Yes, Drake?"

"Mason came to see us yesterday."

I turned abruptly and stared at Drake with no small amount of shock running through me. Drake remained entirely impassive. I took in his appearance, hating the way my body responded to his proximity. The images of the way his indigo eyes had come alive when he fucked me after I'd killed had my cheeks feeling hot. It was the first time I'd ever seen Drake display any sort of real emotion. It had been downright terrifying. In a way, I was more scared of Drake than I was of

West, but at least with Drake, I knew what to expect. He was emotionless, stern, and always in control, except when he wasn't. West was a whole other level of scary. The way he could flip from one mood to another in the blink of an eye left me reeling. No, he was definitely the most terrifying of the bunch, but Drake came a very close second.

"M-Mason?"

"Yes, your… *friend*, Mason."

In all the drama of the weekend, I'd entirely forgotten about what Mason would do when he found me gone. Now I felt guilty. Horrible waves of it made my stomach twist. My nails dug into my palms, trying to quell the sickness.

"Oh. I suppose he wanted to know where I am."

I didn't know what Drake wanted me to say. My feelings towards Mason were very conflicted. I thought I'd killed him. I'd shouted and screamed at the man while stabbing him repeatedly, my entire mind breaking from the strain of the past ten years and the pain I'd endured. How Mason hadn't stopped it, even though he professed to care about me. And then he'd hurt me. All I could feel was betrayal. He'd promised to protect me and keep me safe. He'd done neither of those things.

"Why didn't you tell him he hurt you?"

My eyes went to my arm, where the finger marks were fading fast. It no longer hurt. To be honest, I was more concerned with the way my muscles ached after Francis suspended me from his ceiling with ropes. Perhaps I wasn't as limber as I first thought. If I was going to keep up with this lot, I would need to remedy that.

"Why do you care what I told him?"

His jaw ticked.

"Answer the question, Scarlett."

"How about I don't want to answer your questions, huh? Do you think I want to talk to you outside of work matters? The answer is no. Not after what you did to me."

He leant forward, eyeing me with the same intensity he'd used when the man had fucked me on the sink counter in the warehouse. I raised my chin, not caring if I was being defiant. My anger at his uncaring attitude and the way he'd used me had made me reckless.

"This is not up for debate. You are going to give me an answer."

"Go. Fuck. Your. Self."

Drake sat back and steepled his fingers.

"You want to do this the hard way?"

"I don't want to do this any way."

I wanted to leave but knowing I might run into Prescott again had me faltering. I didn't know if I could keep my resolve if he looked at me with those beautiful blue eyes of his. If he told me he was sorry and he cared about me. My heart was desperate for him. And I hated the traitorous piece of flesh beating in my chest.

"Come here."

I didn't want to be anywhere near Drake. No way in hell I trusted him, nor what he would do to me. He'd kept threatening punishment and hadn't yet delivered on it. I was in no doubt if I went over to him, I would be on the receiving end of his version of discipline. He had warned me he wouldn't tolerate any further disobedience. And what was I doing? Telling him to go fuck himself and refusing to answer his questions.

"No."

"Scarlett."

"No. I'm not coming anywhere near you."

For a long moment, the two of us were at a stalemate. Then Drake put his hand on the arm of his chair and rose from it. I swallowed when he walked out from behind his desk and stood before me. The way he towered over me had my hands trembling at my sides. Even more so when he reached up, gripping my chin between his thumb and forefinger to keep me in place. The other was dug in his pocket as if he knew I wouldn't go anywhere.

"So defiant. I'm going to enjoy breaking that fiery little spirit of yours."

You should have run the moment he stood up.

He leant closer to me, his breath dusting across my cheek as his lips landed close to my ear.

"You're seeing how far you can test the boundaries and that's okay, Scarlett, I understand. It doesn't mean, however, that I'll tolerate it."

His hand dropped from my chin and his long fingers wrapped around my arm. He spun me and pushed me up against his desk, folding my arm behind my back as he pressed me down on it.

"Stay."

Everything inside me protested at his manhandling and the thought of what he was going to do next, but I obeyed. I stayed in place when he released my arm. I didn't dare move. My whole body was rigid with fear. Drake wouldn't grant me any mercy this time.

CHAOS

The sound of clinking and a whooshing noise made me flinch. Then he cracked something against his hand. I looked at him and saw he'd taken his belt off, folding in a loop. He gripped it in his hand and stared at me.

"Drake…"

"Palms flat on the desk and don't move them."

"Are you going to hit me with that?"

"What do you think?"

I didn't know what to do. The thought of him slapping me with a belt sent a shiver down my spine.

"Yes."

"Palms on the desk."

I laid them down on the glass, wondering why I'd been so insistent on refusing to do what he asked. Perhaps I hadn't believed him when he told me I'd be punished. Or maybe I wanted to know what would happen if I continued to push him. Clearly, I had no self-preservation when it came to these men. I ran headlong into dangerous situations without a thought for my own safety.

"You're a danger to yourself."
"It wouldn't be fun if I wasn't."
He shook his head, his indigo eyes darkening.
"Reckless, always so fucking reckless."
"You wouldn't have me any other way."

The vivid image of a younger version of Drake flashed before my eyes. There were no harsh lines to him. Those indigo eyes of his held so much expression, so many emotions. Like he was amused by me, even though I also frustrated the hell out of him.

Where had that come from? It was so at odds with the man behind me right now, I didn't know whether to believe in it or not. I couldn't trust the things in my head.

The first strike of the belt came down hard on my behind, making me flinch again. It was dampened by my clothes, but it didn't stop it from hurting.

"Jesus," I choked out.

He ignored me and struck my other cheek, making me shift on the desk, the pain burning its way up my spine. It worsened with each strike. Tears pricked at the corner of my eyes, but I took it without telling him to stop. Why I was even being so bloody compliant was a mystery to me? Or maybe my sense of self-preservation had finally kicked in and I knew if I pushed Drake, he would only punish me harder. This was bad enough.

There were ten strikes across my cheeks and six across my thighs. I stayed where I was when they stopped, worried he'd continue. Concerned this hadn't satisfied him. My skin was on fire. I didn't think I could take any more.

"Let this serve as your final warning, Scarlett. If you continue down this path, I will make this punishment feel like child's play. Do you understand?"

"Yes, sir."

If this was child's play, then I didn't want to find out what he considered adult playtime. I was going to feel this for hours and sitting down would hurt. A lot.

"Now, answer my question. Why didn't you tell Mason he hurt you?"

"If I told him, he might not have let me come to work... then I wouldn't have been able to tell Prescott what Mason did. He didn't want me to come back here when he found out I'd slept with all of you."

I had left that part out when I told Prescott about it.

"Is that the real reason he was angry with you?"

"Yes."

"I see."

I looked at Drake, who was putting his belt back in the loops of his trousers and not paying attention to me.

"Can I get up now or do you want to ask me something else?"

"You can go back to work."

I pushed myself off his desk. My behind and thighs hurt like the devil, but I ignored the pain and walked around Drake, wanting to be as far away from him as possible. With each step, I wished fervently I had listened to his warnings. I wished I hadn't pushed him.

I'd put my hand on the door handle when his voice brought me up short.

"I warned Mason if he comes near you, he will have us to deal with. You have our protection… for now. If you do anything to jeopardise it, make no mistake, it will be withdrawn. Don't do anything stupid."

His unsaid words hung between us. *Do not contact Mason.* Right then, I didn't want to deal with him. My mind was too fucking full of all the other shit going on around me as a result of asking Prescott to save me from Mason.

I didn't respond to Drake, opening the door and hurrying out of his office. Thankfully, no one else was in the corridor. I didn't think I could deal with Prescott again. Not after Drake had punished me with his belt.

"Some fucking protection," I muttered under my breath on the way back to my office. "Totally fine for you to hurt me, but when someone else does it, that's not okay? Fucking psychos. All of you are."

I didn't understand their logic, nor did I want to. All I could think about was how much my arse hurt and how I hated Drake even more for causing me pain.

Fuck him. Fuck everything. I'm so done.

Maybe I should be more shocked and appalled by Drake's behaviour, but after you've been made to murder a man, everything else pales in comparison. I needed a thick skin to deal with these men. I was pretty sure no matter what he'd said, Drake and the others wouldn't be letting me go… ever.

THIRTEEN

SCARLETT

T he rest of the week passed slowly and with no incidents. Not that I expected it to, but you never knew with these men and their mood swings.

I wasn't sure how Francis felt about me taking up residence in his bedroom. He hadn't complained or anything. It's not like I kicked him out of his own bed, but we hadn't been intimate with each other. After Drake had thoroughly reddened my arse and thighs, I was not in the mood for sex. Francis had eyed it with some amusement and asked me what I'd done to earn Drake's ire. I had to be honest and tell him I'd brought it on myself. He'd been nice about it, but I'm sure he found the whole thing hilarious.

I'd tried to forget about what I'd done on Saturday. Every time I thought about the killing, it made my chest cave in. Talking about it to Francis helped. While it wasn't the same for him, he understood my guilty conscience. Sleeping next to him had kept my nightmares at bay. He was my safe space in messed-up situation I was in. And it kind of helped that he was way too attractive for his own good. I could get lost in his silver gaze and pretend he wasn't as fucked up as the rest of them. Francis was dangerous. I couldn't afford to forget it, even when he made me feel at home by his side.

Friday arrived with me hoping for an uneventful weekend. I'd just left my office to procure Drake's lunch and wasn't looking where I was going when I ran headlong into a very solid body. Taking a step back, I rubbed my forehead before looking up at who I'd walked into.

"Hello, Scar."

My stomach dropped. West stood there with a smirk on his face and those amber eyes of his, full of violence. After he'd been nice to me on Monday, I'd been wary of him and what he might do next. The man gave me whiplash every time I was near him.

"Sorry," I mumbled, not wanting to get into it with him.

I should have known better than to expect him to drop it. He reached up and wrapped his hand around my throat before pushing me up against the wall next to us. I let out a breath as my hands shook.

"You've been avoiding me."

"Doesn't everyone?"

He grinned.

"Yes, but you're different, Scar. You're not scared of me."

I was scared shitless of him, but I stood up to him anyway. As evidenced by what happened with Drake on Monday, self-preservation wasn't high on my list of priorities.

"I am."

My words only made him smile wider. His thumb ran down my neck in a soothing motion.

"Fear makes you stronger… and makes this pussy wet."

I let out a squeak as he cupped my pussy with his other hand. What the hell was wrong with him? We were in the corridor where anyone could see us, and here he was making sexual advances on me. This man knew no bounds. I don't know why I was surprised considering he'd made me come in a public place without a care in the world.

"I've left you alone, Scar," he murmured, leaning closer. "Rest assured, I'll be taking what's mine very soon. I'm going to fuck all your little holes."

The hand around my throat squeezed. I hated the way I responded to him. How my body arched into his as if it wanted him to carry out his threat, especially when he rubbed my pussy.

"I'll make you cry so I can taste your tears again. They're so sweet."

There was a cough nearby. West turned his head slowly towards the source of the noise. His eyes darkened significantly when he spied Tonya standing there looking at the both of us with a raised eyebrow. When she saw West's expression, her face dropped.

"Ahem, Mr Greer, Andrew is waiting for you in the meeting room."

West grunted and released me before straightening his suit. His gaze went to me again.

"Remember what I said."

I swallowed, watching him walk off down the hallway and open the door to the meeting room. My eyes went to Tonya, who hadn't moved. There was contempt in her eyes. She glared at me like I was some kind of wanton bitch for allowing West to feel me up at work. It was hardly my fault he'd done it. The man didn't exactly take no for an answer. He did whatever he wanted. Surely she knew that, considering she'd been here for years. I only knew because Francis had told me. I barely interacted with her on a personal basis. It had mostly been via email and only ever related to work.

She let out a rather judgemental sounding "hmm," and looked me over once more. I pushed off the wall and adjusted my clothes, trying not to think too hard about how my knickers were damp with arousal from West's words and touch.

"What?" I asked, not giving a shit if I sounded peeved.

Who the hell was she to judge me? She didn't know me.

"I'd be careful with that one."

"Who, West?"

"Mr Greer doesn't suffer fools lightly."

I narrowed my eyes.

"Are you saying I'm a fool?"

She gave me a rather fake smile and laughed.

"Oh no, of course not. I'm just warning you, he's rather temperamental. Though, I suppose you didn't look like you were upset by his… attention."

I crossed my arms over my chest and didn't respond. Her attitude was pissing me off.

"Is that how you got hired?"

I frowned.

"Excuse me?"

She flicked her hand up in the air.

"I'm not judging. Us women have to get ahead by any means possible."

Had she actually insinuated I'd slept with the Horsemen to get a job here? Who the fuck did this woman think she was? I dropped my arms and took a step towards her.

"I don't know what type of woman you think I am, but I did not spread my legs to get hired."

The way she smiled at me had my skin crawling. And only proved why I'd got a bad vibe from her from the moment I laid eyes on the woman.

"Oh, honey, you expect me to believe that? The walls aren't soundproof. Besides, I know what they're like. They have rather insatiable appetites." She winked. "Especially Mr Ellis."

I stiffened. Did she just make out like Prescott had slept with her?

"He's been rather lonely this week. I suppose it's why he invited me into his office yesterday."

I didn't want to hear another fucking word out of her mouth. Jealousy and irritation flared inside me. Prescott was *mine*. I might be angry at him, but there was no way in hell I was tolerating this shit. I might have told Francis I didn't care if Prescott slept with someone else, but I hadn't meant it. I cared all right. Far too much.

Even if Tonya was lying and saying shit to piss me off, it didn't stop the pain from driving through my chest. It didn't stop the anger flooding my veins at the very thought of him being with another woman.

Not giving her a chance to say another word, I stormed off, shoving by her without a fucking care for her shocked expression. No, I was going to give the man a piece of my mind and make sure he understood if he ever wanted to earn my forgiveness, this type of behaviour was not the way to go about it.

You're mine, Pres, you're fucking well mine.

I marched down to his office, threw the door open and slammed it shut behind me. Prescott looked up from his desk, his eyebrows shooting up at the sight of me. He rose out of his chair.

"Scarlett—"

"Have you been fucking other women?"

A frown appeared between his brows.

"What?"

"Have you fucked someone else since me?"

He came around his desk, approaching me with confusion in those blue eyes.

"No, of course not. Why would you ask me that?"

I walked right up to him, meeting his gaze head-on. My heart went into overdrive being so close to him. The man it wanted me to press myself against and breathe in. It hurt so fucking much, crippling me with its intensity. I dug my nails into my palms to stay upright, my knees threatening to buckle and give me away.

"Do not lie to me."

He raised his hand. It hovered over my arm as if he wanted to touch me but was hesitant to.

"I'm not. I wouldn't do that to you." Then he touched me. His hand rested on my shoulder, preventing me from backing away. "All I've wanted to do is talk, but you haven't given me a chance."

The calmness of his voice didn't exactly take the wind out of my sails, but it did make me falter. And his touch? Fuck, it was the worst part. I wanted more of it. I wanted him. But forgiveness didn't come easily. Not when he'd hurt me. Not when he'd made me feel as though I didn't matter to him.

"I don't know how to trust you or believe anything you say to me. Not after what you did. But I do know one thing. One fucking thing. If you've touched anyone else, we're done. It doesn't matter if I'm angry with you, Pres, you're still mine." I pointed at my chest. "Mine."

A part of me almost melted at the way his expression softened. And when he lifted his hand from my shoulder and cupped my cheek.

"My little lamb," he whispered. "There is no one else for me but you. I thought you knew."

I wanted to fucking well cry, but I didn't. He called me little lamb. His little lamb.

Fuck, I can't hide it from myself any longer. I can't… Pres, I'm falling for you in the worst way.

"Then why would she say that?" I choked out.

"Who said what?"

Now it seemed so stupid, but my emotions were all over the place. One minute I had West working me up, then Tonya saying shit to me and now Prescott making me want to hold and hurt him at the same time.

"Tonya said you invited her into your office yesterday after she insinuated I'd slept my way into a job."

For a second Prescott didn't react, then he dropped his hand from my face and gritted his teeth, his expression turning deadly.

115

"She did what?"

The rage in his voice made me take a step back.

"She made it sound like you had sex with her."

Prescott's fists clenched at his sides and his lip curled up in disgust.

"What the fuck? I swear the woman is delusional. You couldn't pay me enough money to touch her. In fact, nothing in this fucking universe would be worth it." He looked at me once more. "I promise you, I have never slept with nor do I have any intention of sleeping with her. You are all I need, sweetness, only you."

There were a lot of things I didn't know if Prescott was telling me the truth about or not, but this… well, this I did know. He couldn't fake his revulsion.

"I can't believe she said that to you. What exactly happened?"

Despite everything that had gone on between me and Prescott, the sorry story came out anyway. I told him about West and Tonya interrupting us. By the time I was finished, Prescott looked incensed, like he couldn't believe she had the audacity to speak to me in the way she had.

"That's it. That's fucking it. This bitch really needs to learn her place. I don't give a shit who she is. There is no way in hell I am letting her talk to you that way. She has no right."

Prescott walked around me and strode towards the door.

"Where are you going? We're not done talking," I called after him.

He paused as he opened the door.

"To sort this out, little lamb. No one gets away with giving you shit. Not whilst I'm still breathing."

CHAOS

And with that, he walked out, leaving me staring after him.

FOURTEEN

PRESCOTT

O f all the fucking things Tonya could say to my woman, she'd had to go make up some bullshit about me sleeping with her. Of course, of fucking course. Tonya had been after me for years. I had never once given her the impression I would ever sleep with her or that I was even interested. Couldn't help it if I was naturally charming and friendly. It was a part of the act I put on for the rest of the world. Why I was the face of our company.

Being polite to Tonya was easier than giving her shit when I had to work with her. Maybe I used it to my advantage because she did more for me than she ever did for Francis because of her crush. While she technically also worked for West, he held her in so much contempt, he rarely ever asked her to do anything for him.

I strode down the hallway towards Tonya's desk but was interrupted on the way by West walking out of the meeting room. I paused when he raised his eyebrows at me.

"Why do you look murderous?" he asked, digging his hands in his pockets.

"Tonya."

His eyes narrowed.

"What did the bitch do now? You know, she saw me with Scar not that long ago."

"What did she do? She told Scarlett I fucked her yesterday, that's what she did."

West's expression grew cold and downright scary.

"Are you serious?"

"Yes. I just had Scarlett storming into my office and accusing me of fucking other people."

And she'd told me I was hers. I wasn't going to lie, it gave me so much damn hope knowing her feelings towards me remained. Maybe if I apologised for hurting her, she could forgive me. If I showed her how much I cared and she was my everything. I didn't care what the hell the others said or did any longer. Scarlett was more important than anything else. I needed her to remember me. I needed her to… love me.

"What else did she say?"

"Tonya accused Scarlett of sleeping with us to get a job."

I swear a vein popped in West's temple.

"She did, did she? Well, the bitch has crossed a line for the last fucking time."

The moment the last word left his mouth, he walked off toward reception. I followed him, watching West flex his hands at his sides. The moment we both rounded the corner and I spied Tonya sitting there without a care in the world, I wanted to rip her to shreds. However, I was relatively sure I didn't need to when West strode right up to her desk and leant on it. His expression cleared of all annoyance as he stared at her. A sure sign he was going to do something incredibly fucked up.

Tonya looked up, her eyes going wide. I hung back by the entrance to the lobby, waiting for the shitstorm to happen.

"Can… can I do something for you, Mr Greer?"

West smiled at her that maniacal way of his.

"Why, yes, Tonya, you can."

"And what's that?"

He leant closer and ran his fingers over the wood.

"Explain something to me."

"Yes?"

He dug his other hand in his pocket, flicked open the blade of his pocketknife and without a second thought, stabbed it into the desk right by her keyboard. Tonya jumped, her eyes going wide as she spied the knife.

"Why you think it's acceptable to tell Scarlett you're fucking one of your bosses."

She paled and shifted back in her chair.

"I—"

"I'm not done, Tonya. Not by a long fucking shot."

He ripped the knife out of the desk and strode around to her side.

Scarlett appeared next to me.

"What's going on?" she asked as she took in the scene in front of us.

I glanced at her, noting she was about to move closer to West and Tonya. Reaching out, I tucked Scarlett against my side and put my hand over her mouth.

"Shh, just watch," I murmured.

West put his hand on one arm of Tonya's chair and leant closer, placing the flat side of the knife against her cheek.

"Do you really think Prescott would ever consider your pathetic pussy to be worthy of his dick? You aren't even worth a pity fuck."

She flinched and I wanted to laugh. Scarlett let out a muffled squeak by my side, but I kept a tighter hold on her. I wasn't about to let her interrupt West when he was on a roll.

Tonya looked like she was about to shit herself as West pressed the knife harder into her face.

"This crush of yours needs to end. He doesn't give a shit about you. Look, he's standing right there staring at you like you're fucking nothing." West removed the knife and pointed it at me. "Because that's what you are. Nothing."

Tonya's eyes went to mine. The abject horror on her face when she saw I had Scarlett next to me made this all so worthwhile. I didn't care if I wasn't the one giving her hell. West was annihilating the woman. I was happy to let him.

West ran the back of the blade along her chin, turning her attention back to him.

"You think you're safe because of who your daddy is... but you forget, I don't give a shit whose daughter you are. I will hurt you and I will enjoy every moment of it."

"But... but Drake," she whimpered.

"But Drake what? You think he's going to save you because you're his fucking step-cousin, huh?" He grinned. "Don't make me laugh. If he knew what you'd said to Scarlett... well, there's no telling what he would do, because in case you hadn't realised, that woman over there is ours. If you try to humiliate and hurt what's ours, you don't live very long, you hear me?"

CHAOS

A tear ran down Tonya's cheek. I didn't feel sorry for her. Ever since she'd come to work here, she'd been a nosey bitch who couldn't keep herself out of our personal business. West and I had wanted her gone for a long time. We didn't owe her anything. She was only working here because Drake had given her a job as a favour to her father, his step-uncle, Fletcher. While I respected Fletch Sinclair to an extent, as he'd given Drake the money for us to start Fortuity, didn't mean I liked his daughter. We'd paid him back his investment years ago. We didn't want Fletch in our business for any longer than he had to be.

"I've gutted people with this knife before, Tonya," West told her as he ran it down her neck and pressed the tip into her skin. "I will do it to you. I will turn your fucking insides out and leave you to bleed to death in the most painful way possible. Let this be your last fucking warning. You say another fucking word to Scarlett, I will end you. That's not a threat, it's a promise."

West straightened, flipped the knife closed and tucked it back in his pocket.

"I see we've come to an understanding, so I'll leave you to get back to work now."

He walked away from the woman he'd terrorised and stopped in front of Scarlett. I dropped my hand from her mouth but didn't let her go completely. West leant down and put his mouth to her ear.

"I will end the world for you, Scar. All you have to do is ask."

Then he pressed his lips to her cheek before he shoved his hands in his pockets and strolled away. Scarlett's eyes followed him, her expression one of complete disbelief.

"What the fuck?" she whispered.

Her eyes met mine when West disappeared into his office.

"Prescott, what was that?"

"That was West, little lamb."

Her body was trembling, but I didn't think it was quite as hard as Tonya was shaking right now. I didn't give a fuck about her. Reaching up, I stroked Scarlett's cheek, trying to soothe her because she was clearly in shock. For a second she stayed right where she was, then she wrenched herself out of my grasp and backed away.

"He's psychotic," she said, waving down the corridor. "Actually psychotic. And you? You think that's normal? What the hell is wrong with you?"

I walked after her as she kept moving away down the hallway.

"I thought you understood. This is who we are."

She shook her head.

"He threatened to gut her."

"And? She upset you."

"That is not an appropriate response. I don't want him to kill her, Pres!"

"You can tell him."

"I am not talking to him. He's insane."

This was not how I wanted a conversation with her to go.

"Stop walking away from me."

Scarlett only backed away further, shaking her head.

"No! Jesus, you're all fucking crazy, you know that? All of you!"

"Scarlett—"

"No!"

She looked back and found herself outside Drake's office, which meant she didn't have anywhere else to go. Then she stabbed a finger in my direction.

"If you think I want to talk to you after that, you're mistaken." Her voice had got all high pitched and loud. "You haven't even apologised for all the shit you've put me through and now this? I don't even know why I'm fucking well here any longer."

I caught up to her and took her by the arm, keeping her in place so she could damn well listen to my apology.

"I'm sorry, little lamb. I never wanted to hurt you."

Tears welled in those beautiful eyes and it cut me.

"But you're not sorry for making me... kill someone." She whispered the last part, thankfully. I didn't need her shouting about it for the entire world to hear.

"No, I'm not."

I couldn't lie to her. I didn't regret what we'd done. It was necessary. Everything we did was. Scarlett had proven herself to us. Even if she was still under their control to an extent, we'd started the process of bringing her over to our side. Sure, it was immoral and fucked up, but the four of us didn't play by society's rules.

"What is going on out here?" came Drake's voice as he opened his office door.

Scarlett gave me a wounded look.

"You expect me to understand why when I don't understand a single thing about any of you. I hate what you made me do. I hate it so much, Pres. You stained my fucking soul and you don't even care."

"I do care, sweetness. I care a great fucking deal about you."

Fuck, little lamb, I love you. I'm fucking well in love with you.

She shook her head, tears slipping down her cheeks.

"You only care about how you can use me."

She ripped herself out of my grasp and ran away to her office, slamming the door shut behind her. I was left staring at the place she'd been, hating myself for breaking her trust and making her think she didn't mean the world to me.

"What the hell was that, Pres?" Drake asked.

"That was the result of West threatening to gut Tonya in front of Scarlett after Tonya insinuated she was sleeping with me and accused Scarlett of sleeping with us to get a job."

My tone was flat and void of emotion. Something inside me was so fucking broken right now, I couldn't bring myself to sound any other way.

"Jesus fucking Christ. Can I not leave any of you alone for two fucking minutes?"

"I can't do this anymore, Drake. I fucking can't." I buried my fingers in my hair. "This is fucking killing me." I turned to him. "She hates me."

He gave me a sympathetic look.

"She doesn't hate you, Pres."

I couldn't believe it. Even though she'd given me hope earlier, I was still worried there was nothing I could do to make this up to her. How could I when she kept running away from me?

"You don't understand," I told him, my voice quiet, "I love her."

Then I walked away from him. I'd just confessed the truth to Drake rather than Scarlett. And I was a fucking idiot for it.

FIFTEEN

SCARLETT

I sat at my desk staring at the wall with tears slipping down my face. My mind was a riot of too many emotions. Nothing felt right or good. It was all so very wrong.

I didn't have a handle on anything. On my life. On the expectations placed upon me. On the feelings my traitorous heart was throwing at me. It was all too much. I didn't know what to do with myself. How to even keep breathing any longer. To keep everything together.

And then my phone started ringing, jolting me out of my misery and regrets.

I dug it out of my bag and looked at the screen. My stomach sunk to my feet. Grabbing the box of tissues on my desk, I tugged some out and dabbed my face before answering.

"Hi, Dad," I said in my best fake happy voice.

"Scarlett, I hear from Mason you have moved out."

I didn't like the tone of his voice. The judgement in it. This conversation wasn't one I wanted to have after all the shit I'd dealt with.

I stood up, knowing I still had to go sort out my stupid boss's lunch. Grabbing my handbag, I walked over to the door. Thankfully, no one was in the hallway when I walked out.

"I have."

"For what purpose?"

I almost faltered in my steps. What exactly had Mason told him? And why had it taken almost a week for him to do it?

"I felt like I could work faster if I was closer to them."

The lie wasn't hard for me to tell. I'd been lying to my parents for years. It was safer for me. Got me in less trouble. I didn't have to be scared he might hit me and leave bruises all over my body. The body that had been broken far too much already after my accident. The doctors had said I'd been very lucky the damage hadn't been worse. Not sure what's worse than having a broken pelvis that had to be bolted together with metal rods. Not to mention the fact it had left me with internal scarring. I was still sore over the fact they'd destroyed my ability to have children even though it meant I could walk again. One day, I would have to deal with those emotions, but not today. Not when my life was all fucked up beyond belief.

"I see. And what progress have you made?"

I walked by the reception lobby towards the lifts. The desk was empty but after what happened between West and Tonya, it hardly surprised me.

"I think they're starting to trust me."

Hitting the button for the lift, the doors opened almost straight away. I trotted in and pressed the button for the ground floor. Then I looked myself over in the mirrored walls, finding my face an absolute mess. Hooking my phone between my shoulder and my ear, I dug a makeup wipe from my bag to clean myself up.

"Do you have anything useful yet? Something we can use?"

"I don't exactly have access to their confidential data, Dad."

"What good is you living with them then?"

The quiet irritation in his voice set me on edge. Even though I was miles away from him, safe from his fists, it didn't stop my instincts from flaring up and telling me I was in danger.

"I've been supervised at all times in their penthouse." It wasn't strictly the truth, but he didn't need to know that. "What do you want me to do?"

"Use your brain, Scarlett. Look around when they're asleep."

While it had occurred to me, my issue was I slept next to Francis who would notice if I left the room at night. He wasn't exactly a heavy sleeper. And I sure as hell wasn't going to sleep in one of the other's rooms. Drake and West terrified me. The less said about the current state of my relationship with Prescott, the better. With my dad's phone call, there'd been no time for me to process anything Prescott had said to me.

"I'll try. That's all I can do."

"Get me results or you know what will happen."

I swallowed, balling the used makeup wipe in my fist. He would drag me back to the estate and lock me up again. He'd keep me there for the rest of my life if he could. And all I would face was more abuse. My only option was to stay with the Horsemen and try to do as my father said even though I no longer wanted to.

It was absolutely insane, but I had no desire to hurt the men I was with no matter what they'd done to me. No matter what my parents said they'd done to them. It was something they couldn't prove anyway. It's why they need me. And I hated them for it.

"Yes, Dad."

"Good. I expect a full report in a week."

He hung up without saying goodbye. I sighed, dumping my phone back in my bag. What did it matter if I no longer had any makeup on? It was better than it running all down my face. And now I had to work out how to get my parents something by next week. What a fucking joke.

The lift doors opened. I walked out onto the ground floor, dumping the wipe in a bin on my way and waving at the receptionist. When I got out onto the street, I made my way to the local sandwich shop Drake liked and put in an order. After five minutes, they handed me over a bag and I paid using the company expenses card Drake had given me. As I was leaving, someone put their hand on my arm. I almost jumped out of my skin at the touch. Looking to my left, I found the last person I expected to see. A flood of conflicting emotions raged through me like wildfire.

"Mason?"

The sight of him brought back last weekend when the Horsemen had made me think I was killing my only friend. When I'd screamed at him and let out my long-buried feelings towards the only person I'd ever felt close to in the past ten years. And here he was, standing there very much alive. Relief flooded me, but it was warring with my other feelings of disappointment, regret and pain.

"I thought I would miss you."

I pulled away from him and moved out of the way of the door so we wouldn't block anyone trying to come in.

"You shouldn't be here."

Drake's words from earlier in the week had stuck with me. He'd warned Mason to stay away from me. If they found out Mason was here and I'd seen him, there would be hell to pay.

"I needed to see you."

"How did you know I'd be here?"

"I've been watching you all week, making sure no one ever came here with you."

I rubbed my face, hitching my handbag strap higher on my shoulder. The whole idea of him keeping tabs on me gave me a rather sick feeling in my stomach.

"What do you want?"

His brown eyes were full of concern and sorrow.

"Did I really hurt you?"

My eyes went to the shop window.

"Yes, you did. I had bruises on my arm."

"Why didn't you tell me?"

Meeting his eyes felt impossible right then.

"You scared me, Mase… and I never thought there would come a day where you would do the same thing *he* does to me."

To his credit, he didn't touch me. I would've flinched back away if he had.

"I'm so sorry, Scar. I didn't mean to."

"But you did. You threatened to take me back there," I hissed, finally looking at him again. "Did you think I would trust you after that?"

"Is that why you went to them? Told them you were scared of me?"

I took a step back, not liking the way he was looking at me nor how he'd spat the word 'them'. The Horsemen might be dangerous and twisted, but they weren't out here trying to actively hurt me in the way Mason had, and the way my parents would do if I went back. At least, I didn't think they'd made me kill a man to hurt me. They did it to prove a point.

When Prescott told me he hadn't wanted to hurt me, he'd meant it. No matter how angry I was at him, it didn't change the fact he hadn't lied to me about their reasoning. He hadn't sugar-coated it for my benefit. And it was one of the only reasons I hadn't outright told him I didn't want to be with him any longer. Well... and the fact I'd fallen head over heels for the man. My stupid heart wouldn't allow me to lie to myself any longer or pretend it didn't belong to Prescott. I wasn't even going to question how I could feel this way about him and want Francis at the same time. Not to mention my conflicted feelings towards West and Drake.

"What else did you expect me to do? You gave me a fucking ultimatum. I had to make sure you didn't take me back."

"That's not fair, Scar."

Was he seriously trying to act like I was the one being unfair right now?

The fucking cheek.

"Not fair? What's not fair is everything you and my parents have forced on me, that's what's not fair, Mason." I tried to keep my voice low as people were staring. "I never thought I'd say this, but I'm safer with them than I am with you. And trust me, I wish that wasn't the case."

Mason flinched. It served him fucking right. He should know the truth. I feared him now. I was terrified he would take me away from the Horsemen. They had no reason to come after me if he did. Or did they? I'd been sure Prescott had wanted to say more to me before I ran away. I could see it in his blue eyes. The pain and agony in them reflected in my own.

"You're not safer with them at all. Why can't you see that?"

I stepped closer and lowered my voice to an almost whisper.

"They might be fucked up, but they don't lock me in a room, bloody, bruised and beaten to the point where I pass out because I said the wrong thing to them. They aren't cruel for no reason. And you enable it by not doing a single thing about it. Don't come here again, Mason. They will hurt you if you come near me. You're lucky I'm not going to tell them about this."

I didn't give him a chance to respond, walking around him and out the door onto the street. Nothing about what I'd said to him felt good, but I wasn't going to stick around and listen to him rail against the Horsemen. While I knew my rationale for staying with the boys was probably way off, I was more scared of my father than I was of them. Yes, they'd made me kill, but I wasn't fearing for my life when I was with them. I wasn't scared it might be the last time I took a breath because my father took it too far. I'd already almost died once on the night of my accident, I wasn't about to let it happen again. No, I would do everything in my power to stay away from him.

I should tell Drake I'd seen Mason, but it wouldn't be worth it for either of us. Besides, I did not want a repeat of the belt incident any time soon. Maybe his punishment should have reminded me of what my father had done to me, but it didn't. Everything between me and Drake was about a battle of wills and had a sexual undertone to it. Deep down, I knew I played up on purpose to see what he would do. A part of me couldn't help but want to push his buttons. For some reason, I trusted him not to go too far when I shouldn't trust the man at all.

As I made my way back to Fortuity, all I wanted was to curl up in a ball and escape for a few hours, but I had to work for the rest of the afternoon.

Today had been absolute shit so far.

Could it get any worse?

Knowing the Horsemen, the answer to that was... yes, yes it definitely could.

SIXTEEN

WEST

I fully expected to get a lecture from Drake over what I'd said to Tonya earlier, but all he'd done was ask me what exactly happened. After I told him, he shrugged, said she deserved it and walked off towards the kitchen to start on dinner. When he waved me over a few minutes later, I'd been confused until he told me what he had planned for later. I didn't know what the fuck had got into him, but if he wanted to screw with Scarlett some more, I wasn't going to complain. It meant I had to make a phone call to Gary for a drop-off, but he came through for me as always.

The five of us shared a rather stilted dinner. Drake told Scarlett in no uncertain terms she was going to sit with us. The woman looked resigned to her fate, but it didn't stop her from giving him a mutinous look when he wasn't paying attention. Prescott spent the entire time sulking while Francis was clearly wondering what the fuck had gone on today. I wasn't in the mood to rehash the Tonya shit all over again. She was on her last fucking chance. I hadn't been joking about gutting her. I would do it in a heartbeat. Didn't care if she was Fletcher's daughter. She was Drake's family, not mine. Though mine could go fuck themselves after they decided I was too 'crazy' for them to deal with. The less said about them, the better.

When Scarlett tried to escape after dinner, Francis stopped her. Considering he was the only one she was being civil with, Drake had clearly told him to keep her down here with us.

"Come here," he murmured, taking her hand and pulling her over to the sofas.

She followed him but her face was full of confusion. He sat down and encouraged her to sit in his lap. Scarlett curled herself up in it and pressed her face into his neck as he stroked her back. Prescott watched the two of them from the kitchen where he was filling the dishwasher. There was a definite hint of jealousy in his eyes, but not because he didn't want her close to Francis. His relationship with Scarlett was all kinds of fucked up and he wished she would hold him like that again. It was so fucking obvious he'd gone and fallen for her... not that I could say a word. The woman had dug her way inside me a long time ago. Made a permanent place for herself there. And I didn't hate her for it. If anything, her presence there was the only thing keeping me from imploding.

Drake got some beers from the fridge and dumped them out on the coffee table before taking a seat across from Francis and Scarlett. I wandered over and dumped out the contents of my pockets on the table, picking up a bottle of beer and popping the top off with the opener.

"Want one?" I asked Scarlett who was watching me. She always watched me as if she was nervous about what I might do next.

"I don't like beer," she muttered, pressing herself closer to Francis.

I popped the cap off a second bottle and placed it in his free hand before sitting at the other end of the sofa from them, leaning my arm across the back of it.

"Do you want a glass of wine then?"

Scarlett shook her head.

"Pres, get her some water, yeah?"

He gave me a dark look but did as I asked, bringing it over and setting it on the coffee table. Then he sat down by Drake. I swigged from my bottle before pointing at the baggy I'd dumped out on the table.

"Who wants to start?"

Scarlett's eyes followed the direction of my finger until they widened when they spied the drugs on the table.

"What are those?"

"They're not for you."

She sat up, her eyes narrowing as she looked at me.

"What do you mean?"

"He means you're not taking drugs with us, Scarlett," Drake said, leaning forward and pulling the baggy closer to him so it was out of her reach.

"Why not?"

I tried not to smile. Scarlett didn't like being told she couldn't do something.

"Do you want to?"

"I don't know. You haven't told me what they are, so how can I answer that?"

Francis remained silent, watching the girl in his lap intently. Prescott was ignoring all of us.

"E," I said, answering her question. "And none of the cut with other drugs shit they sell on the streets. This is proper shit."

If Gary tried to sell me Ecstasy cut with Ket or some other shit, I would throw his dead body in the fucking canal. He wouldn't fuck me over. The guy valued his life, not to mention he sold to the crime families. He wasn't a fool.

"I've never taken anything like that."

"And that's exactly why you're not taking any tonight," Drake said. "Too unpredictable."

Scarlett sat back against Francis and glared at Drake.

"Don't treat me like a child. If I want to take a pill, I can."

Like fucking putty in our hands, she was, falling for our game way too easily.

Drake took out one pill and set it on the table, giving Scarlett a hard stare.

"Really now? You want to get high?"

"Maybe I do."

He waved his hand at the table and sat back.

"Have at it then if you want to be reckless."

Scarlett stared at the pill on the table like it would hurt her somehow. I could see the war going on in her head playing out in her expression. She frowned, her eyes flicking to Drake and back to the pill.

"What will it do to me?"

"It's a happy drug, Scar," I said with a shrug. "It'll make you feel good."

Drake had decided he wanted to test Scarlett's boundaries tonight. He wanted to see what drugs might do to her state of mind and if she might remember more of the past. I'd suggested LSD or mushrooms, but he didn't want to send her on a trip. He wanted to see her free and happy tonight after witnessing her tears over Prescott earlier. He'd mentioned it when he was discussing the plan with me. Who'd have thought Drake actually cared? He certainly didn't show it in his approach to Scarlett, but he always kept his emotions locked down. Maybe seeing her cry affected him more than he'd let on.

Scarlett gingerly reached out and picked up the pill. None of us said anything as she put it in her mouth and swallowed hard. Picking up the glass of water, she sipped at it before placing it back on the table. Then she curled herself around Francis again and ignored the rest of us. It would take time for the effects to kick in.

I watched her as Drake turned to Prescott and tried to talk to him, but the miserable fuck was being uncommunicative and clearly didn't want to be around any of us this evening. It started with Scarlett running her hand along Francis' chest with increased frequency as he sat sipping his beer. When she giggled and whispered something in his ear, his cheeks went red and he coughed.

"What?" he hissed.

She said something else and it made him shift in his seat. Then Scarlett sat up abruptly.

"Music. We need music!"

It had hit her system. I leant over to the coffee table and picked up one of the remotes, hitting play on it. The soft tinkle of guitar rang through the room.

"That's not upbeat."

"So?"

Scarlett crawled off Francis' lap towards me. I grinned when she got up in my face. For a moment she stared at me, then she reached out and ran her finger along my jaw.

"That tickles," she giggled.

Then she became fascinated with touching my face. Her fingers traced lines along my cheeks and then my bottom lip. I let her, amused by the fact she'd forgotten about the music and how she was so interested in my features.

"You're pretty," she told me, her voice taking on a dreamy note to it.

I laughed and gave her a wink.

"If you say so."

"You have pretty eyes. They're like amber gemstones." Her eyes fell to my mouth. "Can I kiss you?"

I did not expect her to ask me that, let alone lean closer to me. Placing a hand on her chest, I stopped her from closing the distance.

"I don't kiss, Scar, but I'm sure the others would be happy to let you if you ask nicely."

The pout and disappointment on her face made my heart tighten. Scarlett had been the only girl I'd ever kissed. The only one I wanted to, but I wasn't ready to go there. Not when kissing her would only remind me of the girl I'd lost and how she couldn't remember who we'd been to each other. Something I'd never come to terms with. Something I needed to. The feelings I had involving Scarlett and I were too raw even after ten years.

"Okay."

She went to move away, but I caught her and hauled the woman into my lap. I didn't want her to stop touching me, to stop looking at me with such ardent fascination. She might be high, but none of us were above taking advantage of it.

Scarlett stared at me, her tongue running over her bottom lip. I reached up and cupped her face. She leant into it, rubbing her face against my palm as if she needed to be touched. She craved it. And when she started rocking her hips against mine, I reacted, gripping her hip to encourage her.

"Someone's getting a little frisky," I murmured.

"I want to touch you."

Her fingers went to my shirt, fumbling with the buttons to get them open. I'd long since discarded my blazer and now was just in a shirt with rolled-up sleeves so you could see my tattooed forearms. I dropped my hands from her body and leant them across the back of the sofa, letting her do what she wanted. When she got the buttons open, she spread my shirt and ran her hands down my bare chest. She smiled to herself as she did it as if touching me skin on skin made her happy.

"You feel good," she whispered.

I turned to Francis.

"Pass me the weed and my lighter."

He rolled his eyes but leant forward and grabbed the stuff off the table. Instead of giving it to me, he rolled a joint, lit it and passed it over. I took a drag before leaning my arm over the back of the sofa again. Breathing out the smoke, it coiled upwards from my mouth. Scarlett stared at it in wonder, then her attention was dragged back to the fact she was touching me. And her fingers went to my belt, pulling at it.

"What you doing there, Scar?"

"I want to touch you," she repeated.

"I thought that's what you were doing already."

She shook her head.

"No, I want to touch you here."

Her hand splayed out over my cock. I leant closer to her, taking another drag.

"You do? Say it then."

"I want your dick."

"Then you better ask nicely for it."

I looked over at the others. Drake was smirking, Francis was rolling his eyes while Prescott was still ignoring proceedings. The guy was big on watching, so this wasn't normal. I indicated him with my head. Drake slapped Prescott around the shoulder. Prescott glared at him before his eyes fell on me and Scarlett.

"Please fuck me, West. I want it. Please give me your dick."

"Do your needy little holes need filling?"

"Yes, please… I'm so wet."

Her hands rubbed over my stomach as if she was waiting for my permission. I grabbed a handful of her arse, pushing her down on my hard cock.

"Are you sure you just want my dick, Scar? What if he fucks you too, hmm?" I waved my joint at Francis. "You want that? You want us to double team you?"

She bit her lip, rocking on my cock like she couldn't get enough.

"Please."

Putting my joint to my lips, I took another drag before grabbing hold of her jaw and opening her mouth. Then I blew the smoke into it. Scarlett coughed as the sweet-smelling smoke filled her lungs.

"Take your clothes off if you want us to fuck you, Scar. Give us a little dance, hmm? Show us how much you want it."

For a moment I thought she might disagree, but then she got off my lap and backed away, moving her body to the beat. The music had changed to something slow and sensual, just the right tone to set the mood. And fuck if I wasn't ready to watch her dance for us before I could fuck the living shit out of her for being such a good girl.

SEVENTEEN

DRAKE

Watching her slowly unbutton her blouse while her body swayed to the heady beat had me shifting on the sofa. I don't think any of us could look away from Scarlett and her movements. And the fact she'd begged for dick, begged for more than one, had me hard in an instant.

Giving her Ecstasy was a risk, but the tears streaming down her cheeks earlier when I'd caught her and Prescott arguing in the hallway did something to me. They made me want to give her a night off from her thoughts and feelings. Prescott's accusation that I didn't care about her hit a nerve with me. This might be a fucked up way of showing I cared, but it was my way.

I hadn't, however, expected her to want sex. Not like I was complaining or anything, but shit, watching her strip for us was heaven.

"We going to do this here or upstairs?" Francis asked, waving at Scarlett.

"Not got lube down here," West said with a shrug.

It was easier to fuck her together on a bed. The one we'd had installed in our playroom was bigger than your standard king size for that very reason. Custom built for our need to share.

"Upstairs," I said before sipping from my beer bottle.

Glancing over at Prescott, I found him mesmerised by Scarlett. He rubbed his bottom lip with his finger as his eyes roamed over her body. He'd admitted he loved her earlier. I don't think he was capable of separating her from the girl we'd known as kids and the woman she was now. At least not his feelings towards Scarlett. It wasn't necessarily a bad thing, but we all knew she couldn't be trusted until she remembered us. And even then, I had no idea how she would feel about the four of us.

Scarlett had discarded her blouse and skirt. The underwear she was wearing was basically see-through. I hauled myself up off the sofa and approached her. She stared up at me with this bright smile on her face.

"Did I do okay, sir?"

Fuck did I want to smile. Instead, I nodded and wrapped a hand around her waist.

"Come, we're taking this somewhere more... comfortable." I turned back to the others. "Bring water, wouldn't want her getting dehydrated, yeah?"

I got a nod from Francis. Scarlett came with me willingly as I made my way over to the stairs, knowing the others would follow along behind us. I took her upstairs and down to the end, opening the door and pushing her into our playroom. Her eyes went about the room when I turned on the lights. We'd had dimmers installed, so it wasn't harsh.

"Get on the bed, Scarlett."

She did as I told her. The woman looked so small on the big bed, sitting in the middle of it watching me with wide eyes. She reached out towards me. I walked over to her, hearing the others come in behind us. Leaning down, my hands went to her knickers. She let me pull them off her legs before allowing me to discard her bra too. I wrapped my hands around her ankles and tugged her towards the end of the bed, letting her legs dangle off the end. Lowering myself to my knees, I spread her legs and kissed my way up her inner thigh. She let out a whimper, her hands going to my hair. I smiled against her skin, knowing she couldn't see it.

My tongue delved between her wet folds, tasting her essence and seeking out her hard little nub. She moaned in response, her hips bucking into my face. In my experience, it was harder to come sometimes on E, but I had an ulterior motive for going down on her. Putting my hand out, I waited until one of them slapped a tube into it.

Scarlett's hands left my hair as she was shoved back onto the bed. My eyes flicked up, finding West had his hand around her throat and had pinned her to the sheets.

"Please," she whined, her hands grasping at his arms as if she wanted him closer. "Why won't you kiss me?"

He stared down at her with an intense expression, like he was considering it.

"You can kiss Pres or Frankie, Scar. I'm sure even Drake would consider it, but he's busy between your legs."

Preparing you for what's to come, little wisp.

I don't think she was happy with his answer. She looked like a petulant child and her nails dug into his tattooed forearms. He didn't seem to care about her inflicting injuries on him, but West loved pain with his pleasure. It was his thing.

"I can't," she whispered. "Pres only gives them as rewards. I haven't been good for him."

West leant closer, his expression softening a fraction.

"You want to kiss him right now?" he murmured.

She nodded, letting go of West's arms.

"I think he might be willing to make an exception."

Fuck, the hope in her eyes had me wanting to tell Prescott to get his act together and sort his shit out with her. Clearly, in her drug-fuelled haze, she'd forgotten about their arguments. About how he'd hurt her.

"Pres, come here," West said, looking towards where I was sure Prescott and Francis were, but I couldn't see them.

"Why?" came Prescott's response.

"Because I fucking said so."

I pulled back from Scarlett's pussy and flipped the cap on the lube. Her eyes went to me, her body bowing towards my face. She didn't want me to stop. I stroked her inner thigh, reassuring her I wasn't going anywhere. Then I coated my fingers and slid them between her cheeks, rubbing them around her tight little hole. She pressed herself against me like she wanted me to prep her even though she was distracted by West.

Prescott came into view as he sat on the other side of Scarlett. His expression was cautious as Francis joined West, sitting on the bed by Scarlett's head.

"Ask him, Scar," West said, waving at Prescott.

There was fear in her eyes but she turned to Prescott when West let go of her neck. Her hand moved slowly, reaching out and landing on Prescott's thigh. He stared down at it like he couldn't believe she wanted to touch him.

"Pres."

He leant towards her as if he couldn't help but want to be near her. The moment he got close enough, she wrapped her other hand around his neck and tugged him against her. His hands landed on either side of her as she captured his mouth in hers. I watched him kiss her back with no hesitation. You could see the tension leaving his body as his fingers speared into her hair.

While she was distracted by his kiss, I pressed a finger inside her before lowering my mouth to her clit again. Her moan, muffled by Prescott's mouth, fuelled me. I wanted to give her more, make her explode. As I worked her with my fingers, she thrust her hips almost like a demand to keep going.

"Please," she whimpered into Prescott's mouth. "Fuck me, please."

Prescott released her and sat back, looking like he was in a daze from having kissed the woman he was in love with.

"Is she ready for it?" West asked me.

I'd worked two fingers inside her tight entrance, but I didn't think it would be enough.

"Needs more prep," I told him as I pulled away from her pussy.

"Fine, she can sit on my dick whilst you do it."

I grinned and pulled my fingers from her. West didn't take long to take off his clothes and sit up against the headboard next to Francis, who'd stripped off already.

"Come here, Scar."

Scarlett flipped over onto her hands and knees before crawling over him. West didn't hesitate in grabbing hold of her hips and sliding his cock in her thoroughly wet little pussy. She moaned, gripping his shoulders like an anchor.

"This what you want, Scar? You want dick?"

"Yes, please, more, give me more."

He smirked as he shoved her down fully on his cock. I tossed the lube to Francis and nodded at her. He could have at her first considering that's what West had suggested downstairs. What she'd agreed to.

Francis picked up the lube, flipped the cap and got behind her. She looked at him over her shoulder while she rode West's dick. West leant forward and took her nipple in his mouth, making her whine in response. Francis put his hand around Scarlett's neck, tugging her back against him while his other hand delved between them.

"You want me to fuck you, huh?" he murmured. "You want to take us both?"

"Please."

"What a good little whore you are."

The way she all but preened for him was hot as hell. She let out a choked moan a moment later, indicating he'd penetrated her with his fingers. While I watched him prep Scarlett further for his dick, I stood up and undressed. Prescott did the same. None of us gave a shit about being naked in front of each other. I was secure in who I was, not to mention we'd known each other practically our whole lives. Everything we'd gone through had formed an unbreakable bond.

"Please, Frankie, please fuck me."

Hearing her say that after all these years had me pausing. Francis hadn't mentioned she'd called him Frankie. Considering he hadn't reacted, she must've done it before. He merely pulled his fingers from her and grabbed the lube.

West sat back and eyed her with a smirk.

"You going to ride us both, Scar?"

She leant closer to West, their bodies brushing together as if she was giving Francis better access. Her lips trailed along his jaw, something West didn't stop. He merely held her hips still while Francis put his hand on her back, the other grasping his dick.

"Yes," she murmured against West's skin. "I want to fuck all of you."

"Dirty girl."

Fuck me, little wisp, you are something else. Something I never expected, but I need you. All of you.

I wanted my hands full of her, fucking her like they were as Francis pressed inside her. She gripped West's shoulders, letting out a sharp cry of pleasure and pain. I couldn't help but be drawn closer to her and by the looks of it, Prescott felt the same way. The two of us moved either side of the threesome. I leant closer and nuzzled her neck with my lips. She tilted her head to allow me better access.

"Please, more," she whimpered.

Prescott dug his hand between West and Scarlett, cupping her breast and pinching her nipple. I did the same to her other breast, rolling her nipple between my forefinger and thumb.

SARAH BAILEY

She panted, her head falling back against Francis' shoulder as he pressed deeper inside her. I kissed her neck, running my tongue along her skin. Her hands left West's shoulders and instead landed on my dick. I was pretty sure she was touching Prescott's too judging by the way he grunted. West gripped her hips harder and encouraged her to fuck him and Francis, guiding her so she could stroke Prescott and me at the same time.

This was the closest the four of us had ever been to a woman together. Touching her. Fucking well worshipping her. When we shared, it was often two on one, perhaps three, but this? This was us and Scarlett, the way we were always meant to be.

"Harder, I want it harder, please."

Francis wrapped a hand around her shoulder to get better leverage. She cried and whimpered as he gave it to her, but the sounds were of pleasure, need and desire.

"That's it, my little whore," he murmured. "Fucking take it."

I pinched her nipple harder as Prescott moved his hand lower to seek out her clit. She closed her eyes, turning her face into Francis'. He caught her lips, tangling their tongues together in a messy kiss. When he released her, she turned to me, wanting my mouth. I let her kiss me, my hand curling around her jaw to bring her closer. She tasted so fucking good. It reminded me of the night she'd been covered in blood and it only made my cock throb harder between her fingers. Fuck did I want to do it again. Bathe her in it before fucking her until she screamed.

CHAOS

Scarlett cried out in my mouth, her body shaking as she came violently. I released her, allowing West and Francis to hold her between them. I sat back on my hands, watching them continue to pound into her, both driving towards their own releases. Scarlett let go of me and Prescott, her hands going to West's chest to keep herself steady.

It was then I understood Prescott's voyeurism. Watching the three of them together, the boys barrelling their way to their own climaxes as Scarlett panted between them was alluring in a whole different way. I'd watched before, but something about it being Scarlett had me needing more. Needing to see it. And when the two of them groaned, finding their mutual pleasure in our woman, I was enraptured by the scene in front of me.

They held Scarlett for a few minutes while the two of them came down, before Francis pulled out of her and slumped down on the bed. West lifted Scarlett off him and handed her over to me. She sat in my lap, panting with her eyes closed. Reaching up, I stroked her cheek before waving at Prescott to grab the water off the bedside table. He handed it to me and I pressed it to her lips. Scarlett opened her eyes before she drank from it, staring up at me with a grateful expression on her face. When she was done, I handed the glass back to Prescott.

"Are you going to fuck me now, sir?" she whispered.

I leant closer, my lips dusting across hers.

"Yes, Scarlett. Then you can fuck Pres, mmm?"

She nodded before she kissed me and I was utterly lost in her sweet mouth and the feel of her against me. I let myself drown in Scarlett because come tomorrow, she wouldn't be so pliant or giving. Of that, I was sure.

155

EIGHTEEN

PRESCOTT

Drake laid Scarlett down on the bed next to where West sat. He'd picked up his joint from the ashtray and lit it again, his amber eyes on our friend stroking his fingers down our woman's chest as she stared up at him with wide eyes.

When she'd taken a kiss from me, I swear I almost died, my heart was beating so fast. It was as if she'd forgotten all the pain and heartache between us. She still wanted me... needed me. Fuck did I love this woman. Everything about her. All I did was think about her. Fixate on her. Wanted to be in her presence. I wanted to damn well worship her.

The others accused me of being self-absorbed and to an extent, it was true. I didn't care about the effect my actions had on others. In fact, I liked to watch them in pain and suffering. I wanted to infect them so I could leave them in the dust. But with Scarlett? I wanted none of those things.

Well, I wanted to infect her so I could keep her. And I had up until the night of the killing. Then she'd seen who I really was. A man with no morals like the others. West was right. I'd shattered her illusion. I was worried I'd destroyed her feelings for me completely. Perhaps she couldn't accept me for the way I was. For the way all of us were. But I kept reminding myself Scarlett was one of us. She was meant to be by our sides. She was ours.

Wicked men need a woman to keep them grounded. They need a guiding light. Scarlett had been that for us when we were younger. I wanted her to be that for us again. I needed it.

"She's going to crash hard after this," West said, pointing his joint at Scarlett.

"We'll have to look after her," Francis said.

He'd leant up against the headboard on the other side of Drake and Scarlett with a beer he'd brought up. West eyed him with a pensive expression on his face before taking another drag of his weed.

"Perhaps."

Drake put Scarlett's hands above her head and held them down with one hand. His other ran up her leg, pressing it up to her chest.

"I can rig her up if you want," Francis said to Drake.

Drake raised his head, his eyes curious.

"How?"

"Nothing fancy." He nodded above them. "Tie her hands to the ring."

For a moment Drake said nothing then he gave Francis a sly smile.

"Go ahead."

Francis set his beer bottle down and tugged open a drawer, pulling out a length of rope from it. Drake got off Scarlett who looked puzzled until he encouraged her to stand. She rubbed herself against him as if she was craving human contact. Unsurprising given she was high on fucking E.

"Which one? The centre of the bed or the wall?" Francis asked, nodding to the different metal rings bolted to the ceiling and walls.

"The wall, better leverage."

Francis pried Scarlett away from Drake and made her put her wrists out for him. She let him loop the rope around them before he tugged her closer to the wall and made her put her arms up. He then tied the rope to the ring, making it impossible for her to go anywhere. It made my predatory instincts flare seeing my little lamb trapped and unable to escape.

Scarlett stared at Drake when Francis moved away. Drake approached her, his hands going to her waist as he encouraged her to turn around. There was enough slack in the rope to allow her to do so freely. He tugged her body against his, putting one hand above them and wrapping it around her bound wrists.

"Sir," she whined. "Their cum is running down my leg."

He nuzzled her hair, adjusting her, so she was at a better angle for him to fuck her standing up.

"I don't care." Drake bent at the knees and thrust up inside her, making Scarlett cry out and shift in her bonds. "I like knowing you've been used by them."

None of us has ever been bothered by that shit. It was part and parcel of sharing.

159

West stared up at Drake as he held onto Scarlett and fucked her. The man had a perfect view of Drake sliding in and out of Scarlett's wet little pussy. It was a view I'd normally love, but right now, I was too enraptured by watching the way her lips parted as she looked back at Drake. The way she panted and moaned. Seeing her come alive with her pleasure. She was far more important to me.

My hand went to my chest, rubbing the place where the aching organ inside lay. I wanted to be with her. To hold her close and show her how much I loved her. It's not like I could tell her now. Not when she was high. Besides, I had to make shit up to her first. Prove I was hers and hers alone. The fact she'd even thought I would be with anyone else had cut me. Scarlett had no idea the depth of my devotion to her. How every passing day she dug her claws further into my heart without even trying.

"More," she panted. "Please."

Drake said nothing. He wasn't one for talking much in general and didn't tend to be very vocal during sex. He pressed his lips to her neck and took her harder, their skin singing the tune of their passion.

"You want to come again, Scar?" West asked, blowing out the smoke from his lungs.

"Please."

West set the joint on the ashtray and shifted closer to them. Scarlett's hips weren't flush with the wall so he could stick his head between her and the wall. Her cry when his mouth met her clit while Drake continued to fuck her echoed around the room.

"Fuck," Francis muttered.

CHAOS

He'd sat down next to them again, his eyes fixed on their bodies. Unsurprisingly, he was hard again, his hand wrapped around his dick and stroking slowly. How could you not be turned on by the erotic sight in front of us? It was way better than beating off to porn.

"Oh fuck," Scarlett all but screamed. "Please, don't bite, oh, oh fuck!"

West didn't give a shit if he hurt her, he liked to bite. She writhed against Drake who didn't do a damn thing about West biting her clit. He merely buried his face in her neck and let out a harsh breath.

"Make her come," he ground out. "I want to feel her."

West wrapped a hand around her thigh and fucking went to town on her clit, leaving Scarlett to hang there, tortured by the two of them. Tortured with pleasure and pain. And fuck, when she came, they didn't stop. She bucked and screamed, but Drake and West didn't give a shit. They wanted to drag it out until she was begging, outright begging them to end it.

"Please, please, I can't. I can't take any more," she all but sobbed.

West finally released her, sitting back against the headboard again with a smirk. Drake had his hands full of her body as he continued to fuck her until he shuddered at her back, groaning in her ear with his climax.

When he released her, pulling out and taking a few steps back, she sagged in her ropes, her body clearly feeling the effects of the brutal poundings she'd taken.

"Let her down," I said to Francis.

He did as I asked, letting Scarlett curl up on the bed, her body trembling. Leaning over her, he pressed a kiss to her cheek.

"It's okay, shh," he whispered. "I've got you, Scar."

He stroked her back while Drake sat down on the edge of the bed and stared out over the room.

"I want Pres," she whispered to Francis. "Please."

I didn't hesitate, moving towards her so she didn't have to be without me. I lay behind her and pulled her against my chest, my hand going to her stomach. She turned her face towards mine, her hazel-green eyes full of happiness at the sight of me. Her tear-streaked face made my heart lurch. I pressed a kiss to her temple, which only made her smile.

"What do you want me to do, little lamb?" I murmured.

Usually, I would take what I wanted, but the need to keep the smile on her face drove me to ask her what she needed. She turned around in my arms and wrapped her leg around my waist, rubbing against me with her body. Her cheeks were flushed with her arousal.

"Like how you did in your room," she whispered.

I bit my lip, relatively sure of what she was asking for.

"Your wish is my command, sweetness." I looked over her shoulder at Francis. "Give me the lube."

He shifted, grabbing it and slapping it in my hand. Even though Scarlett was rubbing the other guys cum all over my dick, it wouldn't be enough. I slathered lube over my dick before notching it to her tightest entrance. Given Francis had fucked her here, there was little resistance as I pressed inside. Scarlett held onto me, her eyes fixed on mine as I took her. They betrayed her feelings. For the past week, she'd looked at

162

me with contempt and pain, but now… now she was showing me her desire. I held onto it knowing it wouldn't be the same come morning when she crashed down from her high. Who the fuck knew how she would feel about all of this?

Her fingers speared into my hair, tugging me closer while my body pressed deep into hers. There was nothing quite like her tight, hot little arse, her walls rippling around my cock with each thrust. Her lips brushed against mine, showing me she wanted kisses. I didn't delay, my lips moulding with hers and tasting her sweet mouth. The thought of making her work for it went out the window, all I wanted was to kiss her and fuck her until we were both wrung out.

I gave it to her with short, sharp thrusts, making her moan and pant in my mouth, but I didn't stop devouring her. Her tongue tangled with mine, her nails digging into my scalp. I liked the sharp pricks of pain, reminding me I was still alive. No part of me cared how this looked to the others. I was lost in Scarlett's body and her need… in making love to her.

"Harder," she breathed. "Fuck me harder."

My hand went to her hip, holding onto her so I could give her what she asked for. My hips were practically flush with hers with her leg pinned beneath me.

I love you, little lamb, I love you so fucking much.

The words were on the tip of my tongue, wanting out of my mouth, wanting to whisper in her ear and give my devotion to this woman. I loved the girl she'd been and the woman she was, but we needed to join the two together. Give Scarlett the truth of who she'd been.

"Don't stop, Pres, please, don't stop, give it to me."

Her nails dragged through my scalp, down my neck and across my back. I grunted at the sensation of her dragging them down my spine, raking across my skin and scratching me up.

"Mark me, little lamb," I whispered. "I'm yours."

It was the closest I could get to telling her the truth of my feelings. And to stop myself from saying any more, I released her mouth and bit down on her shoulder. She cried, her body tensing against mine. She needed claiming all over again, reminding who she belonged to. The need to see her skin painted with my marks drove through me.

"Mine," I told her before I bit her again. "Fucking mine."

And with that, she dug her nails into my back, shattering in my arms as I continued to pound into her tight little hole, loving the way she felt as she came. Everything about this was perfect. A moment in time where it was me and her, even though I knew we had an audience. The intensity of it had me letting go, groaning as I came inside her, emptying everything I had into the woman I loved. It was all hers anyway. All of me belonged to this small but incredibly strong and resilient woman in my arms.

The two of us held each other when we finally came down after Scarlett pressed her face into my chest. I didn't want to let her go, but she was clearly exhausted.

"I don't want to fight anymore," she whispered against my skin. "I just want you, Pres. I miss you so much."

I didn't know what to say. How could I respond when she wouldn't feel this way tomorrow? She'd be angry all over again when she was in her right mind. I pressed a kiss to the top of her head.

"I'm sorry, sweetness. I'm so sorry. You have me, I'm right here. I'm yours."

I spent a few more minutes holding her until I pulled away. Scarlett's eyes were drooping and her body was almost limp. We'd worn her out. I sat up and stroked her hair off her sweaty skin, looking around at the others.

"We should clean her up."

The last person I expected to move was West, but he swooped in and picked up Scarlett like she was a child. She curled up against his chest, apparently not fazed by the fact it was West who had a hold of her.

"Wait," Drake said as West moved to carry her from the room. "What are you doing with her?"

West gave Drake a wink from over his shoulder, not even bothering to stop on his way out.

"Don't worry, I've got her."

The three of us looked at each other with confusion.

"He better take care of her," Francis said as he got up, "or I'll deck him in the morning."

"As if he'd let you," I replied.

He gave me a look.

"She's probably going to give him hell," Drake said.

I shrugged as I got up and gathered up my clothes.

"Let her... he deserves it."

Before they could say another word, I walked out. I wasn't going to think about tomorrow. I was going to bed to savour the time I had with her and decide how I was going to tell the woman I loved her. It's all I cared about. All I could care about. There was nothing left for it. I would do whatever it took for her forgiveness, because my life without Scarlett was too depressing for words. And I wasn't prepared to live in misery any longer.

I'll prove myself to you, little lamb, until you learn to trust me again.

NINETEEN

SCARLETT

My brain hurt. Someone had taken a tiny hammer to it and was knocking on my skull. It wasn't the only pain I registered in my body as I regained consciousness. Everything ached. What the fuck had I done last night to cause this? Why was I feeling so… shit? Like I wanted to bawl my eyes out. Nothing made sense. I didn't want to move. I wanted to curl up in a ball and disappear.

My fingers twitched. The pads of them brushed over skin that wasn't my own. Cracking my eyes open, I found myself encircled in the embrace of two tattooed arms. My face was pressed into a solid, muscular chest and I was naked. Completely and utterly bare. My eyes followed the line of his chest up to his chin and found the slumbering form of the one person who terrified the shit out of me.

What the fuck am I doing with West?

I let out a squeak of shock, then pressed my hand over my mouth, trying to shove it back in. No way in hell I wanted to wake the psychopath up. Not when I had no idea what I was doing here. My brain went into overdrive, trying to remember what happened last night and why on earth I would have willingly got into bed with West of all people.

"I want to fuck all of you."

My words rang in my ears. The ones I'd said to him when they'd taken me to what I gathered was the room they fucked women together in. And holy crap, had I really had sex with all four of them again? I'd asked for it, rubbing myself all over West and demanding he give me his dick. What the hell had got into me?

Then I remembered they'd given me a pill after telling me I wasn't allowed to do drugs with them. I'd taken Ecstasy. I'd been fascinated with the Horsemen after it kicked in. Their touch had me craving more, made me horny and want to fuck them. All of them. I'd needed it so badly, I hadn't even cared about the way they'd used me. I'd begged for it.

This was hell. Absolute hell, because now all I could think about was the way West had carried me out of the room and taken me into his own. I remembered asking him to kiss me again and him refusing, telling me it wasn't something he did. Then he took me into his bathroom and washed me in the shower. It hadn't occurred to me it was weird for him to treat me with care. He'd kept my hair out of the spray so it didn't get wet as he cleaned me. Then he dried me, got me another glass of water and insisted I drank the whole thing before he put me to bed. I'd fallen asleep immediately, having been completely worn out from the night's activities.

West took care of me. What do I even do with that?

What did I do with any of what happened last night? I should never have taken the damn pill. All it had done was made me let all my inhibitions fall to the wayside and fuck the men I was mad at. Now I was pissed with all four of them because none of them had stopped it. They'd all participated like it was normal to have a girl begging for them after she'd taken drugs.

Well, fuck them.

I had to get out of this room and as far away from West as possible before he woke up.

Extracting myself from his embrace was accomplished with some difficulty. I moved slowly, wriggling out from his arms and slipping out of his bed.

When I stood, my eyes roamed around the room. One wall was a massive glass window, like the other two had in their bedrooms. West's bed was right in the middle of the room with black sheets and red pillowcases. He had a huge painting on one wall. My feet carried me closer to it without thinking about the fact I needed to escape. The colours matched his sheets. A rider carrying a huge sword on top of a horse set on a dark red background. It reminded me of Prescott's horsemen figurines in his room. Did West have a weird fascination with the mythology of the horsemen too?

I thought the painting was apt for West. It reminded me of violence. He was a rather violent and unforgiving person from what I knew of him.

"Prescott got me that… he thinks I'm War."

I almost jumped out of my skin. Turning on my heel, I found West on his side propped up on his elbow staring at me with a damn smirk on his face. The sheets were pooled at his waist, but I wouldn't be surprised if he tossed them off to let me see him in his naked glory.

I couldn't deny the fact West was hot as hell in the worst way possible. A deadly predator wrapped up in the most glorious bad boy package with those damn tattoos. But this man wasn't a bad boy. No, West was a villain through and through. Stupid me happened to like that about him. I hated the fact I got wet from him telling me he would burn down the world if I asked him to. Who got turned on by the idea of a man destroying shit for you? Me… apparently.

Why had I not run away the moment I got out of his bed? Here I was, staring at this painting of his in the nude rather than escaping the crazy man's bedroom. A part of me was fascinated with West's personal space. I wanted to explore it even though I knew I shouldn't. I hated the fact I was intrigued by him.

His eyes roamed over me, making me incredibly self-conscious and unsure of what to do.

"What are you doing out of bed, Scar?"

I crossed my arms over my chest, covering my breasts.

"Getting away from you."

He licked his lip.

"Are you now? That's not what you said last night."

God. Damn. This. Man.

My cheeks heated. All I could think about was how I'd begged, actually begged him. This was so wrong, but it felt so right. Being with him and the others had made me feel complete.

"I was literally on drugs. What makes you think anything I said wasn't tainted by that?"

He laughed. Fucking laughed. And I got distracted by him running his hand down his bare chest. Why was I thinking about trailing my tongue down those grooves, and lower?

Stop. It.

"So… you didn't mean it when you said 'Please fuck me, West. I want it. Please give me your dick'? Because from what I remember, you were pretty eager to sit on it."

I almost fucking died on the spot, especially since he'd decided to mimic me in this high pitched needy, desperate tone that did actually sound a lot like I had done last night.

"You… you… you… just shut up!"

I hated the way he grinned in a super boyish way, softening his features and making him ten times more attractive.

"Come on, Scar, you can't tell me you didn't enjoy yourself."

"As if I'm *ever* going to admit that to you."

Hell, did I want to be away from this man. I was feeling like absolute crap and here he was taunting me.

"You look upset." He patted the sheets next to him. "Come here and let me make it better."

"How the fuck would you make anything better? All you do is torture me for your own amusement."

He didn't even flinch when I said it, just kept rubbing the sheets with his hand as if to order me over to him. Screw him. I was done, but I also remembered I was naked and going out into the penthouse like this when I was feeling so unnerved didn't feel right.

Instead of going over to him, I stomped over to where I could see his wardrobe doors and ripped one of them open. I could feel him watching me. My eyes roamed over his clothes before I snatched out a black shirt and put it on, buttoning it up to cover myself. When I turned around again, West was smirking.

"Do you think I won't take that off you?"

"You'll have to catch me first."

I sprinted across his room, ignoring the way my muscles screamed. When I got to the door, I fumbled with it and let out a panicked squeak when I found it locked.

How the hell do I unlock this fucking door?

A hand slammed down on the wood above me. I froze, terrified of moving and looking up at him. My skin prickled when I felt his hot breath against the side of my neck. I'd made a grave error of judgement. And now I was in trouble. Big fucking trouble. I'd provoked the crazy man who'd locked me in his room with him. The big bad fucking wolf.

"Going somewhere, Scar?" he murmured.

I didn't answer him. Not sure I could. My body was in flight or fight mode. It couldn't decide which way to go.

My breath whooshed out of me when he nuzzled my neck. And I panted when he wrapped his other hand around my throat, pressing me against his body.

"You can run all you want, but you'll never be able to hide from me. I'll track you down and drag you back here. You know why that is?"

I shook my head.

"You belong to me. I don't like my possessions to go wandering off on their own. They could hurt themselves and we wouldn't want that, now would we?"

I shuddered, feeling all of his hard muscle at my back, caging me in and stealing the breath from my lungs. His fingers squeezed, reminding me to answer him.

"No," I whispered.

"Do you know what I'll do if you get hurt, Scar?"

"No."

He pressed his lips to my cheek.

"I would tear apart the person who has the audacity to lay a fucking hand on you limb from limb and give you their still-beating heart as a trophy. After that, I'd hold you down and fuck you until you're crying as punishment for leaving and getting yourself hurt. I wouldn't even stop to clean up the fucking blood, do you hear me? I'll fuck you in it until you're a panting, whimpering mess and then I'd give you to Drake because he gets off on that shit, and no doubt he'll fuck you so good, you won't know your own name. So don't go wandering off unless you want me to tear apart the fucking world to find you."

Jesus Christ.

What could a girl say to that? What could anyone say to it?

"Now, are you going to be a good girl for me?"

I nodded. There was no other answer I could give. West had never pretended he was anything else. The man was violent and possessive. I shouldn't be turned on by those things, but I was. If he put his hand between my legs, he'd find me wet and wanting despite the fact I'd been thoroughly fucked by the four of them last night. I'd let him pin me against the door and fuck me until I cried if he wanted to.

"Let's go get you something to eat then, hmm? You burnt through a lot of energy last night and I wouldn't want you passing out on me again."

He stroked his thumb down my neck before he released me. I stayed by the door, waiting for him while he put something on before he came back over to me. He put his hand on my shoulder, tugging me away so he could unlock it. I let him take my hand and pull me out of his room. The man had outright terrified the shit out of me and turned me on at the same time.

Maybe West had been right the first time he'd fucked me on his desk. Maybe fear turned me on. And maybe it's why I found this man so attractive when I really, really shouldn't.

Well, fuck.

TWENTY

FRANCIS

West holding Scarlett's hand as he pulled her down the stairs had my eyebrows rising. I glanced at Drake, who was flipping through his tablet next to me at the table. My eyes went back to Scarlett. Her expression was a mixture of apprehension and fear. What had West done this time? And why was she following him so willingly?

After last night, I was concerned about her feelings towards us. Did I regret what we'd done? No. Seeing Scarlett stripped of her inhibitions and everything holding her back was something else. The way she'd begged was damn fucking sweet. But it hadn't stopped my concern over what she would think come morning.

"Morning, dickheads," West said, giving me a wink.

I glared at the idiot. Why did he always have to be such a little shit?

He took Scarlett into the kitchen, picked her up, and set her on the island. Her legs dangled off it, her hands going to the edge.

"Stay," he told her, and she obeyed.

He moved to the kettle and flipped it on. Scarlett looked over at me and Drake. Her eyes narrowed. It confirmed she wasn't happy about recent events. But when the fuck had we ever made Scarlett happy since she'd come back into our lives?

"What do you think he did to make her compliant?" I murmured to Drake.

He looked up, eyes drifting over Scarlett and West before coming to land on me.

"What he does best. Be himself."

I snorted and shook my head, bringing my mug to my lips.

"You've seen the way she stands up to him."

"She always has, Francis. She's the only one who was ever able to control him. Why do you think I've fought so hard to get her back, huh?"

I sighed and sipped my tea. Drake might appear aloof and uncaring, but the man was hiding a fucking dragon inside him. We'd left no stone unturned in our search for Scarlett because of him. Drake never gave up, no matter how many times we ran into a dead end. Me, Prescott and West had told him it was futile on so many occasions, but he kept sending us after new leads until one finally paid off. Then we realised just how fucked we were. You didn't go up against men like Stuart Carver without having some serious clout at your back. Fortuity was not only our baby, but our way of becoming powerful enough to challenge the man who'd taken our woman all those years ago.

CHAOS

"You wanted her back too, so don't act like this is all because of West."

He gave me a sidelong glance and went back to his tablet.

"I'm not."

"Okay, Mr Aloof, you tell yourself that."

Drake clenched his fist on the table, the only outward sign of his irritation.

"I don't trust her."

"This has nothing to do with trust, Drake. You can admit you want her to remember you. The world isn't going to fall apart just because you have feelings."

The way he glared in my direction had me smiling. Then his fist unclenched and he shifted, his expression fading.

"I can't sleep knowing she's here."

"You been spending time in your hideaway then?"

He nodded, flexing his hand on the table.

"Too much time."

"Have you been taking the pills?"

He shook his head. I rolled my eyes. Drake didn't want to medicate his condition. I understood, but the man couldn't run off no sleep forever. He would crack eventually and take the sleeping pills, if only for his own survival.

"You don't have to spend your whole life worrying about the rest of us, you know. We're capable of taking care of ourselves."

"I know that," he muttered.

"Do you? The world isn't on your shoulders, Drake, stop acting like it is."

I got another glare for my comment. It wasn't often I pushed Drake's buttons, but he did like to get in his own way

177

far too much. Overthinking shit all the time and being wrapped up in his own thoughts rather than actually living. Too fucking stubborn for his own good, which didn't help matters either.

"I miss having her there to talk to," he said with a long, drawn-out sigh. "She was always so... understanding."

I nudged his shoulder.

"Then stop being a heartless bastard towards her."

"I'm not."

"You can't expect her to think you actually like her if the only time you're nice to her is during sex. That's not how it works."

My smile as his face dropped and his eyes narrowed only made it worse. Drake looked like he was ready to throw me out the window.

"As if I'm going to take relationship advice from you."

"She sleeps in my bed, so I must've done something right."

I knew I was winding him up, but I was too amused by his attempt at keeping his temper in check to stop.

"Yeah, let's see if she still does after last night. She keeps giving us daggers."

"You did trick her into taking E, Drake."

He gave me a sly smile.

"I wanted to give her a night of freedom. Seeing her smile the way she did... totally worth it."

"Aw, you're getting all sentimental."

His smile dropped.

"Fuck off."

The drugs were Drake's idea, but the rest of us had gone along with it.

"I should go smooth things over with her."

CHAOS

He gave me a look but didn't reply as I got up and wandered into the kitchen with my mug between my fingers. Scarlett watched me when I approached her and leant up against the counter. Her mouth thinned, and her hazel-green eyes narrowed.

West was moving about the kitchen, making her some breakfast. I noted it was French toast with an excessive amount of cinnamon. He remembered Scarlett's tastes as well as I did.

"You mad at me?" I asked her in a quiet voice that didn't carry across the room.

"Let's see... you didn't stop what happened last night, and actively participated in the whole thing, so what do you think?"

I reached out and stroked her arm, amused she couldn't bring herself to admit she'd had a fivesome with us out loud.

"I'm sorry."

"No, you aren't."

I bit my lip and shifted closer, setting my mug down on the countertop.

"Can I make it up to you?"

"How?"

Turning to her, I moved my hand from her arm to her face, capturing her chin between my fingers. The freckles dusting across her nose shifted as she frowned but she didn't stop me.

"I'll teach you how to tie some of my knots and maybe next time... you can tie Drake up."

West snorted and looked over at us with amusement painting his features.

"As if he would ever willingly submit to that," Scarlett muttered, glancing at West.

"No one said anything about him being willing."

179

Her lips parted as if she couldn't believe what I'd just said.

"You'd help me?"

I shrugged.

"Perhaps."

She leant closer until our breath mingled.

"I had no idea you were so…"

"I think the word you're looking for is imaginative," West put in. "Our Frankie is the mastermind behind our more deviant plans, even if he likes to pretend he isn't."

It was almost a compliment coming from West.

Scarlett didn't look at him, her eyes remaining fixed on me.

"Is that true?"

I rubbed her bottom lip with my thumb.

"It is."

There was no hiding it from her now West had sold me out.

"Teach me and I might forgive you."

"I'll take it."

Scarlett didn't hesitate in kissing me back when I pressed my lips to hers. Such a pliant mouth she had. She'd grown far more confident since the first time I'd kissed her, and it was beautiful to see.

"Leave her fucking mouth alone, Frankie, she needs to eat."

Pulling away, I shot West a dark look. Scarlett's smile made dealing with his shit worthwhile. She reached up and stroked my jaw.

"Don't mind him… if he wants to kiss me, he could just say it instead of making snide comments."

West walked over to us and set a plate down for her on the counter. Then he leant over her, his mouth meeting her ear from behind.

"What happened to being a good girl for me today, Scar?"

His voice was deadly and full of promised violence.

"Maybe I like making you jealous," she replied, without taking her eyes off me.

"I'm not going to kiss you, so this little game you're playing here will only end up with you crying and choking on my dick, you hear me?"

Her hand left my jaw and fell on my shoulder. I didn't even bat an eyelid at him threatening her with that. It was West all over.

"Maybe I want that," she whispered. "Maybe I like it when you threaten me."

For a moment, I'm not sure West knew how to react. Then he chuckled and reached up, stroking her hair back from her face before his fingers traced a line down her throat.

"I don't threaten, I only make promises. You carry on, you know what will happen and on your own fucking head be it. Now, turn around and eat your breakfast."

He pulled away and walked back over to the stove. Instead of doing what he told her, Scarlett leant forward and kissed me again. When she pulled away, she smirked before turning and digging into the French toast West had made for her. The woman was playing with fire and she knew it.

"Fire burns, Scar," I said after she stuffed some toast in her mouth. "Remember that."

"You saying you're not going to save me from him?"

I raised an eyebrow.

"You wouldn't want me to."

"I suppose you're right."

Leaning closer, I propped my chin up on her shoulder and curled my hand around her thigh, stroking my fingers across her bare skin. She was only wearing a black shirt, which I'm pretty sure belonged to West. Her clothes were in my room. Having spent all week sleeping next to her, I couldn't help but need to touch her after she'd spent the night with West.

"I missed you last night," I whispered in her ear. "Did you have any nightmares?"

I didn't care about admitting my feelings to her. Not even Drake's warnings about us not being able to trust her stopped me. If I wanted to build a relationship with Scarlett, there had to be some semblance of honesty between us, despite all the secrets and lies. Perhaps then she wouldn't hate me so much when she discovered the truth about her past. When she remembered. I was damn sure she wouldn't be happy with any of us for lying to her about knowing who she was. And she'd be even more annoyed when she realised what we'd done had triggered the catalyst of events leading up to her accident and the destruction of her old life.

"Not that I remember." She stroked her fingers along my hand on her thigh. "Thank you for asking, though. No one really cared about my nightmares nor how they affect me."

I frowned. It struck me as odd no one would care about her well-being.

"No?"

She shook her head. The haunted look in her eyes concerned me.

"Not like they could do anything, you know. So I kept it to myself."

Somehow I didn't think it was the real reason, but I didn't press her on it. Not sure it would have won me any points with Scarlett. There was always an air of despair surrounding her whenever she talked about anything to do with the past ten years, especially in relation to the Carvers.

Scarlett said nothing more, merely finished her French toast and the tea West had made for her. Then she shoved the plate away and stared at his back with a curious expression on her face.

I heard footsteps, so I turned to see who was coming into the kitchen. Prescott had a rather determined look on his face. He'd been down earlier to eat but hadn't been particularly talkative and had disappeared soon afterwards.

He approached Scarlett, grabbed her by the waist, and slung her over his shoulder. She let out a squeak of surprise. West turned around and raised his eyebrow as Prescott carried her off towards the stairs. Scarlett looked up at us from her position, her face a picture of shock and irritation.

"What the fuck, Pres? What are you doing?" she screeched, trying to escape him.

He didn't say a word, ignoring her fists pounding on his back the next moment.

"Let me go!"

The man walked up the stairs with Scarlett, her complaining the entire way, and out of sight. We could still hear her decrying him until a door slammed shut.

"Well, someone woke up and found his balls this morning," West said, coming over to pick up Scarlett's

183

discarded breakfast things. "You reckon he's going to punish her little pert arse for giving him such a hard time over what we did?"

"He's going to tell her he loves her," Drake said.

Both mine and West's heads whipped around to our stoic friend.

"What?"

Drake waved a hand towards the stairs.

"Pres is in love with her. He told me and now he's going to tell her."

"Well, fuck me," West said with a grin. "Pres fell in love. What a fucking miracle, he actually cares about someone other than himself."

Drake scoffed.

"You're a fine one to talk. You think we don't know how you feel about her?"

West's smile disappeared in an instant.

"Fuck off, Drake."

Drake shrugged and went back to his tablet as if it was a normal, everyday occurrence for Prescott to declare his love for a woman. But honestly... I wasn't surprised by it at all. Scarlett was the girl we'd grown up with. The one none of us could ever forget. We'd gone to extreme lengths to return her to us. The only thing that did surprise me was Prescott being the first one to fall. West was the one who had loved Scarlett all our lives. Then again, West was just about as capable of telling a girl he loved her as he was at keeping his violent urges in check. Guess we'd have to wait and see how long it took him to crack.

Could love even enter the equation between the five of us?

Us sleeping with her was one thing, but love and a relationship were something else entirely.

And me?

Well, I didn't know how I felt. I'd not considered it. And maybe I needed to. The future was up in the air, but the bond between the five of us had always been permanent even if our missing piece had forgotten who we were.

TWENTY ONE

PRESCOTT

When I woke up this morning, I decided enough was enough. Scarlett was going to hear me out. I couldn't go another night with this discord between us hanging over our heads. Not when she'd kissed me so willingly last night. When she'd asked for me and told me she missed me. Who gave a fuck if she was high. The woman had said she didn't want to fight any longer. We weren't going to fight. We were going to have a conversation. And I was going to tell Scarlett the truth.

I loved her tenacious little soul. She was my little lamb. And she was going to accept she belonged to me.

I'd tried things her way. Waited for her to give me a fucking chance and it had got me nowhere. This time things were going to be on my terms.

It's why when I'd gone downstairs, I picked her up and took her to my room. She complained, struggled and hit me the whole way, demanding I put her down, told me I was behaving like a caveman and I had no fucking manners, but I hadn't paid her any mind.

I slammed my bedroom door shut and locked it before I set her down. My woman had rage burning in her hazel-green depths when she looked up at me. Her fists were clenched at her sides as if she couldn't decide whether she wanted to pound my chest or tell me to go fuck myself.

"What the hell do you think you're doing?" she demanded. "I am not a fucking ragdoll for you to toss around whenever you please."

I kept my expression neutral as I looked down at her. Fuck, she was so small compared to me, but Scarlett was the strongest woman I knew. The boldest and most fearless. And the one who owned my heart.

"No, you're not."

"Then what the—"

I put my hand over her mouth and wrapped my other arm around her back, tugging her against me. She blinked, then tried to wriggle out of my grasp, but I only held on tighter. Her hands went to my chest, shoving at it.

"You can hit me all you want, sweetness, I'm not letting you go."

The way she glared had me fighting a smile. I dropped my hand from her mouth to hold her closer.

"Why the hell are you being like this?"

"Because you haven't given me a chance to talk to you."

"I gave you one yesterday."

I shook my head.

"No, you accused me of fucking another woman, and we argued. That was not a conversation."

CHAOS

Her mouth snapped shut. She knew I was right.

"I want you to hear me out, okay?"

"What if I don't want to?" she shot back.

By fuck did I want to tell her to stop being so stubborn, but I wouldn't. She was hurt and lashing out at me because of it. I couldn't afford to piss her off any further.

"You don't have a choice right now, sweetness. And before you give me shit, I have a good fucking reason."

"Oh yeah? And what's that?"

My arms dropped from around her and my hands went to her face instead. I needed her to look at me. To really fucking see me and hear me. Her skin was so damn soft against the pads of my fingertips, reminding me of how I loved having her body against mine. How she was perfect in my eyes.

"You're mine, little lamb. You're mine and I'm yours. And you... you fucking well have something of mine. I don't want it back because I expect you to keep it safe. I know you'll keep it safe. I trust you with it."

Her bottom lip trembled, and her expression grew softer.

"You trust me?" she whispered.

I didn't directly answer her question with my next words, but I was determined to get all of my damn thoughts out.

"I'm sorry I didn't show you every part of me, so you weren't prepared that night. I'm sorry I wasn't truthful with you about the real me. I'm not a good man, sweetness. There are things I've done, we've all done, that would make you question who you're with. I've hurt, I've maimed, I've tortured and I've killed... and I liked it. I won't pretend to be anything else other than the man you see standing before you. I like to

189

cause other people harm. It fucking feeds my soul when I infect them and ruin their lives just because I can."

Her eyes fixed on mine. I couldn't read her thoughts, but I couldn't stop. It all had to come out, so she'd believe me when I told her how I felt. So she'd see the damn fucking truth.

"All those things are a part of who I am. The parts you've not seen. And I should have trusted you with them. I fucked up, sweetness. I know that. I'm sorry for it. You deserved more than the crumbs I gave you of myself."

Her hands slid up my chest to my neck, wrapping around it as if she needed an anchor.

"The thing is… the fucking thing is… I have never felt this way about anyone before. I've never looked at anyone the way I do you. You're precious to me, so fucking precious. I never want to harm you. You mean everything to me."

I swallowed, and my hands tightened around her face. It was now or never. Even if I couldn't tell her how I'd known her my whole life. How I loved the parts of her she'd lost. The parts of her she'd gained. And everything in between. I had to tell her this one thing because it was killing me inside being without her.

"I didn't think I still owned a heart, but you showed me I do… because my heart belongs to you."

Tears welled in her eyes. She knew exactly what I was going to say. It didn't matter. I had to say it anyway.

"I love you." I stroked my thumb over her cheek. "Please stop fighting me… please let me love you, my precious little lamb."

Those threatening tears spilt down her cheeks. I waited, allowing my words to sink in. Letting her process them. No matter how much it killed me to watch her in silence, I had to let her work through her emotions. I would fight for the right to be by her side. I would do anything for Scarlett. I loved her.

"Pres," she sobbed, letting go of my neck so she could slap my chest with her palm. "Damn you… why do you have to be so fucking perfect?"

Before I could utter a word, she went up on her tiptoes and kissed me. I wrapped her up in my arms and kissed her back. It was desperate and all-consuming. All our feelings poured out. The hurt and pain. The want and need. The lust… and what I hoped was love.

I lifted her up, grasping her thighs as she wrapped her legs around my waist. I carried her over to the window and pressed her against it, keeping her pinned. Scarlett's hands were in my hair, holding me closer. Our tongues were a tangled mess of passion and desire.

"I love you," I whispered between kisses. "I fucking love you."

Scarlett pulled away. Her tear-filled eyes were wild as she stared at me, holding onto my head so I couldn't kiss her again.

"Show me."

I propped Scarlett up against the window with my body and legs. My hands shoved the shirt she was wearing up to find she was bare underneath. I almost groaned at the sight of her. Then my fingers were at the buttons, tugging them open and exposing her stunning body to me. I ran the tips of my fingers down her chest, listening to her gasp at the physical contact.

"Please, Pres, I want you."

Her hands went to my t-shirt. I helped her tear it off my chest and dropped it on the floor. Then she was unbuttoning my jeans, tugging them down enough to allow my cock to spring free. Scarlett guided me to her wet entrance, staring at me the whole time as I thrust inside her. I couldn't help the groan escaping my lips.

"Fuck me like you mean it," she sobbed, grasping my head again and pulling me closer. "Show me you love me."

Her tears were decimating me, but I did as she asked. I held her tight and fucked her like I meant it. My cock slid in and out of her wet little pussy with rapid, sharp thrusts. I drove into my woman again and again so she'd know I meant it. Meant every single fucking word. And my tongue went to her cheeks, licking away her tears.

"Pres, more, please. Don't stop. Never stop. Fuck!"

Her head banged against the glass as she tipped it back, but Scarlett didn't care. She was lost in us. Lost in the pleasure and the pain. Her thighs gripped me harder, trapping me between her legs. I wasn't going anywhere. This woman was the best part of me. The only part that even mattered.

"I belong to you, little lamb," I ground out in her ear, listening to her panting and loving the way she clawed at me. "Do you believe me? Do you believe I love you now?"

Her nails dug into my shoulder, her body moving back against mine.

"Yes," she cried out. "Yes, fuck, please."

"Say it. Tell me you believe me."

"I believe you, Pres. I know you love me. Just don't stop. Don't stop."

I never wanted to leave her pliant, soft little body. Never wanted to let her go. The way she took me and begged was fucking magical. But there were things I wanted from her too. Things I needed to fucking know.

"Who do you belong to?"

"You," she whimpered. "I'm yours. I never stopped being yours."

She didn't even hesitate. Fuck did I love that about her. Everything about her was perfect to me. She might be broken in half, her memory fractured, but I only saw all of her. And I would protect her with my fucking life if I had to.

"More, please, I'm so close."

I gave it to her harder, adjusting the angle of our bodies to stimulate her better. It only made her cry out louder and dig her nails into me to the point they almost drew blood.

"Yes, like that. Just. Like. That."

I didn't stop. Didn't falter. I drove her into oblivion because I wanted to see her fall to pieces. To shatter under my hands and come all over my cock. The sensation of sliding in and out of her wet pussy was driving me crazy, but I held back. Held on to make sure she got there too.

"Fuck, Pres!"

She came apart, her whole body shaking and trembling with her climax and triggering my own. I grunted, spilling inside her hot body and never wanting it to end. I couldn't let go of her. She'd branded herself on my heart. She owned me. And I didn't even care. I wanted her to have me.

Her fingers left my shoulders, wrapping around my body as she held me against her. Scarlett pressed her face into my neck, breathing heavily against me.

"Pres…"

"Yes, little lamb?"

Her hold on me tightened.

"Even though I can't remember who I was and I feel like I'm not whole inside, it doesn't change the fact I love you too because my heart knows you and that's what matters."

All the tension left my body.

"Your heart knows me?"

She nodded.

"I don't know how, but it does." She pulled back and stared into my eyes. "I love you, Prescott… so you better take care of my heart, okay?"

I pressed my forehead against hers. I shouldn't promise her this because of everything to come, but I couldn't help it. She needed me to reassure her. And she loved me. This woman loved me. I didn't deserve Scarlett, but I'd do everything in my power to love her the way she deserved.

"I will, sweetness. I'll protect it with my life."

She kissed me again. I was lost in her. In this woman I'd known my entire life. And I hoped when Scarlett remembered me, the part of her she'd lost would love me as much as this version of her did. I couldn't live in a world without her again. I refused to.

Don't leave me in the dark again, little lamb. Don't leave any of us. We need you.

The girl we'd sacrifice the world for was in my arms. I would never set her free because she was a part of all of us. And we weren't complete without her.

TWENTY TWO

SCARLETT

Prescott loved me. He loved me. One of the crazy, fucked up psychotic men I'd been sent to destroy loved me. And I loved him back. I loved Prescott Ellis. My heart recognised him and wanted him. I'd finally listened to the stupid organ and admitted the feelings living inside it. How could I not when he'd trusted me with his truths?

All weekend I'd gone back and forth with myself over it. Over the conflicting feelings about the situation I was in. I'd already established I couldn't hurt Prescott, but it was worse now. So much fucking worse. He'd given me his heart for safe keeping. The thought of ruining him or the others made me feel sick. Bile kept rising in the back of my throat. And I hated everything about it.

What the fuck was I going to do?

It's not as if I could tell my father I wasn't going to do his bidding any longer. I dreaded to think what he would do.

Likely have Mason drag me back to the estate and then… the less I thought about that, the better. I didn't want to imagine the beatings and being locked up in the cold room with nothing but the clothes on my back for days on end. There was just me and the concrete floor. The only human contact I'd had was when one of the staff changed the fucking bucket I'd been left with to do my business in and when they fed me. The isolation made my nightmares worse. I would scream for hours at night, but no one could hear me.

I did not want to go back to that life under any circumstances.

It left me in the worst sort of predicament. While I knew the boys would protect me if anyone tried to take me, I didn't exactly have a choice in the matter when it came to my father's demands. What the hell could I even do? Feed him false information? What would it achieve if he found out I was lying to him? Nothing.

I didn't want to hurt the boys either. I had to admit that to myself. I'd fallen in love with one of them, begun to have feelings for another - and the other two? Well, it was up in the air. I wasn't sure Prescott would forgive me if I did something to endanger his friends. I wouldn't forgive myself either.

The only time I wasn't thinking about this shit was during sex. And after his declaration, Prescott had pretty much kept me in bed all of Saturday other than to feed me. Something about being in a blissed-out post-coital haze prevented negativity from encroaching on me. Only when he'd fallen asleep next to me, looking peaceful as ever with his dark blonde hair mussed from my fingers and his chest rising and falling steadily did the guilt eat me up inside. And kept me from being able to stay level-headed.

Sunday came and went with no drama between the five of us. In fact, the others had kept to themselves, leaving me and Prescott to be in a little bubble of our own. I hadn't expected them to be so… considerate.

Monday rolled around and I was tired, but Drake wasn't being too demanding at work. In fact, he gave me a bunch of tasks and left me to my own devices. Didn't mean I was let off from making him coffee.

I carried a fresh cup into his office, noting he was on the phone. Making sure to be as quiet as possible, I placed the mug down on the coaster and was about to leave when he put his hand up. I paused as he waved me closer. Given I never knew what I was going to get with Drake, I was cautious as I came around the desk towards him.

When he grabbed my arm and tugged me in his lap, I tried not to yelp. His arm banded around my chest, holding me in place so I couldn't escape.

"No, that's not going to happen … I don't know what you want me to say … you've already told me that before … no, I'm not going to budge on it."

I shifted in his lap, trying to get a little more comfortable. There was no point in trying to run. I would only get punished for it. Drake did not like me talking back to him or being disobedient. Though after my conversation with Francis about Drake the night of the killing, I had a feeling Drake took great pleasure in punishing me when I stepped out of line.

"What does that matter? We don't need their business … well, it's not my problem."

I almost squeaked when he pressed his face into my neck and breathed me in. What was he doing? This wasn't like Drake at all, from what I knew of him. He wasn't particularly affectionate or demonstrative of his feelings. I mean, I knew he wanted to fuck me. He'd made it pretty clear, but everything else? Not so much.

"Quit moving, Scarlett," he whispered to me while the person on the other end of the phone kept talking.

Why did it make me want to do the exact opposite of what he told me? I don't know why I enjoyed pushing Drake's buttons so much. Was I asking for a punishment like last time when he spanked me with his belt? I shuddered at the thought of it, shifting against him despite him telling me not to. His harsh breath told me he was not happy with me.

My reckless streak decided to rear its ugly head. Without warning, I turned around in his lap so I was straddling him. Luckily I'd worn trousers today or I might have ripped my skirt with the movement. Drake's indigo eyes came into view and there was no mistaking the darkness in them. I gave him a smile as my fingers went to his tie, straightening it for him. His hand came up and gripped mine, stopping me from doing anything further. For a long moment, the two of us stared at each other. He was willing me to back down and I was refusing.

He released my hand and placed his over the bottom of his phone.

"Enough."

The low and deadly tone of his voice made me shiver. But I wasn't interested in obeying him today. Not when he'd manhandled me into his lap for no apparent reason.

He took his hand off the phone.

"This isn't up for debate, Clive, either you sign papers or we have nothing left to discuss."

I slipped off his lap and leant against his desk instead. Then I ran my fingers down the centre of my chest and bit down on my lip. Drake's eyes followed the path of my fingers.

"No, I have already spoken to Francis and he agrees with me … well, you're the one who doesn't want to understand our position. As I said, it's not my problem."

My fingers went to the top button of my blouse. I undid it, exposing the tops of my breasts to him, and the lacy bra I was wearing underneath. I deliberately dropped my eyes to his lap and licked my bottom lip. When I raised them again, Drake's expression was fierce and stern.

He placed his free hand on the arm of his chair and pushed himself up to his full height. I swallowed, knowing I was about to be on the receiving end of his fury. He took my hand, spun me around and shoved me up against his desk, forcing me onto my stomach. The man held my arm against my back, keeping me pinned there while he continued his conversation.

"My final answer is no, either deal with it or don't … I'm not missing out on anything, thank you very much … fine with me, no skin off my nose … goodbye, Clive."

He tossed his phone down on the desk and leant over me. I could feel his hot breath on the back of my neck, as I'd put my hair up in a bun today. Prescott told me yesterday if I wanted to provoke West, all I had to do was put my neck on show. And maybe when I'd come out of his bathroom this morning, he'd smirked, but didn't comment on it. He knew what I was doing. It would serve West fucking well right if he got riled up by it. The man kept threatening me with things and not delivering.

Drake, on the other hand, I knew he delivered, so I had no clue why I'd decided to play with fire.

"I see someone woke up and decided to be a brat this morning," he said, his voice like a caress across my skin. "Tell me, Scarlett, do you enjoy this? I have a feeling you don't want to be able to sit down for the next couple of days."

"You think I enjoyed it when you… spanked me?"

"Yes."

I spluttered, unable to form a damn sentence. I did not want him to do it again… did I?

"We've already established you do this on purpose. You want me to punish you. If you didn't like it, you would have stopped pushing after I did it the first time. So, why don't we both save ourselves this conversation, hmm?"

"I wouldn't have to push your buttons if you just fucking talked to me like a normal human."

He kept one hand pinning my arm to my back while the other dusted over the curve of my arse as if he was testing the waters.

"That's what you want from me?"

"I…"

Was it? I didn't know any longer. Everything about these four men was so fucking confusing. Well, I wasn't confused about my feelings towards Prescott, but I didn't understand why I was so drawn to the other three. Why did I want to knock down Drake's damn iron fortress and make myself a home inside the ruins?

"Maybe," I whispered.

His hand landed more firmly on my behind, almost caressing it with his fingertips as they stroked along my clothes. And for some reason, I arched into his touch like I wanted more.

"I see."

Drake took my wrist from my back and pressed my palm on his glass desk, pinning it there. My other hand was already resting on the glass on the other side. His lips traced a line across the back of my neck, making me tremble.

"You're so soft and pliable," he murmured, his deep resonating voice making me melt on his desk. "No matter how many times you defy me, I will always conquer you in the end."

My breath came out in bursts with my need for him to do something other than stroke my behind. The anticipation made me press back against him. Was I asking to be punished?

"Drake, I wanted to talk to you about… oh, oh my… I'm sorry, I didn't know…"

My head whipped up, almost knocking into Drake's as his body remained over mine. Standing in the doorway was Tonya. Her eyes were wide with shock and her mouth was opening and closing like a fish.

"Leave and close the door," came Drake's firm voice, vibrating across my back.

For a moment, she continued staring at the two of us. It must have looked quite the sight, me bent over Drake's desk with his hand pressing mine down and the other cupping my behind. Her eyes betrayed her disapproval and judgement at finding me in such a compromising position with my boss. Only Drake was kind of more than just my boss. I didn't know how to define my relationship with the Horsemen, but we'd crossed the line between employer and employee the moment West fucked me over his desk. The fuse to a catalyst of events leading up to me becoming theirs to do what they wanted with. And me giving in.

"Can I see you after this?" she asked.

"Now, Tonya."

She put her hands up and backed out, but not before glaring at me. I didn't react. It wasn't worth it. I could tell West about it and he would probably gut her like he'd threatened. Maybe it wasn't the best idea. I didn't want him killing her for me.

The door shut, leaving the two of us alone again. Drake nibbled the top of my ear, making me shudder against him.

"I'm not going to go easy on you, Scarlett."

He straightened, letting go of my hand. Both of his went to the button of my trousers, before he tugged both them and my knickers down, exposing my bare behind to his gaze. I almost flinched when he stroked his hands over my cheeks. And I cried out when he slapped me, the sting radiating up my spine. They came again and again, across each of my cheeks until I was shifting on the desk, trying desperately not to cry.

It occurred to me Drake's punishments didn't remind me of the horrific things my father had done when I stepped out of line. When I'd come here, I'd been meek and obedient because of it, but the girl behind the glass wasn't either of those things. She was fire and brimstone. The more time I spent around the Horsemen, the more I became like her. I could feel it. The change echoing around me and giving me back the person I was. The cracks forming across the glass were small and perhaps I'd finally be able to smash through. I'd see the past and it would explain everything... or at least, I hoped it would.

A particularly hard smack across a sore spot jolted me out of my thoughts and returned me to the room. Who the fuck knew how many times he'd slapped me. All I could feel was the burn across both my cheeks. I knew sitting down would be unpleasant for the rest of the day. And the worst part? I was ridiculously aroused by the entire ordeal.

You do like to push his buttons and get punished for it. It's a game and you like playing it.

I wouldn't admit it to him, but I could tell myself the truth.

The final smack he gave me was harder than the rest. The sound of it rang in my ears. His fingers caressed the sore skin, making me whimper in response.

"I don't make idle threats. Every time you push, you will receive a punishment. And trust me, it will not be this every time. I can be quite creative when I want to be."

I didn't doubt that in the slightest.

"Now, go make me a fresh cup of coffee and get back to work. And if I hear you've been in one of the others' offices for any reason that's not work-related, there'll be consequences. Work hours are not playtime."

I hadn't planned on going to one of the others, but him telling me I couldn't made me want to see Prescott all the more. However, the thought of Drake punishing me further today had me resisting the urge to seek out the man I loved.

I lifted myself off Drake's desk and pulled my clothes back on, hating the way they rubbed over my sore and no doubt red behind. Turning around, I looked up at him. He had his hands shoved in his pockets and his expression was neutral like the whole thing hadn't affected him in the slightest.

I don't know why I stepped up into his personal space and pressed my hands against his chest. He didn't move, but he didn't tell me off about it either. Going up on my tiptoes, I pressed a kiss to his cheek before dropping back to my feet and walking away. I didn't look back to see his reaction as I knew there wouldn't be one. Not a visible one, anyway. Maybe I wanted to leave him wondering why I'd done it. I was pretty sure the last thing Drake expected after he'd left me with a red arse was affection from me in response.

You can wonder all you like, Drake Ackley. If you're going to be so insistent on this punishment shit, then I'm sure as hell going to play you at your own fucking game in return.

TWENTY THREE

FRANCIS

T he concentration on her face as I tied the knots around her wrists made me smile. Scarlett had a little furrow between her brows, her eyes intent on my fingers as I explained what I was doing. She was laid out on her stomach in her pyjamas on my bed, resting on her elbows so I could show her how to tie some very simple knots. My legs were on either side of her.

"Over like this," I said, watching her face rather than what I was doing. "Then under here."

I could probably do these in my sleep, but I had to start somewhere with her. She'd demanded I show her this evening after admitting she'd been punished by Drake earlier for pushing his buttons. I'd expected her to want to spend time with Prescott, but she'd sought me out.

"Can I ask you something?"

I undid the knots around her wrists to show her again.

"If you'd like."

"It's about Drake."

The rope dropped on the bed. Scarlett looked up at me with a rather sheepish expression on her face.

"What about Drake?"

I couldn't keep the suspicion out of my voice. While she'd come in here to make me fulfil my promise to show her how to tie knots that would be hard to break out of, I didn't like her using me as a source of information about the others. Especially not Drake. If she wanted to know things about him, she could ask the guy herself. Didn't matter if he was a locked box. It was his choice what he told her and what he kept to himself.

"I'm not asking you to tell me his secrets."

"Hmm."

"Put your wrists out, I want to try."

I did as she asked, watching her pick up the rope and wrap the length around one of my wrists.

"It's just when West… threatened Tonya last week, he called her Drake's step-cousin. And I was wondering about it."

Drake's family was a sore subject for him. His parents had been through a rather messy divorce when we'd been sixteen, around the time of Scarlett's accident. His father had an affair with his now-stepmother. The only people he was in contact with now were his mother and his step-uncle, Fletcher Sinclair. He'd given us the original funds to start Fortuity. And the only reason he kept Tonya around was because of his uncle, even though we'd already paid him back every penny. I'd done that for us. Drake didn't want it hanging over our heads or for his uncle to have any say in our company. He had no idea why we'd wanted to start it in the first place. Why the girl with me was the reason for everything we'd done in our lives.

"You should ask him about it."

"Asking Drake anything is like pulling teeth."

I snorted. He wasn't the most forthcoming out of the four of us, but he had his reasons. Many of them had to do with the girl currently struggling to tie the knot I'd shown her.

"Not like that, remember, over then under."

Scarlett readjusted the rope and did as I said.

"All I can tell you is Tonya is his step-cousin."

"Do you like her?"

I frowned. After learning what she said to Scarlett, I wasn't particularly impressed. Then again, Tonya had always been a problem. I'd met her long before Prescott and West. Couldn't say I'd ever liked her, but I had nothing against the woman... until now.

"No. She shouldn't have said that shit to you."

Scarlett looked up at me having tied the knot I'd shown her. The knots around my wrists were loose, but they weren't too bad overall. If she tightened them up, she might actually be able to trap Drake with them.

"She seems like a rather jealous and vindictive person."

I wasn't going to dispute it. And I knew from the moment she met Prescott, she'd wanted him. Given the state of Prescott and Scarlett's relationship, I had a feeling our girl wasn't too happy with Tonya's crush on her man.

"She has a lot to be jealous of. You have us, of course she's going to hate it."

Scarlett gave me a look. Clearly, it had been the wrong thing to say. Tonya was likely jealous because Scarlett was beautiful, strong and had captured our attention. She had no idea of our previous relationship with the girl who'd been our everything back when we were kids.

"I have you, do I?"

I traced my finger along her jaw. There was no denying I felt something for Scarlett. She'd been my best friend. Someone I had always cared for. Just because she was trying to destroy us now, didn't change those facts. She didn't know any better. She didn't remember. And unlike the others, I wasn't going to hold it against her.

"Yeah, you do. That a problem?"

For a second, she didn't react, but the wicked glint in her eyes had me narrowing mine. Scarlett shifted up onto her hands and knees, then she crawled under my bound arms, straddled my lap and wrapped her arms around my neck.

"No."

Her mouth was on mine, kissing me as she pressed her body against me. The suddenness of it had me scrambling to stay upright with my hands bound. I landed flat on my back with Scarlett on top of me, still kissing me and rubbing her body on me. My bound hands rested on her back. I didn't try to escape the loose knots she'd made, not when she was all over me like this.

Her hand slid down my body between us and wrapped around my rapidly hardening cock. I groaned in her mouth, unable to help myself. She kissed her way down my jaw, stroking me over my clothes. Fuck, I wanted her. I'd tried not to think about how much I needed this woman. How much I wanted her to remember me. How much I wanted to fuck her while she was chained up with metal wrapped around her body. The way it would leave indents all over her skin. How I'd make it so tight, it would put a strain on all of her muscles and joints.

No, you're not going to do that. Don't forget what you did to Chelsea.

Guilt flooded my senses, making me stiffen. She must have felt it as she raised her head and stared at me.

"What's wrong?"

I shook my head and looked away.

"Nothing."

"Don't you want me?"

The rejection in her voice made my chest hurt. I looked at her again, wanting to reassure her I was in the moment with her.

"Hey, no, I want you, Scar. You have no idea how much. Just got shit on my mind is all… and no, I don't want to talk about it."

Her free hand slid across my jaw, her hazel-green eyes full of concern.

"Why are you and the others not bothered by being with the same woman? Not that we're together or anything, but you know what I mean."

"We've always shared."

It wouldn't make sense to anyone else, but the four of us had been through hell and back. We'd done everything together since we were kids. As we grew up and developed sexual desires most people would baulk at, sharing women who were into it didn't feel like a big deal to us. Maybe we'd all become a little voyeuristic like Prescott. It was the way we were. And it hadn't changed because we'd got Scarlett back. If anything, our need to be with her together was intensified by our connection to the girl from our past.

"So I'm just another notch on your bedposts?"

"That's not what I said."

Scarlett started to slide out from under my arms, but I tightened them around her.

"If I was only interested in fucking you, do you think I'd have taken care of you that night? Do you really think I would have got in the shower with you, held you whilst you cried and made sure you were okay?"

She froze, her eyes widening.

"I care about you, Scar. Don't start trying to think otherwise."

"Or what?" she whispered.

I wasn't like Drake who wanted to punish her for every indiscretion, but her words made me pause. Did she want consequences for doubting me?

"Or... I'll bind you to my bed."

"And do what to me?"

The huskiness of her voice had me slipping my hands from the loose knots around my wrists, but I didn't move them from her lower back just yet.

"Remind you why you're my whore."

She shivered, her pupils dilating as her fingers tightened around my cock. Clearly, she wanted me to do exactly that.

"Frankie," she breathed before I captured her mouth with my own.

My hands ran up her back and tangled in her hair. Her hand resumed stroking my cock. I wanted her pussy wrapped around it. Her hot, wet little pussy. I wanted her to scream my name. Without warning, I flipped us over, pinning her down on the bed with my hands wrapped around her wrists above her head.

"You're such a bad girl," I murmured against her lips. "My little whore."

"Tie me up."

I let go of her wrists and grabbed hold of the discarded rope. Then I looped it around her wrists and tied them together. Standing up, I pulled her up onto her knees. I reached up and looped the rope over the bar bolted to my ceiling, suspending her wrists in the air as I tied it off too. She had to raise up on her knees a little, but she could still move her legs.

My hands shoved her t-shirt up, exposing her tits. I sucked one into my mouth and loved the way she gasped when I bit down. My other hand dug underneath her shorts, seeking her wet warmth. She moaned when I speared her with my fingers, shoving them deep and groaning at the way she clenched around them. I wasn't gentle. I wanted her to fucking well feel it. Wanted to show her she was mine.

"Do you want my cock, whore?"

"Please."

"Good, because I'm going to make you come all over it."

I thrust my fingers inside her harder before biting down on her nipple again. She arched into me, crying out at the intensity I was playing her body with. She couldn't do a damn thing about it other than take it.

"Frankie, please."

Pulling my fingers from her, I shoved her shorts down her legs, tugging them off before freeing my cock from the confines of my clothes. I gripped both Scarlett's hips, pulled her over me and impaled her on it in one brutal, unforgiving thrust. The way she panted as I drove into her again and again made my heart fucking pound. Pressing closer, I kissed her mouth, sucking her tongue and tasting her.

"Mine," I grunted. "You're mine, whore. You better not forget it again, you hear me?"

"Yours."

I bit her lip, making her whine as I continued to drive into her little body. Making her take every inch. I was trying to avoid touching her behind because I knew she was sore from Drake's punishment earlier. Her hips gave me enough leverage to give it to her the way she craved. Scarlett liked it rough and raw. She wanted passion and fire. I could tell from the way she writhed and squirmed with each of my thrusts.

"Frankie," she panted, "don't stop."

I loved the way she said it so easily now. It wasn't even a conscious decision on her part. Every time she called me, Frankie, my feelings for her got more and more tangled up in the web of lies we'd weaved. How would she react when she found out the truth? Who the fuck knew. It was a gamble we'd eventually have to take. And soon. No matter what Drake said, I was done with this farce. Done with the secrets. If Scarlett was ever going to come back to us as the girl she'd been, we needed her to remember the past. Needed her to know who we truly were to each other.

My hand shifted from her hip to her thigh so I could thumb her clit. I wanted Scarlett to come all over me. There was no better sight in the world.

"Come for me, whore. Show me who you belong to. Show me how much you love my cock."

Her back arched and her mouth parted on a silent scream. I'd known she was close. I could feel it. The way she clenched around me was so damn sweet, her pussy milking my damn cock for all it was worth. I choked out a groan, unable to help myself as I emptied myself inside her tight heat.

Scarlett leant against me, panting and trying to regain her equilibrium. I held her close, still rocking my hips into hers with the last pulses of my own climax. She pressed her face into my neck, kissing my pulse point.

"When I first met you, I never imagined you'd be like this."

I stroked my hands up her back.

"Like what?"

"Well, you were so friendly and... nice... but neither of those things are true, are they?"

Moving back, I looked at her. There was no judgement or reproach in her eyes, only understanding.

"No, I'm not... but I think you like that."

I reached up and brushed my thumb along her bottom lip.

"The dark is alluring," she whispered. "And the men who live in it even more so."

I slid my thumb between her lips. Her tongue curled around it. Those eyes of hers burnt with a heady mix of desire and satisfaction.

"It's what we do, Scar, lure you in until you're so deeply involved, you can never escape."

Perhaps I shouldn't have said it, but I didn't care. I wanted her in the darkness with us. I craved it. We all did.

She only sucked on my thumb harder, her tongue sliding over the pad. It sent a jolt right to my cock, which was still half-hard inside her. What the fuck was it about her? She was intoxicating. I wanted to kiss her until she couldn't breathe. Fuck her until her pussy was raw. I wanted to dig myself inside her chest, smash through her walls and truly make her heart as much mine as it was Prescott's. He may have told me she'd reciprocated his love but warned me not to mention it to West or Drake. Her relationship with those two was precarious enough as it was. I had no intention of intervening.

"Bad girl."

She smiled around my thumb, her eyes twinkling. I brushed my nose against hers.

"Have you forgiven me for Friday?"

She nodded before my thumb popped from her mouth.

"You're my safety, Frankie. Please don't ruin that for me."

Fuck.

I couldn't promise her I wouldn't. Not when she had no idea what we did. How the only reason she'd been left broken was because of us.

"I'll try not to."

Digging my hands in her hair, I kissed her. My dick grew hard, so I fucked her again until she was crying, panting and begging me not to stop. Until I made her come so hard, she screamed and thrashed in her bonds. Then I let her down, cleaned her up in the bathroom and tucked her up in bed with me.

She curled up against my side with her head resting on my shoulder, her hand placed directly on my racing heart.

"When's your birthday?"

I almost stiffened but made a supreme effort to stay relaxed as I stroked her shoulder. One question I could not answer under any circumstances. Not my birthday nor the others. It was a sure-fire way of opening up a can of worms I wouldn't be able to shove back in.

"Why? You one of those astrology types who wants to check if we're compatible or something?"

She shoved me.

"No… not that there's anything wrong with it. I'm just trying to get to know you."

"Well, all you need to know is I'm twenty-six and it's not any time soon."

To distract her, I grabbed hold of her chin and kissed her. She didn't need to learn anything more about me this evening. Especially not about that. And if she tried to question me again, I would bury my face between her legs. Make her come enough times, she would be too exhausted to ask me shit.

There were some doors better left shut while she couldn't remember the past. When she did, our woman might realise the significance of her question. And why I had to keep it a secret for all our sakes.

TWENTY FOUR

SCARLETT

I didn't know why, but every time I left my office this week, Tonya was lurking in the hallway. It was like she was watching me. I didn't like it, but I had said nothing to the Horsemen. Knowing if I did I would be signing her death warrant because of West's threats, I kept my concerns to myself. The only saving grace was that she hadn't made any further remarks to me. In fact, she barely acknowledged my presence unless it was to say good morning.

Tonya was the least of my concerns. All day my father had been blowing up my phone with calls and texts demanding I give him an update. With everything going on between me and the boys, going on a night-time spying mission hadn't been top of my list of priorities. I always fell asleep before Prescott or Francis as I was spending alternate nights in their rooms. Being with them kept my nightmares at bay. I didn't wake up screaming or whimpering every night any longer. It was the first time in a long time I'd been at peace, even if I should be on high fucking alert around these men. Didn't matter if I loved Prescott and he loved me, there were too many secrets and lies between all five of us. I could feel them hanging in the air, almost suffocating us and keeping trust and honesty from surfacing.

I couldn't put off the conversation with my father forever. When the penthouse was silent, I crept from Prescott's bed out into the hallway and downstairs. My feet carried me to the view of the cityscape from their open plan living space. I tugged at my sleep shirt, my phone clutched tightly in my hand, staring out over the tops of the buildings spread out before me. Something deep in my heart resonated with this place. It felt more like home than Kent ever did. It was where I'd grown up, that much I knew. In the weeks I'd been here, I'd grown used to the background noise accompanying the place. It was never silent and still.

At first, I hated it. The noise made my nightmares worse and left me feeling more alone than ever. And I'd felt completely alone for the past ten years in my prison. Then the sounds of the city became comforting. They reminded me I'd escaped for the time being. I'd found my freedom. And now, here with the Horsemen, I was in a different cage. One I wasn't sure I wanted to escape. Not when I'd fallen in love. But I loved someone who kept secrets. I could never fully trust any of them.

My fingers went to my chest, rubbing the sore spot where my heart lay beating. I wanted to crawl back into bed with Prescott. I wanted him to kiss away my pain. To call me his little lamb and do dirty things to my body. Never in a million years did I think I would end up needing the man I'd been sent to destroy. I think I needed all of them, even if I was terrified of West and Drake was a locked vault. Then there was Francis who made me feel safe. He'd chased away my demons. He made it okay for me to go on after the night I'd killed a man. It should haunt me. Somehow, when he'd taken care of me that night, he washed away the horror, guilt and regret. He'd re-written my narrative.

I sighed. I wasn't okay with what I'd done, but I had to go on living. There was no other choice.

Raising my phone to my face, I stared down at the screen before I dialled my father's number. He would be pissed off, but what could he do? I wasn't a miracle worker. I wrapped my other arm around my middle and stared outside as the phone rang.

"Scarlett."

"Dad."

"Where have you been?"

The quiet calm of his voice had my limbs trembling. It was the precursor to the rage. An anger I knew all too well. It would result in fists of fury and my battered body being thrown in the concrete room. I hated the place with a passion. Many times I'd wanted to burn it all down. To take a fucking match to the building and watch my prison disintegrate. But it was wishful thinking on my part.

"With them. I couldn't exactly answer when they're watching me."

"You couldn't answer my texts?"

"I'm sorry, things were hectic today."

Learning how to lie effectively had been an early lesson for me. It hadn't always worked, but it kept me out of trouble half the time. The other half? Well, the less said about it, the better.

"That's not good enough, Scarlett."

Nothing I did ever was for Stuart Carver. Sometimes I wondered why they'd even adopted me in the first place when they'd never loved me. I was a burden to them and they never let me forget it. It hadn't started until after my recovery. After I learnt to walk and talk again. After my injuries had healed and my body was almost whole again. No, they'd been loving and caring then. But things gradually began to change. The loving parents morphed into... monsters. And I hated them for it. Both of them.

"I know."

My voice was quiet and meek. My body wouldn't stop trembling. Fear was rushing through my veins even though I knew he couldn't physically hurt me from here. His words would crush me though. Destroy my spirit. He'd ruin my hard-earned progress towards finding myself again.

"Living away from us has made you forget your place. I don't think you're ready for freedom. If I didn't want to nail those bastards to the wall, I would make you come home right this instant. Do you hear me?"

"Yes, Dad."

"They think they can hide in their ivory tower forever. Well, they're wrong. You are going to find out the truth for me and you're going to do it fast. This has gone on long enough. It's going to end with you. All of it. You're going to *end* them."

A tear slid down my cheek at the thought of ending Prescott. I couldn't. My heart wouldn't let me.

No, I won't end them for you. I can't. I love him.

"Now, have you got what I asked for?"

I shook my head, dreading the word I had to utter.

"No," I whispered.

"Why. Not?"

The deadly tone he'd used had me putting my free hand to the glass to keep myself upright.

"They're always watching me. Always."

"They're not watching you now."

I flinched. No way I wanted to sneak around while I was on the phone with him. I wouldn't even know where to start. I knew where the boys' bedrooms were and downstairs they had a gym, but if there were other rooms, they hadn't shown me them. Besides, why the hell would they have kept evidence of what my dad accused them of doing? It wouldn't be very smart. The Horsemen weren't stupid. They couldn't have got to where they were now otherwise.

"What exactly do you want me to find, Dad? A way to get past their security? The layout to their penthouse?"

"All of it, Scarlett. Everything. I need everything. Taking those bastards down is paramount, do you hear me? They need to die for what they've done."

What you think they've done.

"Okay. I'll try."

I needed to placate him somehow. His voice had gone up several octaves.

"Trying is *not* good enough. You haven't given me anything. I'm beginning to think you have no intention of doing what you've been told."

"I do, I swear."

I'd known this would be bad, but I couldn't help my sinking stomach and the sick feeling coiling in it. Knowing he couldn't get to me with his fists was the only thing keeping me from collapsing on the floor in fear.

"You're weak, you know that? You've done absolutely nothing for me. Nothing. We're no further forward at all."

"We are. I'm closer to them than anyone else could ever get, Dad."

"It's meaningless if you can't find a damn thing on them. You are fucking useless, Scarlett. You always have been. Lord knows why we even paid for your private fucking healthcare when you're nothing but a disappointment."

His voice was so loud now. I couldn't deal with it. I was shaking all over, wanting this to end.

"We've given you everything and this is how you repay me?"

"I'm sorry," I whispered.

"Sorry? Fuck sorry. You are going to do as you're told, do you hear me? No more excuses. None. Get me what I need."

A hand clapped on my shoulder. I jolted and spun around so fast, I made myself dizzy. My hand reached out blindly and landed on a solid chest. My dad was still shouting in my ear, but I barely heard what he said. My eyes raised as my head cleared. I found indigo blue ones staring down at me.

Oh, fuck!

"If you don't do what I tell you, I'll bring you home. I'll bring you back here and then your life won't be worth living, you hear me?"

My mouth parted, but I couldn't say a damn thing. And no doubt Drake could hear the volume of my father's voice through the speaker. Probably why he plucked the phone away from me and put it to his ear.

"I'm sorry, Mr Carver, but Scarlett needs to get back to bed. She's had a very busy day."

Drake hung up the phone. I snatched my hand back from his chest and stumbled into the window behind me. My phone dangled between his fingers and he stared at me with an unreadable expression on his face. I'd never been able to decipher Drake's moods, but now I knew I was in trouble.

"Can I have my phone back?" I whispered, putting my hand out.

He placed it between my fingers without hesitation. I slipped it behind my back, holding it there because I was scared he'd change his mind and take it away from me.

"I... I was just..."

What the hell could I even say?

"Talking to your family."

I nodded, unsure if he was going to ask why my father had been shouting at me. It's not as if I could tell him. They couldn't find out what I was really here for. The threat of my father was all too real for me. He would hurt me in unimaginable ways if I revealed the truth to the Horsemen. If I ruined everything.

Drake cocked his head to the side before he stepped closer. I sucked in a breath when he cupped my cheek with his large hand.

"You're shaking."

I hadn't stopped. My body was on high alert from my conversation with my father. I couldn't get rid of the sickly

223

feeling I had inside. The horrific memories of the concrete room kept resurfacing in my mind.

"I'm… I'm fine."

We both knew it was a lie. I couldn't afford to say anything else.

"No, you're not."

And with that, I found my face smashed into his hard chest and his arms encircling me. My body was stiff, wondering why on earth he was being nice and not questioning me about what he'd heard. Surely it should be his first concern, shouldn't it?

"What are you doing?" I whispered into his shirt, my arms hanging limply at my sides with my phone still clutched in one of my hands.

He didn't respond as his fingers traced lines down my spine. The motion was soothing, but I was too jumpy and unnerved by the whole thing to relax. Did he think I was going to melt and tell him everything? Was it why he was doing this? I couldn't help my suspicions given all our interactions with each other.

He must've realised this wasn't working. I wasn't going to calm down. I didn't have that sort of relationship with him. I didn't feel safe letting go. Not in the way I did with Prescott and Francis. Drake was made of stone compared to them. And I didn't particularly want to be comforted by a fucking statue.

The awkwardness between us when Drake let me go settled over the room. It was almost suffocating. He stared at me with those damn beautiful but terrifyingly cold indigo eyes of his. I wanted to be away from him. Away from all of this.

"Are you going to tell me what that was about?"

I shook my head.

"Secrets aren't going to win you any favours, Scarlett."

"There's nothing to tell."

His eyes narrowed.

"I'm sure that's what you want me to think."

"I don't need you to think anything because it's none of your business."

He'd made things worse by hanging up on my father. Now I was going to be in bigger trouble. Maybe I should throw this fucking phone off the roof. Let it smash on the ground so my father couldn't call me any longer. Would I be free of him then? Or would he find a way to get to me?

Could I trust Drake to keep me safe from my father? Could I trust any of them? I had no idea, and it's why I kept my mouth shut. Why I couldn't tell him my father was an abusive piece of shit who'd sent me here to find out the truth and destroy them.

"Are you scared of him?"

The question cut me. I wanted to say yes, but I couldn't.

"Do you really think I'm going to tell you, of all people, anything about me? You don't care. You literally don't give a shit about me other than how you can use me. So no, Drake, I'm not going to stand here and answer your questions. You haven't given me any indication you actually have any feelings whatsoever, so fuck you."

His jaw ticked at my words, but he didn't respond. Deciding I'd had enough, I shoved past him and walked towards the stairs intending to go back to Prescott. I was no longer upset, I was mad. So fucking mad at Drake for being an unfeeling dick. He might have tried to hug me, but it wasn't real. He did it because he thought it would placate me. Then he could fucking butter me up and make me answer his questions.

What I didn't expect was to have him come after me, grab my wrist and shove me up against the wall next to the staircase. And I certainly didn't expect him to lean into me, those indigo eyes dark with repressed emotion.

"You think I don't care about you?" he hissed, wrapping my hair around his fist. "You have no idea. No fucking idea at all."

My mouth was claimed in a hot, searing kiss that made my toes curl. Drake attacked it like he was starving and I was his sustenance. I was utterly helpless against the onslaught. My fingers gripped his waist, pressing my phone into him because I had nowhere else to put it. His body was hard and unyielding, keeping me pinned to the wall so I couldn't escape him. And right then, I didn't want to.

His tongue tangled with mine, demanding everything from me. His large hand gripped my thigh, pulling it up and wrapping it around him. It only brought his body closer to mine. The heat of him was everywhere, burning me up. A needy, high-pitched whine echoed in my throat. If Drake tore my clothes off and fucked me right there, I wouldn't have objected. To be honest, I probably would have encouraged it.

"You're maddening," he muttered in my mouth. "Utterly maddening."

Then he bit my lip so hard, it bled. I cried out from the pain, but it was muted when he sucked my lip in his mouth. When he tasted my blood. My eyes flew open, staring into his intense ones. The possessiveness and desire in them had me trembling. It's like the floodgates had opened and I was seeing the real man hiding beneath all those layers.

He released my lip with an audible pop. I blinked before licking along the inside of it. Tasting what he had. The metallic liquid spread across my tongue, making me wonder why he found it so alluring.

"Go back to Pres, Scarlett," he all but demanded, his voice hoarse and gravelly.

Drake backed away, looking distinctly harassed by the whole experience. Almost as if he couldn't believe he'd lost control. But I'd seen it and felt it. He couldn't hide from me. From us. If I pressed him, I was in no doubt he'd shut right back down and go back to being cold and unfeeling.

Even as everything screamed at me to go to him. To take off my clothes and offer myself to the statue of a man who gave me whiplash, I didn't. I pulled myself away from the wall and walked upstairs.

My feet carried me to Prescott's bedroom and I slipped inside. He was still asleep, his hand resting on his bare chest and the moon bathing him in its light. My heart hurt at the sight of the man I loved. I put my phone on the bedside table, crawled into bed with him and curled myself around him, pressing a kiss to his chest. He stirred, wrapping his arm around me and holding me against his body.

"My little lamb," he breathed, nuzzling my hair.

"I love you," I whispered into his skin.

I did. So fucking much. Being with him made everything else melt away. My stupid altercation with Drake. The kiss... fuck, that kiss. I'd never been kissed with such intensity before. Well, in all honesty, I'd only kissed two other men, and they were both pretty demanding, but Drake... I didn't know how to even go about describing the passion hiding behind those indigo eyes.

Prescott didn't ask where I'd been. He tucked his hand under my chin and pressed a kiss to my mouth. He whispered how much he loved me before cuddling me to him and falling asleep again. His presence soothed me and calmed my racing heart.

I fell asleep hoping he would ease my throbbing pussy in the morning because I couldn't deny I was turned on to high heaven by a certain man who'd utterly confounded me tonight. And I had no idea what the hell I was going to say to him next time we saw each other.

TWENTY FIVE

DRAKE

I'd lain awake half the fucking night cursing myself for the way I'd kissed her. Why did she erode my control? Why did having her here make me so fucking insane? I could barely stand the distance between us even though I'd put it there. And I was utterly done with everyone accusing me of not caring about her. They fucking well knew I did. I'd fought so hard to get her back. Gone to extreme lengths to return Scarlett to us. Me. I'd done that.

My little wisp. I brought her back to us.

Her not knowing I cared was more than I could take. The way I cared for her couldn't be quantified. I was just fucking realistic about what we were dealing with. And after overhearing what Stuart fucking Carver said to her last night, and the way she'd behaved towards me, I was right to be damn well suspicious and reticent when it came to dealing with her.

"I'll bring you back here and then your life won't be worth living."

What the fuck did he mean by her life wouldn't be worth living? Hadn't they treated her well while she'd been with them? Had they... hurt her?

I would fucking gut the cunt if he'd laid a hand on her. I'd drain him dry of his damn blood because he deserved nothing less. If anyone hurt our woman, I would stop at nothing to ruin them alongside Prescott, Francis and West. We'd hunt them down together. And we'd bathe in their misery before the end.

Scarlett wasn't going to tell me what her father meant. And I doubted she'd tell the others. It became very clear to me when she started acting all cagey, she was afraid of Stuart. Terrified of him. In fact, I had a feeling she must fear him more than she did us, because why else would she be here? Why would she have gone to these lengths when she had a glimpse of who we were hiding underneath our façades?

It was why I'd called the others together. Prescott had left Scarlett in his room to watch TV in bed while we gathered in the room next to our home gym. The one she didn't know existed. Francis had dubbed it the war room. It contained everything we'd found in our search for Scarlett. One wall was plastered with pictures of her. Everyone connected to her. Everything we had on the Carvers. All of our memories and mementoes of the girl we'd lost. The things we hoped to show her when she returned to us. But Scarlett wasn't whole yet. She didn't remember who we were. This place had to remain a secret until she did.

West stood in the corner with his arms crossed over his chest and had his eyes glued to the last photo we'd taken of the five of us together at sixteen. We looked so young. All of us were smiling. Scarlett stood in the middle between West, who had his arm wrapped around her, and Prescott. Francis was next to Prescott and me on the end with West. Our little gang of five who had stuck by each other through thick and thin.

Fuck, I miss those days. We had our whole lives ahead of us. And now we're fractured. It's not fair.

Prescott walked over to it and ran his fingers over the photo.

"Little Nyx," he murmured.

He looked at West who narrowed his eyes but didn't comment on our childhood nickname for Scarlett. We all knew why West hated it so much. The reminder of the night everything had fallen to shit wasn't a pleasant one for any of us, but for him… it was worse.

"What's this about, Drake?" Francis asked as he took a seat at the table we had in the centre of the room.

I took a chair at the head of the table and leant my elbows on it. We hadn't been in here since she'd come to work for us. There was no need. But right now, we required somewhere safe to talk where she couldn't overhear us.

"I found Scarlett up late last night in the living room, speaking to Stuart on the phone."

Prescott whipped his head around and stared at me.

"I woke up when she came back to bed, but I didn't ask her what she'd been doing."

None of them were surprised by me being up. They all knew about my bouts of insomnia. Right now, it was so bad I was barely getting a few hours in every night. Francis had commented on it, telling me to take my damn sleeping pills. I knew I should listen to him. However, now I'd found Scarlett in the living room when she should be in bed, it made me want to keep an eye on her even when everyone else was asleep. Prescott should have locked his fucking door last night. That was the agreement, so she didn't wander around in places she shouldn't be. I'd have to remind all of them.

"He was having a go at her."

"Did you hear what he said?" Francis asked, a concerned expression flitting across his face.

I rubbed my wrist with my fingers.

"A little and I didn't like it. Not one fucking bit."

West shoved off the wall and walked over to the table before leaning on it with both hands.

"What did he say?"

The irritation in his amber eyes was very apparent.

"He said something about bringing her back home and her life wouldn't be worth living if that happened. So I took her phone, told him she needed to go back to bed and hung up on him. She, of course, denied anything was wrong, but I don't believe her."

West's hands curled into fists.

"That cunt, if he's hurt her—"

I put my hand up.

"I know, but we can't be sure he has been. I'm not sure of anything right now."

The whole thing had rattled me. Overhearing her conversation. Her denial. The way she'd accused me of not caring about her. And the kiss. The damn fucking kiss. She stole my self-control. Ruined it. She was wrecking me on the inside and I had no clue what the fuck to do about it. How to stop this descent into hell. Because this was absolute hell for me. The worst fucking kind of insanity.

West shoved off the table and paced away, his back rigid with his anger.

"I'm going to kill him. He deserves it. The motherfucker deserves to be gutted. He needs a fucking slow and painful death. He took her. He took what's ours."

Prescott and Francis watched West pace the length of the table. We all agreed with him. Stuart Carver deserved to die for everything he'd done.

"We can't do anything to him," I said after a minute.

West almost slammed his fist into the wall. Instead, he stopped and slapped his palm against it, breathing heavily.

"I know. I fucking hate it, but I know."

There were so many reasons we had never been able to go after Stuart Carver, the owner of the premier league football club, Rotherhithe United. The first being that very fact. He was a prominent and rich man. Not to mention the circles he ran in. Friends in high places. Politicians. Celebrities. The criminal underworld. The man had been rather good friends with Frank Russo before he got offed. And worst of all, his best mate had become the Met Police Commissioner a few years ago. We'd had a run-in with Garrett Jones when he was still a Detective Inspector. No way any of us wanted to get back on his radar.

Our biggest obstacle always came down to one thing. You tried to off a man like Stuart Carver, you'd bring a world of trouble down on your head.

Besides, we couldn't kill him when he had Scarlett and he knew it. He fucking well knew it. It's why he took her. He took her to punish us. To say we had a vendetta against the man was an understatement. The four of us wanted to burn his fucking football stadium to the ground and destroy everything he'd built.

Even now, when we had Scarlett back, going after him would be a gamble. Especially while Scarlett had no idea who she was. Who she'd been. And why we'd even got ourselves into this mess.

"So what do you want to do about this then?" Francis asked when none of us said anything for a few minutes.

"First of all, if you have her with you at night, lock your door so she can't leave. We do not need her finding anything she shouldn't, especially not this room."

Prescott rubbed the back of his neck.

"Sorry, I got a little… distracted last night."

"Let me guess, you were too busy giving her a dick down," West said, pulling away from the wall and smirking at Prescott.

Prescott dug his hands in his pockets and tried not to smile.

"Maybe. You jealous?"

I knew for a fact West hadn't touched Scarlett intimately since the night we'd given her E. He'd kept his distance. I wasn't entirely sure why or what was going through his head.

"As if."

"She wanted it this morning, but *someone* called a meeting."

West's smirk got wider.

"Is that so?"

"Yeah, so I'd quite like to wrap this shit up."

West turned away, but not before I caught him biting his lip as if he was planning something.

"This is important," I said, not wanting to get in between him and Prescott.

I watched Prescott roll his eyes.

"Yes, I know, Drake… but when your woman wants your dick, you give it to her."

"Apparently, I missed the memo."

Francis and West snorted. The way Prescott smiled at me had me narrowing my eyes.

"Well, you see, the way I hear it, it's your fault she's all worked up and in need of release."

I almost choked on my own breath.

What the fuck?

"I don't know what you're talking about."

Francis looked at Prescott.

"I thought you said you didn't ask her what happened."

Prescott shrugged.

"I asked why she was so horny and she placed the blame at Drake's door but refused to say any more. So, tell us, Drake, what did you do to Scarlett last night after you caught her?"

Clenching my jaw shut, I rested my palms flat on the table. No fucking way I was telling them about the kiss. The godforsaken fucking insane kiss between us.

"Hmm, it's not the first time she's been all turned on and shit after an encounter with you," Francis said, crossing his arms over his chest and levelling his gaze on me. "Are you holding out on her?"

"What the fuck is this? Question me about my relationship with Scarlett day? I didn't sign up for that."

West barked with laughter, making my face fall further. Why the fuck were these lot trying to mess with me?

"Well, if you'd just fuck her instead of punishing her, then we wouldn't have to say anything," Prescott said, giving me a wink.

"You're all a bunch of cunts, you know that right?"

"Says the man who seems to be a little scared of Scarlett's cunt right now," West said with a grin.

I stood up and glared at the idiots I called my best friends. They were getting on my last fucking nerve. My ability to keep myself in check was already shot to pieces by that damn woman last night and now this bullshit.

"Fuck. Off."

"Hit a sore spot, have we?" Prescott said.

I clenched my fists, trying to rein in my temper. Trying not to lose my shit with them. This was not what we were meant to be discussing.

"We are here to talk about Stuart, not my relationship with Scarlett."

Francis rolled his eyes.

"What do you want us to do, Drake? Ask her outright if Stuart's been hurting her? She's not going to tell us anything."

"This is why I keep saying we need her to remember the past," Prescott said, waving his hand at me. "And we need to do it soon. She's not going to trust us until she knows the truth."

Shoving my hands in my pockets, I paced away. He had a point. Maybe I was scared of her remembering. Scared of the repercussions. A huge part of me didn't want her to know what happened the night of her accident. It changed everything. But I knew it wasn't fair to keep it from her either.

"We've already deviated from the plan by bringing her here."

"We're gambling with a real person. One we all care about, no matter what happened in the past or why she's here now. Plans change… or we wouldn't all be fucking her now, would we."

I sighed and turned back to them.

"You're right. She is a person and it's something we have to handle delicately. We can't go off half-cocked and fuck her up even worse. Let's revisit this when we've all had time to think about it and come up with a potential solution, okay?"

The three of them gave me a nod of agreement. I needed a minute to work out how we should go about this. What would be the safest way? I mean, we weren't known for doing anything 'safely' but Scarlett and her amnesia weren't something we could afford to mess around with. Our mere presence clearly wasn't working fast enough.

"And don't ask her about Stuart. Do not press her about any of it. We need her to think we're not suspicious. It's the only way she's going to let her guard down."

I wanted to know everything that had gone on in the Carver household, but pressurising Scarlett wouldn't get us anywhere. We needed to approach it from a different angle.

"Yeah, yeah, okay, we get it," Prescott said.

"Good."

"Are we done?" West asked.

I nodded, wanting to be alone with my own thoughts to calm the fuck down.

He looked at Prescott who narrowed his eyes at our friend.

"What are you planning?"

West merely grinned and moved towards the door.

"West."

He unlocked it, pulled the door open and turned his head back to look at us.

"It's between me and her."

West walked out, shutting the door behind him and leaving Prescott glaring.

"I knew I shouldn't have said anything about her being horny," he grumbled. "He's going to fuck with her, isn't he?"

"You should know West will use any excuse," Francis said with a chuckle and a shrug.

Prescott shook his head and rubbed his chin.

"Fuck."

I didn't give a shit what West did. Ignoring Prescott and Francis, I walked out. They could damn well fight it out amongst themselves. I wasn't in the mood to deal with them any longer after they'd given me a hard time. I made my way underneath the stairs and opened the door to the stairwell. If I was ever going to get my head on straight, I needed to get away from these idiots for a while. And try to find my equilibrium again.

TWENTY SIX

WEST

I stalked upstairs, not giving two fucks if Prescott wanted to satisfy Scarlett's urges. He'd had more than enough time with her after his whole 'I love you' declaration. She probably thought I'd given up on fucking with her head. I was merely lulling her into a false sense of security. Psychological warfare happened to be one of the many ways I liked to mess with people. Everyone thought I was a violent piece of shit who couldn't control himself. They were all fucking dumb and had no idea who they were dealing with.

I threw Prescott's door open and walked in. Scarlett was tucked up in Prescott's bed, her eyes glued to the TV. She looked over at me when she heard the door, her eyes going wide.

"West? Where's Pres?"

I didn't answer her, merely stalked over to his bed, ripped the covers from her body and plucked her up from where she was laying. Scarlett was unceremoniously tossed over my shoulder, making her let out a yelp. I carried her from the room, my arm pinned over the backs of her legs.

"What the fuck? Put me down!"

In response, I smacked her arse, earning another yelp from her lips. The verbal abuse I got for it wasn't worth repeating as I took her into my bedroom. I locked the door before I tossed her on my bed. She scrambled into a sitting position, glaring at me as I walked over to my window and looked out across the city.

"What is wrong with you? You could have asked me to come with you."

"Would you have?"

"No."

I smiled and dug my hand in my pocket, extracting a joint and my lighter.

"Then you've answered your own question."

Sticking the joint in my mouth, I lit it and breathed the smoke in, holding it in my lungs before I blew it out. I slid my lighter back in my pocket. It might be early to start smoking, but I didn't care. It always took the edge off.

"What do you even want, West?"

I raised my hand and beckoned her over without looking back. It took a minute, but she joined me by the window, staring at me with a frown.

"I'm here. What do you want?"

Grabbing a hold of her hand, I slid the joint between her fingers. She looked at it with no small amount of suspicion.

"You want me to smoke this with you?"

"You need to relax, Scar. Not everything needs to be a battle between us."

She didn't take a toke.

"I don't want to do drugs with you."

I took the joint back from her, dragged the smoke in my mouth before grabbing hold of her face. My fingers squeezed her jaw, forcing her mouth open. She tried to get away, but I leant into her and breathed the smoke into her mouth, shutting it before she could do a thing. She choked on it for a moment before I released her. Scarlett shoved me away from her, spluttering as I grinned and took another drag.

"You're a dick," she ground out.

"If you'd just taken it without complaint, I wouldn't have to make you."

"I hate you."

"I'm sure you do."

She clenched her fists, clearly perturbed by my nonchalant tone. The woman could say whatever the fuck she wanted to me. I knew she liked it when I had my hand around her throat. When I touched her. When I fucked her. I was in half a mind to give it to her now. To make her come all over my dick. Prescott said she wanted it, so why the fuck not?

Sticking the joint between my lips, I grabbed a handful of her arse and tugged her against me. My other hand captured her wrists and held them behind her back. Then I took the joint from my mouth and held it between her lips instead.

"Breathe it in, Scar."

"Fuck you."

"We can do it the hard way again if you wish."

Her glare made me tighten my hand around her wrists. She winced and did as I asked, sucking in the smoke. She choked

241

again, but she held it for a moment and breathed it out into my face. I smiled at her.

"Good girl."

"I don't want to be your fucking good girl."

Don't you? Hmm, then I think I know what you want.

"You want to be a bad girl, then?"

"No!"

"Oh, Scar, it's okay. I know you want it, you're just too scared to admit it."

She struggled against me. I laughed at her attempt to escape. Even if she wanted to run, there was nowhere for her to go. I would hunt her down and drag her back in here by her hair. And she would regret it because I would make her life hell for a few hours.

"If you keep that up, you'll only get my dick hard."

She stopped, the fire in her eyes mounting with every second.

"Let me go."

"Smoke this with me and maybe I will."

I made her take another toke, watching the smoke curl out of her mouth afterwards. Taking my own drag, I smiled at her and licked my lip.

"Is this something you do all the time?"

"Smoke weed? Sometimes."

"And other stuff?"

I shrugged, adjusting my hold on her.

"On occasion, I do E and LSD. The other three don't like dealing with me when I'm out of my head, so you know, I keep it on the down-low."

Didn't matter to me if she knew about my drug use. I drank whisky and smoked weed more than I did pills. It was my way of keeping my need for violence at bay. And right now, even though we were smoking, I wanted to get violent with her. Very fucking violent.

Pulling Scarlett away from the window with me, I popped the joint in the ashtray on my bedside table. Then I ran my free hand down her throat, gripping it between my fingers and squeezing.

"How about you turn those sharp claws on me, Scar, hmm? If you hate me so much, show me."

I let go of her wrists but kept my hand around her neck. The defiant look in her eyes made me want to push her further. Fuck how I wanted to make Scarlett snap. I shoved her back towards the window and pinned her neck against it.

"Go on, I know you want to hurt me."

She wrapped her hand around my wrist and dug her nails into my skin. I cocked my head to the side and licked my lip.

"You can do better than that."

Sliding her other hand under my t-shirt, she dug her nails into my chest and dragged them down towards my stomach. I let out a breath, feeling myself growing hard under her touch. Then I leant closer, getting right up in her face.

"Hurt me, Scar. Fucking hurt me."

Her hand left my chest and she slapped me across my cheek. The sound rang through the room. It stung, but I loved it. I looked her up and down, running my teeth along my bottom lip.

"Again."

The heat in her eyes made me want to rip her clothes from her body and fuck her senseless. Her hand came up and she slapped me. This time it was harder. She hissed at the impact as if it hurt her as much as it did me. I squeezed her neck. I wanted to bite it and leave marks on her skin. Wanted to remind her of who she belonged to and why she would never be free of me.

"That's it. Let it out, Scar. I want you to hurt me."

"I hate you," she whispered, her nails digging harder into my skin.

"If you're going to tell me you hate me, say it like you fucking mean it."

Her eyes darkened.

"I hate you."

The hand she'd slapped me with came up and gripped me by the throat.

"I. Hate. You. West."

There you are, Scar. There's my girl. Fuck, you're magnificent.

Her fingers squeezed. I tore her away from the window and pressed her down on my bed instead. Her light brown hair fanned out across the black sheets. I was going to show her the real me. All the other times we'd fucked, it had been tame. It was time she saw my true nature. The feral beast lurking inside me.

My free hand slid into my pocket and I drew my knife from it, flipping it out. She watched me place it at the top of her t-shirt, right above her breasts.

"You're about to hate me a whole lot more."

I tore it down her t-shirt, slicing through the fabric. She stared at me with wide eyes as I exposed her breasts. I ran the point over the tip of her nipple before circling her areola with it. She trembled, her nipples hardening under my ministrations. My woman was terrified and it showed. Her breathing was heavy and her heart rate spiked under my fingers. But Scarlett had her legs spread for me as I leant over her. I pressed my knee into her pussy, rubbing the fabric of her shorts against it.

"You're mine, Scar. All fucking mine. I'm going to make sure you never forget it."

I leant closer and ran my nose up her cheek.

"Don't move or it will hurt worse, you hear me? If you struggle and ruin it, you'll only have yourself to blame."

"What are you going to do?" she whispered, her voice shaking on the words.

I pulled back and smiled at her.

"Make sure everyone knows who you belong to."

Releasing her neck, I placed my left hand on her breastbone, holding her there as I pressed the knife tip to her skin just below her collarbone.

"This is going to hurt," I murmured. "But you can take it, Scar. You're my girl."

I dug the knife in, cutting through her skin and dragging it down to form a line. She let out a cry of pain, but she kept still other than her fingers curling around the covers. I was very precise with my cuts. I wanted it to look good on her, not some jacked-up jagged scar, but something beautiful. Pretty almost.

Scars for my stunning Scar.

Her eyes remained fixed on me the whole time. Tears ran down her face and small whimpers erupted from her mouth, but not once did she tell me to stop. She took the pain just like I knew she could.

When I was done, I watched the blood running down her chest, seeping from the word I'd carved into her skin.

War.

For once in my life, I wanted to live up to our name. The one we'd been given when we landed on the financial scene and caused a fucking huge stir. They'd branded us gods. And now I was embracing it.

I'd given her my mark.

She belonged to War.

And War was me.

TWENTY SEVEN

WEST

Scarlett's eyes flicked down. She didn't say a word. She kept staring at the blood and the carving like she couldn't believe what I'd done. Her fingers loosened from the covers, but she kept them by her sides. Her chest rose and fell in rapid bursts, making me think she was in shock.

"If Drake was here, he'd want to lick the blood from your skin," I murmured.

Her watery eyes met mine again. I leant closer and kissed the word, making her whimper. The cuts wept with her life-sustaining liquid. I licked it from my lips. While I wasn't like Drake with his blood obsession, the sight of it here satisfied me unlike anything else.

I put the knife to her mouth. She knew what I wanted her to do. I could see it in her eyes. There was no more mutiny. She didn't know whether to hate me or beg for me to fuck her.

Her tongue slid out and licked the length of the blade. I flipped it over and let her clean the other side. Then I shifted up on my knees and stared down at her. The t-shirt I'd cut lay on either side of her. She wasn't naked enough for me. My fingers dug between her shorts and her skin. I ripped them down her legs. Then I used the knife to slice through her underwear on either side of her crotch. It fell away, revealing her pussy to me. Her dripping pussy, glistening in the sunlight streaming in through the windows.

"Who do you belong to, Scar?"

Her bottom lip trembled. She lay there staring at me with wide, tear-filled eyes and didn't respond. I pressed the flat side of the blade against her pussy. Not like I would cut her with it here, but she didn't know that.

"Who do you belong to?"

"War," she whispered. "I belong to War."

"Good girl. Now get on your fucking hands and knees."

She did as I asked, her whole body trembling with the effort of turning over. I set the knife down next to me before I tore the remnants of her t-shirt from her body and leant down to run my tongue up her spine. Straightening, I pulled my t-shirt off my body and unbuttoned my jeans. When I was bare, I knelt behind her, running my hand up her cheek and along her back.

"This pretty pussy is mine." I pressed my thumb to it, sliding it along her slick entrance. "She belongs to my cock, Scar. I'm going to abuse her the way you need."

I dipped my thumb into her heat. She whimpered but didn't dispute my statement.

"Mmm, you're soaking. Did the pain turn you on, Scar? Do you want me to make it hurt more?"

Pulling my thumb from her pussy, I slid it higher, finding her clit. She jerked, but I held onto her hip, keeping her from moving away. I rubbed her clit in slow circles, eliciting harsh needy pants from her lips. She wanted more. I could tell by the way her hips shifted in my grasp.

Removing my thumb from her clit, I gripped my cock and slid it between her lips, knocking the head against her clit. I repeated the action, slipping back and forth until she let out a whine.

"Please, West."

I notched the head of my cock to her entrance.

"Does this pussy need filling?"

"Please, I need you."

Teasing her entrance with the head of my cock, I chuckled and adored the way she tried to back herself onto it.

"I'm going to hurt you."

"Please."

The desperation in her voice had me slamming inside her in one unforgiving thrust. She cried out, choking on her own breath as her hands gripped the covers below us. I slid back out and plunged inside her again. I curled my other hand around her hip and fucked her. My body pounding into hers with loud slapping noises. They rang through the room with my brutality. I wouldn't give her mercy.

"Your pretty pussy takes my dick so fucking well," I ground out through my teeth.

"Fuck! Fuck me."

Releasing her hips, I dug one hand into her hair and pulled at it, making her head snap back. The way her neck strained as she stared at me was so fucking beautiful. A damn goddess, she was. My fucking goddess. Mine.

I tugged her hair more, pulling her up by it until her back met my chest. My other hand slid up her body and wrapped around her neck. I held her against me, her legs bent either side of mine as I thrust upwards, making her take me deep and hard.

My lips went to her ear and I bit down on the lobe. Her hands curled around my back, holding me to her. If I was in any doubt she wanted this before, I wasn't now. My eyes went to the cuts I'd made below her collarbone. The blood had started to clot. I'd make sure to clean her up real fucking good when I was done with her. First, I wanted to make her come all over my dick and paint her insides with my cum. Show her who owned her sweet pussy. Who would give her everything she ever desired.

"You're my bad girl, Scar," I murmured in her ear. "Only I'm allowed to hurt you and make you cry. No one else gets that fucking privilege, you hear me? No one. If anyone touches you, I will kill them. They'll regret ever laying a finger on your precious skin. It's mine. All of you is mine."

My fingers tightened around her throat, restricting her airway. My other arm wrapped around her waist, giving me better leverage to fuck her with. My thrust grew harder even if they were shallow, showing her I owned her little body. As if she didn't already know that when I'd carved my ownership into her skin.

She let out these beautiful gasps as she tried to suck enough oxygen into her lungs. Fucking perfect. That's what my girl was. Her fingers tightened around me, trying to tell me it was too much, but it would never be enough. Never.

"You want to come, my little Scar? Want to explode all over my dick?"

Her choking whine was the only answer I needed. I slid my hand from her waist up to her chest and gripped one of her nipples between my fingers, twisting it.

"West," she choked out.

"I'll make you come when I'm good and fucking ready."

My fingers slid higher, brushing over the cuts. Then I pressed them into her skin. She cried. Oh, how she fucking cried. I watched the tears running down her cheeks with rapt attention. And licked them away, tasting her pain on my tongue.

"Please," she gasped. "Please."

My hand slid to her nipple again, massaging her breast and slipping her nipple between my fingers. I tightened them around it. She bucked and writhed against me, but she didn't let me go. She held onto me, letting me fuck her and tease her nipples. Her pussy felt so fucking good around my dick. The way she clenched when I squeezed her nipple too hard was the icing on the cake.

This girl had driven me half-mad my entire life. Now I had her back. I had her warm, lithe body against mine. I'd carved myself into her skin. And I'd brand myself all over her heart again. She was mine forever. She'd been destined to be so from the day she was born. Destined for all of us.

"Anyone who's hurt you, I'll take their lives, you hear me?" I whispered in her ear. "I'll destroy them for you. Every single one."

I didn't care if Drake couldn't confirm his suspicions. We were going to kill Stuart Carver regardless of whether he'd hurt our girl or not. But I knew he had. There was no fucking way she'd be scared of him otherwise. Our woman was strong as fuck. She wouldn't let anyone intimidate her. Not even us. So whatever the fuck that cunt had done to her, I would get it out of her one day. I would make her tell me everything. Then I would rid the world of the scumbag who'd stolen her from us ten years ago. I'd rip out his fucking heart.

"West," she whimpered.

"That's right, Scar. I'll burn them all to the fucking ground."

My hand slid down her body and sought out her clit. I stroked it the way I knew she needed. The exact way to make her buck and tremble in my grasp while my cock hammered into her sweet pussy, hitting all the right spots. My fingers tightened around her throat, almost choking her.

"Come on this dick. Fucking milk it."

Her silent cry a few minutes later as she rocked against my cock and fingers was everything. She choked and spluttered as I kept a tight hold on her throat, but she came so beautifully. Her body shook as it raced through her. Her pussy tightened and released, milking my cock in the way only she could.

"My bad little Scar," I hissed in her ear.

I loosened my hold on her neck, allowing her to suck in more air. Her nails dug into my skin, but I liked it. I wanted the pain. It reminded me I was alive and I had her with me.

Her body slumped against mine. Her thoroughly used and wrecked little body. I let go of her neck and pushed her forward onto her hands. Then I gripped her hips and thrust

252

into her over and over. I punished her pussy until I exploded inside her, emptying all my pent up lust and rage into her body.

"Scar," I groaned. "Fuck."

Nothing ever felt so good. No other pussy felt this sweet. She was everything to me. I couldn't admit it to her, but she owned me. Each and every part of me belonged to Scarlett. It always had. The years separating us and her loss of those memories from the past didn't matter. She and I shared a bond. It transcended all of that bullshit. She knew it deep down. She could feel it. It's why she stayed with us. Why she was drawn here. Why she came back.

When my dick was spent, I pulled out of her. I stroked her hip as she swayed on her knees. I climbed off the bed and plucked her off it, cradling her in my arms. Scarlett placed a hand to my chest and stared up at me as I carried her towards my bathroom. She didn't say a word when I kicked the toilet seat closed and set her on it.

I walked over to the cabinet above the black granite sink counter and opened it. Pulling out the items I needed, I set them down on the counter next to Scarlett. Next, I grabbed a washcloth and wet it. Then I knelt at her feet and pressed the cloth to the carving I'd made on her skin, gently wiping away all the blood. My other hand stroked along her bare thigh when she hissed at the touch of the cloth.

In order for it to permanently scar, I would need to make sure she didn't cover it up. I knew all about scarification even if I'd never had it done myself. Penn told me about it during an inking session. It's how I'd met the Fixer. He tattooed on the side.

"Do not let anyone else touch this, you hear me? Only I'm allowed to take care of it."

She placed her hand on my tattooed one.

"Okay," she whispered, giving me a subtle nod.

Leaning forward, I pressed a kiss to it.

"It's perfect, just like you are. A scar for my Scar."

She shivered, her fingers tightening around mine. I wished I could tell her the truth. Tell her of my feelings and remind her of who she was to me. Remind her of our past and everything we'd done together as kids. All of the times I made her laugh. The way her eyes would light up the moment she saw me.

Not a day had gone by since she'd disappeared where I didn't feel her loss. The girl who'd been precious to my damn soul. She was mine to protect. And I would protect the woman she'd become with every part of me. I'd slay our enemies to keep her out of harm's way. We were the only ones who could do anything to her. And even as we hurt her, we took care of her too. We kept Scarlett safe.

I kissed the word I'd carved on her skin again, making sure she knew it would mark her for the rest of her life the way she'd marked me. It might be invisible to everyone else, but I felt it. My little Scar had signed her name on my heart when we were kids. And it would remain there... forever.

TWENTY EIGHT

SCARLETT

I lay on West's bed, completely bare except for a pair of knickers he'd retrieved for me after he'd ruined my other clothes and stared up at the white ceiling. His head was on my stomach, his fingers tracing soft lines along the skin below my breasts. His eyes were closed, and my hand was in his light brown hair, stroking the soft strands. West wasn't asleep, but he was quiet as his chest rose and fell with his breathing.

After the brutality he'd fucked me with, the peace and quiet was alien and almost unnatural. It's as if carving the word 'war' into my skin and fucking me senseless afterwards had calmed him. I hadn't processed my feelings about what he'd done. It was fucked up. So fucked up, but I didn't exactly hate him for it. How did you even go about unpacking that shit?

A man I barely knew, and who terrified the shit out of me, had cut me with the intention of creating a scar. His way of branding me. Showing the world who I belonged to. And I'd given into it. I'd allowed him to do it without complaint. What kind of person did it make me? I had no fucking clue. Perhaps I'd crossed the veil and walked into the darkness with them… or maybe I'd been roped into it. Didn't matter when I was locked in the abyss now.

Where could I even go from here? I was in love with one of them and another had carved his ownership over me onto my skin.

My eyes flicked down to the wound below my collarbone. It really fucking hurt when he did it. Even now, it was still sore. He'd been gentle when he cleaned it and told me it needed to stay uncovered. I hadn't expected care from a man like West. One who went from calm to batshit crazy at the drop of a hat. It's why I hadn't objected to him keeping me in his room now. Besides, I wasn't sure how the fuck the others would react to what he'd done. My sneaking suspicion was none of them would be very impressed.

West's eyes opened. His lips curved up into a smile as his fingers moved higher, stroking the bottom of my breast. I tried not to react to his touch. Tried and failed. Goosebumps rose all over my skin. He didn't speak as he raised his hand and used the pad of his finger to brush over the tip of my nipple. The more he did it, the harder it became until it was a stiff peak, eager for more of his maddening fingers.

"I didn't think you were capable of being gentle," I muttered under my breath knowing he would hear me regardless.

Those amber eyes regarded me without a hint of emotion in them.

"I'm capable of many things, Scar," he murmured. "Things you can't even imagine."

He raised his head only to shift higher and lower his mouth towards my nipple. His tongue darted out and traced a line around my areola before he sucked my nipple in his mouth. I bit my lip, trying not to whimper at the way his tongue bathed it. My hand went to his hair again, brushing through the strands and adoring the way it felt against my fingertips.

My nipple popped out of his mouth and he breathed on it, making me tremble from the sensation of his hot breath on my wet skin.

"I'll show you one day. The way I kill would make your stomach turn, but I'll make you watch, let you hear the screams whilst I rip a man's heart out of his chest with my bare hands."

And here I thought psycho killer West had been contained after he'd been satisfied by me. Clearly not.

"Does everything come down to violence with you?"

He pressed a kiss to my breastbone.

"For the most part." His eyes flicked up to mine and a wicked smile appeared on his face. "You like my violence, you're just unwilling to admit it."

I pursed my lips. There was no way in hell I wanted to incite more of his violent nature right now. He'd already hurt me enough today to last a lifetime. I was in no doubt he would make sure my new scar would be permanently etched on my skin for all to see. The only saving grace was he hadn't made it too big. The word was small, but if I wore anything with a low neckline, it would be visible.

How on earth am I going to explain this to Prescott?

Why was I even thinking about that? It was West's job to explain this shit to them, not mine. It hadn't been my idea.

"If I asked you to be gentle, would you?"

His fingers stroked my nipple as he kissed his way down the centre of my chest.

"Maybe."

I couldn't stop my body from trembling from his touch. All I'd experienced from West was a brutal form of fucking. This was so at odds with what I knew of his nature. And I couldn't help the way one of my walls fractured inside as he chipped away at the bottom of it.

As his mouth met my belly button, he licked his way around it, watching me from under his lashes. I hadn't noticed how long they were before. You couldn't call West anything other than gorgeous, even if he was fucking terrifying at the same time.

"You'd have to be good for me, Scar, then I'll be as gentle as you need."

His fingers curled into my knickers, tugging them down my legs, which he set on his shoulders before burying his face in my pussy. West brought me to not one but two intense orgasms, his tongue bathing my clit and his fingers speared into both my holes. I clawed at his head, but he didn't let up until I was crying, tears streaming down my face at the overwhelming pleasure. I was surprised he didn't try to fuck me again given the way his cock strained in his boxers when he'd finished with me. And I didn't let on how disappointed I was about it. West's dick was something else. At least, the things he did with it were. He knew how to hit me in the right places to send me flying.

CHAOS

West got off the bed and pulled on the rest of his clothes. He made me sit up and dressed me in the things he'd got from Francis' room. Half my clothes were in there and the other in Prescott's room. The loose t-shirt he dressed me in semi-hid the cuts on my skin and was so long it almost covered my jean shorts.

He took my hand and led me from the room after unlocking the door. I fidgeted, following him downstairs where we found all three of the others lounging on the sofas with the TV on. Drake was reading on his tablet while Francis and Prescott spoke in low voices. Their eyes followed me and West as he took me into the kitchen. He gathered up my hair in his fist, brushing it aside so he could place his lips to my neck.

"Go sit with the others whilst I make lunch," he whispered into my skin.

"Will you make me a tea, please?"

He brushed a thumb along my stomach.

"As you wish, my little Scar."

Then West pushed me towards the living room area. I padded over to the sofas, wondering who to sit with. Prescott put his hand out to me, so I chose to sit next to him. He curled his arm around my shoulder and pressed me against his side, kissing the top of my head.

"Okay, little lamb?"

I nodded, unsure of whether to say anything about what happened between me and West. My eyes went to Drake. His indigo ones were narrowed, fixed on my t-shirt. I instinctively pulled it higher on my collarbone and tried not to hiss at the fabric rubbing against the cuts.

259

"What is that?"

The tone of his voice scared the shit out of me. Deadly and cold.

"What's what?"

"Don't be smart, Scarlett."

Prescott looked at me with concern, his eyes falling on where I was clutching my t-shirt over the carving on my skin.

I don't want to show them.

Everything inside me screamed to jump off this sofa and hide in the false safety of West's body. I could hear him moving around the kitchen and knew he'd heard Drake. He wasn't going to protect me from this.

"What are you hiding, sweetness?" Prescott asked, reaching for my hand.

"Don't!"

He gripped my fingers, peeling them away from my t-shirt. Then he tucked his own fingers under the fabric and exposed the word 'war' carved into my skin. For a moment, Prescott didn't react, his blue eyes fixed on the marks. Then he sucked in a breath and his head whipped around to West. The anger in his blue eyes made me attempt to shrink back, but Prescott's arm around my shoulder tightened, keeping me pinned against his side.

My head turned enough to allow me to see West. He stood by the kitchen island, a chopping board full of vegetables set out before him and his fingers clutched around a large knife. The sight of him casually making lunch shouldn't have made me tremble, but West and knives had always brought me a shit ton of trouble.

"Go on," West said, giving Prescott a maniacal smile. "Let's hear it, Pres. You want to have a go at me for what you're going to describe as mutilation. And I'm perfectly willing to listen."

Prescott's mouth pressed into a thin line and he didn't say a word. He didn't have to, as Drake rose to his feet, throwing his tablet down. He moved towards me and Prescott, his indigo eyes almost black with anger. My bottom lip trembled when he leant over me and stared at the word on my collarbone himself. Then his eyes flicked up to West.

"I'm only going to ask this once. What the fuck were you thinking when you decided this was appropriate?"

"She needed a reminder of who she belongs to," came West's explanation. "A permanent one."

I swallowed. It's not as if I stopped him from doing it. But could I have done so if I tried? When it came to West, I didn't think so.

"You carved 'war' into her fucking skin, West."

"You can blame Pres."

"What the fuck? I have nothing to do with this shit," Prescott interjected. "I did not tell you to mutilate our girl."

"What can I say? Your obsession with the horsemen wore off on me."

"Fuck you. I'm not letting you put this shit on me."

"We put up with a lot from you, but this… this…" Drake trailed off.

Without thinking, I reached out and touched Drake's face. His eyes snapped to mine. The harsh breath emitting from his lips when I stroked a thumb across his cheek had me in half a mind to keep my mouth shut.

"It's okay," I whispered. "Don't be mad at him."

Who the fuck knew why I was defending West's actions. Perhaps it was the way he'd cared for me afterwards. And he had made me come three times today.

Drake's eyes narrowed.

"What did you just say?"

"I don't want you all to fight over this."

He straightened, forcing me to drop my hand from his face.

"Are you seriously defending him after everything he's done to you?"

He pointed at the cuts on my collarbone. Prescott released my t-shirt, allowing it to settle back over them. I winced but kept staring up at Drake and his cold expression.

"No, but what is the point in arguing? It's not going to change anything. I'm the one who has to live with it, not you."

I don't think Drake liked me speaking back to him. His jaw ticked and his hands curled into fists at his sides as if he was holding back from grabbing hold of me to teach me another one of his lessons. Pretty sure I'd had enough fucking lessons today after I'd been scarred for life by a psycho who was more than a little obsessed with me.

"We'll discuss this later," was all he said before he walked back to the sofa and sat down.

I had a feeling I would not be included in any discussions the four of them had about what West had done. Not wanting to earn myself another punishment, I kept my mouth shut and curled into Prescott instead, wrapping my arm around him. He rested his head on mine.

"Do you want me to punch him for you, little lamb?" he whispered.

"Who? West or Drake?" I whispered back.

He snorted.

"Both?"

I shook my head and buried my face in his chest, wincing at the movement of my shoulder. It pulled on the cuts. I was going to have to deal with this while it healed.

"No, just hold me."

He kissed my hair and didn't say any more. I was tired and it was barely the afternoon. My father hadn't tried to call me back last night. I hadn't heard from him yet today either. No doubt it was only a matter of time before he got hold of me. And to be honest, I dreaded that far more than anything these four could do to me.

While I didn't know how I felt about West's actions, I did know he would protect me. He'd told me so. And if he ever found out about what my father had done to me, I was pretty sure he would make good on his promise to kill whoever had hurt me.

Did I want my parents dead for what they'd done to me?

It was a question I had no answer to.

No answer at all.

TWENTY NINE

PRESCOTT

I couldn't remember the last time I'd seen Drake this pissed. He paced the room like an angry dragon waiting to strike. His nostrils flared and his fists were balled at his sides. West had done a lot of shit in the years we'd known each other, but apparently, this was a step too far for Drake. And to be honest, I was kind of unhappy about it too. West had never learnt the art of restraint.

Scarlett had been forced to go back to my room by Drake. She'd glared at him behind his back before she'd left with me. I'd had to lock the door under his orders to prevent her from coming out, but not before I'd kissed her thoroughly and told her it would be okay. Scarlett had this look in her eyes like she didn't believe me, but I'd be back for her. I would take care of my girl.

"Of all the fucking things you could do to her, West, of all the fucking things," Drake ground out, not stilling in his pacing.

West didn't say a word. He merely sat on the kitchen island with his legs wide and his hands dangling between them as he lent on his thighs with his elbows. The lunch between the five of us had been stilted and silent, the tension in the air ripe with anger. The only person who'd kept his mouth shut about the whole thing was Francis. I had no fucking clue what he thought with his blank expression. It wasn't like him. Usually, he'd be the first one to be giving West hell. The two of them were at each other's throats more often than not.

"I tell you I'm suspicious of that cunt hurting her and this is what you do in response? You brand her? Fuck. I don't know what to do with you any longer."

West's mouth twitched but he kept staring at Drake without a single hint of emotion in his expression. It meant he was in one of his moods. The kind where he could snap at the drop of a hat and things could get bloody.

"You didn't ask her how she felt about it," I put in, waving my hand at Drake.

His head whipped around, the glare he sent my way utterly chilling.

"Are you excusing his behaviour?"

"Fuck no. I'm just saying… shouldn't we ask her? Like she said, she's the one who has to live with it."

I didn't want to get into an argument over the whole thing. Sure, I could deck West, but would it actually help matters? No. It would merely increase tensions between us. All of us were already on edge after being in the war room and Drake finding Scarlett talking to Stuart last night. I wanted to ask her, but I wouldn't. I might trust Scarlett with my heart. It didn't mean I trusted her to tell me the truth about her home life

266

before she came back to us. Not when she was clearly under Stuart's control.

"This isn't about her. It's about him." Drake pointed at West. "You need to rein it the fuck in, West. We are already walking on thin ice. How is she going to cover that up, huh? Did you think about that?"

"You should know he's not some mindless animal," Francis said. "Everything he does is deliberate."

It was the first time he'd spoken since Scarlett had come downstairs for lunch with West earlier. The guy sat on the sofa with his arms crossed over his chest, his grey eyes narrowing on Drake. West eyed the back of Francis' head, suspicion flitting across his features.

"Now you're defending him. What the fuck is this?"

"This isn't me defending shit, Drake. I'm saying you're asking the wrong questions. Why don't you ask West what happened between him and Scarlett when we were teenagers? Might give you a better idea of why he felt the need to carve himself into her skin."

Drake stilled, his eyes going to West.

"What's that supposed to mean?"

Francis stood up and dug his hands in his pockets.

"I think it's time someone came clean, then the rest of you might stop hating on me for that night."

He walked over to the windows and stared out at the city with his back to the rest of us. West's eyes were on Francis. He didn't look annoyed but he didn't look happy either. I didn't know what to think. I knew West had a crush on Scarlett when we were kids, but as for something happening between them? It was unexpected.

SARAH BAILEY

"Did she tell you?" West asked, his voice low.

"Yes, some of it, anyway. I kept it a secret this whole time so you can thank me later," Francis replied without turning around. "She made me promise not to speak of it. I don't want to break her trust. It has to come from you."

West let out a breath, his eyes falling on the floor in front of him. The last time I saw him look defeated was when we discovered who took Scarlett. He opened his mouth and his words came out hushed.

"A week before her accident, Scarlett came over to mine. She was having a hard time dealing with what happened."

I winced. The memory of the events leading up to the night of her accident descending over us like a black fucking cloud.

"She didn't want to be reminded of it, of that day. She wanted a new memory… and she wanted it with me."

West rubbed his chin. The implications of his words were clear, but he continued on anyway.

"We were going to make a go of it, a real relationship, you know. And we were going to tell you all about it, but then…" he trailed off and closed his eyes.

Then the accident happened. Then our lives were changed irrevocably. And nothing was ever the same again.

"The first time she had sex wasn't when I fucked her in my office. It was when we were sixteen. She was mine. She's still mine." He put a hand on his chest. "She'll always be mine but she doesn't remember it. She doesn't remember that night and the promises we made to each other. So be mad at me all you want. I don't care. But you don't get to tell me I did something wrong when she and I have a history you don't know a fucking thing about."

268

Francis turned around then. West raised his head and they shared a look of understanding between them. Something about it told me West was still holding a few things back, but Francis wasn't going to make him tell us the rest. Wasn't going to force him to confess his other secrets.

"I told her because of your relationship," Francis said. "She deserved to know what her boyfriend was up to on her behalf. What we'd all decided to do."

West jumped off the kitchen counter and shoved his hands in his pockets. His eyes narrowed.

"I know, Frankie, but it doesn't mean I forgive you for it."

Then he walked away towards the stairs without even sparing me and Drake a glance. I'd known West had feelings for Scarlett, but her reciprocating them was something else. West's behaviour over the years started to make more sense in light of his little revelation.

"Well, thanks for the fucking heads up on that shit, Francis," Drake ground out.

"It wasn't my place to tell you. Their relationship is between him and Scarlett, not the rest of us."

I rose to my feet and made my way over to the stairs.

"Where are you going?" Drake asked.

"To be with Scarlett."

I didn't stop to let him ask me anything else. My feet carried me up the stairs and along the hallway. I unlocked my bedroom door, walked inside and closed it behind me. Scarlett was sitting on the floor with her legs crossed staring out of the window. I crossed the room, lowered myself to the floor behind her, curled my arms around her waist and held her against my chest.

"Little lamb," I whispered into her hair before resting my chin on her shoulder.

A big part of me felt for West. She didn't know what she'd lost, but he did. And it was clear being around her tortured him way more than any of us had previously thought.

"I don't hate him for doing it," she murmured, her eyes still fixed on the window. "I might not understand West and why he did it, but I don't hate him."

I held her tighter against me, waiting for her to continue. Scarlett wasn't done. I could feel the words she wanted to let out vibrating inside her. Her hand raised and she brushed her fingers over her t-shirt right over where he'd cut her.

"He scares me, but as he keeps telling me I like the fear. I like how it makes me feel inside." She turned her head to look at me. "The first night we were together you said you wanted to chase me, catch me and fuck me in the dirt… do you still want that?"

My fingers traced a line across her stomach. The thought of giving into my primal side with her had me growing hard. I wasn't sure why she'd brought it up when we were talking about West, but I wasn't going to ask or press her.

"Yes."

I captured her hand and brought it to my lips, kissing her fingertips.

"I feel alive when I'm scared, Pres, so chase me, terrify me the way he does," she whispered, staring into my eyes. "I trust you to keep me safe."

I tilted my face closer to hers so our mouths were almost brushing against each other.

"You want me to take you out to the woods and hunt you down? Make you feel the fear?"

"Please."

I kissed her lips, imagining myself running after her. How I'd make her desperate for me. My hand slid down her stomach and cupped her jean-clad pussy. She rocked her hips back into me.

"Didn't West fuck you after he carved into you?" I asked, my words vibrating across her lips.

"He did."

"And yet you're still needy?"

"I'm always needy for you."

I groaned, attacking her mouth again and rubbing her through her shorts. Kissing this woman felt so natural. There was no need for games and rewards. The way we felt about each other surpassed that. She was my world. My fucking sun.

Scarlett turned in my embrace and straddled my legs, wrapping her arms around my neck. Her hazel-green eyes fixed on mine. They bled with her emotions, searing into me. I reached up and stroked her hair from her face before cupping her cheek. My other hand curled around her behind.

"How pissed is Drake over what West did?"

"Pretty pissed."

"And Francis?"

I shrugged.

"I think he understands."

She leant closer, her nose knocking against mine.

"How do you feel?"

I kissed the corner of her mouth.

"West does as he pleases. He always has. Your feelings about it are the only ones that matter to me, little lamb. Only you."

While I wasn't happy about West's actions, learning about his past with Scarlett made me realise there were too many secrets between all of us. There was too much history between us for this to be something we fell out over.

"I don't know how I feel."

"That's okay, sweetness. You're my concern because I love you."

Her eyes softened. I couldn't stop telling her how I felt now it was out in the open. I'd never loved anyone before. Didn't think I was capable of it. Of allowing someone access to my heart. My need to express my feelings was compounded by the fact I didn't know how long it would be until she remembered the past. And when she did, everything could come crashing down around us. I stole these moments between us where our love wasn't tainted by it. Where she didn't question this thing between us. Our relationship. Where the lies and secrets weren't an issue like they would be when she found out the truth.

Her fingers threaded in my hair before she rubbed her nose against mine.

"You're a little bit perfect."

I squeezed her behind.

"Only a little?"

"You're my kind of perfect, Pres."

I lowered my hand from her cheek, brushing my fingertips along her jaw. Then they hovered over the cuts below her collarbone. I didn't want to hurt her by touching them.

"Is it sore?"

"Yes… and he told me no one else is allowed to touch it whilst it's healing except him."

"Sounds like West."

He was one possessive motherfucker when it came to Scarlett. Most people wouldn't understand why he was okay with us touching her but not anyone else. But the five of us were bound for life. It had always been this way between us. Only now it had become more about sexual desire rather than friendship.

"I didn't think he was into the whole horsemen thing like you are."

I smiled.

"Am I still your Pestilence?"

Scarlett ran her teeth over her bottom lip.

"Always."

"And he's your War."

She grinned.

"Yeah, I guess he is."

She kissed me, her nails digging into my scalp. Then Scarlett pushed me down on the floor and rubbed herself against me. I was completely ready to fuck her senseless like I had planned to this morning before West decided to intervene.

Even as I worked her little jean shorts down her legs, I couldn't shake the feeling a storm was coming in the wake of what West had revealed today. And none of us could ever prepare for the fallout.

THIRTY

DRAKE

The weekend had gone by with far too much drama between the five of us. I swear having Scarlett here was creating more tension between the four of us than ever. West and I were not exactly on speaking terms after he'd decided to carve a fucking brand into her skin. I knew I had to get over it, but fuck, she'd received enough scars to last a lifetime. The worst ones were invisible. They were locked within her memories. And I knew I had to stop procrastinating when it came to the issue of her amnesia.

Scarlett hadn't spoken to me all day. She'd brought me coffee and been as silent as a damn mouse, refusing to make eye contact and looking distinctly uncomfortable in my presence. I suppose she was annoyed at my dismissal over her feelings regarding the 'war' issue.

When she approached me after dinner while I sat reading in the living room on the sofa, I narrowed my eyes at her, immediately suspicious of what she wanted. Scarlett sat down next to me, rubbed her fingers over her thighs and gave me a tentative smile. Her nervous habits had never changed. She was always worrying at something with her fingers.

"Um, so... I need to ask you something," she ventured.

I put my tablet on the arm of the chair.

"Go on then."

She glanced over at Prescott who was filling the dishwasher in the kitchen. West had disappeared off somewhere, probably to smoke a joint while Francis had decided he wanted to work out.

"Would it be possible for me to leave early on Thursday?"

I almost outright said no, but I needed to be a little less closed off with Scarlett. She told me she wanted me to talk to her like a normal human being. And she wouldn't have asked without a reason. I intended to find out what it was.

"It entirely depends on why you're asking for time off."

Her eyes went to her lap. It was clear this conversation made her uncomfortable and she didn't want to have it with me.

"My... my dad wants me to go to a game on Thursday and he wants to see me before kick-off. I don't really care about football, but it's my dad and I haven't seen him since I moved."

I desperately tried to keep myself in check knowing she'd spoken to Stuart again today. I wanted to rip that motherfucker a new one and tell her no, she couldn't go under any circumstances. Not when he might be hurting her. Not when she was ours. And not when there was a risk he'd take her back. He'd take her from us again. I couldn't have that. None of us could.

And why the fuck did he even want to see her? Whatever the reason was, it couldn't be good.

"He wants you to go to a football match."

Her eyes flicked up to mine. My tone was flat. I couldn't afford to let on how much this angered me.

"Yeah, sounds crazy but I've never been before."

It hardly surprised me Stuart had kept that part of his life from Scarlett. He'd hidden her from the world for ten years in a place we couldn't get to her. His estate was almost impenetrable. Security everywhere monitoring everything twenty-four-seven. It was a fortress. And we'd only recently found out it was where he'd been keeping her. Before, we'd had no idea where Stuart had hidden our woman.

"Do you want to go?"

She nibbled her bottom lip.

"I guess so. It would be nice to see my parents."

I could tell it was a lie from the way her voice shook.

I glanced at Prescott who was eyeing us with concern. He'd leant up against the counter, seemingly not wanting to interrupt my conversation with her. Who knew if she'd mentioned this to him before she came to me. I doubted it. Scarlett didn't talk about the Carvers with us. The fact she was now meant Stuart had pushed her into this. He clearly wanted information from her. Maybe I should let her go to see what would happen. To see what he might ask her to do.

"It'll be perfectly safe if that's what you're worried about. And he's sending me two tickets. I don't have to go alone."

Now I really was suspicious as fuck.

"He said I should bring Mason, but as I'm not allowed to see him…"

"Francis will go with you."

Prescott's eyes widened and she looked at me like I'd grown two heads.

"What?"

"You'll go with Francis."

There was no way in hell I would send West with her. It would end up in a bloodbath. Prescott would be way too protective over Scarlett. She wouldn't want me with her so I wasn't going to offer. The safest bet was Francis. I trusted him not to fuck anything up. He could keep a cool head. The only person who'd ever managed to rattle my best friend was West. And it was par for the fucking course. West wasn't exactly known for keeping his mouth shut.

"Francis?"

"Yes."

"But—"

"This is not up for debate. If you want to go, he is coming with you."

I could see Prescott wasn't very happy about my decision, but he could fucking deal with it. If he went, he would act far too coupley with her and it would spell disaster for us. Stuart could not find out about their relationship under any circumstances. Not when it would likely antagonise him. Francis was the safe one. He wouldn't act like her fucking boyfriend when they were there.

"You haven't asked him if he wants to go."

"He doesn't have a choice."

"Do you make all of his decisions for him?"

My hand snapped out and gripped her chin, tugging her closer to me. She let out a yelp, her hands landing on my chest to stop herself from toppling into me.

"Do not question me."

Her hands pressed against my chest, trying to push me away from her.

"Let go!"

"No."

She ripped herself out of my grasp and scrambled away from me. At least, she tried. I grabbed a hold of her leg and tugged her right into my lap. I held her arms behind her back to stop her from struggling.

"Get off me!"

"Do you want me to change my mind, Scarlett? Is that it? Because this is only going to end one way if you don't cut it out."

The way she glared at me made my dick thicken. Fuck. Why did she do this to me? The war between us was intoxicating as fuck. I wanted to pin her down on the damn coffee table and give it to her until she was crying and begging for mercy.

"I want you to stop being such a dick to me."

I raised an eyebrow.

"Are you sure you're not acting out because you want my dick?"

A loud snort came from the kitchen but I ignored Prescott. He was better off staying the fuck out of this.

Scarlett's mouth dropped open. Her eyes widened and her body stiffened in my grasp.

"What the fuck did you just say to me?"

"Isn't this how it goes, Scarlett? You act out, I punish you for it, you get wet and I deny you pleasure, hmm?"

"Go fuck yourself, Drake. Literally, just go fuck yourself. I don't want anything from you."

I leant closer.

"Liar."

Before she could say another word, my mouth was against hers, tasting her fucking intoxicating bratty lips. The ones I couldn't get out of my damn head. Scarlett struggled against my grip, trying to turn her face away but I held it between my fingers and kept her still. I forced her to open up to me, needing to taste every inch of her. Fuck, I'd never wanted someone more than her. Never needed a girl so damn fucking much. She tortured me with her words and constant need to disobey me.

Her tongue tangled with mine in a battle of wills as I kissed her deeper, wanting so much fucking more. Then Scarlett bit my lip so hard, she drew blood. I released her mouth, panting. The metallic taste of my own blood only made my dick throb between us. The wild look in her eyes and the heaving of her chest told me she was just as affected.

I licked the blood before spreading it across my teeth and baring them to her. Her nostrils flared then she ripped herself out of my grasp, toppling backwards on the sofa. She was up and scrambling away from me the next second.

"Fuck you!" she screamed before running towards the stairs.

I stood, watching her attempt to get away. There would be nowhere she could hide from me. Absolutely no-fucking-where.

CHAOS

"Well, that went well," Prescott said.

"Stay out of this," I growled as I strode after her.

That girl was not going to get away with this shit. No, I was going to punish her for biting me even though it had only heightened my need for her.

"Get away from me!" she screeched when she looked behind her as she ran up the stairs.

I didn't answer her, my long legs eating up the space between us. She charged down the hallway when she reached the top of the stairs, but I wasn't far behind her. She'd barely got to the first door when I pounced, grabbing hold of her by the waist and hauling her up against my chest. She kicked out and screamed, but I slammed a hand over her mouth.

"You are trying my patience right now, Scarlett," I murmured in her ear. "Severely."

I carried her down the hallway, not caring about the way she struggled against me. Nothing would stop me from having her now. My self-control was in tatters on the floor. My restraint... non-existent. At the end of the hallway, I kicked open the door to our play space. There was no fucking way I was allowing her in my bedroom when she'd misbehaved.

I dropped Scarlett down face first on the bed, my hand planted on her back to keep her in place. My hand went to my tie, tugging it until it loosened before I pulled it off. I took both her hands and coiled the tie around her wrists, knotting it to restrain them behind her back. She pulled at it, trying to get out of my makeshift restraint.

"What the fuck do you think you're doing!"

"You know your actions have consequences with me, Scarlett. Don't act like you're surprised this is happening right now."

My hands went to her skirt, shoving it up until it sat on her hips. I almost fucking died when I realised she wasn't wearing underwear.

"Was this for Pres, huh? You giving him unfettered access to this pussy now?"

She shook her head, still struggling against the bed while I stroked a thumb down her wet slit. This, she couldn't hide from me. The way she wanted it even when she fought against me.

"No! It wasn't for him."

"Then who?"

She turned her face into the covers.

"Why would I tell you?"

I removed my thumb from her slit only to smack her pussy. She cried out from the impact, shifting on the bed.

"I will punish you if you don't."

"West stole them from me earlier. He said I wasn't allowed to wear them at work," she whispered.

I wanted to roll my eyes. What the fuck was West playing at? Didn't matter. One less barrier for me to deal with. I smacked her pussy again for good measure, earning another yelp from her before my hands went to my own clothes. My dick was so hard, it ached and I couldn't help rubbing the tip along her wetness.

"Just so we're clear, this is for me, not you."

And with that, I thrust inside her. Her cry and the way she tried to escape made me smile. I gripped the tie around her wrists and used it as an anchor. There was no build-up. No gentleness. I fucked her with long, intense thrusts, making her squirm on the bed. The only sounds in the air were the wet sucking noises of her pussy around my cock, my body smacking into hers and her cries.

"If you behaved for me, I wouldn't have to punish you, Scarlett. I wouldn't have to keep teaching you these lessons, but you don't seem to want to learn."

No matter how I tried to keep my voice calm and steady, it was strained. I was lost to her sweet pussy and the sensations of her walls clenching around my dick. She wanted to hate me for fucking her, but she couldn't do a damn thing about the pleasure I was giving her. I knew she wouldn't admit how good my dick was making her feel.

"Fuck you, Drake. Just fuck you," she whimpered. "I hate you."

"No, you hate how much you want me."

"Go to hell!"

"Gladly. I'll take you with me so you can burn too, burn in this with me."

She shut up then and took what I was giving her. I leant over her, still punishing her wet pussy with my cock.

"We're toxic for each other," I whispered in her ear. "So fucking toxic, but it doesn't mean I'll let you go. I'm never fucking letting you leave us."

All my pent up lust and rage was coming out in the way I fucked her. In the way I took from her without mercy, not caring if she wanted it or not. Scarlett was a fucking sickness inside me. She'd infected me the moment she walked through the doors of our damn building. The moment I'd laid eyes on her again after ten years. I'd searched for her for so long, built up this image of the girl we'd lost in my mind, and now she was here... I was lost in her defiance, in her fucking attitude, in her everything.

I let out a grunt as I came inside her. It had been way too fast, but I didn't care. This wasn't about pleasure. It was about punishment. I pressed my forehead into her back, trying to hold back from making further noise as my climax washed over me. Fuck she smelt so good. Like cinnamon.

She smiled at me as I deposited a cinnamon roll in her lap from the local shop.

"You are the absolute best, you know that?"

I shrugged, taking a seat next to her and knocked my shoulder into hers.

"I just know what you like, Little Nyx."

Scarlett leant over and pressed her lips to my cheek.

"Don't be modest, you're a sweetheart... but only when no one else is looking."

"Only for you."

My heart fucking hurt as the memory washed over me. I wasn't always like this. I used to be open and free with my emotions. Then, not only was Scarlett ripped away from us, but my family got torn to pieces by my cunt of a father. I hated him for it, utterly despised the man. He could quite frankly burn for all I cared. We'd all be better off he wasn't in the fucking world any longer.

I hated how she'd reminded me of that shit. How when I'd needed her the most she wasn't there. It wasn't Scarlett's fault, but it didn't matter to my heart. Not when she was so mixed up in my pain.

I moved off her so fast, she cried out from my dick pulling from her abused pussy. Shoving it back away in my boxers, I could feel the tendrils of toxicity suffocating me. I couldn't be near her any longer. Couldn't face this shit between us. I didn't stop to untie her, striding out of the room and hating myself for every moment. My feet didn't stop until I was back downstairs. Prescott was standing by the kitchen island with a beer in his hand.

"Go see to her, she needs you," I ground out as I walked under the stairs and tugged open the door to the stairwell.

"Where is she?" he called after me.

"In the playroom."

I didn't stop to hear his reply. I had to get away from everything, from everyone, before I did something I couldn't take back. I'd already fucked up with Scarlett tonight. And I wasn't sure she would forgive me for it, or if our relationship with each other would ever be the same again.

THIRTY ONE

SCARLETT

hat the fuck happened? What the actual fuck literally just happened between me and Drake? I lay there on my front with my legs dangling off the bed, tears running down my cheeks, feeling as though I couldn't get any lower. My arms were trapped behind my back, making it impossible for me to go anywhere. Besides, how could I move after that? After he'd punished me.

A pitiful sob erupted from my lips. I didn't think I could despise him any more than I already did, but I was wrong. He was right about us being toxic. I pushed him into showing me his emotions and he responded with nothing but brutality. Like his true nature was as dark and twisted as West's. At least with West, he let it all hang out there for everyone to see. He wasn't hiding anything. Drake was a solid wall of coldness, but underneath was an inferno waiting to burn you alive. And I had stoked the flames a little too much.

"Little lamb."

Another sob fell from my mouth with his deep voice encompassing me. I could hear him move towards me, and his hands immediately went to the tie around my wrists.

"Pres," I whimpered.

"Shh, I've got you, sweetness."

He unknotted the tie, freeing me, and picked me up off the bed before sitting down with me in his lap. I lost it then, burying my face in his shirt and letting it all out. My muffled cries echoed around the room while Prescott held me to his chest and stroked my hair.

What the hell would I do without him? This man had become everything to me in such a short space of time. My heart was his. Irrevocably. West might have carved his brand into my skin, but Prescott had carved his name on my heart.

"Take me out of here, please. I don't want to be here."

He stood without saying anything and took me out of their playroom. I curled my arms around his neck and rested my head on his shoulder. A door opened behind Prescott. My eyes met West's a moment later as he stepped out. His amber ones narrowed as he took us in. I couldn't contain my tears or my choking breaths.

"What's going on?"

Prescott paused on the way to his room.

"Drake and Scarlett had a fight."

I was glad he did the talking. I was incapable of speech, of explaining what their friend had done to me.

He continued walking, but what I didn't expect was for West to follow.

"A fight?"

"Mmm."

Prescott opened his door, carrying me into his room. He didn't close it behind him, striding over to his bathroom. He set me down on the sink counter, but I wouldn't let go of him. West came with us and leant against the doorframe.

"Shh, little lamb, let me clean you up, okay?"

I shook my head, keeping my arms wrapped around his neck so he couldn't go anywhere. My legs locked around his waist. If Prescott let me go, I would disintegrate. I was barely holding it together as it was.

"What the fuck happened?"

Prescott turned his head towards West.

"Can you get Francis to go after Drake?"

"Not until you tell me what the fuck this is about."

Prescott kissed my hair and held me, stroking my back. I was still crying. I couldn't stop.

"Just text him, please. I don't know what went on in the playroom between her and Drake, okay?"

My eyes were on West even as I held Prescott to me. His eyes were narrowed while he pulled out his phone and fiddled with it before slipping it back in his pocket. Shoving off the door, he stepped towards us. His hand came up and buried in my hair, pulling me from Prescott's neck. West stared down at me with an unreadable expression on his face. Then he pressed his forehead to mine. I let out another sob, wondering how and when things had changed between me and him. Had him marking me been a turning point? I had no fucking clue.

"What did Drake do, my little Scar?"

"He punished me," I hiccupped.

"How and why?"

I didn't know how to answer him. How to begin to explain the escalation between Drake and me until it reached boiling point. Until we clashed in a mess of unwanted feelings and emotions towards each other.

"My dad wants me to go to a game on Thursday and… and I didn't like the fact he told me Frankie would go with me without even consulting him first. It got out of control and… and he… he…"

"He did what?"

My body shook with the memory of Drake pinning me to the bed, restraining my wrists and fucking me. I hated him for the way it made me feel. For how scared I was of him and how that fear made me wet. And most of all, I hated how he'd used sex as a way to punish me for fighting him. He used something so intimate rather than the pain of his palms or his belt. I would have infinitely preferred that to what he'd actually done to me.

"He fucked me to punish me… to hurt me for talking back to him," I whispered, choking out the words because they fucking broke something inside me. "And I hate myself for it. No matter how much I want to hate him, I can't. I fucking can't. My heart won't let me. It won't let me hate any of you, and I don't understand why."

West said nothing, but I could see my words affected him by the way his eyes darkened. And I knew they affected Prescott, as his arms around me tightened. West pulled away and looked at Prescott over the top of my head. They shared a silent conversation between them for a long moment.

"Undress her," West said before shoving off the counter and moving towards the shower.

CHAOS

My hands around Prescott's neck loosened as he released me and straightened. West flipped the shower on before stepping out, his hands going to his t-shirt. I watched him strip out of his clothes. Prescott's hands were at my blouse, unbuttoning it and tugging it off my shoulders. He unhooked my bra, chucking it away too. Then he helped me off the counter, unzipped my skirt and tugged it down my legs, leaving me bare.

I didn't ask what was happening when West took my hand and pulled me into Prescott's shower with him. The hot water streamed over us instantly. West turned me around and pressed my back against his chest. His body was warm and calmed the war raging inside me a fraction. My eyes went to Prescott who'd started to strip too. West rubbed my arms and pressed kisses to my shoulder. It didn't take long for Prescott to join us, stepping up to my front and picking up my shower gel. West shifted back slightly while Prescott lathered up his hands. Then they were on me, dusting over my skin as he washed me.

The next thing I knew, West's hands were in my hair, applying shampoo to it with a gentle touch as he massaged my wet strands. I didn't know what to do or say. The two of them were taking care of me without having been asked. All of their touches were soft as if they knew I needed soothing.

As West tipped my head back to rinse it, Prescott's hands curled around my face and he leant down to kiss me. His kisses were comforting. The whole experience was. And I ended up crying in his mouth. I knew Prescott could be caring, but I had no idea West was capable of such things until he washed my hair with such reverence. It made my chest ache. Nothing about this was sexual, despite the fact we were all naked in the hot water with our bodies pressed together.

"My little lamb," Prescott whispered against my lips. "My precious little lamb."

I curled my hands around his waist, his wet skin feeling soft against the pads of my fingertips. West's hands roamed down my back, stroking along the wet strands of my hair. I sighed in Prescott's mouth. Their touch was my healing balm.

West pulled me out of the stream of the water to apply conditioner to my hair next. I reached out and grabbed Prescott's shower gel. He raised an eyebrow as I squirted it on my hands before rubbing them over his torso.

"Let me," I murmured over the sound of the shower running.

He didn't stop me from washing him in return. Being able to focus on his body helped stop my thoughts from running at a million miles an hour. My hands ran over his biceps and the taut muscles of his stomach. He watched me the entire time, his blue eyes full of emotion.

When I moved him to rinse off, he gripped my chin between his fingers, tipping my face up towards him.

"I love you, sweetness."

Prescott didn't leave me in any doubt of his feelings when we were alone, unlike certain other people in this household. I hadn't expected him to say it in front of West. My heart swelled. I went up on my tiptoes and pressed my body to his, wrapping my arms around his neck.

"Me too," I whispered into his skin.

Then I let him go and turned around. West pulled me to him and ran his fingers through my hair, tipping it back under the spray to rinse off the conditioner. My fingers itched to touch him. To wash him the way I had Prescott. Did I ask him if I could or did I just do it? The intimacy of the moment made me bold. My hand went to the gel again, and I lathered it up in my hands. I placed them against his chest. It reminded me of the night they'd given me drugs, and I'd wanted to touch him all over. If I was honest, I'd wanted to explore his body for longer than I cared to admit.

A low rumble erupted from West's chest as I washed him. It vibrated through me, making me want to open up to him, even though I knew he was fucking crazy. His spirit was twisted, but something about it intoxicated me. His nature called to mine. Made me want to stay with him in the abyss, no matter how many times he hurt me.

His fingers went to my shoulder, stroking over the cuts he'd made. I hissed in response, making him smile at me in a maddening way. It hurt. He knew it. He didn't care. And right then, I wanted it to hurt. I wanted to bleed out all over the place, to feel something other than the abject misery Drake had brought on.

West traced the word war with his fingertip, reminding me I belonged to him. And for some crazy fucked up reason, I wanted it to be true. I needed to be his.

"You're an addiction, Scar. One none of us can escape," he murmured as he leant closer. "My curse and my addiction."

He nibbled my jaw before biting down on my earlobe, making me arch into his body.

"I'll never be free of you."

His words had a deeper meaning I didn't understand. The soft agony in his voice made me ache. My hands curled around his back, running up his skin to keep him close to me.

If I was his curse, he was mine too. All of them were. I was bound by my word to my father to destroy them, and yet, I didn't want to hurt them.

"Don't leave me tonight," I whispered. "Please."

West didn't respond. He pulled out of my embrace and finished rinsing the conditioner from my hair. Then he turned off the shower and pushed me towards Prescott, who took me out of the shower and bundled me up in a soft towel. I let him dry me off and seat me on the sink counter. My eyes roamed over the two men drying their bodies in front of me before they both pulled underwear on. The way they were so casual about being nude together, like it was no big deal, made me smile. Even if they hadn't shared me in bed, it was clear they had a very close-knit friendship with each other. It didn't stop their volatility, but I'd come to realise it was their nature.

Prescott picked up my hairdryer I'd left on his counter yesterday morning. I didn't stop him from helping me dry my hair. He'd watched me do it enough times now. Then he picked up my toothbrush, squirting toothpaste on it before handing it to me. When I was done brushing my teeth, he plucked me off the counter and carried me into the bedroom. West followed, pulling back the covers when we reached the bed. Prescott laid me down in the middle, giving me a smile as he stroked my hair back from my face.

"You should get some sleep, sweetness."

"Are you coming to bed?"

He nodded.

"Give me a few minutes, okay?"

Prescott didn't wait for my response, pulling the covers over my naked body and tucking me in. He turned on one of the bedside lamps before clapping to turn out the main lights.

"I'm going to check on the others," he murmured to West as he passed by him to grab his dressing gown.

Prescott shrugged it on and disappeared from the room. West stood watching me for a long moment. He stepped towards the bed, knelt on the end and crawled over me, planting one of his hands by my head while the other he laid between my breasts.

"Do you love Pres?"

There was no emotion in his eyes, but his question made me tense underneath him. If I lied to West, I didn't think it would go well for me. And after the shit with Drake, I didn't want to cause any further problems.

"Yes."

West licked his bottom lip and shook his head a little before he smiled. His hand left my chest. He curled it around the covers next to me and pulled them back. He flopped down beside me, tugging them over himself before he cupped one of my breasts in a possessive manner and buried his face in my neck. I didn't know what to make of his reaction, nor the fact he'd laid down next to me.

"What are you doing?" I whispered, even as my fingers entwined with his on my chest.

"Staying like you asked me to."

For a moment I was absolutely stumped. What would Prescott say when he came back and found West in his bed with me?

"Is Pres going to be okay with that?"

"Don't care either way."

I couldn't help smiling.

Typical West, not giving a shit what other people think.

"West?"

"Mmm?"

"Are you ever going to kiss me?"

His breath dusted across my neck.

"No."

I wanted to ask him what his aversion to kissing was. West clearly had demons I wasn't privy to, but it struck me as odd when the others did it.

"What about if I kissed you?"

West's whole body tensed at my words. His fingers tightened around my breast, squeezing my fingers between his.

"Stop pressing the issue, Scar. It's non-negotiable. I don't kiss. Deal with it."

I didn't get to respond as Prescott came back into the room, shutting the door behind him. He didn't comment as he went back into the bathroom. A few minutes later, he came out with two piles of clothes in his hands. He set them on his armchair before getting into bed on the other side to me from West. He turned out the light and pressed a kiss to my forehead before curling an arm around my waist and laying his head next to mine.

"I told you to get some sleep, little lamb."

His fingers stroked my skin, encouraging me to drift off. Clearly, he wasn't perturbed by West being in his bed. I allowed myself to relax against the two of them. And I fell asleep wondering if Drake was okay after what happened between us, even though I shouldn't give a shit about him at all.

THIRTY TWO

FRANCIS

I didn't think I would be happy to be attending a fucking football match today, but after all the shit between Drake and Scarlett, I was glad to be out of the damn building. The aftermath of Drake's loss of control had been messy. I'd found him on the roof, pacing and dragging his hands through his hair. It took me half an hour to convince him to come back downstairs. He'd gone on and on about how he'd totally fucked up, and Scarlett would never forgive him for going too far. If he just apologised to her, things would likely blow over, but I let him work out his feelings until he'd calmed down.

Over the next couple of days, Scarlett refused to go near him and only communicated with him through email. After his whole guilt rant about the situation, it didn't come as a surprise when he acquiesced to her desire not to be around him. He had even taken to making his own coffee, something I'd taken the piss out of him for. Not that he'd been very impressed. Tonya offered to make it, but Drake told her it was none of her business and she should stick to doing the job he paid her for. I had a feeling that after she'd given Scarlett a hard time, Drake was less inclined to be nice to his step-cousin.

Speaking of Tonya, she was getting on my last fucking nerve. She'd had the audacity to ask me about Scarlett and her relationship with us. I'd politely told her our personal lives had nothing to do with work. Not sure she liked my answer, judging by the way she'd started giving me attitude for the rest of the week.

So yeah, I was glad to be away from the fucking drama, even if it meant I had to see the man who'd taken our girl from us.

I pulled up in the car park near the stadium and turned off the engine. Scarlett and I had changed into smart casual clothes for this little outing. She rubbed her fingers along her black jeans, telling me she was nervous. I reached over and stroked her cheek, making her turn her face towards me.

"We don't have to go. I can take you somewhere else instead."

She gave me a tentative smile.

"I promised my dad."

I didn't give a single fuck about watching the game. It hardly interested me. I was here for Scarlett's protection. To make sure Stuart didn't try to take her back. Drake was suspicious about what Stuart wanted and so was I. The fucker wouldn't ask to see Scarlett unless it was for a good reason. And no doubt one we wouldn't be privy to. I was under orders to allow this to play out unless he tried to take Scarlett. Then all bets were off.

CHAOS

I didn't care if Stuart would be unhappy about me showing up with her. There was no way we would have ever let her go with Mason. He needed to stay away from her. And he had so far, but it didn't mean any of us trusted it would remain that way. Mason was a sneaky little fuck.

"Come here."

My hand curled around Scarlett's jaw. I drew her closer, wanting to reassure her everything would be okay. She'd told me I was her safe place. I intended to keep being it for her as long as I could. She'd felt the same way when we were younger. Scarlett always came to me when she was afraid or hurting. Likely why she'd told me about her and West's relationship. She didn't tell me she'd slept with him, only they were making a go of being a couple. Keeping it from Drake and Prescott hadn't been easy, but I didn't want to betray Scarlett's confidence even after she disappeared.

Scarlett's hand landed on my chest right before I captured her mouth. A low moan sounded in her throat when my tongue met hers. She'd braided her hair down her back. I wrapped my fist around it, holding her in place. I didn't want her going anywhere. If anything, I wanted to pull her in my lap, tie her hands to the steering wheel behind her, and fuck her until she screamed.

I shook those thoughts from my head. My imagination kept running away with me every time I got close to her. It urged me to do things to her I'd banned myself from even considering.

I released her, knowing if I kept this up, it wouldn't do me any favours. Scarlett blinked rapidly before her eyes focused on mine. Her fingers curled into the collar of my black shirt. I stroked her face again.

"You make me want things I can't have, Scar," I murmured.

"Like what?"

My hand drifted from her face to her chest, stroking across where her heart lay. I wasn't jealous of her love for Prescott, but I wanted her heart mine too. Fucked up when I hadn't given her my own in return. I was wary of it when she didn't remember us. Besides, trust didn't come easily to me.

I might have grown up in a well-adjusted household with normal parents, but I'd seen the ugliness of the world far too many times, courtesy of my friends. Watching Drake's family get torn apart by his father. Seeing how Prescott was affected by the shit stain that was his absentee father. Not to mention how West's parents had disowned him. Sure, West could be one crazy motherfucker, but they had no excuse for it. You don't abandon your sixteen-year-old kid whose girlfriend was in a tragic accident and subsequently went missing because you can't handle his behaviour resulting from it. They didn't want a son with sociopathic tendencies. Sure, he might have continued living with them until he was eighteen, but they were barely on speaking terms. Now he had nothing to do with them.

Drake, Prescott, West, and I were a family. And we needed the woman who belonged with us to complete it.

Scarlett looked down at my fingers, a frown appearing on her brow.

"I'll tell you later. We should get to the stadium."

I opened the car door and slid out, leaving her staring after me. Waiting while she got herself together, I leant up against the side of the car and shook myself. I had zero intention of telling Scarlett anything, no matter how much I wanted to.

She got out of the car and slammed the door shut before coming around it. I was about to shove off it when she stepped in front of me and ran her hands up my chest. My breath caught at the vulnerability in her eyes.

"You never talk about yourself to me... apart from the rope stuff. I want to know you, Frankie. Why won't you let me in?"

I swallowed. How I wished I could. I'd tell her everything. How much I'd suffered without her. How I'd fucked up and hurt a girl I cared about because I went too far in a sexual game. And how she'd almost died of an overdose, courtesy of West's intervention. It was my fault. I should have paid more attention.

I'm still sorry, Chelsea. I wish I could make it up to you.

Reaching up, I stroked Scarlett's shoulder.

"What do you want to know, Scar?"

"Anything. Like do you have siblings? What's your favourite food? How come you do whatever Drake tells you to?"

I snorted at the last question. Then I removed her hands from my chest and took one of them instead, pulling her away from the car. I locked it and stuffed the keys in my pocket. Scarlett stared up at me as we walked out of the car park.

"I'm an only child. My favourite food is banoffee pie. And Drake is a subject we're not going to discuss tonight. Did you forget you're mad at him?"

"Frankie…"

I sighed and rubbed my cheek.

"I don't do everything he tells me. I've told him to go fuck himself before and I'd do it again. Keeping you safe is an entirely different matter. I don't think you realise how important you are to all of us."

"I don't know why. I'm just a girl."

You're the girl who completed our gang of five as kids. You belong with us.

I leant closer.

"No, you're a rather impressive woman who has captured the attention of the infamous Four Horsemen. I reckon if people knew, they'd be rather envious of your position."

She snorted and batted my arm.

"Shut up."

"It's true."

"Oh yeah? Is that why Tonya hates me so much?"

I shrugged.

"She's her father's least favourite child. Guess she has an inferiority complex and seeing you get what she wants, which is Pres, by the way, has made her mad."

"What?"

Turning to Scarlett, I gave her a wink.

"I said what I said."

While Drake might tolerate his step-uncle, it didn't mean he was unaware of Fletcher's faults. Number one being his eight kids by six different women. Tonya happened to be the result of a one-night stand I was relatively sure Fletch wished had never happened, judging by the way he talked about his daughter and her mother. Getting her a job at our company had been his way of placating Tonya.

"Pres is mine so she can fuck off."

I laughed at the murderous look in Scarlett's eyes at the thought of Prescott being anywhere near Tonya.

"Possessive much?"

She looked up at me, her eyebrows raising.

"I don't know why you're amused. You're mine too. And considering you've seen what I'm capable of, I'd say you better watch yourself, Frankie."

For a moment, I was at a loss for words. My heart hammered in my chest at the fact she'd called me hers. Before I could make an absolute fool of myself by melting before her eyes, I grinned.

"Is that so?"

We reached the stadium, finding queues of fans outside. Scarlett stopped me from walking any further by stepping into my path and putting her hand on my chest.

"Do you have a problem with being mine?"

"No."

"Good."

The next thing I knew, she'd tugged me down towards her and kissed me in front of everyone. I could hear a bunch of cheers in the background and someone shouted, "Get in there, my son." I wanted to roll my eyes, but my mouth was too busy being claimed by Scarlett and her delectable lips.

When she released me, Scarlett's eyes were shining and her mouth was glistening. I swiped my thumb over her bottom lip.

"Was that necessary?" I muttered. "We're getting ogled by a thousand people right now."

"Completely."

"Are we going to have to queue with them?"

She smiled, shook her head before taking my hand again. "Nope."

Scarlett pulled me away from the queuing fans and walked around the building until we came to another entrance. When she approached it, she flashed some passes in her hand and we were allowed through. We stopped inside to talk to someone who directed us where to go to see her father.

"VIP treatment?" I asked.

"Sort of. They don't know I'm his kid. Dad likes to keep his private life... private."

More like he didn't want anyone knowing about the nefarious shit he'd done. For him to invite her to a game, it meant something was up. I didn't comment on it, merely let Scarlett lead the way towards the stairs up to the higher floors where Stuart's box and our seats were.

When we reached his box, Scarlett let go of my hand and looked up at me.

"Is it okay if I speak to my parents alone?"

I nodded. She gave me a shy smile as I followed her into the room and stopped just inside the door, slightly off to the side. I watched Scarlett approach a man and a woman by the large windows, looking over the pitch. Stuart Carver was a short, jacked-up man with beady eyes and a bald head. He was wearing a grey suit with a black open-necked shirt. Next to him stood his wife, Phoebe. She had dyed blonde hair, long manicured nails, a face full of makeup and a ridiculously skin-tight black dress on. I tried not to glare at the two of them and kept my hands loose when they tried to curl into fists.

"Scarlett," Stuart boomed, giving her a pat on the back before Phoebe embraced her.

I could feel the tension in the air between the three of them. Scarlett clearly didn't want to be anywhere near them, judging by the fake smile she'd plastered on her face. I wanted to go wrap my arm around her and stake my fucking claim, but I stayed where I was, hating every single moment. Hating the way he casually touched her as they talked in low tones like she was a piece of fucking property. If I could gut the man right now, I would, especially when he turned his eyes my way and gave me a death stare. To piss him off, I smiled at him.

Fuck you, Stuart. Just fuck you.

Yeah, we might have wronged him, but I didn't give a shit. The cunt deserved it. In fact, he deserved everything coming his way. There was no way in hell any of us would give the fucker mercy when we got our hands on him. And we would… eventually. He stole our woman. We weren't the type of men who forgave easily. And Stuart Carver had signed his own death warrant the day he'd taken Scarlett from us.

THIRTY THREE

FRANCIS

R ight before I was ready to storm over there and tear her away, Scarlett said her goodbyes. Stuart leant down to whisper something in her ear. He pressed his hand to hers in a gesture that looked to me like he was passing her something, but I couldn't be sure. I could only see the back of her head, so who the fuck knew what she was thinking.

Let it happen, remember? Just let it happen.

Scarlett turned and gave me a bright smile. It fell a moment later, her eyes fixing on something next to me. I turned my head and found the very last person I wanted to see, who had just walked into the room.

Mason fucking Jones.

Before he could move any further, I put my hand out and placed it on his chest.

"If you go anywhere near her…"

My voice was low, and I let the threat hang in the air. Scarlett looked between us, her eyes full of panic. I wasn't going to make a scene, but hell if I didn't want to see this fucker's face around here, let alone anywhere near my woman.

"Trust me, I'm aware," Mason hissed, brushing my hand off his chest and glaring at me. "I'm not here for her."

"Then who?"

Mason nodded his head towards a group of people standing by the windows. My stomach dropped. Standing in the middle of a group of men and women was one person I never wanted to lay eyes on again. The Met Police Commissioner, Garrett Jones, who definitely had it out for me, Drake, West and Prescott. He also happened to be Mason's father. The biggest reason we couldn't lay a hand on the fucker. You didn't touch the Police Commissioner's son without consequences.

I needed to get the fuck out of this box before he saw me, but I did not want to alarm Scarlett either. Holy fuck, this was bad. Really fucking bad.

"Surprised you came with her, didn't think any of you would dare show your faces around here."

My hand curled into a fist, but I tried to keep my expression blank. It wouldn't do me any favours to lose my shit. Calm under pressure. It's why Drake sent me. And yet, right now, I was full of anxiety for myself and Scarlett.

"You think we'd leave her unprotected?"

Mason snorted.

"She's perfectly safe here."

"If you think that, you're stupider than I thought. She's not safe with any of you."

The evils he sent my way made me smile.

"As if you're any better. I took care of her."

I scoffed.

"Oh yeah? You took care of her so fucking well," I hissed. "No wonder she came running to us when she realised you don't have her best interests at heart."

"Neither do you."

He had not a fucking idea. We were who Scarlett needed, not him. We were hers and she was ours. It was how it had always been and it would remain so. Nothing he or Stuart did would ever tear apart our bond. They couldn't. It was permanent. Didn't matter if she couldn't remember. Scarlett gravitated towards us because she couldn't fucking help herself. None of us could.

"I am who I am, Mason. I don't claim to be nice, unlike you. Drop the act. You're jealous and it shows."

If we weren't in a room full of people, I reckon he would have decked me for that comment. As it was, his nostrils flared and his eyes were almost pitch black.

"She doesn't belong to you."

I reached out a hand towards Scarlett, careful of making any sudden moves. Didn't want to attract the unwanted attention of Mason's father. He was too busy talking to the people he was with.

I didn't give a shit what Drake said about keeping our relationship with Scarlett under wraps. Mason needed to learn his fucking place.

"Doesn't she?"

Scarlett made her way over, giving each of us a tentative smile. The moment she got near, I took a hold of her hand and tugged her against my side. Leaning down, I pressed a kiss to her forehead as I wrapped my arm around her waist.

"Ready to watch the game?" I murmured into her hair. "We should find our seats."

She put a hand to my chest and looked up at me when I pulled away.

"Yes." Her head turned to Mason. "Um… hey, Mase, you okay?"

It was very clear he wasn't judging by the way the vein in his temple started popping as he stared at the two of us.

"I'm fine, Scar. How have you been?"

"Good. Um, Frankie and I need to go. It was nice to see you."

She smiled brightly at him, but I could tell this whole situation was making her nervous. Her body shook next to mine. Mason stepped away from the door, but not before giving me another death glare. I gave him a wink, then tugged Scarlett out of the box. I glanced back and found not only Mason but also Stuart giving me daggers. I'd probably royally fucked up by making it clear Scarlett was mine, but I didn't give a shit.

Drake is going to kill me.

When we were out of earshot, Scarlett looked up at me.

"What was that about?"

I tugged her towards the doors leading out to the stands where our seats were.

"What was what about?"

"You and Mason."

I shrugged as we walked down to our row. We shifted along it and took our seats, Scarlett having quickly checked our passes. She tucked her bag under the seat and sat back, her eyes falling on the pitch where the footballers were making their way out. I put my hand on her thigh, stroking my fingers along her jeans. Touching her soothed me a fraction. I was still riled up from Mason and the fact I'd seen his father and Stuart.

"It's nothing, Scar."

"If you call male posturing, nothing."

Clearly, she wasn't inclined to let this go.

"You think I'm going to be nice to a man who hurt you?"

Her eyes met mine.

"Well, no, but I don't think this is just about that."

Leaning closer, I captured her chin between my fingers with my free hand.

"You're mine. He thinks otherwise."

Her eyebrow shot up.

"What?"

My eyes went to Stuart's box situated above us to the left. The man himself was standing by the windows looking out. His eyes were on me and Scarlett. I could see the irritation in them. No longer giving a fuck about his opinion nor the fact I was likely thoroughly antagonising him, I turned my attention back to Scarlett.

"I don't know if you've noticed, Scar, but he wants more than just friendship from you. And I'll be fucking damned if he touches you again in any capacity."

"You're beginning to sound like West."

I ran my thumb along her bottom lip.

"If I didn't already make it very clear, anyone, and I mean fucking anyone who tries to touch you or hurt you in any way shape or form, I will end them."

Scarlett swallowed. It was lucky no one else was sitting near us because no doubt if they heard me saying something like that, they'd probably think I was a psycho. And they wouldn't exactly be wrong. Not sure all of those normal people out there enjoyed killing and torture the way me and the others did.

"Now you do sound like West," she whispered.

"You're ours, Scar. We protect what's ours."

She reached up and curled her hand around mine.

"I don't think knowing you'll kill for me should turn me on."

My other hand moved higher on her thigh, making her let out a harsh breath.

"How long is this game?"

"Ninety minutes, not including half-time."

"And we have to stay for the whole thing?"

She nodded. I leant even closer and brushed my lips over hers.

"When we get back, I'll deal with your little… issue."

"Frankie…"

"You telling me you don't want me to bury my tongue in your wet pussy and make you scream, my little whore?"

She shuddered, her fingers tightening on my hand.

"You can't say stuff like that," she whimpered. "My parents are like right over there."

"I don't care. If it wasn't considered indecent, I'd bury my face in your pussy right now."

"Oh my god, Francis!"

My fingers brushed over her crotch before I kissed her. I kept my eyes open, staring up at the box. The hatred in Stuart's eyes made me smile in Scarlett's mouth.

CHAOS

Look at me all you want, Stuart, I don't care. You tried to take her away from us, but she's ours. She will always be ours.

If Drake found out about this, no doubt I would get a lecture, but fuck it. I wanted the cunt to know.

When I released her, Scarlett's face was bright red. I smiled as I sat back. My hand went to her thigh again. Scarlett looked around, her eyes frantic. She faltered when she saw Stuart watching us from the box.

"I… I didn't want him to know about us."

"No?"

She turned back to me, her face paling slightly.

"No! You're technically my boss, Frankie. All of you are. What if he thinks you're taking advantage of me?"

I licked my lip.

"I've taken many liberties when it comes to you, Scar. And I'm going to take a whole lot more later."

She scowled, crossed her arms over her chest and turned away to look at the game. It had already started while I was busy kissing her. I squeezed her thigh, glad she'd not tried to pry my hand off her.

"Are you angry?"

"Maybe."

I couldn't help leaning into her and pressing my face into her hair.

"I'm sorry."

"No, you're not."

"I'll make it up to you."

She ran her teeth over her bottom lip.

"I know you will."

"Is that right?"

She turned her head slightly towards mine.

"Yeah, it is. I've soaked my knickers and it's all your fault. So you better make good on your threat to bury your face between my legs."

"Trust me, I plan on more than that, my little whore."

She shivered but didn't respond. I turned my attention to the game we were meant to be watching. A bunch of men running around a pitch kicking a ball was not my idea of a good evening out, but it couldn't be helped. At least I was here with Scarlett. And I could tease her all I wanted until she was squirming in her seat. I fully intended to make good on my threats.

Maybe I'd turned all my attention on her after seeing people I despised had rattled me. A part of me just wanted her too. To prove to her I could give her as much as the others did. I didn't want to be complacent. And Drake fucking up so badly with Scarlett made me realise we had to be better to her. We needed to take care of our girl.

"You think any of them are attractive?" I asked, pointing down at the players.

Scarlett narrowed her eyes.

"Why?"

"Just asking."

She made a show of looking down at the pitch. I wasn't fishing for compliments, merely interested in how she would respond.

"I prefer my men to be a little more... sophisticated."

"Oh?"

She sat back and gave me a wicked smile.

"They're not bad looking, but a well-dressed man does it for me."

I knew what she was doing, trying to pay me back for asking. I decided to humour her.

"I see. And do you have any examples of such men?"

My fingers dipped to her inner thigh.

"Yeah, I do."

"Care to share?"

"You... you're far more interesting than this lot." She waved at the pitch. "But you already knew that."

I squeezed her thigh.

"I want to take you home."

She blushed again.

"I wish you could."

Fuck this game. Fuck being here. I had to be patient and wait. Soon, I could reap my damn reward. And it would be this woman naked, tied to my bed with nowhere else to go.

Just the way I liked her.

THIRTY FOUR

SCARLETT

The ninety-minute game went on for way too long. By the time it was done, I was ready to get out of there. Not to mention after Francis had outed our relationship to my dad, I wanted to avoid saying goodbye to my parents. Didn't matter anyway. Dad had told me what he wanted. Told me what I was expected to do. And I wasn't looking forward to it.

As we hadn't eaten, Francis took me to dinner. He spent the entire meal sending me lust-filled looks and playing footsie under the table. Well, he was rubbing my leg with his foot the whole time as if he couldn't stop touching me. Or perhaps he was teasing me on purpose. Either way, I was ready to get back home and get naked with him.

After he parked up, we walked into the lift together. I stood next to him, reminded of the first time I'd stepped into Fortuity. I'd been in this very lift with Francis. Glancing at him, I couldn't help smiling.

"What?" he asked, his silver-grey eyes dark with desire and a hint of curiosity.

"Just thinking about the first day I was here. When I met you."

He smirked.

"Oh yeah, when you wanted to kiss me."

I could feel my face growing hot. He turned to me, digging his hand in his pocket. The other he brushed across his mouth. I took a step back as he stepped towards me. Soon I was backed up against the mirrored wall with Francis staring down at me. He placed a hand above my head and leant closer.

"Going somewhere, Scar?"

I shook my head.

"Good."

He took my chin between his fingers and kissed me. My lips parted, allowing his tongue to delve between them. I whimpered when it curled with mine. My fingers speared into his hair, dragging him closer so his body was flush with mine. I was practically throbbing between my legs, desperate for the feel of him against me.

"Frankie," I gasped when he kissed down my neck.

His hand dropped from the wall and curled around my behind, pressing me ever closer. I couldn't stop myself from grinding my body into his. The past couple of hours of being close to him after he'd told me he was going to eat my pussy had been torture. I wanted his tongue on me.

"Please."

"My needy little whore."

I shuddered, feeling hot all over. My desire suffocated me. I dragged my fingers down his neck, curling them into the collar of his shirt before rolling my hips into his. His cock dug into my stomach. I wanted it in me. I wanted him on top of me. I wanted to be at Francis' mercy. And for him to have none for me.

"I want you so fucking bad."

The words left my lips in a high-pitched breathy voice full of unrepressed desire.

"My tongue or my dick?"

"Both."

"So greedy."

He grazed his teeth along my throat. I didn't care if it was. If I didn't have him soon, I would lose my damn mind.

The lift doors opened. We'd reached the penthouse. Francis pulled back only to pick me up. I wrapped my legs around him as he carried me out. My eyes were on his, utterly engrossed by the way his silver eyes glinted with deviancy and mischief. As we reached the stairs, my eyes flicked to the three people standing near the kitchen watching us. It looked like Drake was about to say something but Prescott slapped his chest, signalling for him to keep quiet.

Honestly, I was grateful. If he made us stop to chat, I would have thrown something at his head. Probably my trainer. The man would be pussy-blocking me. And if he ever wanted to earn my forgiveness, preventing me from getting cock from Francis would not be the way to go about it.

My attention went back to the man himself. My fingers went to his dark brown hair again, stroking through the soft strands. He hadn't gelled it tonight. I loved the way it felt against my skin.

"I could stare at you all day," I whispered as he took me down the hallway after reaching the top of the stairs.

"I already told you I'm going to feast on your pussy, there's no need to butter me up."

"I wasn't."

He cocked a brow.

"No? You really find me that attractive?"

Francis entered his bedroom, not bothering to shut the door and brought me over to his bed.

"Yeah, I really do."

He set me down and licked his lip.

"Stay."

As if I would be going anywhere. I needed this man too much to leave.

He took my bag from me, carrying it over to his bedside table before setting it down. He emptied his pockets out too. The next thing he did was open a drawer and pulled a few things out, dumping them on the bed next to me. He kicked off his shoes and padded back around to me. I watched him kneel on the floor in between my legs and take hold of my foot. He unlaced my black trainers and pulled them off along with my socks. The anticipation was absolutely killing me by the time he undid my jeans and tugged those off, along with my drenched knickers.

His big palms spread my legs wider as his head lowered and he kissed his way up my inner thigh.

"Frankie," I whimpered as his tongue met my slit.

"Don't worry, little whore, I'll take very good care of your pretty pussy."

CHAOS

His hand slid up my chest and he pushed me back on the bed, pinning me there. Why did I like him calling me that so much? It only made me throb harder. Then his tongue was on my clit and I couldn't fucking breathe any longer. I put my hand over my eyes and tried to suck in air while Francis sucked my clit into his mouth and slid his fingers into my empty pussy.

"Oh god," I whispered, my fingers curling into the sheets.

He was making good on his threat, and I couldn't get enough. My hips bucked into his face with the thrust of his fingers. There was no doubt about it. Francis knew his way around pussy. I was already close and he'd barely got started. When you'd spent the last couple of hours being teased by the very man who was now between your legs, it wasn't any wonder I was on the verge of exploding. It was too much. All of it. My need. His words. The way he was licking my clit.

"Fuck, Frankie," I cried out, cresting the wave and coming all over his face. I couldn't help myself. He'd mastered the art of seduction and I was a fucking slave to his tongue.

He raised his head as my hand fell away from my eyes. I stared at him. The way his mouth glistened with my cum and the satisfied glint in his grey eyes. Reaching out, he grabbed something from next to me before he pushed both my legs up onto the bed, exposing more of my intimate parts to his gaze.

"I'm not remotely done with you yet," he murmured, flipping the cap of the tube he held.

He bowed his head to me again. I panted when his tongue met my sensitive clit. And again when his wet fingers dipped lower to my back entrance. He circled it a few times. It only made me press myself against him, wanting him to penetrate me. Wanting his fingers inside me any way I could have them.

And when he obliged, pressing one into me, I moaned, my fingers gripping the covers harder.

"You taste so good," he murmured. "I could stay here all night."

His eyes were on me, making this whole thing ten times hotter.

"But I need your cock," I whimpered, desperate for him to fuck me.

The way he chuckled made me tremble, especially when he slid another finger inside me, stretching me out further.

"I'll give my whore whatever she needs."

Francis took his time tonguing my clit while his fingers plunged in and out of me. Then he added a third and I lost it again. By the time I came down, I had to push his head away. My clit couldn't take any more torture. He grinned, pulling his fingers from me and using a tissue to clean them off.

"Sit up against the headboard."

I was slow to obey as he rose to his feet because his hands were at his shirt, unbuttoning it. Crawling backwards, I watched him undress, practically drooling over the man. He was nothing short of a fucking masterpiece. All hard muscle and beautiful edges. The happy trail leading to his hard cock made me want to lick him all over. I wasn't lying. I could stare at Francis all day. Gorgeous didn't cut it. He was perfect.

He crawled onto the bed, picking up the rope he'd left on it as he went. First, he removed my blouse and bra. Then he took my wrists and secured them above my head to one of the metal rings on his wall. When he was satisfied I wasn't going anywhere, he picked me up by my hips so he could sit behind me and placed me in his lap. Taking the bottle of lube, he squirted it into his palm before I could feel him rubbing it all over his cock behind me. He lifted me up again and angled me on his cock. A choked breath escaped my lips when his cock pressed against me. I had been expecting regular sex, but apparently, he had other ideas.

His cock slid into my tight entrance with some resistance no matter how much I tried to relax. He was slow to work it up inside me, giving me ample time to adjust as he held my hip to control the pace. I was at his mercy with the way I was tied to the damn wall.

I let out a long breath when he was seated inside me. The stretch and sensation of him filling me was intense. And I loved everything about it.

"I thought you said you were going to take care of my pussy," I whispered, leaning back into him.

He popped his chin on my shoulder and raised a hand to my breast, stroking my nipple.

"Mmm, does your pretty pussy still need filling? I can get someone to take care of that for you."

Francis started to move inside me, making me moan.

"Really?"

"In case you hadn't noticed, we like to share."

I nodded, shifting in my restraints as he continued to fuck me with shallow thrusts, directing my hip with his free hand. He paused, reaching out to grab his phone. A moment later, he threw it back down and started thrusting again, gripping both my hips. This time it was harder. My pussy throbbed and I clenched around him, making him grunt.

"Fuck, you're so tight," he ground out. "You feel so fucking good. My whore. Mine."

The possessive note to his voice had me whimpering. I'd discovered a whole new side of Francis tonight. He took no prisoners and I couldn't deny I found it incredibly alluring.

My eyes went to the open doorway, my ears pricking up at the sound of footsteps. A moment later, Prescott appeared, his blue eyes widening slightly at the sight in front of him. He leant up against the doorframe and gave us a wicked grin.

"What do we have here?"

"You asked Pres?" I whispered to Francis.

"Did you expect me to ask West?"

"No!"

I wasn't sure I could deal with him right now. Not when I was trussed up with Francis' dick buried in my arse.

"Well then, I know he'll take care of your pussy, isn't that right, Pres?"

Prescott pushed off the doorframe and walked into the room.

"Is that why you asked me up here?"

"Are you complaining?"

His hand went to his shirt, tugging at the buttons.

"Fuck no."

Prescott got naked in record quick time while Francis continued to fuck me from behind. I was squirming in his lap in anticipation of Prescott's cock inside me. He got on the bed and was kneeling between our spread legs seconds later. Prescott gripped my chin and stared down at me.

"My little lamb, is your poor pussy empty?"

I nodded, biting down on my lip. He leant closer, pulling my lip from my teeth before he replaced them with his own. I moaned in his mouth, about ready to combust on the spot.

Before I came here, I would have never thought I'd want two men fucking me at the same time. And yet I was desperate now.

"Please," I cried into his mouth. "Pres, please fuck me."

His chuckle and the soft touch of his fingers along my jaw made me wriggle in my restraints.

"So impatient, sweetness."

"Probably my fault," Francis put in. "I teased her the whole time we were out."

Prescott pulled back and raised his eyebrow.

"Please tell me you did not do that in front of anyone else."

I couldn't see Francis' expression, but judging by the way Prescott's eyes darkened, I figured he hadn't denied it.

"Well, I'm definitely not getting in the middle of you and Drake when you tell him."

"We can talk about it tomorrow. Right now, I think Scar's going to cry if you don't fill her pussy with cock."

Francis wasn't wrong. I wanted both of them and I wasn't ashamed of it.

"I like it when she cries."

Prescott pinched my nipple for good measure, making me whine and arch into him.

"Make her cry on our dicks then."

I watched Prescott take hold of his very hard cock and rub it against my pussy, dragging it through my wet folds.

"Pres, please," I moaned. "Please."

His eyes were dark as he slid inside me, making me cry out from the stretch. A tear leaked out of my eye. It hurt even as it felt good at the same time. I liked the pain of it. The way both of them worked in tandem inside me. Prescott leant closer and licked the tear from my cheek.

"Such a good little lamb. You cry so sweetly."

I couldn't put my hands on him as my arms were secured over my head. All I could do was let them pleasure me. Prescott was taking very good care of my pussy while Francis fucked me from behind. I might not always want this, but right now, it was perfect, especially after Francis teasing the shit out of me all evening. Making me want him so badly, I was breathless with my need. He hadn't hesitated to get Prescott involved when he realised I wanted more. It made my heart tighten. Francis did everything in his power to take care of me. He made me feel… special. Like he really gave a shit about me. It only strengthened my budding feelings for the man. Made me want to explore this thing between us and learn more about him.

"Harder," I panted. "Please, make me come again."

Francis gripped my hips tighter, rocking me on them as Prescott increased the strength behind his thrusts. He pressed his hand against the wall to give him more leverage, grinding into me without mercy. I was lost in them. In the way they fucked me. And when Prescott kissed me, I fell off the edge, my body already over sensitised from Francis' exploration earlier.

"Fuck," Prescott grunted as Francis let out a groan.

They didn't let up as I came all over both their dicks. It was everything I needed and so much more. Both of them followed soon after me, filling me up with their cum and making me twitch around them again.

Prescott was the first to pull out. He loosened the knots around my wrists, allowing me to put my arms down before Francis lifted me off him. Prescott flopped down next to me and stroked my shoulder with his fingers.

"Satisfied, my little lamb?"

I nodded, curling into Francis' side and wrapping my arm around his waist when he shifted lower on the bed. He kissed the top of my head, letting me rest it in the crook of his shoulder.

"Do you want me to stay?"

"If it's okay with Frankie."

Prescott kissed my shoulder and curled himself around my back.

"I don't mind," Francis said, stroking my face with his fingers.

It would make what I had to do once they fell asleep risky as hell, but it couldn't be helped. I wanted them with me. Both of them.

After a few minutes of us being curled up together in silence, I got up and went to the bathroom to clean up un-braid my hair. When I came back, I shut the door, hoping Francis would forget it needed to be locked. Then I curled up under the sheets with the two men who'd rocked my world who both held me close, sandwiching me between them. We made quiet small talk until they drifted off to sleep.

I lay there, staring up at the ceiling, urging my eyes to stay open. They'd exhausted me, but if I was to do what my father asked, I needed to stay awake and try not to hate myself for what I was about to do.

THIRTY FIVE

SCARLETT

S lipping out from Prescott and Francis' arms was a lot
harder than I anticipated. The two of them were
pressed so tightly against me, I was sure I would wake
them up. It was a fucking miracle I wriggled out and dropped
off the end of the bed in relative silence. Straightening, I
looked back at them. They were both fast asleep, their
breathing steady and even.

Thank fuck.

I crept over to the bedside table and fished out what I
needed from my bag. Then I picked up one of their discarded
shirts and slipped it on. It smelt of cinnamon and apples so I
knew it belonged to Francis. Buttoning it up, I forwent
underwear, considering I'd drenched it earlier. If I went
rummaging around in Francis' wardrobe for more clothes, I
would end up waking them.

I slid my feet into my slippers before padding over to the
door and opening it with gentle care. My eyes went back to the

boys in bed but neither of them had moved. I darted out of the bedroom and along the hallway, my feet light on the carpet. When I got to the stairs, I ducked down behind the glass when I noticed a figure standing by the window. I froze in place, hoping he hadn't heard me.

For a minute, he did nothing. Then he let out a sigh and walked towards the stairs. I was about to get up and run when he went under them instead. He opened the door to the stairwell and stepped through, shutting it behind him.

What the hell is Drake doing up at this time and where is he going?

I tucked the memory stick my dad had given me into Francis' shirt pocket before descending the stairs. It probably wasn't a good idea for me to use the lift but Drake was in the stairwell.

Fuck!

This wasn't going to plan at all. I'd have to take a chance. It was my only hope. Not that I wanted to do this, but I was mad enough at Drake to consider doing what my father asked of me... or was I?

He'd fucked up with me, no doubt about that, but my anger had lessened. Especially when he didn't complain about me not wanting to see him at work. In the penthouse, it couldn't entirely be helped, but I avoided being near him as much as I could. The man was a damn menace. Well, I could try telling it to my fucking feelings, but I wasn't talking to them. They kept betraying me.

I steeled myself, trying to hold on to my annoyance at his actions. At the way he'd used and punished me. I wanted to hate him so fucking bad, but a part of me wondered why. What possessed him to take it so far? Our relationship had soured before it had even started. I wanted him to talk to me, yet all I'd done was push his buttons and piss him off. Not a great start. But it didn't mean I would let him off the hook. Nor would I allow him a fucking inch. He would take a damn mile if I did.

I walked underneath the stairs and opened the stairwell door slowly. There were no sounds of footsteps so he must've already left. Creeping into it, I shivered. Sneaking around their building in just a shirt and slippers wasn't my best plan, but I had little choice. It was now or never. I wouldn't get another chance. They were careful about locking the doors behind them at night. My distraction tactic had worked. Didn't mean I felt any less shit about doing it.

Sighing, I descended the stairs to the floor below the penthouse and pushed open the door. I crept out into the lobby and along the hallway towards Drake's office.

Please don't be down here.

There were no lights on anywhere so I could only hope he'd gone somewhere else. When I reached his office, I pushed the door open and found it empty. Breathing out a sigh of relief, I walked in and went right over to his desk. It felt odd to sit in his chair. I'd sat in his lap in it before. All it did was remind me of the way he'd punished me in here. My cheeks heated. I pressed my fingers to them.

Now wasn't the time to be thinking about it. I dragged the chair closer to his desk and moved the mouse. The screen lit up. By some kind of miracle, it wasn't locked. I sat back, staring in disbelief. I thought I might have to break into the system, but no, it was wide open for me.

Sickness coiled in my stomach as I took the memory stick out of the shirt pocket I'd stashed it in and placed it on the glass desk in front of me. This was huge for me. It would be declaring war on the Horsemen. At least, that's what it felt like. If I went through with this, I would be giving my father access to data he should never see. Access to things to help us bring them down.

What do you want to do? Do you really want to hurt them this much?

I shook my head, trying to stop my conscience from rearing its ugly head. It did it anyway. How could I do this without solid irrefutable proof they'd done what my father said they had? No one had proof. It was all conjecture and fucking theories. The truth was tangled up in the web of lies all of us had weaved together.

I dragged my fingers across the glass remembering the way he'd pinned me down on here. When he'd spanked me and how I'd secretly liked it but would never admit it to him. I didn't hate Drake. No matter what he'd done to me, I wanted to know what went on inside that damn head of his. He was a sickness in me. A toxicity. A desperate, all-consuming desire to tear him wide open and rip out all the secrets he was hiding.

You're fucked up.

Perhaps I was. Maybe I was too far gone to care how low I'd sunk. Christ, I was in love with a man who was lying to me. I was falling for another who had outed my relationship with him to my father. One of them had permanently marked himself on my skin, making me his and I'd let him. And the last… he'd infected me in the worst way possible. They all had.

I put my fists to my eyes and dug them into the sockets before slamming my head against the back of Drake's chair.

No matter how hard I tried to justify all of this to myself, I couldn't. I didn't want to hurt any of them. Not really. But if they'd done what my father kept telling me they had... didn't it make them monsters?

You like monsters. Don't lie to yourself.

Dropping my hands, I groaned and shook myself. I had to stay strong. If I didn't do what my father asked then I would land myself in more shit. But if I did, then I would hurt the men my heart told me I could trust even when my head told me I shouldn't.

Which one did I believe?

Which one did I fucking trust in?

It only took me a second's more thought before I stood and snatched up the memory stick, stuffing it back into my shirt pocket. I couldn't do this. Not to them. Not when I didn't have proof of their crimes. Not when I didn't know the truth.

I set Drake's chair back to the way it had been before I came in here and crept out, shutting the door behind me. Leaning back against it, I tried not to allow myself to fall apart. I'd almost done it. Almost gone ahead with sticking the damn memory stick into Drake's computer to give my father access to everything. But my conscience had won out in the end. It wouldn't allow me to hurt Prescott, West, Francis and Drake.

You're an idiot.

But I was the idiot who'd fallen in love.

I straightened and walked back down the hallway towards the lobby. Entering the stairwell, I paused on the first step. If Drake hadn't come down here, where had he gone? I shouldn't be curious about it, but I was.

No, it doesn't matter. You need to get back to bed.

335

I walked up the stairs and reached the door to the penthouse when I stopped dead. There was a faint sound echoing down the stairwell... music of some kind. Turning my head, I looked up at the stairs. My feet carried me towards them and before I knew it, I was walking up the next two flights of stairs to the roof. The music got louder as I went. It sounded like a guitar, but I couldn't be sure.

When I got to the top, I found the emergency exit door wide open. Did I really walk out there in a shirt and slippers? It would be cold. And yet the sound of music made me want to find the source. I stepped out onto the roof, looking back to find the door had been secured to the wall behind it. In front of me, there was a structure with all sorts of equipment surrounding it. I couldn't see anyone else up here.

The music was louder now. I could recognise it as an acoustic guitar playing. If I turned back, I would never know who was strumming it. The wind blew, giving me goosebumps all over my bare legs. I pulled the shirt lower on my thighs, but it was futile.

Unable to help myself, I skirted around the structure and stopped dead in my tracks. Behind it, there was a rooftop garden. Neat rows of wooden planters sat with flowers and other plants spilling out of them. There was a seating area with a couple of sun loungers, a bench, a small table and a few wooden armchairs. While all of that stuff stuck out to me because I wasn't expecting it, it wasn't what drew my eyes. No, it was the glass structure beyond the planters.

I walked towards it down the middle of the planters. On all four sides, it was glass with a white roof. Two glass sliding doors were open and the music spilt out from there. There was a large grey sofa and two armchairs with a low table. And right in the middle of the room sat in the comfiest armchair I'd ever seen in my life was the man who'd become the bane of my fucking existence since the day he'd landed in it. In his lap sat a black acoustic guitar. His fingers worked over the strings with practised expertise. The melody he played was utterly tragic and haunting.

Drake had his eyes closed, his dark hair flopping over them as he played. I'd never seen him look so... unkempt. His shirt buttons were undone and his sleeves rolled up. His feet were bare. And the backdrop of him against the cityscape under the dark sky with stars twinkling above him was more than I could take. He looked utterly tortured as he played a tune that spoke to my soul. A song of death, terror and loss rang through the notes.

I found myself drawn to him even knowing I shouldn't be here intruding on this moment. I leant against the glass door, watching him play, unable to leave because this was the first time I'd seen Drake display real emotion. He played the guitar like he was purging himself of his feelings. And holy fuck, he was beautiful. A fallen god.

After everything that had happened between us, seeing him this way made my heart burn in my chest. What had hurt him so much to make him like this? Closed off to everything. And then there was this, him all alone up here in the middle of the night, playing like his life depended on it. I didn't know what to make of it or him.

The last note rang through the air, making me freeze in place. If he found me here, I would be in serious shit, but I couldn't move, far too captivated by the sight in front of me.

Drake raised his head and opened his eyes, staring right at me. It's as if he'd known I was there and it hadn't come as a surprise to see me. His lip twitched, making me swallow. For a long moment, he said nothing as his fingers brushed along the strings.

"What are you doing up here, Scarlett?"

He didn't sound annoyed. In fact, his voice was gravelly as if his throat was clogged with too much emotion.

"I don't know," I all but whispered.

He let out a sigh and placed the guitar down next to him, leaning it up against the armchair before he sat back. His long fingers dragged along his face. Those beautiful hands I'd admired from basically day one. Now I knew why his fingertips were calloused. He played an instrument. And it was almost more than I could take.

Drake's eyes were still on me. His gaze made me tremble as I stood there unsure if I should stay or go. Then he reached out a hand to me. I looked at it. It felt like a peace offering. I was hesitant to walk over to him after everything that had gone on between us.

"Will you please come and sit with me?" he asked in a quiet voice.

Drake didn't ask or request. He ordered. And knowing this wasn't a demand made the decision of what to do… easy.

THIRTY SIX

DRAKE

I didn't expect to open my eyes and find Scarlett up here in my safe space. The place I came to when the world was dark and I couldn't sleep. It was far more often than I liked to admit. And I knew exactly what Francis would tell me if I told him the truth. To take my damn sleeping pills and stop acting like I was a fucking impenetrable tower..

I'd felt her when she approached, but I was so lost in the music, I didn't look at her until I'd finished the song. Now she was staring at my outstretched hand like it would physically harm her. I had no intention of doing anything to hurt her tonight. Weariness had sunk into my bones. All I wanted was to hold her against my chest and breathe her in. I wanted to tell her I was sorry for the way I'd behaved. I just plain wanted her near me.

Little wisp, I don't want to fight anymore.

"Scarlett, please."

I sounded so fucking desperate. It was pathetic. I was at her mercy and I hated everything about it. And yet I was too damn tired to stop it happening. Too fucking done with it all.

She took a tentative step towards me, making my heart slam against my ribcage. Another brought her closer. Two more closed the distance. Her hand slid into mine. The coldness of it made me want to warm her up. She must be freezing considering she was only wearing a thin shirt.

Her hazel-green eyes were guarded as she looked down at me. I didn't blame her for being suspicious. I wasn't going to ask her to sit with me again. She knew what I wanted. Whether she would oblige me was up to her. After everything, I had no right to order her into my lap. Besides, my walls were down. I didn't have the energy to keep them up and hide how I felt.

Her thumb rubbed over the back of my hand. I bit the inside of my cheek to stop myself from responding to her touch. Her skin was so fucking soft. She was delicate. A little wisp of a thing who haunted my every waking moment. The girl from my past had come back. The one who had always seen me. And I couldn't deny I wanted her to see me again.

Scarlett didn't say a word as she lowered herself into my lap and curled up against me. She rested her head on my chest, her hand splayed out over my heart and my whole body shook with the effort of trying to remain calm. I wrapped one arm around her while the other stroked her hair, holding her close. Fuck, she was so small. So fucking fragile.

Lowering my face, I pressed a kiss to her forehead.

"I'm sorry," I whispered, my lips dusting over her skin.

She let out a breath and tucked her fingers beneath my shirt where I'd left the buttons open. Her cold hand on my warm skin made me shiver.

"The song you were playing, did you write that?"

Her question was asked so softly like she was afraid to break the silence.

"Yes."

"What made you write something so haunting?"

You. You did.

I couldn't tell her. Admitting she was the source of my torment felt like I'd open up the floodgates. There was too much at stake here. Too many secrets I had to keep. Letting her in right now when things were so precarious wasn't an option. But if I didn't give her something, a small piece of me, I might ruin everything between us for good. We may not come back from it.

"It's the only way I know how to express my feelings."

She peered up at me. Our faces were far too close, but I didn't move back. The intimacy of the moment had me holding my breath, wondering what she would say.

"Is it lonely in your iron fortress?"

Fuck. Me.

"Yes."

How could I say no? The truth was I'd felt alone since the day she was torn away from us. I had the boys, but without her, none of us felt complete. Not to mention how my fucking life imploded because of my piece of shit father. And keeping West from doing something to hurt himself was a whole other mission in itself. His reckless behaviour made him a danger to himself. We were sixteen. No fucking sixteen-year-old should ever have had to deal with the events of that night. What we'd done. It was fucked up on every level imaginable.

"What happened to you, Drake? Why are you so cold?"

Her hand was on my fucking heart. She could feel my warmth seeping out of me. But she was also right. I was cold. I'd buried all of my feelings so deep, I didn't know how to find them again. Scarlett had forced them out into the open and no matter how much I struggled against the tide, I was drowning in them. In her.

My hand left her waist and cupped her face, my thumb running along her cheek. She didn't stop me. Scarlett was waiting for my answer. I leant closer, pressing my forehead to hers. Our lips almost met. We breathed the same fucking air and still, she didn't stop me.

"Something happened to us when we were younger and nothing was ever the same afterwards."

"To us?"

"The four of us. We all have invisible scars."

They're there because of you, Scarlett. Because of what we did.

I didn't think any of us were ever going to be able to make it up to her. And yet, we would keep her all the same. Even if she hated us. Even if she never wanted to see our faces again. We couldn't live without her. We weren't okay. We weren't fucking okay.

Dropping my hand from her face, I stroked my fingers across her shirt where I knew the scars West had given her lay. They weren't her only scars from us. The rest were down to our actions. The things we'd done.

Fuck, I'm sorry. I'm so fucking sorry for what we did to you.

But I wasn't sorry for everything. Some of the things we did that night were necessary. I wouldn't take them back. Not under any circumstances. I wish we hadn't hurt her. Our best friend. The girl who stood by us through thick and thin. Who we protected with our lives.

"But it's not just because of that, is it? Not for you."

I shook my head, hating how she could see right through me. My walls weren't there to protect me from this.

"No, it's not, but I don't want to talk about it."

"It hurts too much."

I nodded against her head, my lips brushing over hers. I hated how much I wanted to kiss her. To show her I wasn't cold. To prove I had emotions. She brought them out in me. She was the key. I wished I could be free to show her affection and care like Prescott and Francis did. But I was way too fucked up and keeping far too many secrets.

She trembled as she held onto me. I was shaking too, but mine was with anger rather than the fear she was experiencing.

"Drake, what… what if you hadn't…"

"Shh, I know, I'm here, Little Nyx. I'm not leaving you, I promise."

If I hadn't been there, fuck knows what would have happened to her. It had gone way too far this time. Way too fucking far. I was done with this shit. We weren't going to stand for it any longer. When I told the others, they would agree with me.

"I can't. I can't do this."

I could feel her tears soaking into my t-shirt, but I didn't care. I'd hold her for as long as it took. I'd be right here for her. Scarlett needed me and the others now more than ever.

When she calmed down, I would go to them. And we would do something about this once and for all. Nothing, and I mean nothing, would stop us from protecting our best friend from any and all threats. And this shit? Well, it was the worst fucking threat of all.

I shuddered at the memory. That horrifying day. The one that had set all this into motion. And then I shut it down, locking it away before it could decimate me all over again.

"Will you play me something else?"

Her question made me pull back slightly, breaking our close contact. Those hazel-green eyes of hers were full of emotions, but she looked tired too. Like staying awake had become a chore.

"If you want me to."

She nodded and tucked her face into my neck while keeping her hand on my chest. I adjusted her in my lap, shifting her legs up onto the arm of the chair so I had room to pop my guitar on my knee. I learnt how to play a long time ago, having begged my parents to buy me one. And I'd taught myself, practising for hours to get it right. It wasn't until Scarlett was ripped from us when I started to write my own melodies. There were never any lyrics, just the music.

I picked my guitar, set it on my knee and fit my arms around it while still having Scarlet plastered to my chest.

"Do you want me to play you a lullaby?"

"Play me something you've never played for anyone else."

I didn't tend to play when others were around, though the other three had heard me. Partly why I had this room and the garden built so I didn't disturb them at night.

"None of my songs are happy."

"You wouldn't be you if they were."

Why the hell did she have to be so damn… perceptive?

"Okay, an unhappy tune it is."

My fingers went to the strings, knowing exactly the song I wanted her to hear. The one I wrote about the day we lost her. Probably fucked up of me to play it to her, but I couldn't think of anything more apt than this.

Playing with her in my lap wasn't exactly easy, but I didn't want her to go anywhere. The fact she was allowing this closeness between us had my heart burning for her. It reminded me far too much of when we were younger. When we were free of all these burdens, secrets and lies.

I hummed along to the tune even though there were no words. And when I felt her tears soaking my skin where she was pressed against it, I tried not to falter. The song made me want to cry too, but I wouldn't. I didn't allow tears. I couldn't afford to.

Slowly, but surely Scarlett's breathing evened out until I was sure she'd fallen asleep. I brought the song to a close and set my guitar down. My eyes went to her face as her head had fallen on my shoulder. I stroked her cheek, wiping away the dried tears there.

"I wish you knew how truly sorry I am for everything, my little wisp."

I pressed a kiss to her forehead then gathered her up in my arms as I got up only to pop her back in the chair. I set about closing up my hideaway, putting my guitar on its stand before I picked her up again and carried her back downstairs. Scarlett didn't stir and for that, I was glad. She needed to rest.

When I got to Francis' room, I found both him and Prescott in his bed. I shook my head and smiled, setting Scarlett down on the end of the bed and unbuttoning the shirt she was wearing. As I did it, I felt something brush against my hand. Digging my fingers into the pocket, I drew out a small memory stick. This was why she was out of bed.

I slid it into my pocket, discarded the shirt and then placed Scarlett between Francis and Prescott, tucking her up under the covers. Making my way over to the door, I closed it behind me.

Was I pissed about the device?

Yes.

Did it mean I was going to say something to her?

No.

I'd asked Francis to allow this evening to play out. It meant seeing if she would go through with whatever her father had tasked her with. Now I'd intercepted it, perhaps I could use it to my advantage. Tomorrow, I'd discuss with Francis what happened at the game. And we would make a plan going forward.

As I walked back to my bedroom, I tried not to remember the way she'd cried in my arms as I played her a song I wrote about her. About the loss of her. The woman was already under my skin in the worst way possible. I loved witnessing the last moments of a person's life drain from their eyes... but my little wisp might well end up being the harbinger of my downfall. She was making me feel for her in ways I never wanted to. And I couldn't bring myself to hate her for any of it.

THIRTY SEVEN

SCARLETT

I was woken up by soft kisses across the back of my neck. A warm hand cupped my breast. Another was curled around my back, stroking my skin. Opening my eyes, I stared into Francis' grey ones. He smiled at me in such a heart-stopping way, my breath caught. Behind me, Prescott was rubbing up against me, making it very clear he wanted playtime before work. After I'd got fucked by both of them last night, I wasn't entirely on board with the idea. Besides, my brain was already running at a million miles an hour.

I sat up, making their hands drop from me.

"Little lamb?"

I looked down at Prescott whose brow had furrowed with concern.

"I need the loo."

Before either of them could say another word, I'd jumped out of the covers and off the bed. I shut the door behind me when I got into the bathroom and sunk down on the side of the bathtub. The memory of finding Drake on the roof last night flooded my brain, making me put a hand to my mouth. The strange intimacy of the whole thing had me in absolute knots. He'd apologised to me. He'd actually talked to me. He wasn't... cold. I didn't know what the hell to think. This side of Drake was unexpected and completely at odds with what I knew of him.

My fingers dropped to my heart, steadily beating in my chest. Why did he have to make me feel something for him other than anger and frustration?

I looked down at my naked body realising not only had he brought me down from the roof after I'd fallen asleep, but he'd undressed me. I'd left the memory stick in Francis' shirt. If I rushed out there and searched the pocket, it would make them suspicious.

I got up and did my business before quickly brushing my teeth. As casually as possible, I strolled back out finding both of them sitting up in bed talking. I went over to our clothes and started picking them up, separating them into piles for each of us. My fingers went to the pocket of Francis' shirt as I turned away from the two men in his bed. And my stomach dropped when I found the device missing. My eyes darted around the floor, but I couldn't see it anywhere.

Fuck. Fuck. This is really bad!

It couldn't have fallen out. I didn't think either Prescott or Francis had even touched these since they'd taken them off. It left me with only one explanation. And it was the absolute worst outcome of all.

"Are you okay, Scar?" Francis asked.

I looked at him, plastering on a smile.

348

"Yeah, I'm good."

His eyes were narrowed, indicating he didn't believe me. I didn't know what else to say as I put his shirt on the pile I'd made at the end of his bed.

"Come here."

"I'm up now, I might as well grab a shower. Not sure my boss would appreciate me coming to work smelling of sex."

We all knew Drake wouldn't give a shit since I hadn't gone near him this entire week. After last night, I didn't think I could avoid him any further.

I dashed back to the bathroom, ignoring the way both of them called my name. I was totally acting weird and now they were suspicious. Hopefully, this fucking shower would calm me down. My heart was racing and my body tense. I flipped it on and stepped under the spray. The water did nothing to help my racing mind.

Drake took it. I know he took it. Fuck. What am I going to do?

He'd rattled me last night when I found him playing the guitar on the roof. Especially the way he'd held me against his chest and looked at me. The sadness in his indigo eyes broke something inside me when he said something happened to all four of them when they were younger. He wouldn't trust me with what, but knowing they'd suffered through something devastating made me feel for the four men. It cemented my decision not to go through with my father's plan. And now I was fucked because Drake had the damn device. I couldn't get rid of it.

I washed my hair and my body, hating the fact I was still on edge. When I came out of the bathroom after drying my hair, I found Francis was alone. He came over to me and put his hands on my shoulders. I tried not to flinch at his expression.

"You're a little jumpy this morning."

Reaching up, I stroked his face and gave him what I hoped was a real smile.

"I'm okay, honestly."

He leant closer, pressing a kiss to my forehead.

"You'd tell me if you weren't, right?"

I nodded even though it was a lie. I wasn't okay at all. How could I be when I might well be getting a talking to by Drake? I should not have fallen asleep in his lap.

Francis let me go and walked around me into the bathroom. I went to the wardrobes and pulled out an outfit before putting it on. Then I did my makeup in front of one of Francis' mirrors before making my way downstairs while he was still in the bathroom.

Prescott was in the kitchen with a mug in his hand. Drake sat on the sofa with his morning coffee and his tablet. I swallowed as I walked into the kitchen, trying to appear normal, but clearly, it wasn't working judging by the way Prescott raised his eyebrows. Making a beeline for him, I wrapped my arms around his waist and stared up into his beautiful blue eyes.

"You feeling better?" he murmured as he stroked my arm.

I went up on my tiptoes and kissed his cheek.

"A little. Just tired is all."

"You can sleep in tomorrow when your boss over there doesn't expect you to be up for work."

I shook my head as I dropped back down to my feet. Even in heels, all of them were taller than me.

I let go of Prescott and walked over to the kettle, flipping it on. After I'd knocked myself up some breakfast and tea, I took it over to the dining table and ate. My eyes kept darting to Drake who hadn't once looked at me. It was almost as if last night didn't happen. But it had. I remembered the music he'd played. The sorrow and pain in it. There was no doubt in my mind Drake was hurting inside, but as to why, I didn't yet know. Would he ever tell me?

By the time I was done, Francis had joined us. West was nowhere to be seen, but I'd learnt he had a habit of not turning up to work at least once or twice a week. I never asked why, just assumed he had his own reasons.

I decided I wasn't going to let Drake pretend like I hadn't found him up on the roof last night. Besides, I wanted to know for sure he'd taken the damn memory stick. The only way I could do that was if I talked to him. Both Francis and Prescott watched me as I walked over to the sofa and stood in front of the stoic man himself.

"Morning."

Drake was slow to look up at me from his tablet. And when he did, I had to stop myself from swallowing. His eyes bore no recognition of what had happened between us last night.

"Hello, Scarlett. Did you want something?"

"I was wondering if you needed me to organise that lunch meeting with Mr Sinclair for next week. I forgot to ask you yesterday."

"Yes. Thursday would be best."

"Okay, great. Consider it done."

I gave him my brightest smile. The way his lip twitched told me everything. He knew that I knew he had the device. I wouldn't say anything as it would give me away. He wasn't going to bring it up either. We were at a fucking impasse yet again. I didn't want to fall back into this hate-lust cycle between the two of us, but this wasn't helping either.

"Since when did Scar start talking to Drake again?" I heard from behind me.

"Fuck knows."

Glancing back, I could see Francis and Prescott with their heads bowed together. They had no idea I'd disappeared for a while last night. I turned back to Drake and leant closer to him, bending at the waist slightly.

"Thank you for putting me to bed last night," I murmured, keeping my voice low. "I appreciated it."

"You're welcome."

"I can't help wondering why you put me in Francis' bed."

He set his tablet down in his lap.

"Where else would I put you?"

I didn't answer. He knew what I was getting at, but he'd decided to be obtuse. I wanted to know why he didn't take me with him. The only bedroom I hadn't seen in the penthouse was his. And I couldn't help my curiosity. After seeing his rooftop garden, I wanted to know what style he'd gone for. The boys had unique decorative tastes.

Drake was about to open his mouth when a hand wrapped around my throat and I was pressed against a solid body. Looking up, I found West staring at me with a manic smile on his face.

"West," Drake ground out, "what are you doing?"

"My little Scar needs her scars checked."

Before I could say a word, he dragged me onto the other sofa and sat me in his lap. His fingers went to my blouse, unbuttoning the first couple before pulling it to the side and exposing the word 'war' carved on my skin. I winced when he stroked the word. It was still fucking sore because he kept picking off the damn scabs to make sure it would scar my skin.

"Beautiful," he murmured.

"It hurts."

"I know."

He leant closer and pressed a kiss to it. When West was tender, it made my heart ache so damn badly. Like a part of me craved this side of him. And then he had to go put his hand between my legs, cupping my pussy as if it belonged to him. Well, he'd told me enough times it did, so I suppose in his mind, he wasn't wrong.

"I'm taking you out later," he whispered against my skin.

"You are?"

This was news to me. Then again, West did things on his own schedule and rarely informed anyone else of his plans. I'd learnt as much from Francis and Prescott.

"Mmm."

"Where?"

"It's a surprise."

"Then how will I know what to wear?"

He straightened, his amber eyes glinting with mischief.

"I'll pick something for you."

"If you think I'm going to let—"

He put a finger over my lips.

"What I say goes."

I glared at him, batting his finger away. I didn't stop him when he buttoned my blouse back up.

"It's a good surprise, Scar. I promise."

I wasn't sure I believed him, but I decided not to press the issue. After all the times I'd set him off, I was wary about doing it again. West's ability to blow hot and cold was terrifying, to say the least.

"Fine."

He gave me a boyish smile before encouraging me to get to my feet again. He got up himself and strolled away towards the lift. I looked over at Drake who was eyeing West with no small amount of suspicion. Deciding maybe it was best I didn't push him any further about the whole putting me in Francis' bed thing, I went after West and joined him in the lift. He looked down at me with a grin as if he was pleased I'd decided to go with him instead of waiting for one of the others. When the doors closed, I bit my lip.

"Are you sure you won't tell me what we're going to do later?"

He wrapped an arm around my waist.

"It'd ruin the surprise, Scar."

"Is it that or do you not want the others to know?"

The way his eyes glinted told me the answer.

"Drake wouldn't approve."

I couldn't help the smile forming on my lips.

"If that's the case, I promise not to breathe a word."

West winked.

"That's my girl."

And the way my heart swelled at his praise had me disconcerted. Maybe it was the morning's events, but I was nervous about where West was taking me no matter how much the idea of spending time alone with him excited me. West was dangerous. The fact Drake wouldn't like it had me feeling like we might end up in trouble.

But when did these men ever not get me in any?

The answer to that was... never.

THIRTY EIGHT

FRANCIS

"I s it just me or has Scarlett been acting weird this morning?" Prescott said when the lift doors closed.

Scarlett had gone downstairs with West. Given I needed to talk to Drake about last night, I wasn't upset about it. But I did want to ask her what the hell was up with her. She'd been acting suspiciously since the moment she'd woken up.

"Yeah, not just you, I don't know what's up with her."

There was no reason for it. She'd been happy last night… well, except for the part where I'd exposed her relationship with me to Stuart. Otherwise, she hadn't been out of sorts. This morning was another matter.

"That's easy. She knows I have the memory stick Stuart must have given her yesterday and thinks I'm going to do something about it," Drake said.

Both Prescott and I looked at him.

"Memory stick? So that's what he was passing her."

I hadn't forgotten I'd watched him press something into Scarlett's hand.

"Tell me what happened."

I picked up my mug and sipped, wanting to avoid telling Drake I'd fucked up for as long as I possibly could. Prescott gave me a look. He knew too, just not the details. If I was honest, I didn't care about the fact I'd pissed Stuart off by publicly staking my claim on Scarlett. She belonged to us. He needed taking down a peg or two. The fucker was far too confident.

"Stuart may be aware of my... relationship with Scarlett."

I swear the sheer disbelief on Drake's face was unlike anything I'd seen directed at me before. West and Prescott had got their fair share of Drake's disapproving looks, but I mostly avoided them by not creating trouble.

"I sent you with her because you're the fucking sensible one, Francis. What the hell happened?"

He had no idea what I had to deal with last night. Drake wouldn't cut me any slack, but the situation wasn't what any of us had anticipated. Guess maybe I was a little more possessive of Scarlett than I realised. And I wanted the world to fucking well know it. She was mine. Being around the girl I'd grown up with brought out all my protective instincts. The need to brand myself all over her got stronger with each passing day.

I own Scarlett just as much as the rest of them do. She's my little whore. Mine.

"I went into his box with her and waited by the door, right, then Mason turns up. I warned him to stay away from Scarlett, but he wasn't there for her."

Prescott's eyes darkened.

"That fuck. I swear I want to rip his face off."

Drake sent Prescott a warning look. We all knew we couldn't touch Mason no matter how much we wanted to destroy the piece of shit for everything he'd done.

"Who was he there for?" he asked a moment later.

If Drake had any fucking common sense, he wouldn't have asked the question. He knew exactly who Stuart's best friend was. Knew the person who could and would send us all to prison if he ever found out the truth. He would make a fucking example of us.

"Who do you think?"

His eyebrows shot up.

"You serious?"

"Yeah, I am."

"Fuck."

I set my mug down on the counter. Seeing not one but two men who definitely had it out for us was unsettling. To be honest, it rattled me. And I couldn't help but stake my claim all over Scarlett because of it.

"Did he see you?"

I shrugged.

"Don't think so. I hope not. Anyway, Mason was acting like a dick and it pissed me off."

"Sounds like Mason," Prescott muttered. "He's always been a cunt."

"I made it clear Scarlett is ours. Then I may have also kissed her when we were in the stands in full view of Stuart. I saw him watching us and I couldn't help myself."

There was no point lying to them about what happened. They would find out one way or another. Besides, keeping secrets wouldn't do me any favours.

"Jesus Christ," Drake exclaimed.

Prescott smirked.

"I bet he was pissed."

I nodded. Stuart looked incensed. Like he wanted to rip my face off for daring to touch Scarlett. And it reminded me of something else.

"What do you think Mason told Stuart about her moving out?"

"I think the better question is why didn't he tell Stuart she's sleeping with all of us," Drake said, rubbing his chin with his fingers.

"He knows?"

Drake gave me a sharp nod before he sat back and looked up at the ceiling.

"That's the real reason he was angry with her the day he hurt her. Well, likely angry and jealous."

Prescott scowled and crossed his arms over his chest.

"He wants her for himself. Always fucking has… even when we were younger."

Mason was older than us, but we'd known him since we were teenagers. I wished he was anyone other than the fucking Police Commissioner's son. We would have got rid of him a long time ago if it wasn't for that. And who knew why he hadn't told Stuart about her real relationship with us. If Drake was right and Stuart had hurt Scarlett, no doubt Mason knew about it. And in his own fucked up way, he was trying to protect her. Too bad he was protecting her from the wrong fucking people. We were her safety, not him. Us. We'd fight for Scarlett for the rest of our lives.

"He's not having her no matter what he does," Drake said. "Over my fucking dead body."

He dropped his head back down. I could see the dark look in his indigo eyes. The one telling me he would unleash his inner beast on Mason if he could. I watched Prescott smile at Drake's reaction.

"Oh, so you do care, huh?"

"She's *ours*."

Prescott's smile got wider.

"And what, pray tell, caused this sudden possessiveness?"

Drake gave Prescott a dark look.

"Nothing."

"Oh no, you don't get to do that, Drake." Prescott waggled his finger. "How exactly did you get a hold of this memory stick of Stuart's, hmm? I think me and Francis deserve to know. Do you even know what's on it?"

It took a long minute for Drake to say a word. A haunted look crossed over his features, telling me something had gone on last night none of us were privy to.

"She found me in my hideaway and when I put her to bed afterwards, I found the memory stick in her pocket. And no, I haven't plugged it into anything because I'm wary of what's on it. This shit is not our field of expertise."

Prescott dropped his hands from his chest and dug them into his pockets instead.

"We should get West to contact Penn, he'll know someone who can deal with it safely."

"We already owe him one favour."

"So? He's useful and this time we can just pay him. Not like we're asking him to give us another randomer to off or anything."

Drake looked pensive for a moment. We didn't want to owe the Fixer more favours. One was enough. West trusted him even though he had ties to Zayn Villetti, the mafia kingpin, Gennaro's son. The whole Villetti family was involved in a lot of shady shit. Gennaro Villetti was the head of the mafia here in London. And one person we avoided like the plague. He was ruthless and unforgiving. Not a man you wanted to have a vendetta against you under any circumstances.

"You're right. We need to know what's on it and if she's actually gone through with what Stuart wanted or not. Perhaps we can use this situation to our advantage. I'll speak to West when we go downstairs."

I raised an eyebrow at Drake.

"How did she end up on the roof with you?" I was fucking curious about what the hell had gone on between them. "Does this mean she's forgiven you for fucking up?"

Drake scowled before letting out a sigh and looking away.

"I don't know if she has. And she found me up there, probably heard me playing and came to investigate."

"Did she give you a hard time?"

"No. She didn't. And before you ask, I did apologise for what happened... sort of."

Prescott snorted.

"Sort of? So it was a half-arsed apology then?"

Drake didn't look back at us.

CHAOS

"All of us are going to spend a lifetime making up for what we did. Don't give me shit for attempting to apologise to her. We've all fucked up with her."

The three of us fell silent at his words. It wasn't anything new for me. We were always going to have to make up for the shit we'd put her through. For her accident. For ruining her life. That night was on us, but what happened next? Well, it was on the Carvers. We had nothing to do with what they'd put her through. I wished we knew what had gone on in their household for the past ten years. What they'd done to her.

"She knows you play then," I said after the silence had gone on for too long.

Drake finally met my eyes.

"Yes. I don't know how I feel about it." He leant forward, resting his arms on his knees. "The old Scarlett knew, but she's not that girl… at least, I don't think she will ever be exactly the same. Maybe it's why I'm so conflicted about her remembering who we are. We've been separated for ten years. She's not our Little Nyx any longer. She's grown up and fuck knows what she's been through without us."

The sombre notes to his voice made my chest ache. He was right. She wasn't the girl from our youth, but it didn't make her any less magnificent. Any less beautiful and alluring. If anything, she was so much more now. And the only way we'd set Scarlett free was by restoring what she'd lost. By giving her back the girl she'd been so she could be the woman she was now. The one who wanted out of the cage in her mind.

"She needs to remember, Drake. We're running out of options here. What if you hadn't intercepted the memory stick? I know you told me to allow everything to play out, but it's one close call after another right now. I mean, anything could have happened last night. Me going to the game was a huge gamble in the first place, knowing it's his stadium. His people surrounding me and her. Not to mention Garrett being there. It could have all gone to hell."

Drake dropped his head and stared at the floor.

"Anything to do with Stuart is always a risk, but you're right. We can't keep hiding it from her, but we need to get an agreement from West first before we move forward. We make decisions together or not at all, remember?"

It had always been our way ever since we were kids. The five of us had been a democracy in a sense. Only the four of us had gone behind Scarlett's back and changed everything for good by our reckless actions.

"We'll meet after work then... talk about it then."

Drake nodded. I glanced at Prescott who was also nodding. It was decided. We were going to have to do something to accelerate the process. Find a way to restore Scarlett's memories for her. Whatever it took. It was something we all had to face up to. And our demons were about to be exposed in the worst way. The night that haunted each and every one of us, including Scarlett. Especially her, as she couldn't remember a single damn thing.

"Well, let's get going before we're all late and make a bad impression, eh?" Prescott said, waving a hand at us. "We'll deal with this shit later when we're all together."

As the three of us walked towards the lift, I couldn't help feeling a sense of impending dread. This was the right thing to do, but it didn't stop nausea from coiling in my stomach. And I wasn't sure why my senses were on fire with the knowledge

CHAOS

we were walking headlong into the worst fucking shitshow of
our lives.

THIRTY NINE

WEST

Despite the fact I'd had a text from Drake telling me we needed a meeting this evening, it didn't stop me whisking Scarlett upstairs to change after work before anyone else came up to our penthouse. They could fucking wait. My plans couldn't. And so what if I'd turned off my phone so they couldn't give me any shit? Not like they weren't used to me disappearing off for hours on end. Though, I suppose this time was different as I had our girl with me, but whatever. Those three could just deal.

I'd bought Scarlett new clothes specifically for this evening. She'd raised an eyebrow when I'd presented them to her but put them on without complaint. When she stood there in the black ripped skinny jeans, trainers, a black t-shirt with a red skull on the front of it and a little black and red cropped jacket, it was all I could do to not pin her down on my bed and ravage her little body until she screamed for me. It didn't stop me from running my fingers over the scar I'd given her. It made my fucking heart swell every time I saw it. My brand on her perfect skin.

My little Scar belongs to me. She's my little warrior. She'll go to war with me.

I'd taken her hand and dragged her to the lift, hitting the button for the ground floor. It was a miracle we hadn't been caught by Francis, Drake or Prescott. No doubt I would get an earful over not responding to their demand, but I really didn't give a shit. Tonight wasn't about them. It was about me and Scarlett.

She looked up at me with those beautiful hazel-green eyes but didn't say a thing as we rode down. She was nervous. Her fingers trembled in mine and she kept worrying at the zip of her jacket with her other hand. Some things never changed. Her nervous habits had always made me smile. And I'd soothed her nerves every single time when we'd been teenagers.

Now, things were different. We were different. I couldn't be the boy she'd been close to all those years ago. I wasn't him any longer. Ten years had twisted me into someone the old Scarlett wouldn't recognise. And there was no way of bringing him back. Not after what happened. We'd forge a new path together. We were meant to fucking well be, and I wouldn't accept any other answer. Scarlett wasn't going to leave me again. I wouldn't allow it to happen under any circumstances.

"Do you like what I bought you?" I asked as we walked out into the lobby and along to the front doors.

Scarlett looked down at herself. Her hand brushed over her t-shirt, her fingers lingering on the skull.

"I do," she whispered, almost as if she was afraid to admit it. "Thank you, West."

I squeezed her hand, trying not to allow emotion to clog my throat. She sounded like my Scarlett. My girl. The one who appreciated everything I did for her.

I miss you, Scar. I miss everything about the girl you were. Fuck. I want you back. Every part of you. Especially your heart.

I pushed open the front doors, guiding her out into the cool early evening air. She followed me along to the tube station. I could have driven, but I wanted her to experience the city the way we used to when we were younger, when none of us had driving licences.

"You still not telling me where we're going?" she asked when we stood together in the packed carriage.

I rested my hand on her lower back, pulling her closer. I wanted her near. Needed her like fucking air. This woman was my entire life. She always had been. Always would be. I could never let Scarlett go, no matter how many years had gone by. There was nothing I wouldn't do for her, even if she was shit scared of me now. My girl had always been fearless. She kept standing up to me no matter how much I pushed her. No matter how many times I made her tremble. She tried to hide it, but she liked it. She liked when I made her scared. It got her wet and ready for me.

"No. You'll have to be patient."

The pout she gave me was adorable as fuck. Tonight, I wasn't in the mood to argue or get up in her damn face. This was my way of taking her out on a date. Most people would probably say it was fucked up. I didn't want to think about what Drake would say to me right now. What all of them

369

would. If they knew where I was taking her, they would probably have lost their shit.

It was the first time since she'd returned to us I had a hard time not wanting to kiss her. For all the times I'd told her I didn't kiss, it was a lie. The only woman I wanted to kiss was her. I wanted to ravage that mouth of hers until she bled for me. Until she cried and begged for more. I would never be done with her. Never.

The tube lurched, forcing me to hold Scarlett closer as I clutched the bar above us. She gripped my coat in her tiny fists to stay upright. Fuck me, she was the cutest damn thing I'd ever seen in my life. Even when she was giving me attitude. If only she knew how much I adored her tenacious little soul. But the last ten years without her held me back. The secrets between us. The lies. And most of all, my guilt.

The night of her accident tortured me because of what happened. How it happened. And how nothing was ever the same again. It's why I didn't think about it. Only seeing her made it play out in my mind over and over on fucking repeat. I couldn't escape it nor her.

"Are we going to eat first?" she murmured, releasing my coat to wrap her hands around my waist.

"Is my little Scar hungry?"

She nodded. I gave her a smile, my fingers stroking lower down her back, across her perfect little pert arse. Her eyes widened at my touch but she didn't tell me to stop.

"Don't worry, I'll make sure you're well-fed."

I watched her brow furrow slightly as if she was trying to work out whether I was telling her I'd take her out to eat or intending to feed her my cock. Maybe I'd do both. She'd just have to wait and see. I did want her mouth wrapped around it all over again. Her hot, wet little mouth I couldn't stop staring at. The one I craved with every fucking inch of my being.

We got off at the next stop. I gripped Scarlett's hand tight to make sure she didn't escape me or get lost in the crowd of people. When we were out in the open again, I led her towards a gourmet burger place I liked to frequent. Scarlett seemed rather happy with my choice and wolfed down her fully loaded burger with sweet potato fries. They were all the fucking rage these days. She gave me a sheepish look when she was done, as if the way she'd devoured her burger was completely unladylike. I smirked. She had no idea how much watching her eat with such gusto turned me on. Everything she did had an effect on me. It made me want to keep her forever. And I fucking well would.

"Did that satisfy you enough, little Scar, or did you want something else?" I asked, leaning closer to her. I'd finished my food minutes before she did.

Her cheeks flamed. My hand clamped down around her leg and I ran my fingers along her inner thigh. Fuck, I wanted her little pussy wrapped around my dick after she'd been face fucked so hard, she cried. It was all I could think about. Having her. Especially in that outfit. It was the exact style Scarlett used to have when she was younger. Ripped jeans were her favourites and she was always in a pair of beat-up Converse. I'd loved the way she was so unashamedly herself, refusing to go with the crowd or bow to societal pressure to dress a certain way. Scarlett didn't care. She had us and we always lifted her up. Always encouraged her to be herself just as she did us.

"You're asking me? I thought you took what you wanted."

"Tonight is about you."

Scarlett bit her lip while I ran my fingers higher.

"Take what you want, West."

I pressed my fingers into the seam of her jeans, pushing the fabric against her pussy. She let out a little pant.

"What I want, little Scar, is for you to worship me on your fucking knees," I whispered, my mouth close to hers. "And I want you to do it with this defiant mouth of yours."

I raised my other hand and brushed her lips with my fingertips. Then I shoved two of them in her mouth. Her eyes went wide but her tongue curled around them as if showing me exactly how she would pleasure my dick with it.

"Are you going to be my good girl or my bad one?"

Her tongue swirled around the tips of my fingers. I smiled wider, my fingers digging harder into her jeans, stroking her through the fabric and making her hips jerk under my touch.

"You want to be both, don't you. You want me so fucking bad, you can't stand it. You'd let me fuck you right here."

She let out a little whimper around my fingers, too quiet for anyone else to hear. My eyes darted around the room, taking in the rather shocked faces of the people next to us. The couple nearest to us was giving me a disgusted look.

"You like what you see, huh?" I said to them. "You going to get up and leave if I make her get on her knees under the table for me?"

The woman spluttered and the guy she was with looked as though he was torn between being horrified and wanting me to go ahead with it. If I did, I would likely get us kicked out of the place. Didn't matter since we'd finished our meals.

However, it wasn't part of my plans to get arrested for public indecency.

I looked over the couple again.

"Too bad for you, me and my little pet have places to be. And yes, she will be getting her throat battered later in case you were wondering."

I pulled my fingers from Scarlett's mouth, gave the couple a wink and got up from the table, pulling her with me. As I took her hand and walked her over to the counter to pay, I could hear the woman muttering behind us, "What a disgusting man."

I laughed, not giving two shits about her opinion. Scarlett's face was bright red, but I could see the little smirk playing on her lips as if she'd found it amusing too. We'd always shared the same sense of humour and had never given a shit about what other people thought.

After I'd paid, Scarlett and I walked out into the twilight and back towards the tube.

"You're shameless," she murmured, pressing herself into my side. I let go of her hand to wrap my arm around her.

"Those stuck-up fucks deserved it. Her husband clearly wanted us to give them a little show. He was trying to hide his dick getting hard over the thought of it, whilst she was sitting there looking at us like we were the fucking antichrist or something."

She snorted and gave me a bright smile.

"Probably the most action she's got in a long while."

That made me laugh out loud and Scarlett joined in. Fuck this felt good. Being with her like this. As if we were normal again. As if the last ten years hadn't fucking existed. Just me and my girl, doing whatever the fuck we wanted.

In those moments, I forgot to be worried about where I was taking her. About her potential reaction to it. All I could see and feel was Scarlett, my fucking girl. My whole damn world. My life. She was my home. My family. The only person who had ever given me peace, hope and tranquillity.

I love you, Scarlett Nyx. You're my soulmate. My one and only. Now and forever.

FORTY

SCARLETT

The side to West he'd shown me this evening was unlike anything I'd ever imagined. He was playful, funny and, as always, took exactly what he wanted without fear of the consequences. With him, I felt free. Unrestricted. Able to do whatever the hell I wanted. And what I really wanted was this man who was holding my hand as we walked from the bus stop, and his dick down my throat. It was all I could think about since he'd told me to worship him on my knees. All I could focus on. I needed him with a desperation that threatened to turn me as psychotic and reckless as the man himself.

We'd taken a tube and two buses to get to our destination. Now we were walking up a rather run-down looking street towards fuck knows what. West hadn't told me where we were going. My curiosity had almost got the better of me, but I'd asked him enough times already.

My eyes were fixed on him as we walked, taking in every inch of this absolutely gorgeous but fucked up man beside me. His amber eyes glinted in the fading light. I'd never met anyone with the shade before. It tugged at my memories in an unsettling way I tried hard to ignore. As much as I wanted to remember, I didn't want the past to ruin this time I had with him away from the others.

He was dressed head to toe in black, from his trainers to his jeans that clung to his muscular legs. The black t-shirt he wore bore a red axe on it dripping with blood. And to top it off, he had a black canvas military-style coat on. The man carried himself as if he knew he was a god amongst mortals. And I found it alluring even though he scared the shit out of me most of the time.

"West."

"Mmm?"

He didn't glance at me, only squeezed my hand tighter in his. He already had a death grip on it as if he was worried I'd run from him. No fucking way. I barely even knew where we were. I had no reason to leave his side. Besides, I wanted him to shove me up against one of these houses, force me on my knees and let me wrap my lips around him.

Dare I ask him for it? He said tonight was about me. And he'd already told me he wanted me to worship him.

"I want something from you," I said in a small voice that didn't make me sound particularly confident.

He glanced at me with a wicked glint in those beautiful but deadly eyes of his.

"And what's that, my little Scar?"

CHAOS

I had to swallow first before I gathered my courage. Reaching out with my other hand, I drew us to a halt halfway down the street. My fingers ran down his front until I reached the top of his jeans. I traced a line under his t-shirt, brushing the pads over the fabric of his boxers where they peeked out from his jeans.

"Let me worship you."

The slow upwards curl of his lip made me tremble.

"Say please."

"Please, West."

He chuckled, the darkness swelling in his eyes making me want to throw myself at him. My pussy throbbed with the anticipation of him wrapping my hair in his fist and the other around my neck. The way he'd make me take him in my mouth. I knew he could be rough and I wanted it. I needed it so fucking badly.

"Come with me."

He pulled my hand away from his jeans and tugged me further down the street. I hoped it meant he was taking me somewhere less open to let me wrap my lips around his cock. Abruptly, he stopped and pulled me through a small gap between two fences. It was overgrown with grass and weeds, but it didn't stop West from dragging me along it. My eyes darted around, finding the fence to our right was wooden while the one to our left was metal and beyond it seemed to be a building site. Except it looked as if it had been untouched for years with paint crumbling from the parked JCBs, which included a bulldozer, a digger and an excavator, and stacks of abandoned building materials. Something about it sent a horrible wave of familiarity racing down my spine.

West stopped by a pole and let go of my hand to pull at the metal fencing. It rolled back slightly, allowing him to slip through the gap. He held it for me to dart through as well, before setting it back in place.

He didn't allow me any time to look around, dragging me towards one of the abandoned JBCs. The bulldozer had been fitted with a loader that sat off the ground, its bucket hanging in the air. West let go of my hand to haul himself up into the bucket. It was huge, so he fit there with his legs hanging down. He reached out and dragged me between his legs before placing my hands on his crotch. I could feel his dick and it made my body shiver. Then his fingers went to my hair, tangling in the strands as he stared down at me.

"Do you want to worship me or do you want me to make you?"

His voice was low and gravelly.

"Make me."

The moment my words were out of my mouth, I was pulling at the zipper of his jeans, having flipped the button open. He ran his teeth over his lip as if it was the answer he wanted out of me. When I got his dick free, he pushed my head down, making me bend at the waist. My hands went to his thighs as my face came level with his hard cock.

"Lick it."

The demand in his voice made me flick out my tongue, tasting the tip of his cock and the pre-cum beading there. He growled in response, his fingers digging into my scalp. Then he gathered my long wavy hair up in his fist, pulling it away from my face. His eyes were dark in the low light and full of heat.

CHAOS

"You going to show me how much you love this dick, Scar?"

I nodded, tracing my tongue around the crown to demonstrate my acquiescence. The rumble of his chest had me doing it again.

"Open."

My lips parted, allowing him to push his dick into my mouth. The thickness of it had me opening wider to give him better access. Using my hair in his fist, he shoved me down on it until the tip hit the back of my mouth, making me choke a little around his length.

"Fuck," he groaned. "Let me in, swallow my cock."

I did as he asked, swallowing, and his dick sunk into my throat, causing me to gag, but I kept taking it. My hands curled harder around his thighs, my nails digging into the fabric of his jeans.

"My bad little Scar taking my dick so well. Fuck. That's it, all of it. You're a dirty girl."

I couldn't help but obey him and take the whole thing. Breathing around his length and girth was practically impossible, but I didn't let it stop me. He only held me there for a few seconds. Tugging me back off it, my saliva covered his dick and dribbled down my lip. The way he smiled at me set my whole world on fire as I tried to catch my breath.

A minute later, I was back on his dick, taking it the way he wanted. He let out another groan as he worked my head by my hair. I let him fuck my throat without any resistance. Let him use me and revelled in the way he couldn't help the grunts and groans echoing around the bucket he sat in. For the first time, West didn't hold back his pleasure. He didn't hide the way I made him feel with my mouth around his cock. He showed me how much he wanted this. Needed my tongue wrapped around him, stroking his length.

His fist tightened in my hair, pushing me down further until he was lodged in my throat again.

"Mine," he growled.

Then he emptied himself down my throat, the violence of it making my pussy clench. I couldn't do anything else but hold myself there, feeling his cock pulse in my mouth. He pulled me off when he was spent, letting me swallow before I sucked in air to my deprived lungs. He wrapped his free hand around my throat, stroking it with his thumb. He used my hair to pull me up, allowing me to straighten and stand between his legs again. The glint of those amber eyes had my heart pumping wildly in my chest.

"My beautiful little Scar," he murmured. "Such a good girl."

"My War," I whispered.

He stroked my throat again, telling me without words how he felt. This man would destroy the world for me. He would chase me to the ends of the earth. He would do anything to keep me by his side. And I had no idea why he was so devoted to me.

Leaning closer, he rested his forehead against mine, staring down into my eyes like they were the window to my soul. The intimacy of the moment had me sucking in air. The thickness of the tension between us was almost suffocating.

"What do your tattoos mean?" I blurted out without thinking about it.

He grinned, keeping his head pressed to mine.

"Which ones?"

"The ones on your fingers."

"Every time I kill, I have Penn tattoo a memento of it on my skin."

My eyes flicked down to his hand around my neck. The one on his forefinger was the symbol for the Gemini zodiac sign. It made me wonder what it was about, but I didn't ask. The one on his middle finger was a teardrop. And the next one along was a series of small lines with another diagonally across it, representing five. Finally, he had a little sword on his pinkie.

I reached up and traced a line across the skull on the back of his hand.

"Penn? You mean the Fixer guy... he did these?"

"Mmm."

"He's very talented for a man who also gets rid of people for a living."

West snorted.

"People are not the only thing he fixes. Penn is a crazy motherfucker. He might come across as charming, but he's got a few screws loose. The dude is literally obsessed with some girl he's barely spoken to. He talks about her every time I see him."

"Is that why you get on with him?"

He barked with laughter, pulling his head back as his hand tightened around my throat. When he settled down, he smiled at me.

"Probably."

His hand slid from my hair and traced down my back.

"You're a little obsessed with me," I whispered, leaning closer and pressing myself against his body the best I could.

"Not a little… you consume my every waking moment and my dreams. You're my girl, little Scar. All mine. I'll never let you go."

The fingers around my neck tightened, punctuating his words.

"I don't want you to."

His hand roamed from my back to in between our bodies and lower. He cupped my pussy in a possessive manner. I couldn't stop myself grinding into his hand. It made him smirk.

"I think you want me to stick my fingers in your pussy and make you come."

I bit my lip, staring up at him and trying to convey all my need and desperation for him. What I wanted was for him to fuck me with his perfect dick, but he'd just come and I had no idea how long it would take him to recover.

"Mmm, Scar, you want more than that, don't you?" He rubbed my pussy. "It's written all over your face. You want me to bend you over that fucking stack of bricks over there, rip your jeans down and make you scream on my dick."

I didn't know how he'd read my thoughts, but he pushed me back and jumped out of the bucket, landing on his feet with a thud. He guided me backwards with his hand wrapped around my throat until I hit something solid.

"Wrap your hand around my dick, Scar."

I did as he asked, finding it half hard already.

"Stroke it. Make me believe you want it inside your dripping pussy, the one soaking your fucking knickers with your need. I can almost fucking smell your arousal."

I was squirming inside at his dirty words. At the way he didn't give a shit what came out of his mouth and how it made me tremble. And I almost melted in a puddle before him when he unbuttoned my jeans with one hand and slid his fingers inside my underwear. He smiled wider when he found me wet with need.

"West," I whimpered when his fingers circled my clit. It throbbed at his touch.

"Don't worry, my needy little girl, I take care of my possessions. Your pussy belongs to me."

FORTY ONE

SCARLETT

I was dying. I swear to fucking god I was. West's amber eyes were almost black as he stared down at me, his fingers mastering my clit with absolute precision as I stroked his cock back to full mast. There was something about the fear I felt around West. It made my pussy gush with need for him. And right now, I was shit scared of the man towering over me, telling me he owned my pussy. I was terrified because he saw right through me. He knew me on a level I didn't even know myself on. Like I was intrinsically tied to him.

"This little pussy is so wet for me. So fucking wet and ready for my cock."

The only sound I could make was a high-pitched whine in agreement. My other hand wrapped around his waist, pulling him closer. Wanting him to fuck me until I cried and came all over his dick. I wanted to feel myself clench around his length, show him how much I needed his beautiful cock inside me.

He let go of my neck so he could pull my jeans off my hips, dragging my underwear with it. Turning me around, he forced me against the stack of bricks behind us, pressing my face into them. My hips were tugged back, meeting his body as his cock slid between my wet folds. I moaned, my palms flattening against the bricks.

West didn't enter me, content to rub his dick along my slit and coat it in my arousal. The more he did it, the more I whimpered, my nails scraping along the bricks.

"I want you," I cried out, not caring about how much noise I was making. "Please, West. Fuck me."

He leant over me, wrapping his hand around the back of my neck to keep me in place.

"Do you need this dick? Need it so bad, it's making you crazy, hmm?"

"Yes, fuck, please."

"You told me you need more than good dick, Scar. Has that changed?"

I trembled, trying to push back against him.

"You're more than that to me," I whispered. "I want all of you."

I was tired of lying to myself about my attraction to West. Tired of pretending something about him didn't make my soul sing. Maybe I was crazy, but I was crazy for him. My psycho. The man who'd branded his horseman persona on my skin. He was fucking well mine.

"Take what you want then, Scar. You told me I'm yours, so fucking take me."

My hand dropped from the bricks and reached between us. His cock was slippery from my essence, but I pressed it to my entrance and pushed myself back against him. A low moan sounded in the back of my throat. Fuck, he felt so good. Everything about him.

He took over from me then, thrusting deep and impaling me on the whole fucking thing. My knees threatened to buckle, but he kept me upright with his hand on my hip and the other around the back of my neck.

West took me with brutal thrusts, our skin slapping together in time with each of our grunts of pleasure. Neither of us spoke. We didn't have to. Need had taken over. It consumed the two of us. I didn't care if we were out in the open on a building site. Didn't give a shit if someone stumbled upon us. All I could think about was West. All I could feel was him. His body hammering into mine. And when he pressed his face into my shoulder, his teeth gripping my jacket, I knew he was as affected as me by the experience.

My fingers slipped over my clit, stroking myself into a fucking frenzy as he kept pounding into me. The angle of his cock was almost too much, brushing right up against the right spot and making my vision blur.

"Don't stop," I gasped, trying to gulp down oxygen into my lungs. "Please, fuck."

"Scream for me, Scar. Let the whole damn world know how much you need me."

"I don't want the world to know. Just you… only you."

He shuddered against me at my words, like he was barely holding onto his fucking sanity. Mine was already shot to pieces. Fractured by the events of my life and the way he was fucking me. The way he was owning my body and my pleasure.

"I need you," he whispered. "Don't leave me again. Never leave me."

I didn't know what he meant by again, but I couldn't ask him. I was too overwhelmed by the way his dick kept slamming into my pussy with such brutality, it bordered on painful. But I loved it. I needed it. All of it. All of him.

"Fuck, West!"

I shattered, my world splintering into a thousand tiny specs of dust. My eyes closed and I let bliss wash over me. Allowed myself to be carried away. Nothing mattered but him. I could feel him inside me, drawing out my climax while my fingers continued to brush over my clit. The moment it became too much, my hand fell away, but he didn't stop. He kept pounding my pussy, his dick swelling inside me as I clenched around him.

"My little Scar," he groaned in my ear. "My beautiful girl."

It was everything. This moment between us as he emptied himself inside me, owning me with his cock. Claiming me as his own. I surrendered myself to him. It was my only choice. I couldn't keep fighting against the tidal wave. West drowned me. And I let him.

We were both panting when our bodies finally settled together. West wrapped his arms around me and buried his face in my neck, holding me to him as if his life depended on it. If only I could stay with him like this forever. If only I didn't have to face up to the fact my heart recognised the four of these men. It yearned for them despite everything they'd done. And it wanted West to write his name all over it. It wanted me to brand myself all over his in return.

When he finally pulled away and tugged my clothes up, along with his own, my breathing had returned to normal and my legs were no longer shaking. It wasn't like I could clean myself up, so I would have to deal with his cum dripping from me for the rest of the evening. It was worth it for the experience I'd shared with him.

"I didn't bring you here to fuck you," he murmured, stroking my hair back from my face.

"Then why did you?"

He smiled.

"I'll show you."

He took my hand and we picked our way through the building materials until we came to the shell of a building. It was clearly abandoned, or at least, it must be on a normal night. Graffiti marred the walls. Years old ripped plastic sheeting flapped in the cool breeze. And yet the sounds of people could be heard inside along with music.

I don't know why I got a sick feeling in my stomach seeing this place. It felt almost… ominous. A part of me wanted to recoil from it, but West dragged me towards the opening and inside before I could say a word. There was a large crowd of people gathered. They were cheering and shouting at something happening in the middle of the room.

"What's going on?" I asked West.

He pulled me past the crowd towards the stairwell. We walked up a couple of the steps so I could see above the heads of the crowd. They were in a ring around two bare-chested men with their hands up. One of them snapped his fist out, catching the other one around the jaw.

West had brought me to what I assumed was a bare-knuckle fight, and I had no idea how I felt about it. He wrapped an arm around me, pulling me closer to his body. I watched the two men go at each other. I could feel him vibrating with excitement next to me as if watching this got him going. It shouldn't surprise me. Violence was his thing.

"Is this even legal?" I asked, looking up at him.

"Nope. Underground fights never are, it's why they do it here. No one gives a shit about this place. It was left to rot years ago."

"Why?"

West shrugged even as his body tensed. It made me suspicious about the real reason he'd brought me here, but I didn't comment on it. This place felt wrong to me. So fucking wrong. And I had no idea why. A cold sweat beaded at the back of my neck. I tried to ignore it, tried to focus on the fight in front of me, but the feeling grew and grew until it was almost too much. As if sensing my unease, West pulled me against his front, wrapping his arms around my waist and rested his chin on my shoulder.

"Do you come to these often?"

I needed a distraction. Anything to keep my mind off my unease.

"I used to participate until Drake got me banned. To be fair, I did almost kill a man, but he doesn't like me coming here. He'll be angry when he finds out I brought you."

"You don't care what he thinks."

"Not really."

I did wonder at West's friendship with the other three sometimes. They seemed to tolerate his insanity to a point until he crossed some sort of invisible line. Then all bets were off.

"Why are you all friends?"

"Who? Me, Pres, Drake and Frankie?"

I nodded.

"Just are, Scar."

"That's not an answer."

He chuckled, holding me tighter.

"We've been together through thick and thin. They're my family and I'm theirs, no matter how much they want to punch me in the face at times."

I looked at his face. There was tension lining his brow. Somehow, I didn't think he liked me asking these questions.

"You're just so different from each other."

"And? Does that prevent us from being friends?"

"Well, no, but Drake told me last night that something happened to you when you were younger. Something that changed you all."

West stiffened. I knew probing him was probably a bad idea, but my curiosity got the better of me.

"It did."

"Will you tell me what—"

"Hey, I know you," came a voice from nearby.

I turned my head back towards the crowd, finding a guy standing at the bottom of the stairs staring right at West.

"You shouldn't be here."

West released me before pressing me behind him.

"Says who?"

The guy tipped his chin.

"Says fucking everyone. Bennett banned you from coming back here."

"Bennett doesn't have a fucking say in what I do."

I didn't know who the hell Bennett was, but I didn't like the way the guy was eyeing West, nor the way my man's muscles tensed and his fists clenched.

"Oh yeah?"

"Yeah."

And with that, West jumped down from the stairs and raised his fist, smashing it into the guy's face. His head snapped back as my hand went to my mouth. West hit the guy again before he hit back, catching West around the jaw. The crowd noticed the commotion behind them. The fight was forgotten as West and this guy beat on each other.

I stumbled down the stairs, wanting to intervene even though watching West lose his shit was kind of hot. The way he ducked the guy's attempts to hit him further with a weird sort of grace. The crack of the guy's nose shattering under the impact of West's fist.

"West!"

He glanced over at me and grinned before getting back into the fray. Two other people had joined in, trying to drag the guy away from my man. It was useless. West hit one of them in the face and caught the other in the stomach. I watched in horror as the crowd started to cheer him. He smacked the mouthy guy down on the ground and kicked him in the stomach for good measure. The other two were still trying to stop West, but they couldn't get a good grip on him.

The whole thing was utterly crazy. Then it was over as two much bigger guys dragged West off the one he had pinned down on the ground.

"Dude, chill the fuck out, Jesus!" one of them said as West shrugged them off.

He put his bloody knuckles up in surrender before cracking his neck. Without a glance at the man he'd almost beaten to a pulp groaning on the floor, he stalked over to me. There didn't look like there was a scratch on him. And the blood on his hands wasn't his.

"Let's go," he said, taking my hand and pulling me up the staircase.

He didn't care to deal with the mess he'd left behind. West was carefully controlled chaos contained inside a man who wielded it with maximum efficiency.

On the first floor, there were people everywhere chatting and a few making out by the pillars holding the building up. West ignored them and took me up two more flights. There was no one on this level. He led me over to the other side of the building from the stairs, stopping near the edge and turning to me. His amber eyes were full of emotions I didn't understand.

I stepped closer and took both of his hands in mine, looking them over to make sure he wasn't hurt.

"It's not mine," he murmured.

"Was that necessary?"

He smiled, but it was sad.

"Probably not, but…"

"You're not very appropriate."

"Exactly."

I don't know why I wasn't scared of him for what he'd done. Why it made me want to hold him close and take away the demons circling behind his eyes. West could go from zero to a hundred at the drop of a hat. And yeah, it did terrify the

SARAH BAILEY

crap out of me, but it also made me want to understand him. Want to know the man hiding inside.

I wanted to know his heart.

"Who is Bennett?"

"Bennett Jerome Michaelson. Head of a gang in Hackney, but he runs this underground ring."

"And you don't care if he banned you."

"Nope. This isn't his land, anyway. I can be here if I want to."

The wind blew, ruffling his light brown hair. An image of him became clear in my mind. He stood in this exact place except he was younger. I shook myself. It couldn't be real. Yet this place was too familiar in a way I couldn't put my finger on. And I wanted to dispel the feeling. I wanted it to go away. I wanted the magic of the two of us locked together in ecstasy back. I needed it so fucking badly, I could hardly think straight.

Stepping closer, I let go of his hands and wrapped my hands around his neck.

"West..."

"Yes, my little Scar?"

A tiny furrow appeared between his knitted brows as he looked at me. As if he was worried about what I was planning. Well, he should be after all the times he'd told me this wasn't something he did.

"I'm going to kiss you and if you don't want me to... you have to stop me."

FORTY TWO

WEST

TEN YEARS AGO

The persistent knocking at my door made me let out a huff as I approached it. My parents had gone out somewhere. Fuck knows where. Who gave a shit. They certainly didn't give one about me, but whatever. I didn't want to think about them.

I pulled the door open only to find Scarlett standing there, her eyes full of tears and her body trembling. My hands went to her, pulling her inside, shutting the door and wrapping my arms around her.

"West," she sobbed. "Oh god, I can't. I keep remembering it over and over."

I held her tighter. My best friend had been through an ordeal last week. And only now was it finally hitting her.

"Shh, I've got you, Little Nyx. I've got you."

She gripped my t-shirt in an iron hold, clutching me to her as if her life depended on it. This girl was my universe. I would die for her if I could. So right now, I was going to hold her while she cried. While she sobbed her heart out all over my chest because she'd been assaulted. Drake had saved her from the fuckers in time, but it didn't make it any easier on her. Didn't mean she was okay. She'd told me so last night when we were on the phone with each other.

"They almost… I can't… I don't want them to have that from me."

"They didn't, Scar. Drake stopped them, remember? He stopped them."

She shook in my arms. I wished I could make her pain go away. I wanted to soothe her damn soul. Not just because Scarlett was my best friend. I was in love with her. I had been since the day she'd stomped into the classroom on the first day of primary school, her light brown wavy hair wild and her hazel-green eyes full of determination. Especially when she walked right up to me and broke out into a smile as she put out her hand. This five-year-old girl was fearless as she introduced herself to me as Scarlett Nyx. And she'd captivated me ever since.

Her tiny fists gripped my t-shirt harder. My heart fucking broke. We couldn't stay standing here in the hallway. I wanted her to be comfortable. Pulling back, I took her tear-streaked face between my palms, wiping away her still falling tears with my thumbs.

"What can I do?"

"Just be here for me."

I dropped my hands from her face and took her hand, leading her upstairs to my bedroom. She'd been in here a thousand times before, but something about today felt different. She'd sought me out directly without informing the others. Without even texting me beforehand.

I left her by my bed as I grabbed the box of tissues sitting on my desk and brought them over to her. Scarlett took them from me, giving me a sad smile as she wiped her face. No matter whether she was crying, happy, angry or sad, she was always beautiful to me. The most radiant being I'd ever encountered in this universe.

She sniffled and threw the used tissues in the bin, setting the box down on my bedside table before looking at me.

"Do you want to talk about it?"

She'd told me exactly what happened. She'd explained it to all of us even though Drake had been there. He didn't see them grab her and take her behind the building at school. He didn't see when they'd tried to stick their hands up her skirt nor when she'd made an attempt to push them off. But he did get there right before they tore her knickers down her legs. He did tell them to fuck off and leave her alone. Then he'd held Scarlett while she cried and made sure she was okay.

I didn't care what anyone else said. We were going to make those cunts pay for what they did to her. What they kept getting away with because of who they were. Drake, Prescott, Francis and I weren't going to stand for it any longer. Not now they'd hurt our best friend. Not when they'd tried to do to Scarlett what they'd done to other girls, the fuckers.

"No. I don't want to think about it. I can't. It hurts too much."

I reached out and cupped her shoulder, giving it a squeeze.

"Should I invite the others over? We can break into Henry's drinking cabinet again."

I don't know when I stopped calling Henry, Dad. Maybe when I realised he was an absolute cunt. Didn't call my mother that title either. She was Cynthia. I think she hated it, but I didn't care. The woman always gave me a hard fucking time for no reason.

"Your parents aren't here?"

"No, thank fuck."

Scarlett gave me a sad smile. She didn't like them much either. And they thought she was a bad influence on me. To be honest, they hated the boys too. We were troublemakers as far as they were concerned. Didn't give a shit what they thought. The boys and Scarlett were my best friends, more like family to me than my parents had ever been. I wouldn't give them up for anything.

"I don't want you to invite the others over."

"Then what do you want to do?"

She stepped closer to me. There was something in her eyes. Something that told me she was about to change everything.

"I want you to erase their memory from my skin."

For a long minute as I tried to work out what the fuck she meant, I stared at her as she looked at me. Her eyes betrayed her feelings. I couldn't believe what I was hearing and seeing. My heart raced out of control. It beat so damn hard in my chest, I thought it was going to burst.

"You want what?"

Another step brought her even closer.

"West, don't you know how I feel about you?"

I shook my head. Never once had I guessed she might reciprocate my feelings towards her. We were super fucking close, but as friends. I'd always thought we were friends.

Scarlett stepped right up into my personal space and placed her hand on my heart. It pounded harder against my chest. I was sure she could feel it.

"I love you."

Those words. Those fucking words had me struggling to draw air into my lungs.

She feels the same way. She fucking feels the same way.

"You love me?" I whispered.

She nodded as her other hand found mine and brought it up so she could entwine our fingers together.

"I've always loved you, ever since the moment I saw you." She let out a little sigh. "That's why I went up to you. I was drawn to you. I've always been drawn to all of you, but I saw you first, West. It's always been you."

Never in a million fucking years did I ever imagine she'd come over today and declare her love for me. I didn't know what to do with myself. All I could think about was her. This was fate. Destiny had spun its web and brought us together.

"Why me? Why not one of the others?"

She shook her head and leant closer to me.

"What kind of question is that? You're you. There's no one else like you."

"Scar…"

"There shouldn't be any questions. I love you. That's it. You're the whole world to me, West. I don't know why you can't see that."

I didn't know why I couldn't either. It was insane, wasn't it? The girl I'd loved my whole life had secretly loved me too. How didn't I see it when I knew her like the back of my hand? And why the hell was I questioning it? Fuck, I loved her too. I loved her so much, I thought I might die if I was ever without her.

"Scar, I… I…"

She didn't let me speak. Instead, she went up on her tiptoes and pressed her mouth against mine. She took a kiss from me without permission, but she didn't need it. I'd grant her everything she wanted if she didn't stop pressing her mouth against mine. My fingers went to her waist, tugging her against me as my mouth parted and allowed her in. It was a clumsy kiss because neither of us had done it before, but I didn't care. She tasted like fucking magic.

We eventually found our natural rhythm, neither of us wanting to let the other go. This was everything and nothing like I'd imagined. And I thought about kissing Scarlett more than a thousand times over the years. I was in fucking heaven, never wanting it to end, but I had to. There was something I needed to say to her.

Pulling away, I dropped her hand so I could cup her face in both my hands again. She stared up at me, her beautiful eyes full of affection. Full of fucking love.

"I love you too, Scar. I'm so fucking in love with you it hurts. From the moment you stepped into the classroom all those years ago, I knew deep in my heart, you are it for me. I didn't dare hope you'd ever feel the same way."

She pressed another kiss to my mouth, a tear spilling down her cheek.

"I do. I really do. And I meant it… I want you to erase them from my skin. I want it to be you. Please, make love to me, West. I don't care if neither of us knows what we're doing. I trust you with my body, heart and soul."

I hesitated, unsure if now was the right time to do this. But when the fuck had timing ever been right? She'd told me she loved me. This girl loved me and I loved her. Scarlett Nyx was the world to me just as I was to her.

"Okay, though I don't have protection or anything because I didn't think…"

She smiled and shook her head.

"I do."

I raised an eyebrow.

"Did you come here to seduce me?"

She laughed, the beautiful sound tinkling from her lips and making my heart swell.

"Yeah, I kind of did."

I drew her down onto my bed, pressing her flat on her back before I fit myself between her legs.

"Well, consider me seduced."

"That was easy."

I smiled, leaning down to brush my lips against hers.

"With you, everything is easy, Scar. I'd do anything you asked."

Taking her hand, I pressed it against my chest.

"I love you. My heart is yours. Take care of it for me."

"I will, West. I promise."

And with that, I kissed her, allowing her tongue to meld with mine because I was never letting Scarlett Nyx go again. Not when she was mine… and I was hers.

FORTY THREE

WEST

The memory of the night past Scarlett told me she loved me dissipated, leaving me staring down at my present-day Scarlett who'd warned me she was going to kiss me. I stood there, utterly frozen and captivated by the look in her hazel-green eyes.

None of what happened this evening had gone to plan. I hadn't meant to fuck her here amongst the abandoned diggers and bricks in the place where everything went to shit ten years ago. I hadn't meant to beat the shit out of some guy for giving me attitude, but then again, it was hardly a surprise. I refused to allow anyone to disrespect me or tell me what the fuck I could and couldn't do. This place meant something to me. No one was going to tell me I couldn't be here.

Drake would probably tell me I was torturing myself by coming back here again and again, but I couldn't help it. It was the place where everything ended. And I was drawn back here, replaying the event in my mind like it was stuck on fucking repeat.

We shouldn't be up on this floor. She shouldn't be looking at me the way she was. It was hell. Pure fucking agony. And yet I was powerless at this moment. I couldn't stop it. Not when I wanted her. Not when my chest fucking caved in with all my memories of Scarlett from the past. And now when she wanted to kiss me.

I was losing it. Completely. It messed with my fucking head.

Scarlett pressed closer, going up on her tiptoes to reach me. She'd told me to stop her if I didn't want this. I was so fucking torn between needing her to take the decision away from me and pushing her away because she didn't remember me. She didn't remember us. She didn't know she loved me.

"Scarlett."

She paused, her mouth so damn close to mine. There was disappointment in her eyes, but I couldn't do this. She couldn't kiss me when she didn't know who I was to her. It was a fucking step too far. It shouldn't be, considering I'd been deep inside her several times, but kissing to me meant something far more than just fucking. Kissing her was about love. And her heart wasn't mine again yet. It couldn't be when she was living in a world full of lies and deceit.

"I didn't think you'd say no," she whispered.

My hands curled around her shoulders, pulling her away from my body and forcing her to drop down to her feet again. Her words made my heart fucking crack wide open.

I couldn't do this any longer. Couldn't keep pretending and acting like I didn't know who she was. Who we'd been to each other when we were together. Tonight had proven to me it was damaging all of us further. We were caught up in the web of our own making and I was fucking done.

No wonder Prescott had broken so damn fast. The thought of hurting her further after everything we'd done made me crazy. I didn't want to destroy my girl. I wanted to put her broken parts back together. And the only way I could do that was by reminding her who the fuck she was. I needed to give Scarlett back her memories.

I removed her hands from around my neck and held her in place by her biceps. My eyes darted around the floor. This was the place where it had happened. The place where everything had gone to shit.

You shouldn't have come here with her. This was a mistake.

But was it?

Why would it be a mistake when I could show her the truth?

This was where it all began. If she couldn't remember what happened, then this was where I needed to start. Right at the place that had caused her memory loss in the first place.

"Why are you trying to kiss me?"

She blinked as if the question was unexpected. Then she looked around, taking in our surroundings.

"This place feels... wrong." Her eyes met mine again. "It feels like I shouldn't be here. And I want to focus on something else. On you. You don't feel wrong, West. You feel right."

As if she couldn't fucking torment me any further with the memories of us. This hurt way worse than it was supposed to.

"Do you know why I feel right? Do you know why the fuck that is, Scar?"

I shook her a little, wanting her to understand why this was fucked up.

"No."

"Because you know me and I know you."

She frowned but didn't stop me from gripping her harder.

"What's that supposed to mean?"

I growled, my frustration overflowing. She needed to get it. I didn't want to take drastic measures, but maybe I would have to.

"You know me, Scarlett. Look at me. Fucking look and see."

The girl stared up at me but there was no recognition there. Not the type I wanted to see.

"I see you, West, but I don't understand."

I let her go and paced away, dragging my fingers through my hair. How the hell would I get her to see it?

"This place. You know why it feels wrong. It feels wrong because you know what happened here, you just can't remember it."

When I turned to look at her, she'd taken a step back, her eyes widening.

"What?"

"You can't remember what happened and I hate it. I hate that you don't remember me. You don't remember any of us."

Scarlett took another step back. Her body shook and her face started to pale.

"What are you saying right now?"

I didn't want her running from me. Not when I needed her to see me. Closing the distance between us again, I grabbed hold of her arm and pulled her closer. There was fear in her eyes. True, unadulterated fear.

"I'm saying you forgot who I am but I never forgot you, my little Scar. I could never forget you."

Her bottom lip trembled.

"I don't understand."

I cupped her cheek, feeling her soft skin against mine and wishing everything was different. Wishing she'd never lost who she was. But I would get her back. I would stop at nothing to get her to recognise me. I had no choice left. Not now I'd told her I knew who she was.

"You're mine, Scar. You've been mine since we were kids."

Her little gasp hurt my soul.

"I need you back. I need my Scarlett back."

She swallowed, staring up at me with tears in her eyes. Tears, worry and fear.

"Are you… are you saying… you know me? You knew me before I lost myself?"

"Yes."

I swear the dam broke inside her. She let out a little whimper, a cross between terror and pain.

"What the fuck? What… I don't understand, I don't… West, please don't fuck with me. It's not funny. It's not okay."

I shook my head, my hand tightening around her face.

"I'm not fucking with you."

"No, you have to be… otherwise… otherwise you've all lied to me."

We had. It was the truth. We'd been lying from day one.

"Please, I can't… you aren't telling the truth! You're lying to me."

Leaning down, I pressed my forehead to hers.

"I'm not lying to you, my little Scar. I would do anything to see you look at me the way you did when we were sixteen. I would fucking move mountains to make you remember me."

She hiccupped on a sob, her body trembling all over.

"West, I can't…"

I let go of her arm to wrap mine around her, cradling her to my chest as I kept a hold on her jaw.

"You can. Let me show you the truth. You see this place. You've been here. You came here with us so many fucking times. This was our place. Ours."

She shook her head. She didn't want to remember even though I could see in her eyes she knew I wasn't lying to her. Why the fuck would I tell her I knew her if it wasn't the truth? I had no reason to fuck with her. Well, she probably thought I did, but I wasn't that heartless. Not about this. Not when it came to her knowing who I was.

"This isn't a joke and I'm not lying. You told Pres and Frankie you've remembered things, Scar. Tell me what you've seen. Did you see us? Did you hear us?"

I could see she was breaking apart on the inside, but I couldn't stop.

"Tell. Me."

"I don't know! I don't know what I've seen because I can't remember."

"You can."

She didn't struggle in my embrace. Her expression was fucking heart-breaking, but she didn't try and escape.

"You. I saw you here. A younger version of you. I've seen younger versions of all of you, but I can't trust my own fucking mind, West. I can't. It's all so mixed up."

It gave me a small sliver of hope. A tiny piece to hold onto. If she'd seen me in her memories, then she could find the rest. She could tug on the fucking threads and unravel it all.

"You saw me because I was here when we were sixteen. We were here together. You've seen the rest of them. It's real. All of it."

She shook her head.

"No," she whispered. "No, it can't be real. It can't because why would you hide it? Why wouldn't you tell me?"

"We had to and when you remember, you'll understand why."

She let out a small whimper of pain like I was breaking her open with the truth. I was wrecking my girl.

"I can't remember!"

I didn't have it in me to keep going around in circles. It was now or fucking never. Dropping my hands from her, I took her hand and dragged her closer to the edge. I pointed down at the drop.

"This is where it happened, Scarlett. There's a reason this place makes you afraid. It makes me fucking sick too, but I kept coming back here because it's the only piece of you I had left."

She stared down at the ground. Her body shook all over. Her face was drained of all colour, making me wonder if she was finally getting it. Then she backed away, trying to tug her hand out of mine.

"No. No. I don't remember, West. I don't remember a single goddamn thing and you can't make me."

I don't know why I snapped, but I lost control of the situation when she said it. When she told me I couldn't make her remember. I was fucking damned if I couldn't make her. She was going to see the truth for herself.

My hand wrapped around her forearm and I dragged her back towards me, staring down at the girl who had stolen my heart the day she walked into my life.

"I can make you remember who you are, Scarlett. And I fucking well will."

Making sure my grip on her was as tight as possible, my other hand bracing against the pillar next to us, I pulled her over the edge. Scarlett let out a scream as she fell but came to an abrupt halt. I grunted with the effort, but I held onto her, gripping my girl so she wouldn't fall.

"What the fuck are you doing?" she screamed at me a moment later when she realised I wasn't going to drop her.

"I'm showing you the truth."

She looked around us, her eyes frantic.

"You are fucking insane."

"That may be, but I'm doing this for your own good."

"How the fuck is dangling me off a fucking building for my own good? What the fuck, West? Pull me back up!"

"No. Not until you fucking remember what happened."

This wasn't rational. In fact, it was probably the worst fucking idea I'd ever had, but I'd run out of options. She didn't want to listen to reason, so perhaps she'd listen to insanity instead.

"Remember what!"

"Me! You need to fucking well remember me."

Scarlett wasn't exactly light. I held onto her and the pillar, knowing if I dropped her, it would be the end of everything.

She stared up at me. Her pupils were dilated. She was scared out of her fucking mind hanging there with only me to keep her from falling.

"Look at me, Scarlett. Just fucking look at me."

And she did. She kept looking until her eyes filled with tears and her bottom lip trembled.

"Let me back up," she whimpered. "Please, West."

She reached up with her other hand and gripped my arm. "Please!"

"You remember, don't you? Tell me you fucking remember, Scar! Because you need to. You have to remember what happened that night."

"Please stop this!"

I shook my head. I couldn't stop. Nothing would ever make me stop. Not now. There was no going back.

"West! I will fucking kill you if you don't let me back up!"

I stared at her. My girl, the fire-breathing queen of my whole damn soul.

"Yeah, Scar, you will kill me because the real Scarlett wouldn't let me get away with shit."

She blinked, her hand tightening around my arm. Then she looked down at the ground and her face paled all over again. When her eyes met mine, I could see the cogs turning in her head. I could see it in her eyes. And I knew everything was about to change.

"Do you remember now, Scar? Do you fucking remember who I am?"

She blinked once and I took a deep breath.
"Do. You. Remember?"

ACKNOWLEDGEMENTS

Thank you so much for taking the time to read this book. I really appreciate all of my readers and hope this book gave you as much joy reading it as I did writing it.

My biggest thanks for this book goes out to my amazing friend and alpha reader, Ashley. We've been on quite the journey with the first two books. You've helped me grow these characters in ways I never thought were possible. Whenever I suggested something crazy, you were on board and telling me to write it. You're my biggest champion and support. Chaos wouldn't be the book it is if I didn't have you with me. I'm eternally grateful to have you in my life. ILY!

Thank you to Chrishawn for being there for me, helping me set goals and making sure I get my words in. I'm so glad we connected. Couldn't do without you now, girl!

Big thank you to my author bestie, Elle. We've grown so much over the years together and I'm grateful to have you in my life to share our writing woes and successes.

Thank you to my husband for putting up with my long days of writing to bring this story to fruition. Love you to the stars and back.

ABOUT THE AUTHOR

Sarah writes dark, contemporary, erotic and paranormal romances. They adore all forms of steamy romance and can always be found with a book or ten on their Kindle. They love anti-heroes, alpha males and flawed characters with a little bit of darkness lurking within. Their writing buddies nicknamed Sarah: 'The Queen of Steam' for their pulse racing sex scenes which will leave you a little hot under the collar.

Born and raised in Sussex, UK near the Ashdown Forest, they grew up climbing trees and building Lego towns with their younger brother. Sarah fell in love with novels as teenager reading their aunt's historical regency romances. They have always loved the supernatural and exploring the darker side of romance and fantasy novels.

Sarah currently resides in the Scottish Highlands with their husband. Music is one of their biggest inspirations and they always have something on in the background whilst writing. They are an avid gamer and are often found hogging their husband's Xbox.

Made in the USA
Columbia, SC
13 December 2023

28436512R10230